The Baseball

Joe, Frank, and Biff made their way around the crowd at the baseball card show and approached Elliot Sanford Baird. "Mr. Baird's entire house is filled with baseball memorabilia," Joe said. "Let's ask him."

"I paid ten dollars for this Don Mattingly card," Biff said to Mr. Baird. "Can you tell me if it's phony?"

"Ah, yes," Baird said. "A popular card." Baird put on a pair of glasses and studied the card carefully.

"Is something wrong?" Frank asked.

Baird handed the card back to Biff and said, "I don't know how to tell you this, but I believe the card may be counterfeit."

"So I got taken?" Biff said in disbelief. "I feel like such a fool."

"We'll just ask for your money back," Joe said. Just then Joe noticed a red-haired man rudely push his way past them.

Before Biff could react, the man had grabbed the Mattingly card out of his hand and run off.

"Hey!" Frank shouted. "That man just stole your baseball card. Let's go get him!"

The Hardy Boys Mystery Stories

Available from MINSTREL Books

117

The HARDY BOYS®

THE BASEBALL CARD CONSPIRACY

FRANKLIN W. DIXON

SIDNEY PUBLIC LIBRARY

A MINSTREL® BOOK

PUBLISHED BY POCKET BOOKS

New York   London   Toronto   Sydney   Tokyo   Singapore

This book is a work of fiction. Names, characters, places, and incidents are either the product of the author's imagination or are used fictitiously. Any resemblance to actual events or locales or persons, living or dead, is entirely coincidental.

A MINSTREL PAPERBACK *ORIGINAL*

A Minstrel Book published by
POCKET BOOKS, a division of Simon & Schuster Inc.
1230 Avenue of the Americas, New York, NY 10020

Copyright © 1992 by Simon & Schuster Inc.
Front cover illustration by Daniel Horne

Produced by Mega-Books of New York, Inc.

ISBN: 0-671-73064-9

First Minstrel Books printing December 1992

10 9 8 7 6 5 4 3 2 1

THE HARDY BOYS MYSTERY STORIES is a trademark of Simon & Schuster Inc.

THE HARDY BOYS, A MINSTREL BOOK, and colophon are registered trademarks of Simon & Schuster Inc.

Printed in the U.S.A.

Contents

1 Take a Card

"Hey, Frank! Check out this baseball card!" Joe Hardy called to his eighteen-year-old brother, Frank.

The older Hardy was standing two booths away, trying on a rare Brooklyn Dodgers baseball cap. Their tall, lean, blond friend, Biff Hooper, was next to him. The three boys were attending a huge baseball card and memorabilia show that took up the entire floor of New York's biggest convention center.

Looking around, Joe figured it would take at least two days to see the stuff at every booth. The floor wasn't just packed with booths, either. So many people had come to see the baseball cards on display that Joe had almost lost track of Frank a few times.

1

"This has got to be the biggest baseball card show I've ever seen!" Biff practically shouted.

"Me, too," Joe agreed. He handed Frank a card protected with plastic. "It's a 1973 Brooks Robinson. I got it for three dollars."

"What a deal," Frank said, taking off the cap and pushing his dark hair off his forehead. "Especially if it included the bubble gum."

Biff laughed and punched Frank playfully on the shoulder. "Get with it, Frank," he said. "Most baseball cards don't even come with gum anymore."

"I knew that," Frank said, making a face.

"Sure you did," Joe said, laughing.

Before Frank could pass the card back to Joe, Biff snatched it from Frank's hand. "This is a quality card, Joe. The corners aren't damaged, and the picture doesn't have any hickeys."

"Hickeys?" Frank asked.

"Imperfections," Biff explained. "In fact, if this card weren't printed just a bit off center, it would be considered mint."

"What would it be worth then?" Joe asked, taking the card back from Biff.

Biff looked around the packed floor. "A lot. And all these people would be willing to pay for it, no matter how much it cost."

"I didn't realize baseball memorabilia was so big," Frank said.

"There's a ton of money to be made in baseball cards," Joe said.

"No kidding," Biff said. "I figure at market

prices some of my cards have gone up three hundred percent over what I paid for them. Like the one I got here today. It only cost me ten bucks, and there's a good chance it will go higher some day."

He held up a clear plastic box with a baseball card inside. "It's Don Mattingly. I've been looking for it ever since it came out."

"Ten bucks isn't much," Joe said. "What makes you think it will go up?"

"According to the price guide I use, every card is worth more as the years go on," Biff said. "The guy I bought it from even had a Hank Aaron for seven hundred."

Joe brushed his blond hair out of his eyes while he scanned the convention floor. It was funny to see so many people so serious about collecting baseball cards. For him, it had always been just a hobby. Still, it was pretty exciting to think that there were some rare, cool cards to collect—and that he could find them here.

"I'm glad Dad brought us along," Joe said, stepping out of the way of some people who wanted to see what the booth in front of him had to offer.

Fenton Hardy had come to New York City to do some legwork on an investigation he was conducting. Since Frank and Joe weren't busy, Fenton asked them to come along and help. It wasn't the first time Frank and Joe had assisted their father, who was an internationally famous private detective. The Hardys were crack detectives them-

3

selves, and Fenton often asked for their help and advice.

"Is the case super secret?" Biff asked.

"Not really," Frank said, shoving his hands in his pockets. "A new high-definition computer printer was stolen from DupliTec, a company in Bayport. The chief executive officer at DupliTec, a guy named Victor Newton, hired Dad to find the printer. DupliTec's patent on the printer is still pending, and Newton is afraid whoever stole the machine might beat DupliTec to the market."

"So if we didn't have to come here to help Dad track down his leads," Joe concluded, "you might never have gotten your Mattingly card."

"Actually I might have," Biff pointed out. "I bought this from Bayport's Pasteboard Palace. They've got a booth here. Back home I visit the shop almost every week, but they didn't have the Mattingly when I was in there the other day."

"I bet they bought it from someone here," Frank suggested.

"Could be," Biff said as he scanned the floor eagerly. "Hey," he said, pointing to one of the larger booths one aisle over. "Come on. I think I see something I've had my eye on for a long time."

"What's that?" Joe asked, hurrying to keep up with Biff as he edged his way through the crowd.

"A baseball autographed by Bob Uecker," Biff replied. "You know, that old player who does all those commercials."

The Hardys followed Biff to a double-sized booth marked by a large banner heralding the company's name, Baseball Diamonds Are Forever, and its New York address.

"I take it the Pasteboard Palace doesn't carry Bob Uecker's autograph," Joe said to Frank.

"You looking for a Uecker?" interjected a thin man in his late twenties who wore wire-framed glasses. He was standing behind a table covered with baseball cards, old World Series programs, and baseballs. "You've come to the right place. I've got the *only* authentic Uecker autographs at this show." He handed Biff a signed baseball in a box.

"Have you ever actually seen Bob Uecker's signature?" Frank asked Biff.

"Hey!" the man snapped. "I don't sell phony memorabilia."

"He wasn't saying you did," Joe put in quickly. "It's just that the average person might not know what Bob Uecker's signature looks like."

"You're absolutely right," the man said, nodding several times. "For all you know, everything in this booth could be phony. That's why you have to buy from someone you trust." His hand shot across the table. "Name's Forest Rader. I've been a dealer for ten years."

Frank and Joe both shook his hand.

"I personally saw Bob Uecker sign that ball at a show over in New Jersey," Rader said, looking at Biff and making his pitch. "I paid him to sign ten

5

of those and a dozen eight-by-ten glossy photos of himself. This is the last of the baseballs."

"What do you want for it?" Biff asked.

"Thirty-five."

Biff's eyebrows shot up as he looked at the man. "That's a lot," he said.

"You've got to be kidding," Rader said, taking the ball back from Biff. "Uecker's signature is going nowhere but up. You'll double your money in no time."

"Then why don't you hold on to it?" Joe asked.

"I've already got one," Rader said with a smile. "In a safe deposit box."

"I'll give you twenty," Biff offered eagerly. Joe could tell that Biff was having the time of his life at the show. He enjoyed haggling over the prices of the items as much as he did owning his favorite pieces.

"Can't do it." Rader shook his head. "No less than thirty."

While Biff thought it over, Frank asked to see the autographed baseball. Taking the ball from Rader, Frank strolled over to the end of the booth.

Joe edged up next to him. "What's going on?" he asked.

Frank studied a photograph on the table in front of him, then the signature on the baseball. "I just wanted to check and see if the handwriting on this photograph of Bob Uecker," he said, "is the same as the signature on the baseball."

6

"Of course they're the same!" Rader insisted. The dealer had followed Frank to his end of the table. "I told you, I'm an honest man."

"Excuse me." A silver-haired man standing next to them turned to face Frank and Joe. "I myself can vouch for Mr. Rader's honesty."

"Why, thank you, Mr. Baird," Rader said. "That means a lot, coming from one of the foremost collectors of baseball memorabilia."

"Are you by any chance the Elliot Sanford Baird from Bayport?" Joe asked.

"I am," Baird replied, his black eyes looking directly at Joe.

"Mr. Baird's entire house is filled with memorabilia," Rader explained. "His collection rivals that of the Hall of Fame."

"You're too kind," Baird said modestly.

"I've read about you in the Bayport paper," Joe said. "I'm Joe Hardy, and this is my brother, Frank. That's our friend Biff. He's the real collector."

Baird shook hands all around. "I was at the show where Bob Uecker signed that baseball, and that most definitely is his handwriting. But you're right to be suspicious. There isn't a lot of phony memorabilia, but to those of us who love the hobby, even one bad baseball card is cause for alarm."

"You mean people have actually forged autographs?" Biff asked.

"They certainly have," Baird said sternly. "In

7

recent years many counterfeit baseball cards have also turned up."

"Really?" Joe asked.

"More than you might think," Rader said, shaking his head. "There was a phony Bo Jackson rookie card in circulation a couple years ago. A lot of people got taken on that one—even dealers. Mr. Baird here is an expert in detecting counterfeits. Aren't you, Elliot?"

Baird smiled slightly. "Well, yes, I suppose I am."

"Can you tell if my Brooks Robinson card is phony?" Joe asked, handing the card to Baird.

Baird put on a pair of glasses, then took the card and held it under a lamp that illuminated the Baseball Diamonds Are Forever merchandise. After studying the card for several seconds he announced, "It's genuine," and handed the card back to a relieved Joe.

"I paid ten dollars for this Don Mattingly," Biff said hesitantly, handing Baird the card.

"Ah, yes," Baird said. "A popular card."

Holding the card under the lamp, Baird turned it over several times, then asked Biff if he could remove it from its case.

"Is something wrong?" Frank asked.

Baird peered closely at the card, holding it to the light. Then he took a magnifying glass out of his inside coat pocket and looked at the card even more carefully. Finally he handed the card and the case back to Biff.

8

"What's wrong?" Biff asked. "Did I pay too much?"

Baird cleared his throat and removed his glasses. "I don't know how to tell you this," he said gravely, "but I believe the card may be counterfeit."

Biff gasped.

"How can you tell?" Frank asked.

"There are ways," Baird explained.

"Bad logo?" Rader asked knowingly.

Baird nodded. "Baseball card companies take pride in making sure their logos can't be copied. They use special colors and extremely high resolution in the printing," he explained. "Also, if you can see through the card—that is, if the photograph appears on the other side—chances are you have a counterfeit. I'm afraid the logo on your Mattingly isn't printed with the right color."

"So I got taken?" Biff said in disbelief. "I feel like such a fool."

Baird patted Biff on the shoulder. "You needn't," he said. "A number of collectors I know were fooled by the Bo Jackson card. My advice is to take the card back to where you bought it."

"If you'd bought it from me," Forest Rader said, "I'd give you a refund."

Looking disappointed, Biff stared at the counterfeit card.

"We'll just go over to the Pasteboard Palace booth and ask for your money back," Joe said.

9

As the Hardys and Biff were thanking Baird for his help, Joe noticed a red-haired man rudely push his way past them.

Before Biff could react the man had grabbed the Mattingly baseball card out of his hand and started running toward the exit.

"Hey!" Frank shouted. "That guy just stole your baseball card! Let's go get him!"

2 The 5:07 to Trouble

Joe Hardy leapt into action. The guy's red hair was easy enough to spot in the crowd. The fact that he left a trail of overturned tables and flying baseball cards behind him made it even easier.

"I'll cut him off at the exit!" Frank shouted, racing ahead of Joe.

"Stop that guy!" Biff yelled as he joined the chase.

Joe lost sight of the red-haired man for a split second when he disappeared behind a throng of people at a busy table. Suddenly the thief reappeared near the exit. Joe put on the speed, dashing through the crowd in the direction of the main doorway.

When he was no more than twenty feet away from the door Joe heard a scream. At the same

11

time someone shouted, "Hey, what's the big idea?"

Joe pushed his way through the crowd and found himself standing right in front of the red-haired guy. An older man had the thief pinned against the doorway, but the red-haired guy was struggling to get free. Joe saw that Biff's card was still clutched in the red-haired man's left hand.

Before Joe could react the thief had scrambled out of the older man's grasp and was about to slip out the doorway. Without wasting another moment, Joe made a diving grab. He caught the thief's right ankle, pulling him to the floor.

"Let go of me!" snarled the red-haired man.

"Hold on, Joe!" Joe heard Frank call out. "We're on our way."

Apparently realizing he'd lost the chase, the thief flipped Biff's baseball card toward Joe, then kicked out viciously with his left leg. The blow landed squarely on Joe's jaw and made him lose his grip.

The red-haired man scrambled to his feet and raced out the door. Joe lay on the ground, holding his jaw. Frank and Biff arrived moments later.

Several people in the crowd asked Frank if they needed help, but when Frank shook his head no the group started to disperse. Frank knelt by his brother. "You all right?" Frank asked Joe.

"I'm fine," Joe said, sitting up.

"I can't believe we lost him," Frank said under his breath.

"I'll go after him," Biff said, and ran off.

"That guy threw Biff's card down somewhere," Joe said, looking around the floor.

"I've got it right here," a voice said.

Frank and Joe looked up to see the card in the hand of Forest Rader. "Let me help you," Rader said. He held out his other hand to pull Joe up, then he passed the card to Frank.

At that moment Biff came jogging back into the hall. "I lost him on the street," he said.

"I'm sorry I let him get away," Joe said, rubbing his chin. "But he really distracted me by throwing the card away."

A security guard came rushing over, his walkie-talkie squawking. "What's going on here?" he asked. "I got a report of some trouble."

Frank quickly explained to the guard what had happened, and that they had gotten Biff's card back. "Everything's fine now, but maybe you could keep an eye out for the guy. We'd like to find out why he wanted my friend's card in the first place."

The guard nodded, spoke into his walkie-talkie, and finally took off when they'd convinced him Joe was okay.

"Why do you think that guy tried to steal my card?" Biff asked after the guard left.

Frank rubbed his chin. "I think I remember him standing in the crowd at the Diamonds booth while we were talking with Baird."

"If he was that close and heard Baird say it was fake, it's all the more confusing," Joe said.

"I can tell you right now he wasn't anybody from the business," Rader said. "I know most of the dealers, and I've never seen him before."

"Maybe he was just some nut." Biff shrugged. "Let's forget about it and go over to the Pasteboard Palace booth so I can get my money back."

While Rader went back to his table, Biff led Frank and Joe across the convention hall toward the Pasteboard Palace booth.

"The manager is Nora Shadwick," Biff explained as they made their way through the crowded aisles. "Her store's got the best selection in Bayport."

When the three boys approached the booth Joe saw a man in his middle twenties sitting behind the table. He was a tall, broad-shouldered man wearing a jersey from the Bayport Blues, Bayport's minor league baseball team.

"Hey, guys, this is Cecil Corbin," Biff said. "Cecil works for Mrs. Shadwick. These are my friends, Frank and Joe Hardy."

"You're not the same Cecil Corbin who played for the Bayport Blues, are you?" Joe asked excitedly.

"One and the same," Cecil said. "Pleased to meet you both."

"You had a great fastball," Frank said.

"I still do," Corbin said glumly, "even though none of the owners seem to think so."

"Are you retired now?" Joe asked.

Corbin nodded. "At the ripe old age of twenty-five," he said bluntly. "The team put me on injured reserve, but after I went through surgery on my elbow they decided they didn't want me at all."

"That's their loss," Frank said. "But you can always coach."

"You're right about that," Corbin said, smiling. "In the meantime, I'm working some of the shows for the Pasteboard Palace. How can I help you today?"

Biff handed Cecil the fake Mattingly card. "Elliot Sanford Baird told me this card is counterfeit," Biff explained.

Corbin exploded. "That old fraud! I wouldn't believe a word that crook says. He's the one who owns the Bayport Blues, you know. He lied to me while I was recovering. He said, 'No problem, Cecil. As soon as you're ready, you're coming back to the team.' Then he cut me."

"That's a rough break," Joe said diplomatically, "but Baird seems to know his baseball cards."

Corbin studied the card. "Looks all right to me. You're telling me you think Nora Shadwick sells phony cards?" he asked coldly.

"Not at all," Biff replied. "I've bought a lot of cards from her. She could have been fooled by it. A lot of people are fooled by counterfeits."

"Well, she's not here now," Corbin told them. "She's already left for Bayport. I can't give you any money back without her say-so."

"Do you have any idea how she got the card?" Joe asked Corbin.

"I don't know," he answered. "Both of us bought some cards here. She probably got it here

15

at the show, because I don't remember us having this card in the shop a few days ago."

Frank checked his watch and saw it was almost time to meet his father. "We've got to catch up with Dad at Grand Central Station," he pointed out. "First thing tomorrow we can go downtown to the Pasteboard Palace. I'm sure Mrs. Shadwick will want to straighten out the problem."

"If Nora wants to give you back the money," Corbin said, "that's up to her. But if it were up to me, I'd say let the buyer beware."

The Hardys thanked Corbin and headed out of the convention hall.

"Cecil Corbin sure is a bitter guy," Joe said as they stood on the street searching for a cab. "Not to mention the fact that he seems to have no use for Elliot Baird at all."

"He's not being fair," Biff said, shouting over the noise of rush hour traffic. "Anyone who plays sports has to know that even one injury can ruin a career. Corbin was a good pitcher while he was healthy, but he never bounced back after his surgery."

Frank managed to get a cab to stop for them, and all three friends piled into the backseat. "Grand Central," Frank said, leaning forward to instruct the driver. He checked his watch and looked at the traffic jams around them. "I hope we make the train."

Joe held on to the front seat as the driver swerved out into traffic, nearly sideswiping a bicyclist. "I have a feeling we will," he said, his eyes wide.

Ten minutes later Frank, Joe, and Biff climbed out of the cab. While Frank paid the driver Joe looked for his father. Finally he spotted Fenton Hardy getting out of a cab.

Joe jogged up to him. "How's the case going?" the younger Hardy asked his father.

Fenton greeted his sons and Biff. "Let's just say I hope you had better luck trading baseball cards than I did following leads," Fenton said. "I'll tell you all about it on the train."

Joe and his father led Frank and Biff into Grand Central Station. They hurried down the stairs to track level and boarded the commuter train to Bayport. Minutes after they got on board the train began to move out of the station.

Frank found four seats together, two on each side of the aisle. "I want to hear all about the case," Frank said, "but since we haven't had anything to eat since noon, I thought I'd run back to the club car and pick up some chips."

"Sounds good," Joe said. "Grab me a hot dog while you're at it, okay?"

Frank nodded and started making his way to the back of the coach. As he opened the door leading to the passage between cars he heard the rhythmic noise of the train on the rails, which was louder since there was a gap where the cars connected. He could see the houses and country-side fly by as the train sped along.

17

Just then another passenger came up behind him. Frank held the door open for him and stepped across the connecting walkway toward the club car door.

Suddenly Frank felt his arm being wrenched from behind in a hammerlock. He struggled, but before he could pull himself free his assailant had an arm clamped around Frank's neck.

Reacting swiftly, Frank hooked one leg around his attacker's leg and tried to pull the guy off balance. But the man easily sidestepped Frank's maneuver and tightened his grip.

"I know all about you and your brother," the man growled into Frank's ear. "If you know what's good for you, leave the baseball card business alone."

Frank could hardly talk with the man's arm constricting his neck, but he managed to croak, "I'm not in the baseball card business."

Feeling for an instant that the man had loosened his grip, Frank summoned his strength and backed up, slamming the man against the door of the train. The man groaned but didn't give up his grip. Instead he held on to Frank's neck, keeping up the chokehold.

Suddenly the guy let go of Frank, and Frank spun around to face his attacker. Frank got one good look at the guy and saw with a shock that it was the same red-haired thief from the baseball card show.

Before Frank had time to react, the red-haired man lowered his head and, like a linebacker, plowed into Frank. He grabbed Frank at waist level and pushed him backward, toward the gap between cars.

As all the wind was knocked out of him Frank realized his assailant was about to push him from the train. The only thing separating Frank from the speeding blur of ground below were two chains. His attacker would have no trouble pushing him over them.

In the next second Frank felt himself being forced backward over the chains, headed right for the rails that were whizzing by.

3 The Sky Is Falling

Just before he fell Frank reached out desperately. He had only a split second in which to save himself from falling off the train. In the last moment his fingers found a handhold on the outside of the train car.

Gritting his teeth, he swung his feet up and landed on the floor of the car. The train was moving so fast that just holding on to the handle gave him searing pains in his arms. His shoulder felt as though it was being torn from its socket.

Frank tried not to look down. The ground shot by at what seemed like a million miles an hour. Grabbing the side of the car, he climbed over the chains and then steadied himself against the lurching motion of the train.

Gasping for breath, Frank struggled back into the car's vestibule.

By now the red-haired man was gone, of course. Frank raced into the club car and scanned its occupants. His assailant was not there. Moving quickly back into the car where Joe and the others were seated, Frank told them about the attack.

"It was the guy from the card show," Frank said. "I'm sure of it. He was trying to adjust my itinerary."

"Unless he's willing to jump from a moving train," Joe said, "he's still on board."

"Let's fan out," Fenton suggested. "Biff and I can take the back of the train. You boys take the front. That way we can make sure we get a good look at everyone."

Frank and Joe immediately started toward the front of the train. "Mostly business people and students," Joe said under his breath as he made his way up the aisle.

Once Frank had reached the end of the train he turned and started back toward Joe. "I don't see anyone who looks even remotely like him," Frank said.

"Maybe he jumped after all," Joe said.

"Or else he's in disguise," Frank suggested. "Let's look everyone over again on our way back."

Frank led the way through the swaying railroad cars. He stopped beside a man in a window seat. The man was wearing an Atlanta Braves baseball cap and a pair of reflective sunglasses.

Hearing the faint rhythmic snoring that meant

21

someone was sound asleep, Joe gave his brother a questioning look.

"I can't tell," Frank whispered. "That cap is hiding his hair."

Suddenly the train jerked, then began to slow. The conductor called out the town of Seaview Bluff.

Frank watched the man in the baseball cap. "That guy's out," Frank decided. "The change in the train's motion didn't even faze him."

Joe nodded. "Let's see if Dad and Biff came up with anything."

"No luck," Fenton Hardy admitted when the group met back at their seats. The train jerked noisily to a stop. Out the window Frank saw the guy in the baseball cap getting off the train. He gave the man a close look but couldn't tell if he was the guy who had thrown him off the train or not. He wasn't wearing the same jacket as the man who attacked Frank, but he could have put it in the knapsack he carried. He didn't seem to have red hair, although it was hard to tell, since he was wearing a baseball cap.

"What you have to do is find out who printed Biff's counterfeit card," Fenton told the Hardys. "That's the secret to why this guy is after you."

"Dad's right," Frank agreed. "There's got to be something more at stake than Biff's ten bucks. That guy wanted to steal the card so we wouldn't be able to do any more investigating."

"He must have overheard your names at

Rader's booth," Biff said. "How else would he know you guys are detectives?"

Joe nodded in agreement. As the train started up again he turned to Frank and said, "I say we get to the Pasteboard Palace first thing tomorrow morning. We've got to find out where Nora Shadwick got the fake Mattingly."

The next morning Joe steered the van down Packer Street in Bayport's waterfront district. He found a parking space several doors down from the Pasteboard Palace. The three friends got out of the van, careful to step around a yellow plastic ribbon that blocked off most of the sidewalk in front of an abandoned old store.

"What's this ribbon all about?" Frank asked.

"Watch your head," Joe told them. "I read in the paper that some molding fell off this empty building the other day. It missed hitting a pedestrian by inches."

"This is an old part of town, all right," Frank said, stepping between the van and the curb.

Biff led the Hardys along the street to the Pasteboard Palace. It was next to the abandoned building, with an alley in between.

A bell jingled when Biff opened the card shop's front door. There were already several customers checking out the cards in the rows of glass showcases. A man in a baseball cap and glasses was looking through a narrow cardboard box jammed with old baseball cards.

23

"Hey, Biff," a young woman in her late twenties said. "How did you like the show?"

"It was great," Biff answered. "I looked for you there, but Cecil said you'd already left."

The woman finished ringing up a sale and stepped around the counter. She tucked her short brown hair behind an ear and reached out a hand to introduce herself. "Nora Shadwick," she said.

Biff introduced Frank and Joe, who each shook Nora's hand. Her grip was firm, and she had a no-nonsense way about her.

"Oh, sure," Nora said, nodding. "I've read about your cases in the newspaper. Gosh, I hope you're not in here on business," she joked.

"Actually . . ." Biff said, handing over his Mattingly card.

Frank stepped in for his friend. "We wanted to find out how and where you purchased this card," he said, explaining what had happened at the show the day before. He added that Baird claimed the card was counterfeit.

Nora's bright blue eyes went wide as she took the card. She reached over to the counter for a magnifying glass and examined the card in silence. Finally she let out a deep breath and looked at the three friends with a serious expression on her face.

"This card *is* counterfeit," Nora said. "I'm so sorry, Biff. I hope you don't think I sold you the card on purpose." She immediately walked to the cash register, took out ten dollars, and gave it to Biff.

"Do you know where you got that card?" Frank asked. "We talked with Cecil Corbin at the show, but he wasn't very cooperative."

"Cecil bought the card along with a large lot when he was working Thursday night," Nora said, shaking her head slowly. "Usually he's more careful about checking for counterfeits. Maybe he got sidetracked. Maybe I should have looked at them more closely, but I was pretty busy myself, setting up and all."

"You let Cecil buy for you?" Joe asked.

"I trust him," Nora said firmly.

"Did either of you sell any of the other cards you bought from that guy?" Frank asked.

"I didn't," Nora told him, "but Cecil might have. And the show's still on." She looked up suddenly. "Which means I'd better call him. If those other cards are bogus and he sells them, my reputation as a dealer could be ruined."

She picked up the phone and made a call to Cecil Corbin. "I had to leave a message at the convention center," she told the boys when she hung up.

"Did Corbin say anything about the person who sold him the cards?" Biff asked.

Nora thought for a moment. "I really don't remember," she said. "But I'll tell you this: I want to find out who that person is and whether or not he knowingly sold me phony baseball

25

cards." She looked from Joe to Frank. "You guys are detectives. Can you look into it for me?"

"No problem," Frank said eagerly. "Even if you didn't ask, I think Joe and I would have offered."

Joe nodded in agreement, and Biff slapped them both on the back. "All right!" he shouted. "The Hardys get another case."

The phone rang, and Nora stepped behind the counter to answer it. "It's Cecil," she mouthed to the Hardys.

While Nora spoke with Cecil Corbin in New York City, Frank browsed through the Pasteboard Palace. The shop was jam-packed with cards, team T-shirts, posters, sports trivia books, and collector supplies. Some of the browsers who'd been in the store when Frank, Joe, and Biff walked in had left, and still others had arrived. The Pasteboard Palace sure was a busy place.

"Call me back when you know whether those cards are still in stock," Nora Shadwick said into the receiver as Frank returned to the front counter. Joe and Biff were looking at a real Mattingly that Nora had pulled out for them.

"Cecil's going to pull the rest of the cards we bought in New York," Nora told the Hardys and Biff. "He's also going to check and see if we accidentally sold any other bad ones."

"Is there anyone who would want to try to ruin your business by planting fake cards?" Frank asked Nora, thinking about possible motives. "Maybe one of your competitors wants to give you a hard time."

The store owner thought for a moment. "Not that I know of," she said finally. "I've always had a lot of repeat customers. I'm on friendly terms with all of the other collectors and owners."

"Nora runs the best shop outside of New York City," Biff said. "All the collectors know that."

"Whoever faked this card has some pretty good printing equipment," Joe pointed out. "I think we ought to visit a couple of Bayport print shops to find out exactly what kind of press would be necessary to produce this card."

The phone rang again, and Nora went to answer it. In a few minutes she hung up. "That was Cecil," she explained. "The good news is we didn't sell the other cards. The bad news is Cecil thinks two of them are counterfeit."

"Time for us to get to work," Frank said. "We'll let you know what we find out." He held up Biff's counterfeit card and said, "I know you bought this back from Biff, but do you mind if we take it?"

"No problem. And good luck," she said as Frank opened the door to leave the shop.

Frank led the way past the alley and the abandoned building onto the sidewalk next to their car. Suddenly, high above, a scraping sound caught his attention. He looked up at the top of the empty storefront.

"Frank!" Joe yelled out. "Move out of the way!"

Frank looked up just in time to see that a huge chunk of limestone molding was falling from the building next to them. And it was plummeting right toward Frank!

4 Down in the Dumps

Joe immediately hurled himself at Frank, knocking his brother out of the path of the falling limestone.

"What the—" Frank started to say. But Joe fell to the ground on top of him, muffling the older Hardy's question.

In another second Joe heard the crash as the chunk of stone came hurtling to the ground and crashed into hundreds of pieces.

"Frank! Joe!" Biff yelled. Joe looked up to see their friend standing in the street, safely out of the line of the falling molding. Biff was pointing to the top of the building, where a guy stood at the edge of the roof.

"Someone's on the roof!" Joe cried, helping Frank to his feet. "We've got to get up there."

Frank brushed himself off and quickly saw what Biff and Joe were talking about. "You guys go around to the back of the building," he said. "See if you can find a fire escape or something. There can't be too many ways down from that roof. I'm sure we can cut him off."

While Joe and Biff went around to the back of the abandoned building, Frank worked at getting in the front. All that was keeping the rotting door from falling off the frame was a rusted chain. Frank quickly broke the chain apart by taking a running jump and kicking in the door. Once inside, Frank hurried through the main show-room. Signs and debris told him it had once been a hardware store.

Finding the stairs, Frank raced up them two at a time. After climbing the second set he stepped out onto the littered tar-paper roof. The wind was brisk, and Frank zipped up his jacket and stuck his hands in the pockets.

The man was nowhere to be seen. Frank scanned the roofs of nearby buildings. The stores were close enough together for someone to jump from one store to another, but when Frank looked down the row of buildings he didn't see a soul.

Something shiny on the roof by the front wall caught his eye. Walking closer, he saw a plastic-handled screwdriver. He picked it up with a tissue to protect any fingerprints.

Frank looked over into the alley behind the building and saw Joe climbing up the fire escape.

When his brother got to the roof Frank gave him the bad news.

"He got away," Frank said, kicking an empty can on the roof in frustration. "Where's Biff?"

"Keeping a lookout down in the alley. Did you see where he went?" Joe asked.

Frank shook his head. Then he handed Joe the screwdriver. "I'd say our man used this screwdriver to pry off the molding."

Joe nodded. "And I think I know why, too."

Frank looked at his brother curiously. "What do you mean?"

"The one glimpse I got of the guy, I saw he was wearing a baseball cap. I also saw some red hair peeking out of that cap," Joe said.

"Whoa," Frank said, letting out a low whistle. "You think it was that same red-haired guy?"

"It might be a coincidence," Joe responded, "but he did warn us against investigating the counterfeit card, and we haven't exactly taken his advice."

"Let's see if Biff saw anything down on the street," Frank suggested. "We've also got to find out if there are any prints on this screwdriver."

Frank led the way down the fire escape. Biff was standing in the alley when Frank swung himself off the ladder at the bottom of the escape and jumped to the ground. Joe was right behind him.

"Did you find the guy?" Biff asked, a worried expression on his face.

"Nope," Joe said.

"But I bet he's still in the area," Frank said. "Let's split up and do a quick search." He pointed toward the end of the alley, where it met the street. "We'll meet at that diner in half an hour."

Twenty minutes later Frank had scoured the area around the abandoned building and the Pasteboard Palace. The red-haired guy was nowhere in sight.

"It's as if he just vanished," Frank told Joe when he and Biff showed up in front of the diner. "Into thin air!"

Biff held open the door to the place. A sign out front read Rube's Restaurant, and there were dozens of photographs of baseball stars hanging on the walls inside.

"Seems like everywhere we go we run into baseball fans," Joe said, scanning the walls.

"Nora mentioned to me that Rube is a friend of hers," Biff explained. "He's the one who found her the location for her store."

"He's got a pennant for every team in both leagues on these walls," Frank noted. "And those photographs of ball players are all autographed."

The rest of the decor, Frank noticed, was from the fifties and looked worn out. The black and white tiled floor was chipped and discolored, the booths upholstered in red plastic. He noticed they were ripped and lumpy.

32

"You boys hungry?" a booming voice called out from behind the stainless steel counter.

Frank turned around. The man who'd shouted was wearing a white shirt and apron. His graying hair told Frank he was about sixty years old. "Welcome to Rube's Restaurant," the man said, coming over to their booth. "No menus here. You tell me what you want, I'll fix it."

"Sounds good," Frank said. He introduced himself, then Joe and Biff. The three friends all ordered burgers, fries, and sodas.

"This is quite a collection of memorabilia," Joe commented. "Do you collect baseball cards, too?"

"Got a million of 'em!" Rube exclaimed. "Some worth a couple hundred bucks, most worth two cents. You a collector?"

"I've got a few," Joe told him. "I picked up a counterfeit Mattingly card in New York yesterday. You ever get stuck with bogus cards?"

"Not recently," Rube answered. "Every once in a while you'll hear about a bad card. It's a shame when it happens, especially when some young kid takes the loss." He wrote down their order. "The guy who knows all about counterfeits is Elliot Sanford Baird. He owns the Bayport Blues, lives in the old Larkin mansion on the edge of town. I hear he's got the largest collection of baseball memorabilia east of the Mississippi. A guy I talked to said the house is so full of stuff you can hardly walk through."

"We met Baird in New York," Frank said. "I had the impression that all the dealers had heard of him."

"He's respected, all right," Ruben assured them. "But there've been rumors that he's got money problems. Some say he's going to sell off part of his collection, maybe as soon as the big armory show this weekend."

Ruben finished taking their orders. "Hey, Justine!" he called.

Frank looked up and saw a waitress coming their way. "Yeah?" the woman responded.

"Get these fellows three sodas, will you, while I put their burgers on the grill?" Rube said, walking back to the kitchen after a quick good-bye.

Justine brought their sodas and, when their order was ready, came back with their food. "This hamburger's great," Frank called over to Ruben after taking a couple of bites. "We're going to have to come in here more often."

At that moment Frank heard the crash of cans in the kitchen. Ruben nearly dropped his spatula.

Justine screamed and ran out from behind the counter. "There's a man!" she cried. "A man in the kitchen!"

Just then the red-haired guy came rushing out of the kitchen, kicking restaurant supplies out of his way. He raced past their booth and toward the doorway. Before Frank could react Joe jumped up to follow the guy.

"Who was that?" Ruben cried out angrily.

"We'll explain later," Frank called out to the startled restaurant owner. He quickly threw some money down on the table as he and Biff jumped to their feet.

Out in the alley Joe quickly looked both ways and groaned in disgust. The red-haired guy had disappeared yet again.

But how far could he have gotten? Joe asked himself. He listened closely, but the noise from a garbage truck several blocks away dominated the street sounds.

Joe hazarded a guess that the guy would probably run deeper into the waterfront area, where there were more places to hide. As soon as he turned the corner away from Rube's, Joe felt a glancing blow to the back of his head. He staggered. Turning slightly, he caught sight of the red-haired man. He had a two-by-four in his hand.

"Now you've had it!" the man growled. Before Joe could recover, the man began to loop stout packing twine around Joe's arms, pinning them to his sides.

"I knew you kids would be searching for me," the guy said, tightening the knots, "so I hid out in the kitchen of that restaurant. But when that waitress found me, I had to make a break for it."

"My brother's right behind me," Joe said, regaining his senses. He kicked out at the red-haired guy and connected with his shin. Yelping in pain, the man whacked Joe on the side of the head once more.

35

Joe collapsed in the alley. The man picked up the twine and wrapped it repeatedly around Joe's legs, tying them together.

Above the roaring in his head from the two vicious blows Joe could hear the hydraulic hissing of a garbage truck. The clanging and slamming of dumpsters being emptied echoed up and down the narrow brick canyon.

"Good riddance to bad rubbish!" the red-haired man said gleefully. He struggled with Joe, finally throwing him over his shoulder and tossing him into a nearby dumpster.

Joe felt himself tumble to the back of the steel container. The odor of rotting garbage stung his nostrils.

The crash of the closing lid deafened him, and the sudden darkness left him blind.

Joe struggled with the bindings. He knew he didn't have very much time. The garbage truck was moving closer by the moment. If he didn't get out of the dumpster—and fast—he'd be crushed to death!

5 Counterfeiting Made Simple

Frank Hardy came racing around the corner just as the garbage truck lurched forward and connected with the dumpster.

"I know I saw Joe come around this corner," Frank said, staring at the garbage truck. "But where'd he go?"

The alley was a dead end. "There's no way out of here," Biff said, peering around the truck. "He's got to be around somewhere."

"Maybe the driver saw Joe," Frank said.

Frank led the way toward the truck. Biff followed close behind. Just as they got to the back of the truck Frank heard a loud clanging coming from the dumpster.

"Do you hear that?" Frank asked Biff.

"Yeah," Biff said.

"Stop!" Frank yelled.

The driver looked over at Frank in alarm. His hand was on the controls, and he was about to push the throttle on the crank that raised the dumpster into the truck.

Frank scrambled up on top of the huge steel container. "Wait!" he shouted.

Wrenching open one of the heavy doors on the top, Frank was horrified at what he saw. There, lying in a tangle of garbage and trash, was Joe.

"Frank!" Joe cried, his eyes wide with relief. "Just in time. I could have been landfill."

Frank quickly jumped down into the stinking refuse. He opened his pocketknife and cut the twine binding Joe's arms and legs.

"Are you okay?" Frank asked.

"Fine," Joe said, rubbing his wrists. "Except for the fact that I'm burning mad. That red-haired guy is starting to get on my nerves."

Frank was relieved to hear that Joe was all right. "Besides which," he said, helping Joe to his feet and noticing his brother's garbage-stained jeans, "he owes you some new clothes!"

The Hardys pulled themselves up out of the dumpster, and the truck driver made sure Joe was okay. He apologized several times and finally drove off.

As Frank, Joe, and Biff were walking back to their van Joe explained what had happened. "I don't know what scam that guy's involved in, but it must be something big."

38

"That's why I was telling Biff we've got to find out something about printing," Frank said, "and I think we ought to have a talk with Elliot Sanford Baird. He knows the baseball card business. Let's run over to Copy City now and see if they can tell us what kind of press might have printed Biff's phony card."

"They ought to know something," Biff observed. "I've heard that's the most up-to-date print shop in Bayport."

While Frank drove, Joe dusted the plastic screwdriver for prints. "I've lifted one thumb and a partial finger," he announced. "I'll give these to Chief Collig at the police department and see if he can match them."

"I remember when I used to collect stamps," Joe continued, "there were several extremely rare stamps."

"Isn't there one with an airplane printed upside down on the stamp?" Biff asked.

"Sure there is," Frank said. "The 1923 airmail stamp. One of those stamps would run six figures."

"How many baseball cards are worth that kind of money?" Joe asked Biff.

"There's a 1967 Tom Seaver rookie card that might bring a thousand," Biff said. "Then there's a Mickey Mantle rookie card that recently sold for twenty-four thousand. That's the exception, though."

"There's also the Honus Wagner card, don't forget," Frank added.

39

"Oh, yeah. How could I forget?" Joe said. "That one's worth a hundred thousand dollars."

Several minutes later Frank steered into a parking spot near the front door of the print shop. "It's as big as a supermarket," he said of the brightly lit building.

Inside the air hummed with the sound of presses in the back and a bank of high-speed copy machines toward the front.

Joe led the group to the desk where customers could place their orders. A young woman in a red Copy City T-shirt with a badge that read Adrienne asked if she could help them.

Frank placed the phony Mattingly card on the counter. "If a person was thinking about bringing out a line of sports cards," Frank said, "could your shop do this type of work?"

"Sure," the woman said. "Baseball cards are printed on five-color presses using twelve-point cardboard stock."

Adrienne opened a drawer and took out a combination magnifying lens and lamp. She held it over the card and looked at it closely.

"This wasn't printed on a conventional press," she said. "And it doesn't look like it was done on a color copier either. Whatever it is," she added, "it's very good printing."

"You don't recognize the process?" Joe asked.

"No, I don't," she admitted. "I'd say it's some new copier technology."

"What about the card stock?" Biff asked. "Is this the kind of stock used for baseball cards?"

40

"Does it seem right to you?" Frank asked.

"Have you seen this kind of stock before?" Joe asked before the woman could answer.

"Hey, one at a time, please." Adrienne tossed her hair out of the way and smiled at the three boys. "To answer your questions: Yes. Yes. And yes."

"Yes, this is the right stock for a baseball card," Frank concluded.

"Exactly," Adrienne said. Another customer came up to the desk, and Frank, Joe, and Biff stepped aside to let her help the man. The three friends thanked Adrienne and returned to the van.

"I've got it!" Joe snapped his fingers. "What about the guy who hired Dad to locate that stolen printer? He could probably help us out here. He might even be able to tell is if this card was printed on some new kind of desktop publishing system."

"It's worth a try," Frank agreed. "Didn't Dad say the guy's name was Newton?"

"Vic Newton," Joe confirmed. "And the company was Dupli-something."

"DupliTec," Biff said.

Within ten minutes the Hardys and Biff were headed toward the western outskirts of town, where DupliTec's Bayport offices were located.

"This is the new industrial park," Frank said as he turned the van into a large complex near a small airfield.

"There it is," Biff said, pointing. "On the left."

41

Frank parked in the tree-lined parking lot. They piled out of the van and headed for a door that had the company's logo stenciled on it. Just inside DupliTec's front door a receptionist asked if he could help them. Frank introduced himself, then Joe and Biff.

"We'd like to talk with Vic Newton," Frank told him.

He watched as the receptionist pushed a couple of buttons on his console, then repeated Joe's request.

A few minutes later a tall, husky man wearing a white shirt and red tie came through a door into the reception area. "Frank and Joe Hardy," he boomed. "Welcome to DupliTec! I'm Vic Newton."

Frank introduced Biff. Newton invited the three of them back to his office.

"Working with your father on my case, are you?" Newton asked when the brothers and Biff had been seated in his large office.

"Actually, we're working on a case of our own," Frank told Newton. He took the fake Mattingly card out of his shirt pocket and pushed it across Newton's desk.

"You collect baseball cards, too?" Newton asked in surprise. "I've got a little collection of cards myself, plus several autographed bats. I don't like to brag," he added, "but my prize possession is a pair of Babe Ruth's socks."

Biff was clearly impressed. "I'm the collector,"

he told him. "I bought that card yesterday at a show in New York."

"I hope you didn't pay a whole lot," Newton said. "It's all bent up."

"I know," Biff said. "Someone tried to grab it away from me."

"Really?" Newton said. "How odd. People at those shows are usually a decent bunch."

Newton picked up the Mattingly. "This isn't a really valuable card, is it?" he asked.

"It would be worth something," Frank said, "if it weren't counterfeit."

Newton looked up sharply. "Counterfeit?" He looked at the card again, this time more closely. "Are you sure it's not a reprint?" he asked, opening his desk drawer. Removing three nine-by-six pieces of cardboard, he handed one to each of the teens.

"These are uncut baseball cards," Biff said, his eyes wide with surprise. "Wow. Even major collectors don't have access to entire sheets of cards."

"I don't understand," Frank said to the executive. "How in the world did you get these?"

"It wasn't terribly difficult," Newton said, a grin on his face. "I printed them." Newton shrugged. "I don't know whether or not to brag about this, but I bet I can print any baseball card ever made. Even your Mattingly."

6 Collision at Home

Joe was stunned. He exchanged a look with Frank and Biff. Was Vic Newton printing unauthorized baseball cards?

"Is this great printing or what?" Newton asked enthusiastically.

"You're printing baseball cards here at DupliTec?" Joe asked, keeping his voice neutral.

"Not at all." Newton chuckled. "But I do print business cards."

Frank turned over the uncut sheet of six baseball cards. "That would explain the message on the back," he said. " 'Let DupliTec handle all of your computer and desktop publishing needs.' "

Joe and Biff found the same message printed on the backs of their sheets.

"I get it," Biff said. "These are your business cards, right? They're really good copies."

"Thanks. They were done on my new high-definition printer," Newton said proudly. "Come on out back to the lab, and I'll show it to you."

The three friends followed Newton through the DupliTec offices to the lab at the back of the building. Once they got there, Joe noticed that the laboratory was kept locked. Vic Newton took a key from his pocket and opened the heavy door. He flipped a switch, and the lab was flooded with bright fluorescent light.

Frank spotted the printer immediately. It was completely compact and, with its matte black surface, almost futuristic.

"Sleek design," Frank commented.

"Kind of like something from a sci-fi movie I saw the other night," Biff said.

"There's nothing else like it on the market," Newton bragged, booting up the computer on a nearby table. With red, green, and yellow lights flashing, then burning steadily, the HD printer came alive.

"It's completing its initial checkout," Newton explained.

"This is what you printed those Catfish Hunter cards on?" Joe asked.

"Just watch," Newton said. He keyed in several commands. The HD printer's hum increased slightly in pitch.

Frank watched intently. From a slit in the side of the printer a sheet of cardboard suddenly emerged. The three friends found them-

45

selves staring at six fresh images of Catfish Hunter.

"That's amazing," Joe said, reaching for the sheet of cardboard. "Can you tell us what kind of printing system was used to make Biff's Mattingly?" Joe handed the sheet of fake cards to Biff.

Frank took the card from his shirt pocket and handed it to Vic. Newton studied the bogus card, holding it up to the light and examining it with a pocket magnifying glass.

Newton's eyes widened as he looked at Biff's Mattingly card. A frown came over his face.

"I don't like to admit it," Newton said finally, "but this could have been printed on my machine." Picking up an artist's razor knife from one of the tables, Newton took the sheet of Hunter cards from Biff and carefully scraped a corner of it. "If you look closely, you'll see that my printer overlays the surface with a microthin image."

Joe took the offered cardboard and looked at it under the light.

"May I use the knife on your Mattingly card?" Newton asked Biff. The Hardys' friend nodded.

"It's the same," Newton pronounced when he was done. "Either it was printed on one of my machines, or someone has developed a process just like it."

"How many of your machines exist?" Joe asked.

"There are four here, besides the one that was stolen, and one in our New York office."

"About the stolen printer," Frank said, frowning. "Our dad hasn't told us all of the details, but I'm assuming you think the theft was an inside job. Is there someone working here that you don't particularly trust?"

Newton sighed. "Your father asked me the same question. I told him that I trust every one of my regular employees. However, I do use a temporary service, a company called Hired Help. Who knows if one of the temps was involved?"

"It's possible," Joe said. "Can you get together a list of all the temps who worked here around the time of the theft?"

"Your father already has one," Newton said. "I believe he's been checking out all the names on the list."

Joe thanked Newton for his help. "We've got to find out where Biff's counterfeit card came from," he said, "and whether there are any more of them."

Newton looked surprised. "You kids should check out the card and memorabilia show that's going on at the armory this weekend. There's also a flea market tomorrow at the mall in Southport."

"That's right!" Biff looked excited. "I forgot all about those two shows. Maybe some other collectors have gotten ripped off, too."

"It's a shot," Frank agreed. He reached out to shake Newton's hand. "Thanks for all your help," he said.

"No problem," Newton said. "Let me know if I can help you out again."

Newton showed them out of the building, and the Hardys and Biff headed back to their van. Joe suggested that the three of them get together again the next afternoon to take in the flea market. "We might turn up something interesting," he said.

Frank drove to Biff's house, which was located in one of Bayport's newer housing developments. After they'd dropped Biff off Frank steered the van back out onto the street and headed for the police department.

"Let's drop off the prints from the screwdriver at the station, then head home for dinner," Frank said.

When Joe brought the fingerprints to the front desk at the station he asked the crime lab to process them as quickly as possible.

Frank and Joe were starved by the time they walked into the house and found their parents cooking in the kitchen.

"First order of business—raid the refrigerator," Joe said after greeting his parents.

While Frank and Joe snacked on cheese and crackers their father told them that Nora Shadwick, the owner of Pasteboard Palace, had just called.

"She wanted you to know she heard from Cecil Corbin at the card show in New York. It seems a number of dealers found they've got a few counterfeit cards."

"Do they know where they got them?" Frank asked.

"She didn't say," Fenton replied. "But she's waiting for you to return her call."

Frank and Joe then took turns telling their father about what they'd learned from Vic Newton at DupliTec.

"It's entirely possible we're all looking for the same person," Fenton concluded. "I've gone through the names of those temps who worked for Newton. So far none of them has a record."

Joe thought for a moment. "What I wonder is why would someone who stole a high-tech printer bother counterfeiting baseball cards?"

"If you printed them by the thousands, there might be real money in it," Frank pointed out. "At ten dollars a pop, and no one paying much attention to the cheaper cards, you could get away with it for a while."

"At least until the card seller is caught," Fenton added. "All you can do right now is keep investigating. Since I've got to go to New York again tomorrow, why don't you two concentrate here in Bayport? Ask around at the flea market. See what you find out."

Frank and Joe went into the living room. Joe put in a call to Nora Shadwick. He caught her just as she was closing up the shop. She sounded upset.

"Cecil called from the show late this afternoon," Nora told him. "He said he overheard a number of dealers talking about counterfeits."

"Could he tell if they were all talking about the same counterfeit card?" Joe asked.

"That's the horrible part," she groaned. "Cecil said the convention is flooded with bogus cards."

"What about the other cards in the lot that included Biff's Mattingly?" Joe asked. "Any more counterfeits?"

"You bet," said Nora grimly. "Corbin's pulling them out as we speak. There were at least ten Mattinglys, a Ken Griffey, Junior, Darryl Strawberry from when he was with the Mets. And more, I think. This whole thing just makes me sick," she said woefully. "You've got to find out who's responsible. It's schemes like this that ruin a great hobby."

Joe assured Nora that he and Frank would get to the bottom of the counterfeits. Just then he heard the signal on the receiver indicating another call was coming in. He said goodbye to Nora and took the other call.

"It's the police department," Joe informed his brother, signaling for something to write with.

Frank handed his brother a pencil and a notepad and watched as Joe wrote down a name. He also scribbled down an address in the waterfront area.

"The prints belong to a guy named Mark Wormley," Joe said, hanging up the phone. "He just happens to be redheaded, by the way. Two burglary arrests. And he's on parole. I've got his address."

"Let's pay a call to Mr. Wormley," Frank said, "right after we've eaten. Mom said we're having fried chicken."

After dinner Joe took the wheel of the van, and the two brothers headed downtown to the waterfront district.

"It must be up there," Frank said, pointing at an old building. "Park around the corner."

Frank led the way into the dimly lit lobby of the rundown apartment building. "Doesn't look as if the maintenance crew's been here for several years," he commented as he kicked past a torn bag of trash.

"Wormley's on the fourth floor," Joe said.

Frank went up the stairs as quietly as he could. He winced every time he stepped on some debris and the sound echoed up and down the stairwell.

Placing a finger to his lips, Frank slowly approached Wormley's door. He listened, then knocked. There was no answer. He knocked again.

The door creaked and slowly swung open. Cautiously, Frank looked beyond the doorway and into the living room. The apartment was empty.

"He's cleared out," Frank said, disappointed. He scanned the few pieces of furniture.

"Check the other rooms," Joe said. "Maybe he left something we can use to find him." He headed for the bedroom while Frank sifted through some papers on the coffee table.

51

A scrap of ruled paper caught Frank's eye.

"What do you make of this?" he asked his brother as Joe came back out of the bedroom. Frank handed Joe the paper.

"I don't know," Joe replied. "It looks like a figure you'd use in geometry—parallel lines with a back slash."

"You're right," Frank said. "It's what they call a transversal. But is it a clue to anything? If Wormley drew it, was he just doodling?"

"That's another mystery for us to solve," Joe sighed. He took a last look around the apartment.

Frank led the way back outside, and the Hardys headed home.

"The living room lights are off," Frank said as they pulled into the driveway. "Dad said he was going out, but Mom said she was staying home. It's too early for her to be in bed. I wonder what's—"

"Look! Over by the garden!" Joe yelled. He caught sight of a figure dashing out a back door and through the gloom.

"Someone broke into our house!" Frank cried. "Don't let him get away!"

7 Sniper Attack!

Leaping out of the van, Joe raced across the yard after the fleeing figure.

Frank hurriedly parked and ran into the house. The living room was pitch black. "Mom!" he called. "Are you all right?"

A light came on in the hallway. "I'm fine," Laura Hardy told her son as she emerged from the den at the back of the house. She was holding a baseball bat.

"Did you see the man?" she asked nervously, her voice quavering with fear. "I think he went out through the sliding glass door just as you pulled up. Where's Joe?"

"He went after the burglar," Frank said. "I came in to see if you were all right."

"I'm okay," she said. "Go help Joe."

Frank rushed back outside. From the back of

53

the yard Frank heard the rustling sounds of someone in the bushes. Frank raced toward the heavy foliage. At that moment a figure broke into the open.

It was Joe. "He got away again," Joe said disgustedly. "But I saw the guy. He had red hair."

"Wormley," Frank guessed.

"He didn't hurt Mom, did he?" Joe asked.

"She's okay," Frank assured his brother. "But we'd better see if anything's missing."

"He was in your father's study," Laura Hardy told her sons when they reentered the house. "I was watching television in the den when I heard something in the hallway."

Joe asked, "Did you see who it was?"

"No," she said. "He ran out before I could get a good look. I turned off the lights when he left the house so he couldn't see me inside."

"If he was in the hall outside Dad's study, he could have gone upstairs," Frank said.

"I'll check our room," Joe offered. "You see if any of Dad's records are missing."

Ten minutes later Frank heard Joe calling down to him. "Do you have Biff's Mattingly card?"

"The last time I saw it, it was on the desk in your room," Frank called back up.

"It's not there now," Joe said as he came bounding down the steps to join Frank in their father's office. "I bet Wormley broke in to look for the counterfeit card."

"I think you're right," Frank said. "Especially since nothing seems to be missing here."

Laura Hardy appeared at the doorway. Just then the phone on Fenton Hardy's desk rang. Joe picked it up.

"It's Dad," he told Frank and their mother.

Laura Hardy took the phone from Joe and spoke with her husband. She told him about the break-in but reassured him that everything was okay. After a few minutes she hung up.

Turning to Frank and Joe, she said, "Your father's in New York, following a lead on the DupliTec matter. In case you need to reach him, he wanted you to know he's staying at the Van Hooten."

Frank and Joe checked that all the windows and doors were locked. Laura called the police and, after she'd explained the details of the break-in, asked them to patrol the neighborhood.

"Now," she said, "it's time we all got to bed. We've had more than enough excitement for one day."

"I've been thinking," Frank said as he and Joe headed for the stairs, "before we run over to the flea market tomorrow, we ought to pick up the rest of the cards Nora Shadwick bought when she got the bogus Mattingly. Then maybe we can stop by Baird's place and show them to him."

"What for?" Joe asked, stifling a yawn. "We know the cards are counterfeit."

"We can ask him some more questions about

the ins and outs of counterfeiting," Frank said. "The guy sure does know a lot about it."

"I guess you're right," Joe said, kissing his mom good night. "At the rate we're going on this mystery, we can use all the help we can get."

Eager to get started, Frank was the first one up the following morning. Right after breakfast he called Nora Shadwick and Elliot Baird to make arrangements to stop by. As soon as Joe was up, Frank told him about the plans.

"Nora said she'd meet us at her shop," he said, pouring himself another glass of juice while Joe sat at the kitchen table eating breakfast. "Baird seemed happy to show us his collection."

Ten minutes later Joe was at the wheel of their van. After stopping to pick up Biff they headed for the Pasteboard Palace. Frank ran in for the cards, then hurried back out. Soon they were driving along streets in the wealthier part of Bayport. The houses on these blocks were large, made of brick and stone with lots of windows and chimneys.

"Baird's place sure is huge," Frank commented as they approached the three-story brick mansion. "It's pretty gloomy-looking, too."

Joe steered the van between the stone pillars and started up the curving drive. "Maybe it's haunted," he said. "You know, all those old baseball ghosts."

"Right," Frank said. "Actually, I heard somewhere that Baird bought the house from the heirs of the guy who started the Bayport Blues, way back in the eighteen nineties."

Joe pulled up in front of the stone steps and stopped. Shutting off the engine, he jumped down from the driver's seat. As they walked up the flagstone path Frank noticed that someone was staring at them from the glass pane beside the door.

Joe strode across the porch and pressed the doorbell button. The face disappeared from the glass, and a moment later the door was opened by a big man dressed in a black suit with a white shirt and a red tie.

When Joe introduced himself and his brother the man identified himself by simply saying, "Murphy." He stood aside and said, "Please come in. Mr. Baird is expecting you."

"That I am!" Elliot Sanford Baird said as he stepped in front of Murphy. "Welcome to the Haunted House of Cards.

Joe nudged Frank. "See? Even Baird thinks the place is haunted," he said in a low voice.

"Would you like something to drink?" Baird asked.

Before the boys could answer, he told Murphy to bring them three glasses of soda. Frank's attention was drawn to the confusing jumble of baseball memorabilia on the walls, in cases, standing in corners—in every available place.

"Wow! Babe Ruth's uniform!" Frank exclaimed in awe.

Baird smiled. "The Babe wore that uniform in

nineteen twenty-seven. And the bat in that case over there was the one he used to hit his famous home run at Wrigley Field in nineteen thirty-two."

Frank laughed when he saw Biff's jaw fall open. "You mean that time he pointed to the right-field fence and hit it out of the park?" Biff asked.

Baird nodded. "That's right."

"Wow," was all Biff could say.

"How about this umpire's mask?" Joe asked, pointing next to the uniform.

"That was used in the final game of the forty-nine World Series. It's worth a king's ransom," Baird said. "One of my most prized possessions."

Joe whistled. "This place is better than the Smithsonian," he said.

"Thank you," Baird said proudly, leading them from the hallway into the huge living room to their right. "But the time may come when I'll have to part with my treasures. Please, have a seat."

Frank sat on the edge of the sofa while Biff and Joe each took a seat in one of the large leather wing chairs opposite. Frank was dying to ask Baird what he meant by having to "part" with his treasures, but the collector remained silent. Finally Frank took Nora Shadwick's baseball cards from his pocket and handed them to Baird.

"We think these are counterfeit cards," he said. "Could you check them over and tell us if we're right?"

"I'd be glad to," Baird replied. "You know, this bogus card thing is out of control. There were rumors flying all around the New York show."

Joe asked, "Did you see any phony cards after you looked at Biff's Mattingly card?"

"Actually, I did," Baird told them, a look of disgust passing over his face. "Some young boys had bought fake Mattinglys. And there were at least two Griffeys and a Strawberry that turned up."

Frank and Joe exchanged a look. Those were exactly the same cards that Nora had discovered.

Frank followed Baird over to his desk. Baird switched on the light, then removed a large magnifying glass from a drawer. "Where'd you get these?" Baird finally asked as he put on his glasses.

"Nora Shadwick," Joe replied.

After studying the cards for a few minutes Baird said, "They're all fakes except for this Nolan Ryan." He handed the card to Frank.

"How can you tell?" Joe wanted to know.

"First the logo," Baird said. "Every card company makes its logo very difficult to duplicate. Hold on just a moment," he said, excusing himself.

The collector returned with several long, narrow boxes full of cards. He quickly found what he was looking for.

"Here's something you might be interested in," he said, handing a card over to Biff.

"This is a Mattingly card!" Biff exclaimed.

Baird smiled. "And I'll let you buy it for exactly what I paid for it."

Biff hesitated.

"Which was ten dollars," Baird added. "I've got another one," he explained, "and I'll feel good knowing this one will be going to a serious collector."

Biff eagerly took out his wallet. "You've made me an offer I can't refuse," he declared.

Baird showed them the difference between the logos on the real card and the bogus one. He also explained that the picture on the front of the card shouldn't show through if the card was held up to a light. Finally, he explained that the picture shouldn't be hazy at all.

"Counterfeiters have to take a picture of the card itself," Baird explained. "Then they blow it up and copy it exactly. That's why the photographs themselves are often hazy."

Frank made sure he understood exactly what to look for in a counterfeit and thanked Baird for taking the time to explain all the details.

"Are you fellows trying to find out where the bogus cards are coming from?" Baird asked them.

Joe nodded. "Nora Shadwick asked us to trace them."

"Well, I hope you catch the crook," Baird said. "If there's anything else I can do to help, I'll be right here."

Glancing at his watch, Frank told Joe and Biff they should be leaving. "We've got to be in

Southport at noon," he said, "and it's a good hour's drive."

"Especially if we take Shore Road," Biff added.

"That old road can be dangerous," Baird said, showing them to the door. "Especially after all the rain we've been having. I think it's even washed out in places, so be careful."

After thanking Baird for the information and the tour, Joe took the wheel again. Within minutes the three friends were driving south of Bayport. Out the passenger window Frank watched the waves crash against the rocky coast a hundred or more feet below road level.

"I'm not sure it was such a good idea to tell Baird which route we were planning to take," Joe said, his eyes on the rearview mirror.

"Why's that?" Biff asked.

"Only because we're being followed."

Frank turned around. A battered black pickup truck with darkened windows was some two hundred yards behind them. "Whoever it is seems to be speeding up," Frank said, frowning.

"You're right," Joe confirmed.

Joe pulled the van over as far as he dared. The black truck suddenly accelerated, then roared around the Hardys. The opaque glass made it impossible to see who was inside.

"Guess I was wrong," Joe said, watching the truck pull ahead.

"Maybe the guy is just in a hurry," Biff said, "but he sure does drive like a maniac."

Joe continued driving in silence until Biff said, "Play some tunes, Joe."

Joe turned on the radio and searched for a station that wasn't playing a commercial.

Just then Frank heard a loud pop. The van swerved.

"The front tire!" Joe shouted. "It's blown!" Frank watched his brother fight the wheel as the van swayed violently.

Suddenly there was a second unmistakable crack, then another pop. The van swerved.

"Somebody's shooting at us!" Frank yelled. Glancing out the front window, he saw nothing but sky and water.

"We're going over the edge!"

8 A Hot Time

"Brace yourselves!" Joe shouted. As he glanced in the rearview mirror to make sure no vehicle was behind him, his stomach lurched. He saw a car about thirty feet back, coming around a turn. But Joe had no time to spare.

He turned the wheel sharply away from the edge, doing a one-eighty into the opposite lane. The tires screeched, and the three boys, as well as everything else in the van, slid to the right as the van careened in a hairpin turn.

The driver in the car that had been behind the van hit his horn as he drove by, giving Joe a look that said, "Are you crazy?"

Joe pulled over and put the van into park, then let out a big breath of relief.

"Great driving," Biff said. "You pulled us through."

"Those were shots we heard," Frank said, an alarmed look on his face.

"Damage check." Joe set the emergency brake, and all three friends hopped out of the van.

"The shots came from up on that ridge," Biff said, pointing. He shook his head. "I never thought going to a flea market would be this dangerous."

Joe knelt down by the front wheel wells. "Both front tires are shredded."

Joining him, Frank examined a groove in one of the wheel rims. "Here's where one of the bullets grazed metal," he said. "I'd say from the size of this mark that the sniper must have used a high-powered rifle."

"There was a gun rack in the back window of that black pickup," Joe recalled.

"Let's get these tires changed, then go back to where we heard the first shot," Frank said. "Maybe there's a clue."

Joe took the full-size tire from off the back of the van. Frank had already removed the left front tire. After they replaced that one, Joe pulled a spare out from the back, which they put on in place of the other blown tire. Minutes later Joe started the van and headed back down the road, parking at a spot where the bluffs rose above the road.

"Fan out," Frank instructed. "Look for footprints, scraps of paper, anything that might have been left by the gunman."

Frank scrambled up an opening in the terrain. He made his way steadily toward the top.

"Over here!" he shouted several minutes later.

Joe and Biff came running.

Frank smiled as he pointed to footprints in the dust. "The sniper sat right here and fired at us as we approached."

"Why didn't we see the truck if it pulled over for the gunman to get out and shoot?" Biff asked.

"Good question," Joe said. "I never saw it alongside the road." He walked to the edge of the bluff, which had eroded on one side. Looking down, he found his answer.

"There are the tire tracks where the truck pulled over. And I can tell someone has recently climbed up this way." Joe pointed to a trampled path of leaves and dirt.

Frank looked down at the road, then out over the cliff and across the bay. "I wish I'd paid more attention to his license number."

"I didn't catch it either," Joe admitted.

"If someone's trying to keep us from going to that flea market," Biff pointed out, "then that's exactly where we should be heading."

Frank nodded. "You're absolutely right," he said. With that he started hiking back down the hill toward the van.

"The Southport Mall is on this side of the city," Frank told his brother when they were back in the van.

Joe started up the van and pulled out onto the

65

curving road, being especially careful to slow down when they came around bends.

"I think that's the place up ahead," Biff said, pointing at a large mall and parking lot at the foot of the hill.

Joe quickly found the entrance to the parking lot and cruised around until he located an empty space. The three friends hopped out of the van, and Frank led the way through the crowded lot to the nearest entrance.

Once they got inside the mall Joe was momentarily speechless, surveying the vast number of display tables. "Look at all this stuff!" he said, amazed.

The whole center of the mall was filled with tables. Jewelry, knickknacks, and clothing were on sale. Crowds of people were milling around the tables, checking prices and making purchases.

"I haven't seen any baseball cards yet," Biff said. "But if you want to buy a cheap set of tools, this is the place."

"Yeah, and there's a vendor selling homemade birdhouses," Joe said.

Finally Frank spotted a table loaded down with baseball memorabilia. He signaled his brother and Biff, and they made their way to the display. When he got there Frank noticed that the vendor had only old uniforms and equipment.

"I'm looking for a Mattingly card," Frank told the man behind the table.

"I don't sell cards," the man said. "Try another booth."

"This is great," Joe said, picking up a cracked and dirty first baseman's glove and pounding the well-worn pocket with his fist.

"It's still a pretty good glove," Biff said.

"How much?" Joe asked the vendor.

While Joe haggled over the price of the ancient glove, Frank kept moving.

At a table with old comic books, road maps, and outdated magazines Frank saw several note-books filled with baseball cards.

"Looking for anything in particular?" a young woman behind the table asked him. Frank guessed she was about his age.

"A Don Mattingly baseball card," Frank said.

"What a coincidence," the girl said with a smile. "I happen to have just bought several." She looked through a large mailing envelope, then pulled out a card. It was in a hard plastic case.

"What'd you find?" Joe asked as he walked up. He was wearing his new baseball glove. Biff was with him.

The girl handed the card to Frank and said, "Near mint condition."

Frank examined the card closely. Finally he asked Biff if he could look at the card Baird had sold him.

"Do you think the card is counterfeit?" Biff asked in a whisper, handing his card to Frank.

The girl behind the table must have overheard Biff, because she exclaimed, "Counterfeit! Are you guys accusing me of being dishonest?"

"No, not at all." Joe was quick to reassure her. He smiled and stuck out his hand, the one with the new baseball glove. "I'm Joe Hardy," he said, and he also introduced Frank and Biff.

"My name's Erin," she told them. She hesitated, then laughed and shook Joe's glove.

"There have been some fake cards floating around," Frank explained. "Biff bought one by mistake in New York. Did you say you bought this card today?" he asked Erin.

"Not fifteen minutes ago," she replied. "Why? Is there something wrong?"

"What did the person who sold it to you look like?" Joe asked.

She thought for a moment. "She had blond hair, and she was pretty. Kind of tall. Really nicely dressed. She sold me five Mattinglys and three other cards. She said they were all presents from her ex-boyfriend, who told her they'd be worth something someday. But since she broke up with him, she decided to get rid of them."

"Weird," Joe said. "That's a strange gift."

Frank handed the two cards to Joe. "What do you think?" he asked his brother.

Joe held the cards under one of the gooseneck lamps on the table. "I think it's bogus," he said after a few moments.

"Let me see!" Erin demanded. Taking the two

cards from Joe, she held them side by side under the light. "They look the same to me," she said.

"Look at the logo," Frank suggested. "It's not the same. And the picture is hazy. You can see the outline of the player through the back of the card, too. That's a sure sign that it's fake."

"I was cheated!" Erin said angrily. She emptied the mailing envelope. "What about the other cards? Did I get ripped off?"

Erin handed the cards to Joe. "They looked all right to me," she said in a pouting tone, "but so did the Mattingly."

"All the Mattinglys look bogus to me," Joe told her. "This Darryl Strawberry is also questionable."

"That's what they said when they traded him," Joe heard a familiar voice say. He turned to see Nora Shadwick standing behind them. "Hi, guys," she said. "How's it going?"

"I thought I saw a sign for the Pasteboard Palace across the way," Biff said.

"You've got a table here?" Frank asked Nora.

"I sure do," she said. "I saw you guys and came over to tell you that someone just tried to sell me another phony Mattingly. This time it was some blond-haired woman. I went to a light to check the card, and when I turned around to tell her I couldn't buy it because it was counterfeit, she was gone."

"That sounds like the same woman," Joe said.

"It sure does," Biff agreed. "But why is a

69

woman trying to sell fake cards? I thought we were looking for a red-haired guy."

"We were," Joe said with a frown. "I mean we are." He paused for a moment. "Maybe they're working together to dump their phony Mattinglys."

"What I want to know," Frank said, "is why these counterfeiters keep pushing the same card. They've got to know someone's going to notice a lot of Don Mattingly cards floating around."

"Think of it this way," Nora explained to them. "You hit every dealer and sell ten or twenty of one card at a time. At ten dollars a card, that adds up. By the end of the day you could make several hundred dollars and not have worked very hard. The next day you drop by another fair in a different place and do the same thing all over again."

Erin shook her head sadly. "And to think I got taken. I bought five of them, plus some other fakes. I thought I was getting a deal."

Joe asked Erin for her phone number. "I'll call you if we catch the guy," he told her, writing in a small pocket notebook. "If we don't recover your money, you can still file with the state for victim compensation."

"Thanks," Erin said breathlessly. "Thanks a lot. You guys are great."

"It's nothing," Joe told her, blushing slightly.

"Let's check out the rest of the mall," Frank urged his brother. "Maybe we can find that woman. If she's working with Wormley, he might be around, too."

Nora said she had to get back to work, and Erin told the guys she hoped they found the crook.

"Let's split up," Frank suggested when they reached a large atrium at the junction of the mall's three long shopping wings. "We'll meet over there at that fountain in fifteen minutes."

Joe took the left fork and was back at the rendezvous point a few minutes early.

"I didn't see either of them," Joe reported when Frank and Biff returned. "There weren't any card dealers down that way, either."

"I drew a blank, too," Biff said. "I saw some cards, but they all looked like the real thing."

Glancing at his watch, Frank said they'd better start back to Bayport. Once outside in the parking lot Frank led the group toward the section where they'd parked the van.

"Somebody's gas tank must be leaking," Joe commented, changing the subject. "I'm getting a strong whiff of gasoline from somewhere."

"There's the reason," Frank said, pointing. "See that puddle, right over there by our van?"

Joe stopped. "Frank," he said, "that puddle's *under* our van."

Suddenly, ahead of them a man stepped from between two cars out into the driving lane. His face was hidden behind an umpire's mask, and his hair was tucked under a cap with the peak turned back.

71

"This time you won't get away!" the umpire rasped. He held up something shiny in his gloved hand.

There was a clicking sound, then a flash of fire in the umpire's hand. The man had lit a butane torch and turned the flame up high.

"Watch out! He's got a torch!" Frank warned.

The umpire went into a windup, then hurled the flaming torch right at the pool of gasoline.

9 The Long Arm of the Law

Joe Hardy sprinted into action. Realizing that he was still wearing the old baseball glove he'd bought at the flea market, he stretched out to make a diving one-handed catch. He snared the burning torch just as it arced into the spreading pool of gasoline.

"All right!" he heard Biff and Frank shout in unison. "I'm going after him," Frank shouted.

When Joe felt the torch slap into the glove's webbing he twisted his body, rolling on the ground away from the flammable liquid. When he was completely out of harm's way Joe shut off the nozzle on the torch. It sputtered and died.

"Great catch!" Biff exclaimed.

"Let's get that guy!" Joe shouted as he picked himself up and brushed off his jeans.

Frank was already rushing through the parking lot. Joe couldn't see the guy Frank was chasing.

"Where'd he go?" Joe shouted to Biff.

"Maybe Frank lost him," Biff said, running beside Joe.

Sure enough, ahead of them Frank stopped dead in his tracks. Suddenly, Joe heard an engine roar to life nearby. He turned in the direction of the sound.

It was a black truck with darkened windows. Joe recognized it as the same one that had passed them on Shore Road. The truck backed out of its space, jerked to a halt, then laid rubber as it rocketed toward the exit. Joe wasn't sure, but he thought he saw a passenger in the cab along with the driver.

"There he goes!" Joe yelled across the lot. He tried to catch a glimpse of the license plate, but the numbers were covered with mud.

Meanwhile, Frank and Biff had already seen the truck and were racing back to the van.

"We'll have to follow him on foot," Frank said when Joe reached the van. Frank was on his knees looking at the van's underside. "That guy punctured our gas tank."

Frank walked around the van, then, taking out his handkerchief, picked up a small object.

"It's a spike for putting holes through concrete," he said. "Gas tanks are made out of thick steel, but he could have punctured it with this." Frank put the spike into a small plastic bag that he took from the glove compartment.

Joe looked at the ground around the van. "The guy would have needed to use a hammer to get that spike through our tank. I don't see one around here, but we haven't checked the space where his truck was parked."

Joe jogged several rows away until he found the general area where he had seen the black truck. The space had already been taken by another shopper, but Joe was able to narrow the spot down within two or three spaces either way.

Looking around, Joe tried to see if the red-haired guy had left behind a hammer. What caught his attention instead was a small black square. It was lying right beside a parked car.

Joe picked up the piece of plastic, which turned out to be a three-and-a-half-inch computer diskette. There was a small white label on the diskette that said Home Run.

Looking around to make sure he hadn't missed anything, Joe tucked the diskette into his jacket pocket and headed back to the van.

"The guy also broke into the van," Frank told his brother, "but I can't see that anything's missing."

"If he used a hammer to drive that spike into the gas tank, he must have taken it with him," Joe said. "But I did find this." He showed Frank and Biff the disk.

"We'll run it through our computer when we get home," Frank said.

"And just how are we going to get home?" Biff asked.

"We can call a garage for the van," Joe said. "Then we catch a bus."

Joe sprinted back to the mall and quickly called for a tow truck. Within half an hour a wrecker showed up in the parking lot. Frank and Joe made plans to call about the repairs later in the day. From the van they took their gym bags, which they always had packed for emergencies. Then Frank, Joe, and Biff made their way to the bus stop. As they were waiting for the bus Frank asked Joe what he thought the clues added up to so far.

"We know Biff's counterfeit Mattingly card isn't the only phony card around," Joe said. "From what Nora said, we'll probably find more bad cards."

"But even if they printed up several thousand," Biff said, "we're not talking enough money to buy a luxury sports car or anything."

"No," Joe said. "It's still a decent enough amount of money, though. You could make a living just by traveling around to all the shows and selling phony cards to every dealer you met."

"Wouldn't someone catch on eventually?" Biff pointed out. "People would start to talk."

Joe had to agree his friend was right.

"Maybe that's not the only thing they're printing," Frank said suddenly. "If they can print baseball cards, they can print other things, too."

"You mean, like money?" Biff asked.

"Exactly!" Joe exclaimed. "Or stock certificates, or—"

76

"Anything that uses the same printing process," Frank concluded. "We keep getting around to the fact that the stolen printer is a very important missing link. I wonder if Dad's making any progress on that end."

"Let's call him as soon as we get home," Joe said, checking his watch. "Maybe he's come up with a lead."

The bus stopped for the three boys, and an hour later Frank, Joe, and Biff were back in Bayport. Biff transferred to another bus that took him back home, and the Hardys walked to their house. As soon as they stepped in the door their mother greeted them.

"I'm worried about your father," she told the boys. "I tried to call him at his hotel in New York, but he hadn't checked in yet. That seems strange, considering he left last night. Where do you think he could be?" A worried expression came over their mother's face. "I have to take your aunt Gertrude to run some errands. Would you boys see what you can find out?"

Frank nodded. He and Joe headed straight to Fenton's office while their mother went upstairs to get ready to go out. Frank glanced at the answering machine. "The light's not flashing," Frank said, "so he hasn't called."

"You phone the hotel," Joe suggested. "I'll look through his papers and see if he left any notes about what he might be up to."

Joe opened his father's desk appointment book —the one he kept at home so Frank, Joe, and

77

their mother would know where he was when he was out.

"The desk clerk at the Van Hooten says Dad still hasn't checked in," Frank said, hanging up.

"Here's something," Joe announced. He read aloud from the appointment book. "To New York overnight to investigate Newton's former company—Transversal Industries."

Joe slid open the top drawer in Fenton's file cabinet. Leafing through the manila folders, he stopped suddenly and pulled one out. "Here it is," he said. "Transversal."

Frank looked over his brother's shoulder at the open file.

"It's a list of people who invested in Newton's first company," Joe pointed out. "Most of them have Manhattan addresses."

"Not that one." Frank pointed to one of the names on the list. "According to this, Elliot Sanford Baird invested in Transversal."

"Hmmm . . ." Joe paused. "Very interesting."

"Hey," Frank said, "you remember that doodle in Wormley's apartment?"

"Parallel lines with a back slash." Joe snapped his fingers. "A transversal."

"If Dad's disappeared during his investigation of Transversal," Frank said, "and Wormley is connected to Transversal—"

"Then Dad could be in big trouble," Joe said, looking seriously into Frank's eyes.

Frank checked his watch. "It's late, but if we

hurry, we can catch the next train and still be in Manhattan before seven."

Joe stepped into the hallway and called up the stairs to his mother. "Mom! Can you take us to the train station? We've got to get to New York!"

"It's a good thing we didn't leave our spare overnight bags in the van," Frank commented as they pulled up in front of Bayport's rail depot.

"I'm sure Dad's not in any danger," Joe assured their mother as they got out of the car.

"I hope you're right," said Laura Hardy. "But it's not like your father to forget about calling home when he has to go out of town."

"We'll get to the bottom of it," Frank said, waving goodbye. "Come on, Joe, we've got a train to catch."

Joe watched the bags while Frank went to buy tickets. Frank was at the counter when out of the corner of his eye he saw two men approach. One of them was a uniformed policeman. Frank instantly recognized the other as Con Riley of the Bayport Police Department. Riley had helped the Hardys out on a lot of cases, and he was normally in high spirits. This time, though, the detective looked anything but happy.

"Con," Frank said, reaching to shake his hand. "You taking the train to New York?"

Riley held back, looking uncomfortable. "Unfortunately, no," he said. "And I'm afraid you're not either, Frank."

"What?" Frank asked, confused.

"I'm going to have to ask you to come with us," Riley said, avoiding Frank's eyes.

"Do what?" Joe asked as he approached. "Come with you where?"

Con Riley sighed. "We'd like you to accompany us downtown," he said officiously.

"We can't, Con," Frank explained. "We're on our way to New York. Our father might be in some trouble there."

"You'll just have to wait," Riley said. "We got a tip you two are carrying counterfeit baseball cards across state lines."

"What?" Joe exploded.

"We received a call," Riley continued. "I took it myself. The caller said you'd be trying to leave town with your bags stuffed with counterfeit cards."

Frank stared at Joe, then back at Con Riley. "The caller," Frank said, "was it male or female?"

"If you must know, it was a woman," Riley answered. "She identified herself as being from the biggest baseball card company in the business. Now are you going to cooperate and come down to the station with me?"

Joe gritted his teeth. Frank, however, chuckled and told the police officer, "We're not carrying any baseball cards, but if you want to search our luggage, can't you do that right here?"

Detective Riley hesitated. He glanced at the

uniformed officer. "I suppose we could do that,"
Riley said finally.

"Then be our guests," Frank said.

"Here," Joe said, handing over his bag. "Check
out my socks and underwear while you're at it."

Joe watched without interest as Riley carried
his bag over to one of the benches. The other
officer followed with Frank's.

Riley began rummaging through Joe's bag.
"You two sure do travel light," Riley commented.
Suddenly the detective stiffened. He looked up at
Joe, then removed his hand from the bag.

"Sir," the uniformed officer said to Riley, "I
think I found something."

"I think I did, too," Riley said, holding up a
pack of baseball cards.

Frank thought there were about fifty of them,
wrapped in plastic and sealed with transparent
tape. He glanced at the cards in Riley's hand,
then at a similar pack held by the uniformed
officer.

"Let me see those!" Frank insisted.

"Please don't touch them, Frank," Riley said.
"You know this is evidence."

"Evidence of what?" Joe exploded.

"Possibly dealing in counterfeit baseball
cards," Riley responded.

"How do you know they're counterfeit?"
Frank asked angrily. "You haven't even looked at
them."

"Unfortunately, Frank, I've got probable

cause," Riley told him. "First, someone reports you are in possession of counterfeit cards. Next, you deny having any such cards. Third, we search your luggage, and it turns out you do have cards."

Frank sagged slightly, and Joe's look of disgust turned to one of worry. Detective Riley opened one of the packs and fanned the cards.

A particular card immediately caught Joe's attention. It was a Don Mattingly.

"I hate to do this, guys," Riley told them, "but I don't have any choice. I'm placing you both under arrest."

10 Hardball Pitcher

"You have the right to remain silent," Con Riley started to recite.

"Just a minute!" Joe interrupted. "There's an explanation for this."

Before the officer who came along with Riley could put his handcuffs on Frank, the older Hardy said, "Joe's right. We've been investigating counterfeit baseball cards ourselves," he explained hurriedly. "I think the cards you found in our luggage were planted."

"Our van was broken into at a flea market down in Southport," Joe said. "Nothing was taken, but that's probably when the cards were planted in our bags. We carry packed bags in case we have to stay somewhere on one of our cases."

Riley thought for a moment. "Are you kids telling me the truth?" he asked.

"Nothing but the truth," Frank said.

"Me, too," Joe added.

Con looked at the bag full of phony cards. The officer standing next to him shrugged. Finally Riley said, "Tell me exactly what the case is that you're investigating."

Frank quickly explained to Con about the cards and Wormley and what had happened at the mall earlier that day. After telling the detective the whole story, Frank ended by explaining that he and Joe were going to New York to track down their father, who seemed to be missing.

"We think the stolen printer might be connected to the counterfeit cards," Joe put in.

Riley let out a deep sigh. "I'll have to keep these cards as evidence," he said, signaling the officer to collect the cards.

"I guess you're free to go," Riley said to Frank and Joe. "Just let us know how the case is going."

"Don't we always?" Joe said with a grin.

Detective Riley raised an eyebrow and gave the Hardys a sidelong glance. Then he and the officer walked out of the station.

"That was a lucky break," Frank said. "Let's run! We've got exactly two minutes before the next train leaves."

"No, Mr. Hardy hasn't checked in," the night clerk at New York's Hotel Van Hooten told Frank in response to his question.

"We're going to need a room here ourselves," Joe explained. "We'll take a suite so there will be

84

room enough for all of us when our father finally arrives."

"Very good, sir," the clerk said.

After the brothers had settled into their hotel room Joe called home to see if his mother had heard from Fenton. She told him she hadn't.

"We're going to start looking for him first thing tomorrow morning," Joe promised Mrs. Hardy. "It's too late now to do much of anything," he said, checking his watch and seeing that it was after nine o'clock. After saying goodnight Joe hung up the phone.

"Let's start with Transversal," Frank suggested. He looked in the phone book but didn't find a listing for the company. A call to information didn't get them much further. They got a number for Transversal, but when Frank made the call he found out that the line had been disconnected.

"Try DupliTec's New York office," Joe suggested.

"DupliTec is listed," Frank said, copying down the number. "But we'll have to find Transversal in an old directory. The library would have it."

"Good idea," Joe agreed, and he pulled up the covers on his bed, eager to get some sleep. "Wake me when it's morning."

Frank was awakened the next morning by the sound of a car alarm going off in the street below. He hauled himself out of bed, then roused Joe.

"There's no time to lose. We've got to find Dad," Frank reminded his brother.

After a fast breakfast in the hotel restaurant Joe and Frank hurried to the public library. They quickly found the reference room. While Joe checked the phone books Frank went to the nearest computer terminal to search for news articles about the company, Vic Newton, Elliot Sanford Baird, or any of the other names in their father's Transversal file.

"I've got an address," Joe said quietly, joining Frank at the microfilm viewer. "And get this. The old Transversal address is the same as that of the new DupliTec office. If I didn't know any better, I'd say Newton simply changed the name of his company."

"Newton might have had a long-term lease on the building," Frank said. "According to this article, Newton claimed to have an advanced printer technology when he set up Transversal."

"That's the same thing Newton claims to have now," Joe said.

"Only this time Elliot Sanford Baird is not one of Newton's investors. Baird put several million dollars into Transversal. When Transversal went under, Baird lost his money. I found an article that says Baird is suing Newton for ten million dollars."

"Why is Baird suing?" Joe asked. "People lose money in bad investments all the time."

"Baird is claiming fraud. The article says Transversal sold very few of the printers, and the ones that were purchased were returned because they didn't perform as advertised. Newton's lawyer admits that Transversal was too eager to get its product on the market, that the bugs weren't out of it yet. Newton insists there was no intention to defraud anyone. In the meantime, with all the Transversal printers being returned for refunds, the company went bankrupt."

"Dad's always been a pretty good judge of character," Joe said thoughtfully. "I can't imagine him taking Newton's case if he thought there was anything crooked about the guy."

"I can't either," Frank agreed, "but in the meantime, let's visit the DupliTec office."

Joe looked at the address Frank had written down. "We can take the subway," he noted. "Then we'll have to do some walking."

Frank nodded and led the way out to the street.

"If Newton's on the level, we're still left with the question of who might have stolen his printer," Joe said as they headed down the stairs to the subway.

"Not to mention who might have stolen Dad," Frank added. "Baird has a motive to steal the printer," Frank pointed out. "He believes Newton cheated him. You remember Ruben said he'd heard rumors Baird is going to raise money by selling off some of his memorabilia at the armory show this weekend."

"Printing phony baseball cards would be one way to raise a little cash," Joe said. "But if you're right about Newton's new printer being capable of counterfeiting all sorts of documents, why would anyone start with baseball cards? I mean, why not start right at the top of the list and just print money?"

Frank shook his head and went to the line to buy a token for the subway. "You got me," he said, "but that's exactly what we have to find out."

Half an hour later the Hardys reached DupliTec's offices. The building was located in a warehouse district right on the river. There were several abandoned piers across the street.

"Not exactly the high-rent district," Joe commented. Although there was a lot of traffic on the street, there weren't many pedestrians at all.

"And this isn't the Ritz," Frank added as he looked at the corner building. The ground floor was occupied by a lighting fixtures shop, which was closed. Frank found a small sign above a door on the left side of the building. It read DupliTec Corporation. On the inside of the glass door was a notice announcing that the office would open next week.

Looking through the glass door, Frank could see a narrow hallway and an even narrower flight of stairs leading to the second floor.

Frank tried the door handle. "It's locked."

"Let's try the back," Joe said, starting down the side street.

Frank moved to fall in beside his brother, but Joe stopped short.

88

"What—" Frank started to ask. Then he, too, froze in his tracks.

Frank guessed that the man was no more than half a block away. He was wearing a nylon Cincinnati Reds jacket and an Atlanta Braves cap—with a bit of red hair sticking out from under the cap. His eyes were hidden by sunglasses. He was holding something in front of him, but Frank couldn't tell what it was.

"Careful, I think it's Wormley," Joe cautioned his brother.

"I think you're right." Frank began to advance. "Let's put some space between us."

Joe stepped off the sidewalk and into the street. Frank made the move to approach Wormley directly, and Joe took the flank.

In a flash, though, Joe realized the man wasn't going to play their game. He turned toward Frank and moved his arm into a windup. Joe finally figured out what Wormley was carrying. It was a baseball!

At that second Wormley let fly a hardball that went skyrocketing in Frank's direction.

Joe knew his brother was pretty fast on his feet, but he quickly realized that the guy in the Reds jacket had a very mean fastball.

Joe Hardy watched, transfixed, then horrified as the ball caught Frank square on his forehead. It all happened so quickly that Frank never had a chance to duck.

"Ahhh!" Frank cried, dropping to the pavement.

Joe turned to sprint over to his fallen brother. Before he knew what was happening, a second fastball caught Joe in the neck, slamming hard into the space just to the left of his Adam's apple. The impact and the intense pain stopped him dead in his tracks.

He reached up to his throat, and as he did a red blur raced directly at him. Joe caught only a glimpse of the guy in the Reds jacket. It was Wormley, all right. And he was holding a baseball bat. Joe reached out to fend him off, but in his dazed condition he was too slow.

Wormley brought the bat down sharply on Joe's head. That was the last thing Joe saw before he crumpled, unconscious, to the street.

11 More Headaches

Frank opened his eyes and found himself staring at a cement sidewalk, his head aching. As he slowly regained consciousness he felt as if it had swollen to twice its normal size.

Then he remembered Joe. Struggling to pick himself up, Frank saw a body lying in the street.

"Joe!" he called. But his voice was so feeble he could barely hear it himself. He tried again. "Joe!"

Frank heard a groan. Struggling to his feet, Frank staggered out into the street. When he finally focused on his brother he saw blood on the side of Joe's head.

"Are you all right?" Frank asked, rushing to help Joe.

Joe groaned again, then started to get up.

"Never felt better," he gasped. He touched his head. Frank helped him to his feet.

"Let me get my bearings," Joe said, looking around and blinking several times.

Frank took out a handkerchief and wiped the blood at the back of Joe's head. "It was Wormley, all right," he said. "I only got a quick look at him, but I saw the red hair."

"That guy's in the wrong business," Joe said with a sigh. "If you put radar on that pitch, I bet it would register ninety miles an hour."

"If you're up to it," Frank said, "I think we should still try to get inside DupliTec's offices and look around."

Joe nodded. "I'm with you. Let's see if we can find a way in."

The Hardys walked around the front of the building. The iron gate covering the lighting store windows had been pulled back, and the sign on the front door read Open for Business.

Frank tried the door leading to the DupliTec offices upstairs and found it was still locked. He pointed at the lighting fixtures store. "Maybe there's a way into DupliTec through the store," he said.

"It's worth a try," Joe agreed.

As the two brothers entered the store a bell rang to announce their arrival. An old man in a blue workshirt came over to help them. While Joe distracted the man, Frank wandered through the store looking for a way into DupliTec. Finally he found a set of stairs that led to the basement.

He went back to find Joe and saw that the old man was back behind the counter, busy with some paperwork.

Frank quietly pulled Joe over to the basement door. Frank eased it open, and the two Hardys quickly disappeared down the stairs. Careful not to make any noise, Frank and Joe stepped down into the dusty cellar, making their way past dozens of cardboard boxes. Soon Frank located another door. This one led out onto the building's main staircase.

"We're in luck," he whispered, prying open a lock.

Frank and Joe slipped through the door, climbed up the main staircase, and quickly found themselves in front of the DupliTec offices on the second floor. There a high-powered security system greeted them.

"You spoke too soon," Joe said, grimacing. "We should have known it wouldn't be so easy to break in."

Frank stared at the keypad with flashing red lights. "We'll probably have three chances to get the combination right before the alarm goes off."

"Any guesses?" Joe asked.

"Probably six digits," Frank said, taking a deep breath.

"Or letters," Joe reminded him. "Try *Trans*," he suggested.

"That's too obvious," Frank said. He thought for a moment. "What about the date the company was started?"

Frank pulled out his notepad and found the date he was looking for. He tried the numbers, but nothing happened. The lock beeped twice, and the light still flashed red.

"Allow me," Joe said. He reached over Frank's shoulder and punched in five digits. The lock let out a long beep, and the light flashed green. Joe turned the knob, and the door opened. "We're in!" he announced with a triumphant grin.

"What did you just punch in?" Frank said, following his brother inside.

"Trans," Joe said smugly. "Nothing's too obvious when it comes to combinations."

"I'd say this place needs a lot of work before it's ready to open," Frank said once they were inside.

The office's reception area was cluttered with furniture and large cardboard boxes containing desk chairs and file cabinets. Lights on the receptionist's phone indicated it was hooked up. There was also a brand-new computer. Following the wires and cables, Frank could see it was plugged in.

"We want to check all of the rooms," Frank reminded his brother. "I'll start in the back."

Joe nodded agreement and, using a tissue to avoid leaving fingerprints, began looking through the receptionist's desk drawers.

Frank walked into a room that appeared to be Vic Newton's office. The impressive mahogany desk faced the door. Behind it was a high-backed leather chair. There was a window looking out onto a side street.

Frank searched the drawers, then flipped through the folders in a new four-drawer file cabinet next to the window.

The metal shelving next to the file cabinet was filled with different weights and colors of paper. Kneeling down, Frank saw the bottom shelf was stacked high with cardboard. It appeared to be the same type of stock used to print baseball cards.

What caught Frank's attention was the impressive computer setup covering a long table on the adjacent wall. The main computer unit was an upright tower with several drive slots and a number of light indicators, several of them digital. Connected to the computer was one of DupliTec's HD printers.

As Frank flipped the switch the monitor came instantly to life. The computer's operating system information scrolled past in a blur.

"Talk about fast," Frank said admiringly.

When the main prompt flashed on, Frank typed in a drive change and inserted one of the disks from the receptionist's desk.

The directory showed job application forms, tax withholding forms, and other business forms. On a hunch Frank reached into his pocket and pulled out the diskette Joe had found in Southport. He slipped it into the drive and typed "Home Run."

95

Frank found himself reading a list of baseball players' names. "Don Mattingly, Darryl Strawberry, Ken Griffey, Junior," he read aloud.

Using the system's mouse, Frank highlighted Don Mattingly's name. He clicked the mouse twice.

The darkened screen on the monitor burst into color and displayed a life-size Mattingly baseball card. It was exactly like the counterfeit one Biff had bought at the show, with the player in the same pose. Across the top of the screen was a menu of choices. Frank moved the pointer to "Print" and clicked the mouse twice in quick succession.

The DupliTec high definition printer whirred. Lights flashed. In another instant Frank saw a cardboard sheet of six full-color Mattingly cards emerge from a slit in the side of the printer.

Frank had his hands on the sheet before it could hit the tray.

"Joe!" he exclaimed. "You've got to see this." He hurried out of the office into the hallway and ran into Joe as he was leaving the back room in the office suite. Joe saw the baseball cards as Frank approached.

"These were on that disk you found," said Frank. "It worked perfectly in the HD printer."

"Wow," Joe said, his eyes wide with surprise. He took the set of baseball cards from Frank. "That means the person who had the diskette works on a system compatible with DupliTec's."

"Bingo," Frank said. "That person could be the same one who stole the printer from Vic Newton."

"You're right," Joe said. "Are you thinking what I'm thinking?"

"That the disk could have fallen out of Wormley's truck," Frank said, nodding slowly. "It would be too big a coincidence for the real DupliTec printer thief to just happen to be in the same area Wormley was in." He paused for a moment. "Did you find anything in the back?"

"Nothing," Joe said. "That whole area is being used for furniture storage, as far as I can tell. There are several file cabinets still in their packing cases."

"Wait a minute," Frank said suddenly. "I think I hear something."

"I think you're right," Joe said. "Maybe someone's unlocking the office."

Folding the sheet of Mattingly cards and slipping it in his pocket, Frank started down the hall toward the reception area. Suddenly he stopped and sniffed the air.

"Smoke!" Frank exclaimed. He rushed into the reception area. "The building's on fire!" he called, looking out a window and seeing smoke billow up from below.

Joe came running into the room and raced for the front door. He tried the knob and stared at Frank helplessly. "It's locked!"

97

"We'll have to go out the back," Frank said.

"There are bars on all the windows," Joe said, following Frank to the storeroom.

"Hand me that broom handle," Frank said, coughing. The smoke was filling the hallway and drifting into the room. "And close that door."

Joe grabbed the broom and threw it to Frank. Closing the door was a harder task. There were heavy boxes piled in front of it.

While Joe strained with the boxes, Frank tried lifting the window that led out onto the fire escape. "Some idiot's painted the window shut!" he cried out.

"Break it," Joe urged. "We don't have any time."

Frank smashed the glass with the broom handle. "Come on!" he urged his brother.

Frank swung his leg over the peeling window-sill and eased himself onto the fire escape.

Joe was right behind him. Slipping hurriedly out the window, he glanced back into the storeroom, which was filled with smoke.

"Frank!" he cried. "Look!"

Frank looked where Joe was pointing and saw the storeroom door engulfed in flames. Beside the door the box containing the file cabinets was rocking back and forth, almost hopping.

"There's someone in that box!" Joe exclaimed, ducking back inside the room.

"Joe!" Frank cried. "Stop! You'll get killed!"

Frank Hardy looked on in horror as his brother raced through five-foot-high flames toward the cardboard box.

But Frank got an even bigger shock when Joe managed to rip open the cardboard box and out fell Fenton Hardy.

12 Fire Escape!

Joe gasped when he saw his father. Fenton Hardy was bound and gagged, his eyes were closed, and his face was white from shock.

"It's Dad!" Joe shouted. "He's unconscious."

With flames roaring all around him, Joe pulled his father from the crate.

Frank came running back through the room to help his brother. Hurriedly Frank ripped the gag from Fenton's mouth. Taking his pocketknife, Joe cut the bonds that held the detective's hands behind his back.

"I hear sirens," Frank said. "Somebody must have called in an alarm."

"We've got to get out of here," Joe said. "This old building will collapse."

Frank helped his brother half carry, half drag

their father to the fire escape. The fresh air seemed to revive Fenton. Some color came back into his face, and he began to groan.

"Dad!" Frank shouted, slapping his father lightly on the cheeks. "Dad, can you hear me?"

"Wha—" Fenton blinked, then stared.

"Come on, Dad," Joe said. "We've got to go down this fire escape."

Frank and Joe put their father between them, holding him up under their arms. Slowly the three edged sideways down the fire escape, with Frank in the lead.

Joe heard the sounds of the fire trucks arriving out on the street. Footsteps pounded closer as a detail of firemen ran around to the alley to see if there were any people trapped in the back windows. The three Hardys were just reaching the ground when the crew arrived.

One of the firemen pulled the fire escape ladder to the ground and held it in place. Frank went down the ladder first, Fenton was next, and then Joe.

When they got the ground the firemen quickly pulled them all to safety, away from the burning building.

"You kids saved my life," Fenton said, taking one of his sons under each arm.

"What happened?" Joe asked.

Before Fenton could answer, an emergency worker came rushing over to the three of them. The man, dressed in white, asked them if they needed oxygen or wanted to be taken to the hospital. Despite his condition, Fenton Hardy declined.

"All I really need," he said, "is a good breakfast and a decent cup of coffee."

Joe was relieved to see that his father was back to normal. "I think we'd better get out of here before someone asks us what we were doing in the DupliTec offices," Joe said, watching the firemen work to put out the flames.

"We passed a coffee shop on the way over here," Frank said. "Let's go."

With that Frank led the way down the alley and toward the street. A few blocks later the Hardys found a restaurant. Frank held open the restaurant door for Joe and Fenton.

"There's a booth toward the back," Frank said.

After the three detectives had given their orders to the waiter, Joe turned to his father and asked, "What happened back there?"

"We knew you hadn't checked into your hotel," Frank added. "But we had no idea where you were."

Fenton calmly took a sip of coffee. "When I got into the city I contacted a couple of people who had invested in Newton's first company."

"Transversal," Joe said.

"That's right," Fenton said. "When Transversal folded, all of them lost their money."

"Did you come up with any leads?" Frank asked.

"No, and it was getting late," the detective

102

continued. "But instead of checking into the hotel, on a hunch I caught a cab and came down to the old Transversal office." He paused in his story when the waiter brought their food. "I didn't realize it at the time, but I was being followed."

"Did you see who it was?" Joe asked eagerly.

"Not until it was too late," Fenton admitted. "Newton had given me a key and the combination to the office. I let myself in, but I locked the door behind me. I suspect the person who followed me has a key and the combination as well."

"Did you see who it was?" Joe asked.

"I know it was a woman, and I know she had blond hair," Fenton replied.

Frank and Joe exchanged a look. "That could be the same woman who sold Erin the phony cards," Joe said, quickly explaining to their father what had happened to them since they'd last talked.

Frank nodded in agreement. "It's a good possibility. What happened?" he asked his father.

"She conked me out," Fenton said. "When I came to I was tied and gagged and inside some kind of box. As far as I'm concerned, there's not much doubt now that we're all working on the same case."

"Where to now?" Joe asked, digging into his omelet.

Frank thought for a moment. "Doesn't Forest Rader have a shop in the city?" he asked.

Joe shrugged. "I guess so. Why?"

"Maybe we should stop by before heading back to Bayport," Frank suggested. "We can find out if he's seen any more bogus cards."

"Sounds good to me," Joe said, taking a bite of his toast. "What are you going to do, Dad?"

"There's one more name on my list of investors," Fenton said. "A guy named Keith Burke. I want to see if I can track him down. Why don't we all meet back at the hotel in time for the 5:07 train to Bayport?"

With that, Fenton Hardy went to pay the check. Frank finished his juice and stood up. "I'm amazed," he said to Joe. "Dad's just been stuck in a cardboard box overnight, and after a tiny breakfast he's right back on the case."

Joe looked at his father in admiration. "I know what you mean," he said. "The guy's an inspiration, isn't he?"

"You bet," Frank said. "Come on. Let's show him we know what it means to be a Hardy!"

When Joe opened the door to Baseball Diamonds Are Forever, Forest Rader was nowhere to be seen. Joe looked again, wondering if Rader was hidden in the gloom behind the clutter. There wasn't a space on the walls or on a shelf or in the glass display case that wasn't crammed with baseball cards and memorabilia.

"How would you ever find anything in here?" Frank asked, following Joe into the store.

"It's easy," came a voice from behind a curtain. Forest Rader stepped out from a back room. "I simply remember where every item is kept."

"Amazing," Joe said. "The Pasteboard Palace is twice as big as your shop but probably doesn't have half as much stuff."

"Space is expensive in the city," Rader reminded the Hardys. "Besides, I think the clutter gives the place atmosphere."

Joe unfolded the sheet of Mattingly cards and handed them across the case to Rader. "Have any of these turned up in the past few days?" he asked.

Rader looked at the cards closely under a light. He used a magnifying glass to look at the logo and the photograph, then held the cards up to the light. "These look exactly like the bogus Mattingly card your friend bought," Rader said finally.

"They came from the same source," Frank said.

"Have you figured out who it is yet?" Rader asked.

"Not yet," Joe said.

Rader shook his head and made a face, handing the sheet of cards back to Joe. "I hope you catch whoever is making the counterfeits," Rader said, "and fast. More and more bad cards are starting to show up. As far as I'm concerned, this kind of thing really ruins the business."

"You said more bad cards are turning up?" Frank asked.

Rader nodded, turned, and removed a cigar box from a shelf behind him. "I bought these yesterday." He placed three cards face up on the glass counter.

"You paid market prices?" Joe asked, looking at a Mattingly card identical to the one Biff had bought. There was also a Strawberry and a Griffey.

"I got them from a kid," Rader said. "I lost money, but I wanted to take the cards out of circulation."

"Did you ask the kid where he got the cards?" Frank asked Rader.

"At the Southport flea market," Rader said.

Frank asked, "Do you have the kid's name?"

"No, actually I don't," Rader admitted.

Joe and Frank exchanged a look. Another dead end. "Have you seen other instances of counterfeiting like this in your career?" Joe asked.

Rader thought for a moment. "Once or twice. The counterfeiter has to know a lot about collecting. He needs accomplices, too. The same guy trading bogus cards would get noticed, you know?"

"Sure," Frank said. "How much money could someone make from counterfeiting?" he asked.

"Depends on how many cards you print and how much they go for," Rader said. "A couple hundred Mattinglys at ten bucks a pop, you won't get rich. But you will get out of debt!" he said with a laugh.

Joe thought about Elliot Baird and his financial problems.

"Speaking of which," Rader said, almost reading Joe's mind, "you guys are going to be at the Bayport Armory show this weekend, aren't you? It ought to be one of the memorabilia events of the year, what with Elliot Baird selling off some of his collection."

"You know for a fact Baird's going to be selling a few items?" Frank asked.

"I got it from a good source that Baird's having big money problems," Rader confided.

"Do you think Baird could be behind these counterfeit cards?" Joe asked.

"I didn't say that," Rader replied quickly. "I just think because of his being well-known in the hobby, he'd be in a good position to sell a lot of phony cards before anyone caught on."

Glancing at his watch, Frank thanked Rader. Joe said they'd see him at the armory show.

Out on the street Joe hailed a cab and told the driver, "Stop by the Hotel Van Hooten, then go on to Grand Central Station."

Traffic was heavy. By the time they reached the hotel, Joe saw Fenton Hardy waiting beside the front entrance with Frank's and Joe's bags.

Joe rolled down the window and called to his father. Jumping into the cab's backseat, Fenton told the driver to hurry. "We've only got ten minutes or so before our train." The driver nodded and pulled out into traffic.

During the cab ride Fenton told Frank and Joe that Keith Burke, the last Transversal investor, seemed to have disappeared without a trace. "But a banker told me that Elliot Sanford Baird was the major investor in Transversal," Fenton said. "He owned almost ninety percent of the stock. Baird lost the most when Transversal failed."

"That tends to confirm what we heard," Frank said. He told his father of the rumors about Baird's money troubles.

After they'd pulled up in front of the station Fenton paid the fare, and Frank asked the driver to open the trunk. The driver got out and walked around to the back.

Joe opened the door on the street side while Frank and Fenton stepped out onto the curb. Fenton went to collect their bags from the trunk.

Looking up, Frank saw a white limousine with darkened windows coming toward them from behind. It veered out of traffic, then accelerated.

Joe was halfway into the first driving lane, and the speeding limo was heading straight toward him.

"Joe!" Frank called sharply. "Watch out!"

With a roar the long white car turned slightly toward the right. The ornament on the gleaming chrome radiator grille looked to Frank as though it were actually aimed at Joe.

"Joe!" Frank shouted again.

Joe, concentrating on the luggage, looked up. He was only seconds away from being run over!

13 The Man in the Leather Mask

Frank sprang into action. "Joe," he yelled, "look out!"

Joe had turned around just in time. The white limousine sideswiped the cab as Joe jumped back onto the curb.

Yelling for everyone to get out of the way, Frank raced onto the street to get the number of the limousine before it could disappear into traffic.

"My cab!" the driver yelled. "That clown hit my cab!"

Although Frank strained to see, the darkened windows made it impossible to tell who was inside the limo. The fact that the limo kept right on going didn't make identifying the driver any easier. Frank did manage to get the license plate number, though. He wrote it down in his notebook and walked back over to where Joe and Fenton stood on the sidewalk.

"I got the license," Frank told them above the roar of the traffic. He copied the number a second time in his pocket notebook, then handed one copy to the cab driver.

"Give this number to the police," Frank told the man, "when you call in to report the accident."

"What about you?" the driver wanted to know. "You're my witnesses!"

Joe pointed to the crowd standing around the cab. "Any one of these people can help you out. Sorry!" he yelled, running to catch up with Frank and Fenton, who were already racing to the station's entrance. "We've got a train to catch."

Frank was up early the next morning. After eating a large breakfast he phoned the garage in Southport to check on the van.

"Should be done later today," the mechanic told Frank.

After hanging up Frank asked his mother if he could borrow her car. Laura and Fenton Hardy were still lingering over breakfast. They'd all been up late the night before discussing the case. Fenton filled them in on the names of the temporaries who had worked at DupliTec. He'd narrowed the list down to two women, Gina Lynd and Tracy Simon. Both had left DupliTec suddenly, right after the thefts. Fenton Hardy was going to continue checking up on both of them. Frank wanted to follow their most promising lead: Elliot Baird.

Frank went upstairs to rouse Joe. "I got us transportation," Frank told his brother. "Our first stop should be Baird's mansion. A lot of the evidence seems to point in his direction. He showed us his collection, but we really didn't get a chance to look around the place."

"If he lost all that money in Newton's first company," Joe said sleepily, "it isn't too hard to imagine him trying to get revenge."

"Very true," Frank said, pulling the covers off Joe. "But we won't know a thing unless you hurry up and get ready."

Joe went to shower and get dressed. Frank took the car keys his mother offered and told Joe he'd back out the car while Joe finished his breakfast.

"If Baird's the counterfeiter," Joe said a little while later as he and Frank drove toward the Baird mansion, "and if the bogus baseball cards are made on the stolen DupliTec printer, how did Baird manage to steal the printer?"

"And how are Wormley and his blond accomplice connected?" Frank added. "Are they the brains behind the operation, or do they do the dirty work?"

"I'm sure Baird provides the brains," Joe concluded as they drove up to the mansion. "You know, it doesn't even look like anyone lives here."

Frank turned into the drive leading up to the

front entrance. "You're right," he said. "Look at all the weeds. Baird's really letting the grounds go."

"There may not be anyone home," Joe said. "I don't see a car."

Frank pulled over to one side of the driveway and put the car's shift into park. He walked up the steps and pressed the doorbell.

Joe joined Frank. "Hear anything?" he asked.

Frank pressed the button a second time.

When the front door began to open Frank didn't see anyone at first. Then a scowling face appeared out of the gloom and asked, "May I help you?"

Frank recognized the man as Murphy, Baird's butler. "We're the Hardys, remember? We came to look at Mr. Baird's collection," Frank told the man. "We were here the other day, but we didn't have time to see everything. Mr. Baird told us to drop by if we were in the neighborhood," Frank added, thinking quickly. If Baird wasn't home, he figured, now was a great time to snoop.

"He's not here," the butler said simply. "Mr. Baird won't return until later today."

"Mr. Baird is out of town?" Joe asked.

Murphy paused. "He had to go to New York," the man said. The butler pulled the door open wider. "You say you're the Hardys?"

Frank nodded.

"I suppose it wouldn't harm anything to let you come in and look around. Mr. Baird just acquired

Bo Jackson's Royals uniform. It's one of the most valuable pieces in the collection."

Frank followed the butler into the hallway. The man switched on the overhead lights, then slid open the heavy oak doors leading into what he guessed had once been a parlor.

"The uniform is through here," Murphy said.

While Frank kept up with the butler and distracted him with small talk, Joe hung back and surveyed the hallway. Frank turned around at one point and saw Joe staring at a glass cabinet.

"Something is missing back there," Joe whispered to Frank when the two Hardys finally entered the parlor. Murphy was pointing out a white uniform with the number sixteen sewn on right under the Royals logo.

"What?" Frank asked under his breath.

At that moment the phone rang, and Murphy excused himself.

"I don't know," Joe said, answering Frank's question. "Something. It's bothering me that I can't figure it out, but something is missing."

"I can't talk now!" Frank heard the butler exclaim in a loud whisper from the next room. Right afterward Frank heard the phone slam in its cradle.

"I'm sorry about the interruption," the butler said, returning. "That was a call from Mr. Baird. He told me to tell you to make yourselves at home."

Judging from how the butler had been speaking on the phone and the fact that Murphy had slammed down the receiver without saying good-bye, Frank doubted the butler was telling the truth. Even so, he pretended to believe him and said, "That's really nice of him. I think I could look at this collection for days. It would be a real shame if he had to sell it off."

Murphy gave Frank a blank stare. Joe was about to jump in when the phone rang again.

Looking extremely irritated, the butler excused himself again and went into the next room. He was back in seconds.

"It's for you," the butler announced. "It's Fenton Hardy."

"I'll take it," Joe said, and he hurried into the next room.

While Joe took the phone message from their father, Frank continued studying the treasures in the parlor.

"Thank you for showing us around," Joe said, coming back into the room. "But unfortunately, we have to be going. Our dad was calling to remind us about an important meeting."

Frank played along. He knew they didn't have any important appointment, but he also realized Joe was trying to find a way for them to get out of the mansion quickly. He, too, thanked the butler and then followed Joe out into the hall and through the front door.

"What's up?" Frank asked when he slipped into the passenger side of their mother's car. Joe took the wheel.

"Biff called the house," Joe said, starting up the engine. "He wants us to meet him down at Rube's Restaurant. Dad said it sounded important."

Joe shifted the car into gear and headed down the gravel drive to the street.

"Did you figure out what was missing from Baird's collection?" Frank asked.

Joe nodded. "On the way out I looked at the display case in the hallway."

"And?"

After Joe took a turn onto the street he looked over at Frank. "The other day when Baird showed us around his house he made a fuss about the umpire's mask on display in his hallway. He made it sound as if it was priceless."

"I remember. 'Worth a king's ransom,' Baird said, right?"

"Right," Joe said. "And remember that the guy who threw the burning torch in Southport was wearing an umpire's mask?"

Frank nodded.

"Well, that glass case is empty." Joe paused. "The umpire's mask is gone."

14 Striking Out

"You mean you think Baird's the counterfeiter,"
Frank said slowly. "You think he's the one who
sent Wormley after us?"

Joe kept his eyes on the road but reasoned out
the facts for his brother. "It could be. The mask is
missing. Wormley was wearing one."

While Joe guided the car through the downtown area and headed toward the waterfront
Frank was quiet. "What do you think?" Joe
finally asked his brother.

"It's all so clear, and yet . . ." Frank paused.
"It's too easy. When Baird showed us that umpire's mask he talked like it was a national
treasure. Even if we assume Wormley is working
for Baird, I can't imagine Baird giving Wormley a
valuable baseball artifact to use as a disguise
when he followed us to Southport."

Joe realized his brother was right. He took a right turn and looked for a parking place. They were close to Rube's Restaurant.

"I guess Wormley could have bought an umpire's mask at any sporting goods store," Joe admitted with a sigh. He steered the car into a spot and shut off the engine.

"Don't worry," Frank said, reassuring his brother. "We'll get somewhere on this case, and soon."

"I hope you're right. So far it's been one dead end after another. If Wormley gets away one more time, he may not come back."

Frank nodded. "I think we should plan to visit the Haunted House of Cards again tonight," he suggested, getting out of the car. "If Baird is responsible for the counterfeits, my guess is we'll find the stolen DupliTec printer right there in his house."

"Do you think Baird would admit anything if we pressed him?" Joe asked, holding the diner door open.

"Probably not," Frank said, "but he might slip up."

"You kids came pretty quick," Ruben Pierce said when the Hardys entered the diner. "Your friend was here. He stopped by for a soda, since he was in the neighborhood. Then he had to leave really fast. But he left you this note." Rube handed a slip of paper over to Joe.

Joe unfolded the note and read it aloud:

" 'Spotted Wormley. Am following. Will call.' It's signed 'Biff.' "

"How long ago did he leave?" Frank asked Rube.

Rube rubbed his chin. "Not more than five minutes ago."

"Did he drive?" Joe asked.

"I think so," Rube said. "He had his keys out."

"There goes our chance to follow him," Frank said. "You didn't see which way he went, did you?"

"Sorry, boys, I didn't," Rube said. "Listen, why don't you fellows have some lunch while you're waiting? Today's special is the hamburger deluxe."

Frank glanced at his watch. "It is getting close to noon," he said.

"We'll take two," Joe said, steering Frank to a nearby booth. Within ten minutes they were digging into two of Rube's delicious hamburgers. Not more than two minutes later the phone behind the counter rang. Rube answered it.

"Yes," Joe heard Rube say. "They're right here." Joe got up and headed for the counter. Before he could stop Rube the restaurant owner said, "Sure, I'll tell them," and hung up.

"Was that Biff?" Joe asked excitedly.

"It sure was," Rube announced. "He said to tell you he followed Wormley to the Bayport Mall. He said to hurry over. He's by the fountain, and he's got Wormley in sight."

Jumping up, Joe paid the check and caught up

118

with Frank, who was already out the door and sitting in the driver's seat of Mrs. Hardy's car. Joe slipped into the passenger seat, and Frank drove off with a squeal of rubber. In just a few minutes the Hardys were pulling into the mall entrance and searching for a space.

"Hurry," Joe urged his brother. "Wormley's not going to sit by the fountain all day."

"I'm doing the best I can," Frank said. He swerved the car into a spot that a station wagon was just leaving, snaking a guy in a Mercedes who had been waiting for the spot. The Hardys rushed out of the car while the guy in the Mercedes leaned on his horn.

"He'll get over it," Frank muttered to Joe.

"We'll have to be careful we don't lose Wormley in the crowd," Joe noted while they made their way through the large department store that anchored one end of the mall.

"You take one side of the fountain, I'll take the other," Frank said as they entered the mall's indoor atrium.

As Joe approached the fountain in the center of the mall he caught a glimpse of red hair. Moving closer, Joe found himself looking straight at Mark Wormley. And Wormley, who had been preoccupied up to that moment, was staring right back.

Hurriedly Joe scanned the other side of the mall for Frank. He spotted him not more than fifty feet away, but Joe saw that there were a lot of shoppers between him and his brother.

Joe signaled to Frank.

At the same moment Wormley jumped up. Joe realized that Wormley had recognized him. But the red-haired guy was also gesturing to someone.

That's when Joe saw the blond woman. She was approaching Wormley from the same direction Joe had come. Wormley was trying to warn her away.

Joe sprinted toward Wormley. Seeing Joe start for him, Wormley broke into a run. People scattered, and the red-haired man knocked over one man and sent a baby stroller careening across the terrazzo floor.

On the other side of the mall Frank had seen Joe's signal. He also saw Wormley get up from the bench where he was sitting by the fountain. Then, in a flash, Frank saw the blond woman approach. Right behind her was Biff Hooper.

The woman saw Wormley start to flee and froze momentarily. It seemed to Frank that she didn't know what to do.

But Frank did. He raced over to her. "The police want to talk to you," he said firmly.

The woman stared down Frank with icy blue eyes. "You wish," she said with a sneer.

As the woman tried a fake to the left with a run to the right, Frank deftly grabbed her right arm. She tried to pull away, but Frank held tight. When he finally did relax his grip it was because Biff, accompanied by a mall security guard, had her boxed in.

"Hold on to her," Frank told the guard, "and call the police. I'll be right back."

Joe, in the meantime, found himself on the floor wrestling with Mark Wormley. He had Wormley's arm pinned behind his back and was listening to the culprit beg for mercy.

"I give up!" the red-haired man gasped.

"I see Wormley didn't disappear this time," Frank observed as he jogged over to Joe. "Biff and I caught his accomplice. The police are on their way."

"I'm not talking to any cops!" Wormley spat out.

"That's your choice," Joe responded. "But what you don't tell them, my brother and I can easily fill in."

Joe put some pressure on Wormley's arm and told him to get to his feet. Frank tensed, ready to prevent any fresh attempt to escape.

"Frank, Joe," a Bayport police officer said as he approached the group. He was walking with Biff and the mall security man. They were escorting Wormley's blond accomplice, who was wearing handcuffs.

"Your friend here tells me you've captured some counterfeiters," the man from the Bayport Police Department said.

"This is Mark Wormley," Joe told the officer. "That woman is his accomplice."

"Yeah, right," the woman said. "Try to prove it."

The police officer took Frank, Joe, and Biff

121

aside. "The woman says her name is Gina Lynd, but she won't admit to knowing that red-haired guy."

Joe ran his hands through his sandy blond hair. "Officer, on several occasions that man and woman assaulted our father and both Frank and myself," Joe said, relating the central points of the counterfeiting case. "Even if they don't admit it, we're completely willing to press charges," he concluded.

Joe's speech was enough for the officer. He went over to read Wormley and Lynd their rights and took them both off in cuffs.

"That was great work," Frank complimented Biff after the culprits had been taken away. "How'd you happen to be following them?"

"Wormley was in the Pasteboard Palace," Biff explained. "I saw him try to sell Nora some baseball cards. She wouldn't buy them. I guess she figured out they were fakes. He left before she could call the police, so I followed him down to Rube's, where he had lunch. That's when I called you guys. Then I tailed Wormley to the mall. I think he just came here to pick up Gina."

The Hardys said a quick goodbye to Biff, who was going to stay at the mall, and headed for home. Once they got there Joe called the garage in Southport. The mechanic told him the van would be ready the next morning.

After supper the Hardys headed back out, making their way to Elliot Sanford Baird's house.

Within twenty minutes they were in front of the Haunted House of Cards.

"Someone's home," Joe said. "His place is all lit up."

"Forget about breaking in then," Frank said.

"Why don't we just ask Baird point-blank," Joe suggested as they cruised up Baird's long, dark driveway. He parked the sedan just short of the front walk and got out.

"Ask him what?" Frank wanted to know. "'Excuse me, Mr. Baird. My brother and I would like to ask you if you're a counterfeiter.' Like that?" he asked, making a face.

"We can be more roundabout than that," Joe insisted. "We know how to be subtle. Leave it to me."

Reaching the front entrance, Joe pressed on the doorbell. Murphy answered. "We'd like to speak with Mr. Baird, if he's in," Joe said politely.

The butler started to close the door but stopped when he heard the voice behind him.

"I'm right here," Elliot Sanford Baird told his butler. "Please invite the Hardys inside."

Frank stepped into the hallway past the scowling butler. Joe was right behind.

"It's been a long day," Baird said, reaching out to shake their hands. "I've got to return to New York again tomorrow for a few days. But you're welcome to visit." He ushered Frank and Joe into the parlor, then asked them to sit down.

"We won't stay long," Joe assured him, "but we had a few questions we wanted to clear up."

"I'll be glad to help you if I can," Baird said.

Frank began, "About your lawsuit against Vic Newton—"

Baird jumped up. "That is my business," he said coldly. "You know, I'm really rather tired, so if you don't mind . . ."

Before Frank or Joe could apologize, Baird had pressed a button on the wall, and Murphy entered purposefully through a door at the back of the parlor.

"I changed my mind, Murphy. Show the boys out, would you, please?" Baird instructed the servant.

Joe felt the butler grip his arm hard. Joe was about to ask Murphy to go easy when his attention was drawn to the room from which the butler had entered.

There, on a large worktable, was a sleek black printer. Colorful copies rolled out one end into a tray. Unless Joe was totally wrong, it definitely looked as though Elliot Baird was the proud owner of a DupliTec high definition printer.

15 Inside the Haunted House of Cards

"How much more proof do we need?" Joe asked Frank as they walked away from Baird's mansion. "The guy needs money. He knows about baseball cards. He invested in Vic Newton's company, so he knew about the HD printer."

"So?" Frank asked, opening the car door.

"So Baird obviously got Gina Lynd or Mark Wormley or both of them to steal the printer from DupliTec," Joe concluded. "And he's been using them to pass phony cards. I bet Baird gave Wormley that umpire's mask after all. You saw what a cold shoulder he gave us—"

Frank put out a hand to calm his brother down. He started the engine and pulled away from Baird's house. "Take a chill pill, Joe," Frank said. "First of all, we need to be positive that the printer you saw is the same as the one stolen from DupliTec. Second of all, if you had a stolen printer, would you leave it practically out in the open so anyone who walked in could see it?"

"No," Joe muttered. "I guess not."

"There's a simple solution," Frank said, heading back toward their house.

"What's that?" Joe wanted to know.

"We come back when Baird's not there. He told us he has to go out of town again tomorrow. Let's come back then."

"Makes sense," Joe admitted. "And if it turns out the printer I saw is Newton's, we've got Baird."

"It certainly looks that way," Frank said thoughtfully. "In the meantime, we need to find out if it really was Lynd who stole the printer from Newton."

"Let's ask the chief for copies of Wormley's and Lynd's mug shots," Joe said. "We can show them to Vic Newton."

"Good idea," Frank agreed. "We can press charges while we're down at the station. Then let's get some rest. We've got a lot of investigating to do tomorrow."

Frank and Joe met at the breakfast table the next morning. Frank had already found out the van was ready and asked their mother to drop them off at the mechanic's.

When Joe was sitting down at the kitchen table

with a glass of juice, Frank pushed a section of the Bayport morning newspaper across to him. "This armory show must be a big deal in the world of baseball card collecting," Frank said. "Full-page newspaper ads aren't cheap."

"Did you read the auction list?" Joe asked. "Half this stuff is from Baird's collection. The rumors were right about him selling off part of it." Joe scanned the list. "In fact, look right here." He handed the paper over to Frank. "The umpire's mask. He's going to sell it."

"That's one way to get rid of incriminating evidence," Frank said.

"On the way back from Southport we can stop by DupliTec's office in Bayport," Joe said, "and let Newton see the mug shots. I can't believe that both Wormley and Lynd refuse to talk," he added.

Frank shrugged and stood up. "Con can't make them," he said. "They've both pleaded 'not guilty.' We'll just have to see how the evidence stacks up. Our testimony is going to be pretty incriminating."

Joe nodded and took his dishes to the sink. "Especially when we find out that there's a solid connection between Wormley, Lynd, and Baird. Let's go," he said excitedly. "I have a feeling today's the day we crack this case!"

Standing in DupliTec's Bayport office two hours later with Frank, Joe handed Wormley's

127

and Lynd's mug shots to Vic Newton. "This man assaulted us several times," Joe explained. "We think he may be in on the theft."

"I'm sorry," Newton said. "I don't recognize him."

"How about the woman?" Frank asked. "Her name is Regina Lynd, and she worked for the temporary agency you've done business with."

Newton looked at the picture and shrugged. "She doesn't look familiar to me," he said. "Let me ask my secretary."

Newton called across the reception area to a young woman sitting at a computer. "Rose," he said, "would you please come here?"

Newton showed the woman the photograph of Lynd. "Does this woman look familiar?" he asked Rose.

"Sure, I remember her," Rose said. "She only worked a couple of days, and I wouldn't call it work."

"What was her assignment?" Frank asked.

"She was supposed to answer the phones and do some filing," Rose said, "but every time I looked up she was gone. She spent most of her time talking with the guys back in the lab."

"How soon after she left was the printer stolen?" Frank asked.

"You know," Rose said, furrowing her brow, "I think it was the next weekend."

Joe felt his excitement building. "Did Gina have office keys?" he asked.

"We keep them in the supply room," Rose explained. "It's unlocked during the day."

Turning to Newton, Frank asked, "Can you tell us the serial number of the missing machine?"

"No problem," Newton said. He checked a computer printout on his desk and jotted down a number on a piece of scrap paper.

Frank took the paper from Newton and thanked him for his time. "We'll get in touch as soon as we have any new information," he said.

With that Frank and Joe left DupliTec and headed back to their car. "If the serial number on that printer in Baird's house matches the one Newton just gave us," Joe said eagerly, "this case is solved!"

Late that night Frank and Joe were heading back to the Baird mansion. They'd spent most of the afternoon with their father going over the facts of the case. The police were still questioning Wormley and Lynd in the presence of their lawyers, but they both denied everything.

The Hardys hadn't told their father where they were going, just that they wanted to take in a late movie. They felt it was better not to worry him or their mother.

As they drove Joe watched lightning streak across the sky.

"It's going to be a bad storm," Frank predicted. Thunder rumbled in the background, and rain began pelting the van's windshield.

"Better get our raincoats," Joe told Frank once they had parked the van on a side street near the Baird mansion.

Frank took the rain gear and a flashlight from a console next to the backseat and handed it forward. Joe slipped into the black jacket, then opened the van's door.

Joe silently led the way down the street and around to the front of the house. The plan was to slip through the gate, then head around the back of the house and sneak in through a ground-floor window.

"This place is so dark it doesn't even look like the butler's home," Frank whispered.

Finding the gate open, Joe slipped inside. Frank was right behind him.

"Keep low," Joe whispered, "and let's try the back of the house first. Maybe there's a window that isn't latched."

Joe reached the peeling, rain-streaked house first. He tried several side windows. Frank darted past him and went around to the back. He found a window that was being repaired. The iron bars that had covered the window had been removed and were lying on the ground nearby.

Frank returned in minutes. He signaled to Joe. "I found a basement window," he said. Leading Joe to the spot, Frank eased open the window.

"I'll go first," Joe said around a crash of thunder. "Keep a lookout."

Turning around, Joe dropped to his knees and

backed into the opening. Once inside he reached up and took the small flashlight Frank handed through.

Joe played the beam about the room and saw he was in a shallow basement with a dusty cement floor.

"All clear," Joe told Frank. "Come on down."

Frank caught up with Joe by the cellar steps. A gleam of light appeared under the door at the top of the stairs. Joe whispered, "I'm going up."

Quietly, one step at a time, Joe moved toward the door. Reaching the landing, he stopped to listen.

"I don't hear a thing," Joe whispered. He gripped the doorknob and turned it. He opened it just a crack, then stopped abruptly when the door squeaked.

"I'm going to open it fast," Joe whispered to Frank. "That should prevent the squeaking."

Joe steadied himself, then swept the door back in one swift motion. Except for the rush of air there wasn't a sound.

Cautiously Joe entered the mansion's back hallway. The light under the door had come from a bulb in a wall fixture. Aside from that lone bulb the hallway was dark.

With Frank protecting his back, Joe headed toward the front of the house. Within a few seconds he had entered the front entranceway.

"The printer is in the room behind the living room," Joe whispered.

Frank led the way into the living room, sliding open its heavy wooden doors. Lightning flickered outside, casting weird shadows about the room.

"This way," Joe said in a low tone. Moving swiftly to the door at the back of the parlor, he pointed to the floor. Bright light filtered through the crack between the door and the floor.

"Someone's in there," Frank whispered.

Joe pressed his ear to the door. "I don't hear anything. Maybe Baird just left the light on. Let's check."

Joe quietly turned the knob. Bright fluorescent light greeted them. The black printer sat on the worktable where Joe had seen it earlier. Next to it was a large high-resolution monitor.

"That's Mickey Mantle," Frank said, pointing to the monitor.

"Specifically, that's Mickey Mantle's rookie card," Joe said. "Biff said that one of those in perfect condition sold recently for twenty-four thousand dollars."

"From the looks of it, our counterfeiter is hoping collectors will think these are all in perfect condition," Frank commented. He picked up a piece of cardboard from the tray at one side of the printer and handed it to Joe. The stock held six freshly printed cards.

"I can't believe it!" Joe exclaimed. "Baird will never get away with this. Six Mickey Mantle rookie cards!" He turned the cards over. "How'd he ever find the right paper? This feels like the right weight of card stock." Joe looked up at his brother. "It looks as if Baird was planning to move from a nickel-and-dime operation to the big time—all at once! Let's check the serial number on this printer," he said eagerly.

"I've got it," Frank told his brother. Taking the slip with the number from his pocket, Frank went around to the back of the printer and trained the flashlight on a metal plate where the number was engraved.

"Joe, this doesn't make sense," Frank said. As he stood up to tell his brother about his discovery he discovered something else. Joe was gone.

"Joe, where are you?" Frank asked. "This isn't any time to play around."

Frank hurried to the parlor. He looked across the room toward the hallway door. A light had been turned on.

"Joe?" he called.

Suddenly Frank heard a noise behind him. He turned quickly. What he saw was the business end of a Louisville Slugger.

And then everything went blank.

16 "Ready, Aim . . ."

The first thing Frank noticed was a throbbing in his head. The second was his brother's voice calling out to him.

"I hate to say this, Frank," Joe said hoarsely, "because I know it's not funny. But guess what—the butler did it."

"Murphy?" Frank said in disbelief. When Joe nodded, Frank asked, "You saw him?" He tried to reach up to ease the pain in his head, but he found that his hands were tied. So were his feet.

"Right before he beaned me," Joe said. "I've been working on these ropes," he added, "and I think I've just about got my hands free." Joe struggled against the rope, twisting his hands to put pressure on the loosened knots.

"Got it!" he exclaimed. Finding he still had his

pocket flashlight, Joe located Frank in the darkness. After he got his legs free he hurriedly untied Frank's hands.

"Thanks. Now let's get out of here," Frank urged. "You know, while you were getting knocked out I was checking the serial number on that printer. We're not going to solve this case quite as soon as we thought."

"The serial numbers don't match?" Joe asked, turning to give his brother a puzzled look as they ran out of the room.

"The label on the back of the printer is stamped Transversal," Frank said. "The serial number is completely different. My guess is Baird got that printer from Newton as part of the deal when he put his money into Transversal."

"But the baseball cards it was printing looked like nearly perfect copies," Joe protested, as he ran down the cellar stairs. "The Transversal printer wasn't supposed to work that well."

"I know," Frank said. "I don't understand it myself." He looked around for the first time. "Where are we?" he asked.

Scanning the room with his light, Joe said, "The basement, as far as I can tell."

Frank saw the room was huge, dark, and wet. Cobwebs hung from the ceiling. "We've got to find a way out. Fast."

"I'll check the window," Joe said, jumping up. He returned in a few moments, shaking his head. "No luck. Murphy must have figured that's how we got in. He put the bars back over it."

135

With that Joe went for the stairs, dashing up two at a time. He quickly came back down to report. "The door's been locked from the other side. I hate to say this, Frank, but we seem to be stuck."

Frank tried to pick the lock but found there was a bolt on the other side that wouldn't budge. "Look, this place was built before cement blocks," Frank pointed out when he was back down in the cellar. "Sandstone is pretty soft stuff. Maybe we can dig our way out around that coal chute over there."

Joe looked to where Frank was pointing. The mortar around the coal chute was decaying. "It's worth a try," Joe agreed.

"Find something you can dig with," Frank said, getting up. He walked around the perimeter of the room and found a rusty chisel head in a corner. Using it as a trowel, he started attacking the mortar. Joe grabbed an ice pick and went at it, too.

Four hours later Frank was gasping from the effort of trying to dig a way out of the basement.

"It'll be daylight soon," he said, breathing heavily. "Murphy's probably long gone."

"Don't give up now," Joe urged. "Look, the chute's about ready to come out. Just a bit more digging."

When they'd finally punched a hole through to the outside, Frank found himself looking out at a

136

foggy morning. Frank and Joe squeezed through the opening one at a time. The rain had stopped.

"We're going right back inside," Frank insisted once they were outside, standing in Baird's driveway. "I want to search this house thoroughly, and if the butler's still there, he's going to jail."

"Agreed," Joe said. "The garage is empty," he noted, looking toward the back of the property.

"Let's try the back," Frank said. "There's got to be a way in."

He and Joe jogged around to the back of the house. The kitchen door was locked, but Frank found the lock easy to pick. Soon Frank and Joe were back inside Baird's mansion.

"The house doesn't seem quite so spooky in the daylight," Frank commented as the brothers made their way back to the front hallway. He slid open the heavy wooden doors leading to the living room.

"Look at this," Joe told Frank. He gestured at several cartons piled near the window seat in the living room. "I didn't notice those boxes last night."

"Let's check it out," Frank said, going over and opening one of the boxes. "Well, what do you know!" he exclaimed. Reaching in, he pulled out an umpire's mask.

"Do you think it's the same one Wormley was wearing when he threw that lighter at the gasoline?" Joe asked.

"I don't know," Frank admitted. "I doubt if we

can get any prints from the leather, but there might be something on the wire face cage."

Joe looked in the box, then removed the lids from two more. "This is George Brett's batting helmet," he said, holding up the blue plastic hat.

"This has to be the stuff Baird is selling at the armory show," Frank said. "The rumors were right." Closing up the boxes, Frank walked through the living room and opened the door into the small room off it. There the monitor screen was dark, the printer turned off.

"Here's another surprise." Frank whistled. He handed Joe a sheet of six Mickey Mantle cards. "Read what it says down there at the bottom of each card," he instructed.

Joe looked closely. "Reproduction," he read. "That means these are meant to be copies."

"Obviously Baird's not trying to defraud anyone with these," Frank concluded.

"That means Baird's not a counterfeiter after all," Joe said.

"That's right," Frank said.

"But what about Murphy?" Joe asked, confused. "Do you think he's the counterfeiter?"

"I'd say he's involved in something," Frank said simply. "Otherwise, why would he have attacked us and tied us up? We just don't know how he's involved, or why."

"There's one way we can find out," Joe said. "Let's search his room."

After a quick tour of the area behind the

138

kitchen Frank and Joe found Murphy's room up a flight of back stairs. Frank scanned the butler's room. The furniture included the bare necessities, nothing more. He rummaged through the dresser while Joe searched the nightstand and the closet.

Frank removed a baseball card price guide from the top drawer of the butler's dresser. Stuck inside the guide were three Mattingly cards.

"Jackpot!" he said, handing the cards to Joe. "Don't they look a lot like the card Biff bought?"

Joe nodded, holding a card up to the light. "You can see the photograph through the back, all right. And the colors on the logo don't look right, either."

"Check this out," Joe said, handing Frank a business form. "It's a written estimate from a body shop. I found it in the nightstand. It says there that our butler's real name is Keith Burke."

"According to this, he's got a white limousine that needs its fender hammered out," Frank said, reading the form.

Joe smiled. "What are the chances we're *not* talking about the same limousine that almost ran me down in New York?"

"About zilch, I'd say," Frank agreed. "But look at the address Burke gave the body shop."

Joe studied the form. "That's in New York," he said. "You know what else? It's the same address as Baseball Diamonds Are Forever."

"We've got enough evidence here to get the

police to bring Murphy in for questioning," Frank said. "Let's get out of here before Baird or Murphy comes back."

"Good idea," Joe said, collecting the papers and leading the way out of Murphy's room.

Frank and Joe went down the back stairs and out the kitchen door, the same way they'd come in. Soon they were back in their van planning their next move.

"Let's stop off at home," Frank said. "We can check our messages and change into dry clothes."

"Sounds good," Joe said. "Maybe Dad has a lead or two. If not, I say we head over to the armory and try to find Elliot Baird. We've got some serious questions for him."

The Hardys finally pulled up in front of their house. It had been a long night. Laura Hardy was waiting in the front room and jumped to her feet when she saw Frank and Joe come in.

"Your father's at the station," she said. "He went to put in a missing persons report on you two. Where on earth have you been?"

Frank and Joe quickly reassured their mother that they were all right, then went upstairs to change.

Back downstairs Frank checked the answering machine and found Nora Shadwick had called.

"Guess what?" he said to Joe, listening to the message. "Cecil Corbin thinks he remembers who sold Biff the bogus card in New York."

140

"Oh, really?" Joe asked, buttoning up a fresh shirt. "Who?"

"Forest Rader," Frank said, smiling. He picked up the phone and punched in a number. "I want to clear up one loose end. I'll ask Vic Newton how it is that Baird has one of the old Transversal printers."

The receptionist quickly put Frank through to Newton. Just as Frank had guessed, Newton revealed that Baird had been given one of the Transversal printers as a part of his investment in the company.

"The Transversal printer looks a lot like the new DupliTec model," Frank said. "How different are they on the inside?"

"Actually, they're quite similar," Newton admitted. "Two circuit boards. That's it."

Frank thanked Newton, then called Biff. The Hardys' friend agreed to meet them at the armory. Frank tried to call Elliot Baird at his house, but there was no answer.

Half an hour later, after reassuring their mother that they were well enough to go out, Frank and Joe were heading for the Bayport Armory.

"You don't think Murphy would be stupid enough to try passing phony cards here, do you?" Joe asked, pulling up in front of the low brick building.

"Not if he knows we're on his trail," Frank replied. "He's got to realize by now that Lynd and Wormley have been arrested."

141

"How do you think Forest Rader fits in?" Joe asked. "Could he be helping Murphy pass the cards?"

Frank shook his head. "It's possible. Hey look," Frank said, pointing to a sign out front. "At least we'll have plenty of protection if something goes wrong. There's a guard unit meeting in the firing range."

Frank held open the heavy door. Joe entered the armory's large assembly room and glanced around. "This is a big show," he commented as he looked at the collection of memorabilia. More was being carried in and set up by dealers as the Hardys watched.

"Let's get the lay of the place," Frank suggested.

"I see Baird's booth," Joe said, pointing. Except for the collector's name card the table was empty.

Frank called Joe's attention to an arrangement of tables by a stairway in the corner. "There's Rader's booth," Frank said.

Heading over that way, Frank could see it was already stocked with cards, pennants, and posters. The cases filled with cards were locked.

"Maybe Rader's out getting breakfast," Joe guessed.

"Let's see what's downstairs," Frank suggested, leading the way. There was a long hall in the lower level with military-green walls.

"The guard must meet down here," Joe said.

142

Frank paused by a door marked Firing Range. Easing it open, he looked inside.

The room wasn't being used, but several lights were on. Thirty-five feet across the room paper bull's-eyes were suspended from metal bars.

"They can swing those bars in to change targets," Frank explained.

"More than a few of the guardsmen missed," Joe noted. "Look at all those holes in that wall back there." He gestured toward the unpainted wallboard behind the paper targets. As he went to look back at the firing line he heard a dull thud.

There wasn't time to find out what had happened. Before Joe could react he felt a solid object come down hard on his head. And then everything went black.

Joe had no idea how long he'd been out. As he raised his head and tried to speak he discovered there was tape over his mouth. And his hands were tied.

Joe struggled, then stopped. He could hear talking and shouting.

Then what seemed like a hundred tiny lights appeared in front of him. The light showed Joe how narrow the space was in which he was trapped. Next to him, slumped unconscious, was Frank.

As he looked around the tiny dots came slowly into focus in front of him. Joe leaned forward, lined an eye up with one of the holes, and stared.

What he saw horrified him. Across the room stood ten men in khaki—guardsmen. And each one was shouldering an M-14 rifle.

Suddenly Joe understood. He and Frank were right behind the thin wall directly behind the targets. They might as well have been standing before a firing squad.

"Ready on the firing range!" called an officer sharply. "Ready!" There was a pause, then, "Aim . . ."

17 Home Run!

In desperation Joe wrenched free one of his legs. He kicked the plaster wall with all his strength, expecting at any moment to hear the officer yell, "Fire," and then the sound of the deadly gunshot. He kicked harder and felt the plaster wall break apart beneath his feet.

"Don't shoot!" he heard the officer shout.

Joe kept kicking. By the time the soldiers reached the wall, he had opened a large hole.

The officer untied Joe's hands and pulled the tape from his mouth.

Immediately Joe began pulling Frank out. Frank groaned. He began coming to as soon as he was placed on the firing range floor.

"What happened?" Frank sounded groggy.

"Somebody thought we'd make good targets,"

Joe said. "And there's only one way to find out who." He turned to the guard officer. "If you wouldn't mind," Joe said, "just go ahead and fire away. We want the guy who did this to us to think his little plan was successful."

The officer gave them a surprised look but eventually nodded when he realized they were serious. "Okay, boys," he said reluctantly. "Ready on the firing line," he barked.

While the guardsmen were busy firing their shots, Frank and Joe raced down the hall to the stairs. Joe heard voices from the main floor. At that same instant shots rang out from the firing range.

"Hear the gunfire?" a voice asked. "That's the end of our problem." The speaker laughed.

Joe started quietly up the stairs. Frank was right behind.

The talk was muffled, then Joe heard a familiar voice say, "Wormley's a loser. After all the effort it took to steal the printer, he dropped it."

"It's lucky for him he didn't break the circuit boards," said a second person.

"You've got to admit," said the first man, "it's pretty slick the way I upgraded Baird's old Transversal model. There we are, printing counterfeits right under his nose."

"Once we get them right," said the second man, "there's nothing we can't print. Including money!"

As Joe turned to say something to Frank, Biff Hooper's voice drifted down the stairs.

"Hey, how're you doing, Forest?" Biff asked. "Have you seen Frank and Joe?"

"Haven't seen them," Forest Rader muttered.

Frank eased farther up the stairs. Straining forward past his brother, he saw Rader. Biff thanked him, turned, and walked away from Rader's booth.

"I'll keep an eye on them," Frank whispered to Joe. "You go call Con Riley. We're going to need backup."

Joe nodded. "After that speech we've got enough to put them away for a good while."

After Joe slipped back downstairs Frank decided to make sure of the second man's identity. Placing his foot on the last step, he pressed down on a piece of plastic. The resulting crack echoed like a gunshot.

"What's that?" Rader snapped.

Frank shrank back, but he was too late.

The second man was right at the top of the stairs. Frank found himself staring up at Keith Burke, Baird's butler. And Burke was holding a gun.

"Get up here!" Burke ordered.

Frank obeyed. Rader stepped around the side of his booth. He was also holding a pistol.

"Where's your brother?" Forest Rader demanded.

"He's around looking at the other booths," Frank replied. "He says he wants a 1960 Willie McCovey card. A real one."

"Find Joe Hardy!" Rader instructed Burke.

147

"Yeah, Burke," Frank said. "You and Wormley haven't done very well so far."

Burke was shocked. "How'd you find out who I am?" he asked, his face flushing.

"We not only have your name," Frank told the criminal, "but we know you're the Transversal investor Dad couldn't locate in New York."

Rader interrupted. "It doesn't matter," he barked. "Bring the other Hardy back here, and we better get their friend Hooper, too."

Burke hesitated, his eyes darting around the room. Frank could see the man was close to panic. Finally Burke hurried away.

Frank knew he had to play for time. "One thing we've been trying to figure out," Frank said, "is why anyone would want to counterfeit baseball cards."

The card dealer seemed to be mulling over the question. "I might as well tell you," Rader told Frank, "since you aren't going to be around to use it against me."

Wanting to learn all he could, Frank didn't argue.

"It's simple, really," Rader explained. "If we could print our own baseball cards with DupliTec's new printer, and no one caught on, we could also print our own Stanley Cup tickets— tickets to the Super Bowl, even cash."

"But someone caught on," Frank pointed out. "Your counterfeits weren't good enough to pass for the real thing."

Rader sneered. "It was just a matter of time. I've been reworking the system. We've gotten close to perfection, really close by now. The definition's there, and the colors are dead on. With you nosy teens out of the picture," Rader said ominously, "we'll be able to continue as planned."

"How'd you get the printer?" Frank asked.

"Regina Lynd got a temporary job at DupliTec in Bayport," Rader said. "She made wax impressions of several keys, then Wormley walked in one night and took the printer. I knew I should have gone in myself," Rader said, shaking his head. "Especially after Wormley dropped the printer. But we salvaged the new circuit boards and put them in Baird's old Transversal printer."

"What's Baird's connection with all of this?"

"He and Burke both invested in Transversal," Rader explained. "Only Baird never met Burke, and he doesn't know Murphy's real name. We were going to take another HD printer, but DupliTec installed the security system. So Burke took the butler's job to get access to Baird's printer."

"Pretty smart." Frank complimented Rader to keep him talking. "What about Wormley and Lynd?"

"They were supposed to do the dirty work," Rader continued. "I played baseball with Wormley in high school, and he needed work. I used him at the shop. Then at the New York show

149

I told him you guys were detectives and to get that bogus card away from Hooper. Wormley blew it.

"I told him to scare you off. He attacked you on the train. That didn't work, but at least he got away. Then he tossed that plaster off the old building next to the Pasteboard Palace. That accomplished nothing." Rader shook his head. "Next he followed you down to Southport, and he even knocked you out and tried to burn you up in the DupliTec offices in New York. Again, a failure."

"It was Gina who attacked my dad, wasn't it?"

"Yeah," Rader said disgustedly. "Mark's her boyfriend. She went with him to New York to follow your dad. She nailed him with a baseball bat."

"If I'm not mistaken," Frank said, "they stole Baird's limousine to make the trip."

"They *borrowed* it," Rader corrected. "Baird was out of town, so Burke told them to take it. Burke tells me they hit a cab instead of you kids."

"Another fine miss," Frank quipped.

Rader scowled. Suddenly he jammed his gun in Frank's stomach. "This time we won't miss!"

Frank backed up, but from the corner of his eye he spotted flashing red police cruiser lights. The car was outside the armory's front entrance.

"I've got one last question," Frank told Rader. "Did you have any particular reason for selling the phony cards to Nora Shadwick?"

"I've known Nora for years, and I knew she

150

would trust me. I also knew the colors were off on the logo of those cards, but I couldn't wait to find out if the cards could go undetected. I figured Nora wouldn't expect any bad cards from me. Cecil Corbin wouldn't know a bogus card if it hit him in the face."

Without warning Frank smashed Rader hard in the stomach. The other hand chopped free the gun. The weapon flew from Rader's hand, then clattered down the stairs to the basement. Rader started to run, but Frank grabbed him by the shirt and threw him to the hardwood floor.

"You're under arrest!" Detective Con Riley barked as he ran up to the fallen Rader. Three officers followed the detective.

Rader stood up slowly, then raised his hands. The crowd at the armory was frozen in place as they watched the action.

"Thanks, Detective Riley," Frank said. "Did you see Joe when you came in?"

"Negative," said the police officer.

Frank looked at Riley with concern. "I sent him to make that call to you. I wonder where he went."

At that moment Joe came up the stairs with Keith Burke in tow. Joe had Burke's arms pinned in a tight wrestler's hold behind his back.

"Look who I ran into," Joe said, handing Burke over to Con Riley. "He tried to jump me," Joe said. "And he even had the nerve to try pulling this on me," Joe added, handing over Burke's gun.

151

"Good work!" Frank exclaimed.

"Both you boys will be happy to know that Lynd and Wormley finally started talking," Con Riley said, watching his men cuff Burke and Rader. "In fact, when an officer told them we were going to arrest Rader and Burke, they couldn't start talking fast enough. I told your dad about what was going on down here. He's with them now, listening to them give their statement."

"They're not pinning it all on me," Burke said.

"Oh, yeah? Who burglarized our house?" Joe asked Burke.

"That wasn't me!" Burke insisted. "Wormley did that. And he's the one who pounded holes in your gas tank. Then he went and lost the baseball card disk." Burke looked disgusted.

"What about the umpire's mask?" Frank asked. "It's gone from the case in the mansion hallway."

"Baird took it out," Burke said. "He's planning on selling it here at the show. I just lent it to Wormley."

"Enough chitchat," Con Riley ordered. "Let's get the bad guys downtown to jail where they belong." He prodded Burke toward the exit.

Frank and Joe followed. As they reached the door Frank saw Nora rushing up. Biff was with her.

"You did it!" Nora cried. "And the timing couldn't be better. Now there won't be a cloud hanging over the Bayport card show."

"I knew you guys could do it," Biff said, patting both his friends on the back.

"Well, look at that," Frank said. He pointed toward the entrance where Elliot Sanford Baird and Vic Newton had just stepped in. Frank saw they were talking together and smiling as they approached him.

"Fine work," Newton said to Frank. He shook hands all around. "Your father called me at the office. I wanted to come here and thank you two personally. I also wanted to find my friend Elliot Baird and settle our differences."

"Vic offered me a generous share of DupliTec stock," Baird said, "and I'm dropping my suit."

"Not only that," Newton said, "Baird and I have been talking. I've decided to put up the money needed to turn Baird's mansion into a museum for baseball memorabilia. That way, Elliot won't have to sell his collection after all."

"That's great!" Biff said with enthusiasm. "Now all the fans can see everything in your collection."

"Sounds good to me," Joe agreed. "But here at the show I've got my sights set on a 1960 Willie McCovey rookie card."

"Let's see if we can find one still in its wrapper," Frank suggested. "That way you get Willie, and I'll have my favorite thing about baseball cards."

"What's that?" Biff asked.

Frank smiled. "A stick of good old fashioned bubble gum, of course."

153

PENGUIN

THE FOUR V̶O̶
CHRISTOPHER

J. M. COHEN, born in London in 1903 and a Cambridge graduate, was the translator of many volumes for the Penguin Classics, including versions of Cervantes, Rabelais and Montaigne. For some years he assisted E. V. Rieu in editing the Penguin Classics. He collected the three books of *Comic and Curious Verse* and anthologies of Latin American and Cuban writing. With his son Mark Cohen he also edited the *Penguin Dictionary of Quotations* and the two editions of its companion *Dictionary of Modern Quotations*. He frequently visited Spain and made several visits to Mexico, Cuba and other Spanish American countries.

J. M. Cohen died in 1989. *The Times'* obituary described him as 'one of the last great English men of letters', while the *Independent* wrote that 'his influence will be felt for generations to come'.

The Four Voyages

OF

Christopher Columbus

Being his own log-book, letters and
dispatches with connecting narrative drawn
from the Life of the Admiral by his
son Hernando Colon and other
contemporary historians

EDITED AND TRANSLATED BY
J. M. COHEN

PENGUIN BOOKS

PENGUIN BOOKS

Published by the Penguin Group
Penguin Books Ltd, 27 Wrights Lane, London w8 5TZ, England
Penguin Books USA Inc., 375 Hudson Street, New York, New York 10014, USA
Penguin Books Australia Ltd, Ringwood, Victoria, Australia
Penguin Books Canada Ltd, 10 Alcorn Avenue, Toronto, Ontario, Canada M4V 3B2
Penguin Books (NZ) Ltd, 182–190 Wairau Road, Auckland 10, New Zealand

Penguin Books Ltd, Registered Offices: Harmondsworth, Middlesex, England

This translation first published 1969
9 10 8

Copyright © J. M. Cohen, 1969
All rights reserved

Printed in England by Clays Ltd, St Ives plc

To Mark

who suggested the subject and gave
me most generous help
with the book

CONTENTS

CONTENTS

LIST OF MAPS

INTRODUCTION

CHRISTOPHER COLUMBUS's four voyages of discovery to the New World were recorded in a number of letters and dispatches written by him and the officers who sailed with him. The story was taken up by a talented writer of news-letters to the great, Peter Martyr, and later by the royal historian Captain Gonzalo Fernandez de Oviedo and by Fray Bartolomé de las Casas, in particular, both of whom knew the Indies, and by Columbus's own son Hernando, who accompanied his father on his fourth voyage and wrote his biography. A great library of documents was collected in the Casa de las Indias at Seville (where American affairs were initially handled) and afterwards taken to Hispaniola, and in addition Hernando himself had many papers which were read also by Bartolomé de las Casas, who was a friend of the Columbus family. During the litigation concerning that family's claims to wealth and governorship, facts were discussed and interpreted in a variety of ways. When Oviedo published his official *Historia general y natural de las Indias* in 1547 – fifty-six years after Columbus's landfall – it might have seemed that everything relevant to the voyages had been read and written.

It was not until the quatercentenary of 1892, which inspired a number of books and articles on the man and his discovery, that Christopher Columbus emerged as a mysterious figure about whom many cardinal questions can be asked and few conclusively answered.

Oviedo, with whose narrative this book begins, accepted Columbus as a Genoese of no great lineage, education or attainments, one who had sailed on various commercial voyages, and who conceived and tirelessly advocated from court to court a scheme for crossing the ocean from Spain to China and opening up a direct trade route to the west, by

which the gold, jewels and spices of the Orient could be brought to the ports of Castile: a reasonable trading venture, which he made more attractive to the Catholic sovereigns Ferdinand and Isabela, by offering them the prospect that the inhabitants of the intervening lands, perhaps of China and Japan themselves, might be converted to Christianity on the way. The royal pair were enthusiasts for the conversion of Jews and Moslems, and Columbus carried on his first voyage a converted Jew with a knowledge of Arabic, who would be able to expound the Christian mysteries to the Chinese, Japanese and Indians, who were presumed to speak Arabic.

Oviedo, as the royal historian, takes care to refute Columbus's claims to having presented the sovereigns with a new world. This so-called new world was already known to the ancients, and, as Oviedo tries to prove by a resort to legends which could surely have convinced nobody, had actually belonged to the earliest kings of Spain.

Oviedo's legends are transparent nonsense. But they are no more foolish than most of the arguments which Columbus himself put forward when trying to find backers for his first voyage, and even when theorizing about the probable shape of the world just after the discovery of Trinidad on his third voyage. Ever since the time of the Greek cosmographers Marinus of Tyre and Ptolemy, there had been theories that the world was a sphere and that it would consequently be possible to go to the east by sailing west. Two things were in dispute: the distance, which could only be calculated by computing the circumference of the world at some given latitude; and whether or not there were lands or islands on the way. As for the distance, the shortest possibility was advanced by Marinus of Tyre, and this figure was accepted by Paolo Toscanelli of Florence, an aged cosmographer, who had been approached by the Portuguese and with whom Columbus had exchanged letters. Toscanelli thought Columbus's

project feasible, but does not appear to have respected his learning. However, he sent him a map, which Columbus undoubtedly carried and consulted. Indeed, we find him discussing it with the captain of one of his caravels, Martin Alonso Pinzón, when he was already in the latitude of the Indies on his first voyage.

Columbus's theories were more rigid and even more optimistic than Toscanelli's. He mentally fixed the distance between Portugal and Chipangu (Japan) at 2,760 miles. The actual distance is 12,000. We can no more accept Hernando Colon's claim that his father was a man of education than that he was of noble descent.

In relation to the possible islands lying between Spain and China, of which he was granted the governorship by the Catholic sovereigns at Granada before his first voyage, Columbus was equally credulous. There were many stories of islands lying out in the Atlantic – Antilla, Brasil, St Brendan's Isle – which were either pure inventions or sailors' tales of cloud banks or ice-floes. In Ireland, the Azores, the Canaries and the Cape Verde Islands there were stories of lands to be seen on clear days to the west, but the only western lands that had been visited – Greenland, Labrador and Newfoundland, which had been colonized by the Vikings – were not mentioned in any of Columbus's letters or notes. The Danes, with a Portuguese pilot aboard, had actually revisited Labrador only fifteen years before he landed in the Bahamas. But having visited Iceland, on a trading voyage, Columbus had no interest in the discovery of more frozen wastes. His goal was the rich lands described by Marco Polo and the romantic Sir John Mandeville, lands flowing with gold and spices and eager to be awakened to the true faith.

Impelled by his fixed idea of a westward voyage of less than three thousand miles, Columbus hawked his project around the courts of Portugal, England and the twin kingdoms of

THE FOUR VOYAGES
OF COLUMBUS
(for continuation of second
journey see detailed map)

Miles 0 100   500   1000

SPAIN
Cadiz
Palos
Lisbon
AFRICA
Tenerife
Madeira
Grand
Canary
Gomera
Hierro
CANARY Is.
S. Maria
S. Miguel
AZORES
C. VERDE Is.
Santiago

First voyage return
Fourth voyage
First voyage
Second voyage
Third voyage

Guanahani
Long Island
PUERTO
RICO
Guadalupe
Dominica
Martinique
LEEWARD
ISLANDS
Trinidad
Margarita I.
CUBA
JAMAICA
HISPANIOLA
Cape Gracias
a Dios
Cape
Honduras

Castile and Aragon. Every year the Portuguese were sailing farther down the coast of Africa. Soon they would round its southern cape, still to be discovered, and sail up the east coast to the Red Sea and so along the Arab trade-routes to India and China. To do so they had never to depart far from the sight of land. But with the invention of the ship's compass, a journey far from the sight of land was theoretically possible. Spanish sailors had experience of carrying wine, in round flat-bottomed boats like Columbus's flag-ship the *Santa Maria*, to Bristol, and of bringing furs and whale blubber from Iceland. But these routes had been known to pilots for centuries. To journey out into the ocean, a pilot would have to use the compass and check his position each night with the quadrant, measuring the altitude of the Pole Star. But even on his third voyage, Columbus was theorizing wildly about the apparent deviations of the Pole Star, which he could only explain by the crazy supposition that the earth was pear-shaped and he was sailing uphill. Columbus's theoretical knowledge of navigation was clearly not exceptional. Yet when on his third voyage he decided to sail by dead reckoning from Trinidad (which he had just discovered) to Hispaniola, which he knew from his first and second voyages, with no point of reference nearer than the Cape Verde Islands, he sailed a correct course, though it brought him a little west of his destination on account of currents which he could not reckon with. Columbus was seemingly a good natural pilot, who knew how to take advantage of winds and currents, and who learnt almost intuitively how to sail out with the trades and back with the westerlies.

Whatever Columbus's skill as a pilot, he was extremely inept in his handling of men. His pretensions were great, and he could share no power with a subordinate; he quarrelled with his captains, and his crew were several times on the point of mutiny. He could not control his settlers in the island of

Hispaniola, and was frequently at odds with Bishop Fonseca and the office at Seville which was responsible for his supplies and ships. He trusted no one except members of his own family. Yet so long as Queen Isabela lived, he was able to sway the court to his side. Even the tragic episode of his arrest at Santo Domingo and his return loaded with chains turned eventually to his advantage. In the eyes of all, even of his enemies, he was a man of destiny who had vastly extended the dominions of his sovereigns and the bounds of Christendom.

But what was the relationship of the islands and the possible mainland he had discovered to the Asian continent he was seeking? Having assumed that the island of Hispaniola was in fact Japan, the Chipangu of Marco Polo, he was compelled to accept Cuba as the Asiatic mainland, the 'extreme end of the East'. Although, on first reaching it, he had believed a native account that it was in fact a large island, on his second voyage he compelled his officers and crew to swear under heavy penalties that it was beyond any doubt the mainland of Asia. By an even greater piece of fictional geography the Orinoco, whose delta he discovered on his third voyage, was one of the four rivers of the Bible, flowing from the earthly Paradise, and had a common source with the Tigris, the Euphrates and the Ganges. Whether to the last he still believed that the coasts of Panama, and Costa Rica and the Mosquito coast of Nicaragua, which he explored on his fourth voyage, were also parts of Asia is uncertain. But it would seem so. Alonso de Ojeda and Amerigo Vespucci, a Genoese clerk who accidentally gave his name to the new continent, perhaps believed otherwise, after their expeditions to the north coast of South America. But Columbus was hard to shake from his illusions.

Columbus's principal illusion, that he had made the voyage to Asia, was fostered by his need to provide rapid

successes or victories in order to get renewed backing for his explorations. The islands that he discovered were not rich. The quantities of gold he claimed to be just about to discover were always on the next island. The Arawak fishermen and the Carib cannibal raiders who preyed on them had only a few gold ornaments; the inhabitants of the South American coastlands alloyed such gold as they had with copper, which they in fact valued more highly. Despite Columbus's frequent lists of valuable plants discovered, he was no botanist and made frequent mistakes. The islands had some gums, but no valuable spices. They had timber, it is true, suitable for ship-building, and parrots. In future, the sugar-cane, the banana palm and tobacco would thrive there. But for the present they had little but fish and maize, sweet peppers, yucca and sweet potatoes, the food of the natives – and when European crops were planted there, they speedily shot up and withered. The only wealth of the country lay in its human inhabitants, who could be made to work as slaves either in Spain or at home. The settlers quickly forced them to dig for non-existent gold, and Columbus advocated almost at the start their export to Spain as labourers. But these ideas offended the religious fervour of the sovereigns. The natives must be converted, and Christians might not be enslaved. Such was their view, and that of the historian Bartolomé de las Casas, the bishop of Chiapa and historian of the Indies, who offended all Spanish settlers by his advocacy of native rights and the tales of oppression he gathered from all parts of the sovereigns' new dominions. Only criminals and prisoners of war might be enslaved, and the settlers deliberately increased the numbers of these by provoking Indian rebellions and placing the cannibal Caribs outside natural law.

On their first arrival the Spaniards were favourably re-ceived and entertained by the Arawak people, who traded food and water and a few gold ornaments for such trifles as

newly minted copper coins, brass bells and even bits of broken glass and pottery. They believed that these white strangers in their tall ships had come down from the sky. One finds similar illusions even in the present century on remote islands of the South Seas, as is evidenced by the cargo cult of Melanesia. The Arawaks at first welcomed the newcomers with awe and affection, hoping for their protection from the marauding Caribs, who descended on them from the Leeward Islands to steal their women and castrate and fatten their young men for food. But soon the Arawaks were as frightened of the Spaniards as of the Caribs, and in the end attacked them. When they landed, Columbus's men found the villages deserted. The inhabitants had fled, taking all their possessions into the bush. It is fairly evident, from a chance observation of Columbus that he took care that a certain girl who came aboard with her relatives on the first visit to Hispaniola should not be molested, that sexually hungry Spanish sailors undoubtedly seized Indian women. Quarrels about women led to the massacre of the first settlers at La Navidad.

It is more or less proven that syphilis, a disease unknown in Europe before the end of the fifteenth century, was brought by the Spaniards from America. The Indians suffered from it in a mild form, but it attacked the Spaniards more severely. This explains Columbus's frequent allusions to the sickness and exhaustion of his men. Columbus's own illness, which prostrated him and caused him temporary blindness, is not so easily explicable. He drove himself hard, remaining for days and nights on end in the forecastle, watching the course. He says that all this time he did not sleep. Certainly he did not go down to his cabin. Twice at least, on his return to Hispaniola from Cuba on the second voyage, and on leaving Trinidad on the third, he was prostrated, but whether the symptoms were physical or neurotic is far from clear. We know that when he was in this condition he thought and acted most

unreasonably. This perhaps accounts for his head-on collision with the settlers on his arrival at Isabela, and for his strange theorizings of the earthly Paradise, set down in his log-book on the third voyage. Columbus not only drove himself obsessively forward but confided in nobody except his brothers, Bartolomé, who had treated with HenryVII on his behalf, and on coming out to the Indies took charge of the settlers on Hispaniola, and Diego, a less clearly defined figure. Bartolomé was a good map-maker but no administrator, and Diego, sent for from Italy, had no experience of government. His other lieutenants were of uneven quality. Pedro Margarit, who was to have obtained the gold of Hispaniola while Columbus was exploring Cuba and Jamaica, went home in disgust on finding that the Admiral had given him office but no authority. Columbus did not wish to administer settlers but to go on exploring, and such was the disorder created by his indeterminate policy that after the third voyage he was forbidden to return to Santo Domingo.

The settlers were difficult men, all bent on making swift profits. Those who remained from the first voyage were wiped out. Those that came on the second consisted largely of men under sentence for crimes, who had been pardoned on condition that they joined Columbus's expedition. By now the idea of permanent settlement was taking shape. But most of those who were free to, left for home with Pedro Margarit. Pardoned criminals, however, were compelled to stay, since their pardons were conditional on their remaining away from Spain. They were not suitable colonists, and even after some women were sent out to them from Spain they continued to raise factions. They opposed the Council of Santo Domingo (the Columbus family and their friends) calling them new Christians, or Jewish converts (*conversos*) and boasting of the purity of their own Christian blood.

On the basis of their accusations and some even less sub-

stantial arguments Columbus himself is sometimes said to have been of Jewish descent. The most extreme story is that he was no Italian but a Majorcan Jew, and that the reason for his ambitions for noble rank was to exact private compensation for the humiliation of that people, who were, as he notes in his log-book, expelled from Spain on the day on which he made his terms with Ferdinand and Isabela for the first voyage. Certainly his backers at court, Luis de San Angel in particular, were *conversos*, and he himself wrote in Castilian, the natural language of a *converso*, not in Italian, which he claimed as his native tongue. Columbus's Castilian is spattered with Portuguese and Catalan words, which would not be unexpected in the language of a man whose experience was chiefly of the sea. His Christian faith is not in doubt. It was a very enthusiastic kind, and much affected by a private cult of the Trinity.

Columbus felt himself to be guided by a supernatural destiny to make the discoveries that he did and to add greatly to the dominions of the Catholic sovereigns. As Christopher, he was fated to carry his Redeemer on his shoulders into distant lands. It is this supernatural sense of mission, to be read in all his writings, that impelled him to the Indies and caused him to continue his search, whether for the mainland of Asia or the earthly Paradise, almost to the end of his life. His gains in happiness were small, in wealth not enormous, but in patents of nobility, which he valued highly, very great. On his return from the first voyage he rode beside King Ferdinand through the streets of Barcelona, the equal of the dead prince Juan who had once ridden beside his father. He had done mighty service to his God and his King; in this lay his chief reward.

*

I have endeavoured to arrange the documents which I have translated for this book in such an order as to give a con-

secutive narrative of events. I have, therefore, begun, after a short prelude by the royal historian Oviedo, with the digest of Columbus's lost log-book made by Bartolomé de las Casas for his history. It frequently quotes Columbus's own words, especially his words of wonder at the new lands discovered, that seemed to have a climate 'as mild as Andalusia in May'. I have followed the log-book as far as the Cuba landfall. For events on Hispaniola, the defection of Pinzón, the loss of the *Santa Maria*, and the first half-hearted attack by the natives at the Bay of Arrows (Golfo de las Flechas) I have turned to the *Life* of the Admiral by his son Hernando, which also frequently quotes Columbus's own words, taken from the lost log-book. This account of the first voyage then reaches its conclusion with a letter written by Columbus a few days before landing at Lisbon, copies of which he addressed to various personages. The letter tells, as if for the first time, of matters which will be known to the reader. It is, however, the most important document for the first voyage, since it attempts to sum up the Admiral's discoveries and achievements. It tells nothing of any adverse events, however, for it is after all a success story that he wishes to tell, a story that will bring him fame, honours and ready backers for a second expedition.

The second voyage opens with a letter from Doctor Chanca, physician to the fleet, who accompanied it to Hispaniola but returned with the first convoy to sail for Spain. He is circumstantial in his description of the country, though he shares the Admiral's unsubstantiated optimism concerning its riches. At the moment of his departure for the Old World, reports were just coming in from the reputed gold-fields of Cibao, which can hardly have been as categorical as he asserts. Nor had he thoroughly sifted the history of those events between the first voyage and the second, which had led to the death of all the Spanish settlers at La Navidad. He passes over

the quarrels among the settlers themselves and their treatment of the Indians, especially the women, though this last would have sufficiently explained the burning of the fort and the annihilation of the garrison.

The events of the third voyage are described in two highly emotional letters from the Admiral, the first of which tells of the discovery of Trinidad and develops some very strange theories about the shape of the world, and the second, written in chains, protests grievously against the wrongs done to him by the royal emissary, Bobadilla. The linking narrative drawn from his son's *Life*, though strongly favourable to the Admiral, suggests some of the reasons for his arrest and deportation. Not even his most powerful advocate could entirely justify his quarrels with all his collaborators except those who were members of his own family.

The fourth voyage, which brought Columbus to the mainland of Central America, is told in his own report, supplemented by the story of his loyal lieutenant Diego Mendez, drawn from that gentleman's last will. And the final chapter is contributed by Hernando, who tells of his father's swift decline after his final return to Spain.

Hernando Colon and Bartolomé de las Casas both had access to Columbus's papers, and both give full accounts of the Admiral's life and voyages. Las Casas' *History of the Indies* (*Historia de las Indias*, second edition 1965, Fondo de Cultura Economica, Mexico) is by far the larger book, since it covers the whole history of American exploration up to 1520. It suffers, however, from prolixity of style and from the too frequent introduction of Las Casas' favourite theme, the ill-treatment of the natives. In his advocacy of the rights of the Christianized Indians against the predatory Spaniards, Las Casas made himself extremely unpopular, since the right was always on his side. His history is deeply affected by his humanitarian views, one or two examples of which I have

fitted into the narrative. I have generally preferred however, where no first-hand document exists, to take my story from Hernando's life of his father, a work of scholarship and style, which has too often been slighted by modern historians.

Hernando was the Admiral's illegitimate son by his Spanish mistress Beatriz Enriquez. As a boy he was put as page at the royal court and afterwards accompanied his father on his fourth voyage. But Hernando was a scholar rather than an explorer, and collected a large library. In 1571, his *Life of the Admiral*, which purported to be a translation of a Spanish original, was published in Italian. The history of Columbus and the claims of his family were by then matters of dispute in Spain and publication in Spanish might have been inadvisable. The unpublished Spanish original is lost. Though one nineteenth-century scholar actually suggested that it was no more than the compilation of an Italian bookseller, its authenticity is supported, in my opinion, by the son's exaggerated claims for his father's noble descent and scholarly education – in which no objective critic will believe – and, more strongly still, by his frequent quotations of his father's log-book and other writings, which agree with those of Las Casas and with such originals as survive. None of this material would have been available to an Italian hack working for the book trade. Las Casas' history (begun in 1523), with which he in so many respects agrees, was not published till the nineteenth century. I have no hesitation therefore in accepting Hernando's *Life of the Admiral*, and have translated many chapters from it, working from the most recent Spanish version (*Vida del Almirante Don Cristobal Colon*, published by the Fondo de Cultura Economica, Mexico, 1947).

My source for the chief documents has been the Austral reprint *Los cuatro viajes del almirante y su testamento* (fourth edition, Buenos Aires, 1954), which I have compared in

most cases with the Hakluyt Society's versions and translation, edited by Cecil Jane (London, 1930 and 1933).

Those who want full-length studies of the Admiral's life should read Samuel Eliot Morrison's *Admiral of the Ocean Sea* (Boston, 1942), which is strongest on the side of navigation, since its author followed most of the Admiral's journeys from port to port in his own yacht; and Salvador de Madariaga *Christopher Columbus* (London, 1949), an exhaustive psychological study, which advances an interesting theory of Columbus's Jewish origins. The latest work, Björn Landstrom's *Columbus* (London, 1967), is particularly illuminating on the subject of Columbus's ships, their provisions and equipment.

J.M.C.

April 1968   Knappswood

FIRST VOYAGE
1492–3

GENERAL AND NATURAL HISTORY OF THE INDIES BY CAPTAIN GONZALO FERNANDEZ DE OVIEDO

BOOK II

CHAPTER 2

The origin and character of Christopher Columbus, first Admiral of the Indies, and common opinions of his motives in embarking on his discoveries

SOME say that these lands were first known many centuries ago, and that their situation was written down and the exact latitudes noted in which they lay, but their geography and the sea routes by which they were to be reached were forgotten, and that Christopher Columbus, a learned man well read in the science of cosmography, set out to make a fresh discovery of these islands. I am inclined to believe this theory for reasons that I will explain in later chapters. But it is right to accept this man, to whom we owe so much, as the prime mover of this great enterprise, which he initiated for the benefit of all now living and those who shall live after us.

I will say that Christopher Columbus, as I've heard from men of his nation, was a native of the province of Liguria, in which lies the city and lordship of Genoa. Some give his birthplace as Savona, or a small town or village called Nervi, on the Levant coast two leagues from Genoa, but the most reliable story is that he came from Cugureo, which is also near Genoa. He was a man of decent life and parentage, handsome and well-built, and of more than average height and strength. His eyes were lively and his features well proportioned. His hair was chestnut brown and his complexion

rather ruddy and blotchy; he was well spoken, cautious and extremely intelligent. He had good Latin and great cosmographical knowledge; he was charming when he wished to be and very testy when annoyed. His ancestors came from the city of Piacenza in Lombardy, which lies on the banks of the Po, and were members of the ancient family of Pelestrel. In the lifetime of his father Dominico, Christopher Columbus, now a well-educated young man who had attained his majority, left Italy for the Levant and travelled over the greater part of the Mediterranean, where he learnt navigation and put it to practical use. After several voyages in these restricted waters, having a mind for greater enterprises and wider prospects, he decided to see the great ocean and left for Portugal. Here he lived for some time in the city of Lisbon. From there, or wherever else he was, as a grateful son he sent some part of all he earned to his old father, whom he helped to support and who lived in some poverty with hardly enough money for his bare needs.

There is a story that a caravel sailing from Spain to England with a cargo of merchandise and provisions, wines and other goods, not to be found in England and generally sent there from Spain, was overwhelmed by such violent contrary winds that it was forced to run west for many days, in the course of which it sighted one or more of the Indies. A landing was made on one of these islands and naked people were seen like those found here today. When the winds, which had brought them here against their will, died down, they took aboard water and wood and sailed back on to their previous course. The story goes on to say that as the greater part of the ship's cargo consisted of food and wine the crew had sufficient to keep them alive on this long and arduous voyage and to make the return passage, meeting with favourable weather. They reached Europe safely and made for Portugal. The voyage had been extremely long and dangerous and they

had all the time been greatly afraid. Moreover, though the winds had driven them swiftly on their course, the journey there and back had lasted four or five months, or possibly even more. In the course of that time almost all the ship's crew died. The only men to land in Portugal were the pilot and three or four of the sailors, and all these were so ill that they also died a short time after their arrival.

The story goes that this pilot was a close friend of Christopher Columbus and had some knowledge of the quadrant, and that he marked the position of this land he had discovered. He is said to have given this information very privately to Columbus, asking him to make a map and place upon it this land which he had seen. Columbus is said to have welcomed him into his house as a friend and got him medical treatment, for by now he was very sick. Nevertheless he died like the others; thus Columbus remained with sole knowledge of these islands, and this he kept to himself. According to some accounts, this pilot was an Andalusian, others make him Portuguese, others a Basque. Some accounts say that Columbus was at that time in the island of Madeira, others in the Cape Verde Islands and that it was at this or that place that the caravel arrived and there that Columbus heard of these lands. Whether these events took place or not cannot be decided with certainty, but this romantic story is in common circulation in the form that I have set down. In my opinion it is a fiction. As St Augustine says: 'When the facts are obscure, it is better to exercise doubt than to argue an uncertain case.' It is better to doubt what we do not know than to insist on facts that are not proven.

CHAPTER 3

*The author's opinions concerning the alleged
discovery and description of the islands by the
Ancients*

IN the last chapter I gave a common story concerning the previous discovery of the Indies. Now I will set down my beliefs concerning Christopher Columbus's motives and the knowledge which emboldened him, as a man of some learning, to undertake this great enterprise, so memorable to the men of his and future times. He rightly recognized that these lands had been forgotten, for he had found them described – and of this I am in no doubt at all – as one-time possessions of kings of Spain. I should like to quote Aristotle on this matter. On leaving the Straits of Gibraltar for the Atlantic ocean, he said, some Carthaginian merchants discovered a large island which had never been discovered before and was inhabited only by wild animals. It was therefore entirely wild and covered with large trees. It had great rivers on which ships could sail and was very fertile; everything that was planted there germinated and produced an abundant crop. This island was very remote, lying far off the coast of Africa at a distance of several days' sailing. On reaching it, these Carthaginian merchants, inspired by the fertility of the soil and the mildness of the climate, began to settle and build farms and villages. On learning this the Carthaginians in their senate proclaimed under pain of death that thenceforth none should sail for this land and that all those who had been there should be put to death. For the fame of this island was so high that if any other nation or empire were to hear of it it would conquer it and thus become a very formidable enemy to Carthage and its liberties.

This story is included in the repertory of Brother Theophilus de Ferrariis of Cremona, in his *Vitae regularis sacri ordinis predicatorum* which cites Aristotle's *De admirandis in natura auditis.*

[*Oviedo now tells the story of the legendary Hesperus, twelfth king of Spain in descent from Tubal Cain, who was present at the fall of the Tower of Babel. He bases a long and fanciful argument on the fabulous histories of Beroso and Isidore of Seville, and on the evidence of various early geographers proves that the Fortunate Islands, known as the Hesperides after King Hesperus, were not the Canaries, as was generally assumed, but the Indies themselves. From this he develops an argument that, while admitting Columbus's courage, minimizes his achievement and suggests that he was not discovering but rediscovering the New World.*]

The islands known as the Hesperides mentioned by Sebosus and Solinus, Pliny and Isidore must undoubtedly be the Indies and must have belonged to the Kingdom of Spain ever since Hesperus's time, who, according to Beroso, reigned 1,650 years before the birth of Our Lord. Therefore, if we add the 1,535 years since Our Saviour came into the world, the kings of Spain have been lords of the Hesperides for 3,193 years in all. So by the most ancient rights on this account and for other reasons that will be stated during the description of Christopher Columbus's voyages, God has restored this realm to the kings of Spain after many centuries. It appears therefore that divine justice restored to the fortunate and Catholic Kings Ferdinand and Isabel, conquerors of Granada and Naples, what had always been theirs and belongs to their heirs in perpetuity. In their time and by their commands, the admiral Christopher Columbus discovered this New World (or a very large part of it), which had been completely forgotten: during the reign of his Imperial Majesty, our Lord Charles V, these regions have been more widely explored and his empire thus largely extended.

All the authors whom I have mentioned indicate that these Hesperides were in fact the Indies, and I believe that Columbus followed their authority (or perhaps that of others that were known to him) when he set out on his long voyage, boldly risking so many dangers in search of the lands that he found. Whether or not he was guided by this knowledge, he undertook a journey into these seas which none had undertaken before him and which neither he nor any other sailor would have risked without the authority of these early geographers.

CHAPTER 4

That Christopher Columbus was the first to teach the Spaniards to navigate by taking the altitudes of the sun and the North Star. He goes to Portugal and other lands, seeking help and support for his project of discovering the Indies. The Catholic sovereigns, Ferdinand and Isabela, receive information about him, and at their command he makes his discovery

MANY are of the opinion (which is well supported by convincing arguments) that Christopher Columbus was the first in Spain to teach the art of navigating the wide ocean seas by measuring the height in degrees of the sun and the North Star. He was the first to practise the art, for, before his time, though it was taught in the schools, few (in fact none) had dared to try it out at sea. For this is a science which cannot be translated into actual knowledge unless it is practised in very large stretches of sea far from the coasts. Till then steersmen, pilots and seamen had exercised their craft by trial and error, relying on the knowledge of the captain or pilot, but not scientifically as is done today with our present knowledge of

the seas. They steered as in the Mediterranean, along the shores of Spain and Flanders, the rest of Europe and Africa, and everywhere else, by hugging the coast. But in order to sail in search of provinces as distant as the Indies are from Spain, the pilot must make use of the science of the quadrant, which is practicable only in such vast expanses of sea as those lying between here* and Europe or our possessions in the Spicelands at the western end of the mainland of these Indies.

Impelled by his desire for discovery and having achieved practical mastery of the secret of navigation (touching the plotting of the course), Columbus set about seeking support. Perhaps he relied on this scientific mastery, perhaps on information received from the pilot, who is said to have given him an account of these unknown lands, either in Portugal, or in the Azores (supposing this story to be true), perhaps on the authorities mentioned in my last chapter or perhaps he was impelled in some other way. In any case, Columbus worked through his brother Bartholomew on King Henry VII of England (father of the present King Henry VIII) to support him and equip him with ships in which to discover these western seas, offering to give him great wealth and to increase his realm and estates with new kingdoms and lordships. After consulting his counsellors and certain men whom he had asked to examine Columbus's proposals, the King laughed at the idea, considering all that Columbus said to be nonsense.

In no way disconcerted when Columbus saw that his services would not be accepted in England, he began to open negotiations of the same kind with King John II of Portugal. King John was no more convinced by Columbus, although he was living and had married in that kingdom and by his marriage had become a subject of Portugal. Uninfluenced by this, King John refused either to support or aid Columbus in his project and put no trust in him.

*Santo Domingo, where Oviedo was writing.

He decided therefore to go to Castile, and on arriving at Seville made the acquaintance of the illustrious and brave Don Enrique Guzman, Duke of Medina-Sidonia. Not finding in him the support that he was seeking, he moved on to open new negotiations with the illustrious Don Luis de la Cerda, first Duke of Medina Celi, who also found his proposals fantastic, though some say that this duke agreed to equip Columbus in his city of Puerto de Sancta Maria, but was refused a licence to do so by the Catholic sovereigns. Therefore, since theirs was the highest authority, Columbus went to their most serene Catholic Majesties – King Ferdinand and Queen Isabela, and spent some time at their court in great poverty, meeting with no response from those to whom he spoke.

Remaining there in great straits he endeavoured to persuade those fortunate sovereigns to support him and equip some caravels, in which he might discover this new world (or regions unknown to him at this time) in their royal name. But this project was alien to the ideas of those to whom he proposed it. It did not please them, nor did they share the hopes of its great success in which Columbus alone believed. Not only did they attach little credit to his ideas; they actually considered that he was talking nonsense. He persisted in his suit for almost seven years, repeatedly holding out great prospects of wealth and riches for the crown of Castile. But as his cloak was poor and ragged, he was considered a dreamer and everything he said was taken to be fantastic. Being an unknown foreigner he found none to back him. What is more, the projects which he laid before them were great and unheard of. But see God's care in giving the Indies to their rightful owners! The offer had been made to the mighty kings of England and of Portugal and to those two rich dukes I have mentioned. He did not permit any of them to risk the small sum that Columbus asked. Disappointed by all these princes, Columbus went in search of the Catholic sovereigns,

whom he found occupied at that time in their holy war against the Moors of the Kingdom of Granada.

It is no marvel that such Catholic princes should be more concerned with winning souls for salvation than with treasure and new estates which would only increase their royal cares and responsibilities, nor that they decided to back this project of discovery. But let no one believe that this alone could account for their good fortune, for eye had never seen, nor ear heard, nor human heart dreamed of the rewards prepared by God for those who love Him. These and many other blessings fell to our good sovereigns for their faithful service to Jesus Christ and their fervent desire for the spread of His holy faith. It was for this purpose that the Lord brought Christopher Columbus to their notice, for He sees the ends of the earth and all that happens beneath the sky. And when in due season this great business was concluded, it was God's purpose that was to be fulfilled.

During the time when Columbus was at court he lodged at the house of Alonso de Quintanilla, chief accountant to the Catholic sovereigns, a man of importance greatly devoted to their service and anxious for the extension of their power. Pitying Columbus's poverty he gave him food and sufficient money for his needs. In him Columbus found more support and understanding than in anyone else in Spain. On this gentleman's introduction, Columbus was received by the most reverend and illustrious Pedro Gonzalez de Mendoza, Cardinal of Spain and Archbishop of Toledo, who, on giving Columbus a first hearing, recognized him as a man of fair speech and learning who argued his case well. Realizing that he had a good intelligence and great knowledge he formed a favourable impression of Columbus and took pains to back him.

Thanks to the support of the cardinal and of Quintanilla, Columbus was received by the King and Queen and they immediately attached some credit to his written proposals and

petitions. The business was finally concluded while the sovereigns were besieging the great and famous city of Granada,* in the year 1492. From their royal camp which they had built in the midst of their army and had named Santa Fé the blessed sovereigns concluded their agreement with Columbus; there, in the camp-city of the Holy Faith and in the holy faith that lay in their Highnesses' hearts, this discovery had its beginnings.

Not content with the holy and victorious enterprise which they had in hand, and by which they finally subdued all the Moors in Spain, who had insulted and maltreated Christians since the year 720 (as many chroniclers agree), these blessed princes, in addition to bringing the whole of Spain to our Catholic religion, decided to send an expedition in search of this new world and propagate the Christian faith there, for they devoted every hour to the service of God. For this holy purpose they ordered Columbus to be dispatched, giving him authority under the royal seal to hire three caravels of the type he required in Andalusia, with all necessary crews and provisions, for this long voyage whose only hope of success lay in the pious zeal and holy purpose of these Christian princes, under whose auspices and by whose commands this great adventure began. And since he needed money for his expedition, sufficient to prepare his ships and set out on the first discovery of the Indies, on account of the costly war this was lent him by Luis de Santangel, the financial secretary. A first grant and agreement was made by the sovereigns to Columbus in the city of Santa Fé, in the Kingdom of Granada, on 18 April 1492, before secretary Juan de Coloma. And the agreement was confirmed by a royal appointment given to him thirteen days later in the city of Granada on 30 April of the same year 1492, and with this authority Columbus departed, as has been said, and went to the city of Palos de Moguer, where he prepared for his voyage.

*The last Moorish city in Spain.

DIGEST* OF COLUMBUS'S
LOG-BOOK ON HIS FIRST VOYAGE MADE
BY BARTOLOMÉ DE LAS CASAS

ON 2 January in the year 1492, when your Highnesses had concluded their war with the Moors who reigned in Europe, I saw your Highnesses' banners victoriously raised on the towers of the Alhambra, the citadel of that city, and the Moorish king come out of the city gates and kiss the hands of your Highnesses and the prince, My Lord. And later in that same month, on the grounds of information I had given your royal Highnesses concerning the lands of India and a prince who is called the Great Khan – which means in Spanish 'King of Kings' – and of his and his ancestors' frequent and vain applications to Rome for men learned in the holy faith who should instruct them in it, your Highnesses decided to send me, Christopher Columbus, to see these parts of India and the princes and peoples of those lands and consider the best means for their conversion. For, by the neglect of the Popes to send instructors, many nations had fallen to idolatory and adopted doctrines of perdition, and your Highnesses as Catholic princes and devoted propagators of the holy Christian faith have always been enemies of the sect of Mahomet and of all idolatries and heresies.

Your Highnesses ordained that I should not go eastward by land in the usual manner but by the western way which no

* This digest was made by the historian Bartolomé de las Casas from the log-book of the Admiral, which has since disappeared. The frequent quotation of the Admiral's actual phrases makes it the prime authority for the voyage itself, and it is used here up to the landfall on Cuba, from which point the narrative is taken up by Columbus's report written on his homeward voyage, copies of which he sent to various important persons. Where the narrative is in the first person Las Casas is using the Admiral's words. Where it is in the third he is giving his own rendering.

one about whom we have positive information has ever followed. Therefore having expelled all the Jews* from your dominions in that same month of January, your Highnesses commanded me to go with an adequate fleet to those parts of India. In return you granted me great favours bestowing on me the titles of Don and High Admiral of the Ocean Sea and Viceroy and perpetual governor of such islands and mainland as I should discover and win or should in future be discovered and won in the Ocean Sea, and that these rights should be inherited by my eldest son and so on from generation to generation.

I departed from the city of Granada on Saturday, 12 May, and went to the seaport of Palos, where I prepared three ships very suitable for such a voyage and set out from that port well supplied both with provisions and seamen. Half an hour before sunrise on Friday, 3 August, I departed on a course for the Canary Islands, from which possession of your Highnesses I intended to set out and sail until I reached the Indies, there to deliver your Highnesses' letters to their princes and to fulfil your other commands. I decided therefore to make this careful daily report of my voyage and of everything I should do, see or experience. In addition to a report of the day's events recorded each night, and of the night's sailing recorded each morning, I decided to make a new chart for navigation, giving the correct disposition according to their bearings of the land and water in the ocean sea. I intended also to compile a book which would contain everything mapped by latitude measured from the Equator and by longitude from the west. Though all these things will be a great labour it is essential that I should neglect sleep and carefully watch my course.

*After the fall of Granada the sovereigns gave their Jewish subjects the choice of conversion or exile.

FRIDAY, 3 AUGUST. We set out at eight o'clock from the bar of Saltes and travelled with a strong breeze sixty miles, that is to say fifteen leagues,* southward, before sunset. Afterwards we changed course to south-west by south, making for the Canaries.

SATURDAY, 4 AUGUST. They continued south-west by south.

SUNDAY, 5 AUGUST. They continued on this course and covered more than twenty leagues in the day and night.

MONDAY, 6 AUGUST. The rudder of the *Pinta*,† whose captain was Martin Alonso Pinzón, jumped out of position; this was said to be the doing of one Gomez Rascón, and Cristóbal Quintero, the owner of the ship, who disliked the voyage. The Admiral says that before they sailed these men had been grumbling and making difficulties. The Admiral was much disturbed, since he could not help the caravel without danger to himself, but comforted by his knowledge that Martin Alonso Pinzón was a courageous and an intelligent man.

TUESDAY, 7 AUGUST. The rudder of the *Pinta* was unshipped again and repaired, and they set their course for the island of Lanzarote in the Canaries...

WEDNESDAY, 8 AUGUST. The pilots of the caravel differed as to their position and the Admiral proved to be the most

* Columbus's league was of four Roman miles, approximately three nautical miles.
† Columbus's three ships were the *Santa Maria*, his flagship, the *Pinta* and the *Niña*.

correct. He was anxious to go to Grand Canary and leave the caravel *Pinta* there, since she was steering badly and shipping water. He wished to get another caravel there if one were to be found.

THURSDAY, 9 AUGUST. The Admiral could not make Gomera until Sunday night, and by the Admiral's command Martin Alonso remained off the coast of Grand Canary, being unable to steer. The Admiral went to Canary or Tenerife, and thanks to the diligent work of himself, Martin Alonso and the others, the *Pinta* was very well repaired. Eventually they reached Gomera, on the island of Tenerife, which is remarkably high, and there saw a great fire.

The *Niña*, which had been lateen rigged, was fitted with square sails. They returned to Gomera on Sunday, 2 September, with the repaired *Pinta*. The Admiral says that many trustworthy Spaniards from the island of Hierro who were at Gomera with Doña Inés Peraza, the mother of Guillen Peraza, afterwards the first count of Gomera, swore that every year they saw land to the westward of the Canaries in the direction of the setting sun, and some men of Gomera also affirmed this story under oath. He also remembers having heard the same thing in the Azores and that all accounts agreed as to the direction of the land, the time of its appearance and its size. When the Admiral went to Canary to repair the *Pinta* he put some men ashore on the island of Gomera, where they obtained a quantity of provisions. These provisions, together with meat, wood and water, were now brought on board and on Thursday, 6 September, he finally sailed from Gomera with his three ships.

THURSDAY, 6 SEPTEMBER. He set out that morning from the harbour of Gomera and set course to continue his voyage. He learnt from a caravel which came from the island of

Hierro that three Portuguese caravels were cruising there with the intent of capturing him. The reason for this must have been the King of Portugal's annoyance at his having gone to Castile. He sailed all that night and day in a calm and in the morning found himself between Gomera and Tenerife.

FRIDAY, 7 SEPTEMBER.   All Friday he was becalmed.

SATURDAY, 8 SEPTEMBER.   At three o'clock in the morning it began to blow from the north-east, and he shaped his course to the west. Much water broke over his bows which made progress slow. That day and night he went nine leagues.

SUNDAY, 9 SEPTEMBER.   He made fifteen leagues that day and decided to score up a smaller amount so that the crews should not take fright or lose courage if the voyage were long. In the night he went 120 miles, which is thirty leagues, at ten miles an hour. The sailors steered badly, falling off to west by north and even to west-north-west; the Admiral scolded them many times for this.

MONDAY, 10 SEPTEMBER.   That day and night he went sixty leagues at ten miles ($2\frac{1}{2}$ leagues) an hour. But he reckoned only forty-eight leagues so as not to alarm the crew.

TUESDAY, 11 SEPTEMBER.   That day they sailed on their course westward and made more than twenty leagues. They saw a large fragment of the mast of a 120-tonner, but could not secure it. That night they went about twenty leagues, but he reckoned only sixteen.

WEDNESDAY, 12 SEPTEMBER.   During that night and day they kept to their course and made thirty-three leagues. The Admiral again reckoned somewhat less.

THURSDAY, 13 SEPTEMBER. Continuing on their western course they made another thirty-three leagues and the Admiral reckoned three or four less. Currents were against them. At nightfall the compass needles moved to the north-west, and in the morning returned slightly to the north-east.

FRIDAY, 14 SEPTEMBER. That day and night they continued on their westward course for twenty leagues, the Admiral again reckoning somewhat less. The crew of the caravel *Niña* said they had seen a tern and a tropic-bird, neither of which go more than twenty-five leagues from land.

SATURDAY, 15 SEPTEMBER. That day and night he sailed somewhat more than twenty-seven leagues westwards. And early in the night they saw a marvellous streak of fire fall from the sky into the sea four or five leagues away.

SUNDAY, 16 SEPTEMBER. They sailed westwards all that day and night and must have made thirty-nine leagues. He reckoned only thirty-six. During the day there were some clouds and a little rain fell. Here the Admiral says that from that day onwards they met with very temperate breezes and the mornings were most delightful. There was nothing lacking except the sound of nightingales. 'The weather,' he says, 'is like April in Andalusia.' Here they began to see many patches of very green seaweed, which appeared only recently to have been uprooted. All considered therefore that they were near some island, but not the mainland according to the Admiral, who writes: 'I take the mainland to be somewhat farther on.'

MONDAY, 17 SEPTEMBER. He continued his course westwards for fifty leagues and reckoned only forty-seven. They were helped by the current. They saw much weed, which was very fine and had grown on rocks; it came from the west.

They decided that they were near land. The pilots took and marked the north and found that the needles declined a full point to the north-west. The sailors were frightened and depressed, and did not say why. On observing this the Admiral gave orders that they should take the north again at dawn, and the needles were found to be true. The cause of this was that the star apparently changes its position and not the needles. That Monday morning they saw much more weed, which was like the weed from rivers, and in it they found a live crab which the Admiral kept. He says that this is a certain sign of land, for such weed is not to be found eighty leagues from land. They found the water less salt after they left the Canaries, and the breezes always more gentle. All now sailed on very happily, and whichever ship could sail fastest went ahead. They saw many dolphins and the crew of the *Niña* killed one. The Admiral says here that all these signs* came from the west, 'Whence I trust that the high God, in whose hands are all victories, will very soon give us land.' On that morning he says he saw a white bird called the tropic-bird, whose habit is not to sleep on the sea.

TUESDAY, 18 SEPTEMBER. During that day and night they made more than fifty-five leagues but he reckoned only forty-eight. On these days the sea was as smooth as the river at Seville. That day Martin Alonso sailed ahead in the *Pinta*, which was a fast ship: because, as he called to the Admiral from his ship, he had seen a great flock of birds flying westwards and hoped to sight land that night; this was his reason for not holding back. To the north there appeared a great bank of clouds, which is a sign that land is near.

WEDNESDAY, 19 SEPTEMBER. The Admiral continued on his course and, since it was calm, made twenty-five leagues,

*The dolphin, birds and weed.

43

but reckoned only twenty-two. At ten o'clock that morning a booby approached the ship and in the evening they saw another. These birds are not accustomed to fly more than twenty leagues from land. A little rain fell without wind, which is a certain sign of land. The Admiral didn't wish to stop and beat to windward in order to make sure that there was land there, but he was certain that there were some islands both to the north and south, as in fact there were. He sailed between them because he was anxious to press on to the Indies. 'There is plenty of time,' he says, 'for God willing we shall see everything on our return voyage.' These are his actual words. Here the pilots set down their positions. The pilot of the *Niña* reckoned that he was 440 leagues from the Canaries, the pilot of the *Pinta* 420 and the pilot of the Admiral's ship 400 exactly.

THURSDAY, 20 SEPTEMBER. This day he sailed west by north and west-north-west, because in the prevailing calm the winds were very variable. They made about seven or eight leagues. Two boobies flew to the ship and later a third, a sign that they were near land, and they saw much weed, although they had seen none on the previous day. They caught with their hands a bird like a tern; it was a river-bird, not a sea-bird. It had feet like a gull. At dawn two or three small land-birds came to the ship singing, and afterwards towards sunset they disappeared. Later a booby came from the west-north-west and flew away to the south-east, a sign that it had left land to the west-north-west, for these birds sleep on land and fly out to sea in the morning to look for food and do not fly further than twenty leagues.

FRIDAY, 21 SEPTEMBER. Most of that day was calm, but there was some wind later. That day and night they must

have gone about thirteen leagues on their course and off it. At dawn they found so much weed that the sea seemed to be thick with it. It came from the west. They saw a booby. The sea was as smooth as a river and the breezes the sweetest in the world. They saw a whale, a sign that they were near land, for whales always remain near land.

SATURDAY, 22 SEPTEMBER. He sailed west-north-west, more or less, veering a little to one side or the other, and making roughly thirty leagues. They saw hardly any weed. They saw some petrels and another bird. Here the Admiral says: 'This head-wind is very necessary, because my crew were much agitated by the thought that no winds blew in these seas that could carry them back to Spain.' For part of the day there was no weed, but afterwards it was very dense.

SUNDAY, 23 SEPTEMBER. He steered north-west and at times north-west by north and sometimes along his course westwards. He made some twenty-two leagues. They saw a pigeon and a booby and a small river-bird and other white birds. The weed was plentiful and they found some crabs in it. As the sea was calm and smooth the crew grumbled, saying that since there were no heavy seas in these parts no wind would ever blow to carry them back to Spain. But later the seas rose high without any wind and this astonished them. The Admiral says at this point: 'I was in great need of these high seas because nothing like this had occurred since the time of the Jews when the Egyptians came out against Moses who was leading them out of captivity.'

MONDAY, 24 SEPTEMBER. He sailed on his westward course fourteen and a half leagues and reckoned twelve. A booby came to the ship and they saw many petrels.

TUESDAY, 25 SEPTEMBER. Much of this day was calm, but later there was wind and they followed their western course until night. The Admiral had a conversation with Martin Alonso Pinzón, captain of the *Pinta*, about a chart which Columbus had sent three days before to his caravel and on which – as it seems – were drawn certain islands supposed to be in that sea. Martin Alonso said that they must be somewhere near them. The Admiral replied that he was of the same opinion and that the reason why they had not reached them must be that the currents had driven the ships northeastwards and they had not gone as far as the pilots said. Having reached this conclusion the Admiral asked him to return the chart, which he did on a line. The Admiral then began with his pilots and sailors to fix his position on it. At sunset Martin Alonso went up into the poop of his ship and called most joyfully to the Admiral claiming a present,* since he had sighted land.

The Admiral says that when he heard this positive statement he fell on his knees to give thanks to God, and Martin Alonso and his men said the *Gloria in Excelsis Deo*. The Admiral's men did the same and the whole crew of the *Niña* climbed the mast and rigging and all affirmed that it was land. The Admiral believed so too and that it was about twenty-four leagues away. Until nightfall they all continued to claim that it was land. The Admiral ordered the course to be changed from the west to the south-west where the land had been sighted. They had sailed four and a half leagues westwards that day. That night they went seventeen leagues south-west, a total of twenty-one. The Admiral, according to his custom, told the men they had gone thirteen leagues, for he was still afraid that they would consider the voyage too

*It was the Spanish custom at the time to celebrate all good news by a present. The contemporary English word for such a present, now obsolete, was a Handsel.

long. Thus throughout the voyage he kept two reckonings, one false and the other true. The sea was very smooth so that many sailors went swimming. They saw many dorados* and other fish.

WEDNESDAY, 26 SEPTEMBER. He followed his course westwards until midday and then sailed south-west until they discovered that what they had taken for land was no land but cloud. They made thirty-one leagues in the day and night and he reckoned twenty-four. The sea was like a river and the breezes sweet and very gentle.

THURSDAY, 27 SEPTEMBER. He continued on his westward course. That day and night he made twenty-four leagues and told the men twenty. Many dorados came to the ship and they killed one. They saw a tropic-bird.

FRIDAY, 28 SEPTEMBER. He kept on his western course and owing to calms made only fourteen leagues and reckoned thirteen. They did not find much weed, and took two dorados; the other ships took more.

SATURDAY, 29 SEPTEMBER. He kept on his westward course and made twenty-four leagues, reckoning only twenty-one. All day and night they were held up by calms. They saw a frigate-bird, which makes the boobies disgorge what they've eaten and eats it itself. This is its only food. It is a sea-bird but does not settle on the sea, and does not fly more than twenty leagues from land. There are many of these birds in the Cape Verde Islands. Later they saw two boobies. The breezes were very sweet and pleasant, and the Admiral says that nothing is missing except the song of the nightingale. The sea was

* The dorado is the Coriphaena, a tropical fish about four feet long. It is bright gold in colour and feeds on flying fish.

as smooth as a river. Later there appeared, three times, three boobies and a frigate-bird. They saw a great deal of weed.

SUNDAY, 30 SEPTEMBER.   He kept on his westward course. And owing to the calms went only fourteen leagues, reckoning eleven. Four tropic-birds came to the ship, which is a strong sign of land, for so many birds of one species altogether is an indication that they are not straying or lost. Twice they saw four boobies; there was much weed.

NOTE: 'At nightfall the stars which are called the "Little Dipper" are near the arm on the west side, and at dawn they are in a line below the arm to the north-east, so that they appear to move only three lines, which is nine hours, and this is the same every night.'* These are the Admiral's exact words. He says also that the needles decline a point northeast at nightfall and at dawn they are exactly on the Pole Star. It appears therefore that the Pole Star moves like the other stars and that the needles always point true.

MONDAY, 1 OCTOBER.   He kept on his westward course. They made twenty-five leagues and he reckoned twenty. They ran into a great storm of rain. At dawn the Admiral's pilot calculated that since leaving the island of Hierro they had gone 568 leagues westwards. The lower figure which the Admiral had shown to the men made it 584. But the Admiral's true calculation, which he kept to himself, was 707.

TUESDAY, 2 OCTOBER.   That day and night he followed his course westwards for thirty-nine leagues, which he reckoned as thirty for the men. The sea was always smooth and calm.

* The position of these stars was used to tell the time at night. For this purpose an imaginary figure was drawn with outstretched arms and legs together, with the Pole Star on his breast. The reckoning was by 'lines' drawn on this figure.

'Great thanks be given to God,' the Admiral writes here. The weed was floating from east to west, which was unusual. Many fish appeared and one was killed. They saw a white bird, apparently a gull.

WEDNESDAY, 3 OCTOBER. He followed his usual course and went forty-seven leagues, reckoning forty to the men. Petrels appeared; there was much weed, some very old and some very fresh, bearing something like fruit. The Admiral believed that they had passed the islands which were depicted on his chart. The Admiral says that although he had some information about islands in this region he had not wished to beat about on those days in the past week when there had been so many signs of land, since he did not want to linger, his purpose being to journey to the Indies. He says that he would have been foolish to delay.

THURSDAY, 4 OCTOBER. He continued on his westward course and that day and night he went sixty-three leagues, reckoning only forty-six to his men. A flock of more than forty petrels came to the ship; also two boobies, and a boy in the caravel hit one of these with a stone. A frigate-bird came to the ship and a white bird like a gull.

FRIDAY, 5 OCTOBER. He continued on his course, making eleven miles an hour and went fifty-seven leagues that night and day, since the wind freshened somewhat in the night. He reckoned forty-five to his men. The sea was calm and smooth. 'Great thanks be given to God,' he says. The breeze was very sweet and temperate. Weeds none. Birds, many petrels. Many flying fish flew into the ship.

SATURDAY, 6 OCTOBER. He kept on his westward course for forty leagues in the day and night, reckoning thirty-three

to the men. That night Martin Alonso said that it would be well to sail south-west by west, and the Admiral thought that he had the island of Cipangu in mind, and saw that if they missed it they would not so easily come to the mainland and that the best thing would be to go there first and to the islands afterwards.*

SUNDAY, 7 OCTOBER.   He continued on his westward course and for two hours made twelve, and afterwards eight miles an hour. Up to an hour after sunrise he went twenty-three leagues, but told the men eighteen. All the ships sailed at the utmost speed in order to be the first to sight land and to secure the reward promised by the sovereigns to the first man who should sight it, and at sunrise that day the caravel *Niña*, which was the fastest sailer and ahead of the others, hoisted a standard at the masthead and fired a lombard as a sign that they had sighted land, for these were the Admiral's orders. He had also ordered that at sunrise and sunset the other ships should join him, since at these two periods the mists clear and visibility is greatest. In the evening they did not see the land which the crew of the *Niña* thought they had sighted, and a great flock of birds came from the north and flew south-west. The Admiral concluded that either they were going to roost on land or they were flying from the winter, which was about to set in in the lands from which they came. The Admiral knew that the Portuguese had discovered most of the islands in their possession by observing the birds. He decided therefore to abandon his westward course and steer west-south-west an hour before sunset. They made five leagues that night and twenty-three in the day; thus going twenty-eight leagues in all in the day and night together.

*I accept Salvador de Madariaga's opinion that Columbus also wanted to find Chipangu (Japan) first, but on this occasion rejected Pinzón's advice, at least in his log-book entry, out of jealousy.

MONDAY, 8 OCTOBER. In the day and night together he went about eleven and a half or twelve leagues west-south-west, and at times in the night, unless the text is corrupt, they seem to have made fifteen miles. They found the sea as smooth as the river at Seville. 'Thanks be to God,' says the Admiral, 'the breezes are as sweet as in April at Seville, it is a pleasure to breathe them, they are so laden with scent.' The weed seemed very fresh; there were many small land-birds and they took one which was flying south-west. There were terns and ducks and a booby.

TUESDAY, 9 OCTOBER. He went five leagues south-west, then changed course and ran four leagues to the west by north. In the end he made eleven and a half leagues in all by day and twenty and a half in the night, and for the men reckoned seventeen. All night they heard birds passing.

WEDNESDAY, 10 OCTOBER. He sailed west-south-west, making ten miles an hour but sometimes dropping to seven and sometimes rising to twelve, and in the day and night together they went fifty-nine leagues, which he counted as no more than forty-four for the men. Here the men could bear no more; they complained of the length of the voyage. But the Admiral encouraged them as best he could, holding out high hopes of the gains they could make. He added that it was no use their complaining, because he had reached the Indies and must sail on until with the help of Our Lord he discovered land.*

THURSDAY, 11 OCTOBER. He sailed west-south-west. They ran into rougher seas than any they had met with on the

---

*Columbus says, according to Las Casas' *History*, Bk I, Chap. 39, 'reached'. This suggests that he was confident of having reached them, even though he had discovered no land.

voyage. They saw petrels and a green reed near the ship. The men of the *Pinta* saw a cane and a stick and picked up another small stick, apparently shaped with an iron tool; also a piece of cane and some land-grasses and a small board. Those on the caravel *Niña* saw other indications of land and a stick covered with barnacles. At these signs, all breathed again and were rejoiced. That day they went twenty-seven leagues before sunset and after sunset he resumed his original western course. They made twelve miles an hour and up to two hours before midnight had gone ninety miles, which are twenty-two leagues and a half. The caravel *Pinta*, being swifter and sailing ahead of the Admiral, now sighted land and gave the signals which the Admiral had commanded.

The first man to sight land was a sailor called Rodrigo* from Triana, who afterwards vainly claimed the reward, which was pocketed by Columbus. The Admiral, however, when on the sterncastle at ten o'clock in the night, had seen a light, though it was so indistinct he would not affirm that it was land. He called Pero Gutierrez,† butler of the King's table, and told him that there seemed to be a light and asked him to look. He did so and saw it. He said the same to Rodrigo Sanchez of Segovia, whom the King and Queen had sent in the fleet as accountant,‡ and he saw nothing because he was not in a position from which anything could be seen. After the Admiral spoke this light was seen once or twice and it was like a wax candle that went up and down. Very few thought that this was a sign of land, but the Admiral was quite certain that they were near land. Accordingly, after the recita-

*This was probably Juan Rodriguez Bermeo.

†Pero Gutierrez was actually a steward, not a butler in the literal sense.

‡Rodrigo Sanchez de Segovia was a high official whose duties as accountant or *veedor* were to keep count of the gold, treasure or spices, and see that the sovereigns got their share.

tion of the *Salve* in the usual manner by the assembled sailors, the Admiral most seriously urged them to keep a good lookout from the forecastle and to watch carefully for land. He promised to give a silk doublet to the first sailor who should report it. And he would be entitled also to the reward promised by the sovereigns, which was an annual payment of ten thousand *maravedis*.*

Two hours after midnight land appeared, some two leagues away. They took in all sail, leaving only the mainsail, which is the great sail without bonnets, and lay close-hauled waiting for day. This was Friday, on which they reached a small island of the Lucayos, called in the Indian language Guanahani.† Immediately some naked people appeared and the Admiral went ashore in the armed boat, as did Martin Alonso Pinzón and Vicente Yanez his brother, captain of the *Niña*. The Admiral raised the royal standard and the captains carried two banners with the green cross which were flown by the Admiral on all his ships. On each side of the cross was a crown surmounting the letters F and Y‡ (for Ferdinand and Isabela). On landing they saw very green trees and much water and fruit of various kinds. The Admiral called the two captains and the others who had landed and Rodrigo Escobedo, recorder of the whole fleet, and Rodrigo Sanchez de Segovia, and demanded that they should bear faithful witness that he had taken possession of the island – which he did – for his sovereigns and masters the King and Queen. He further made the required declarations, which are recorded at greater length in the evidence there set down in writing. Soon many people of the island came up to them. What follows are the Admiral's actual words in his account of his first voyage and the discovery of these Indies.

*A small copper coin.
†This is generally assumed to be Watling Island in the Bahamas.
‡The contemporary spelling was Ysabela.

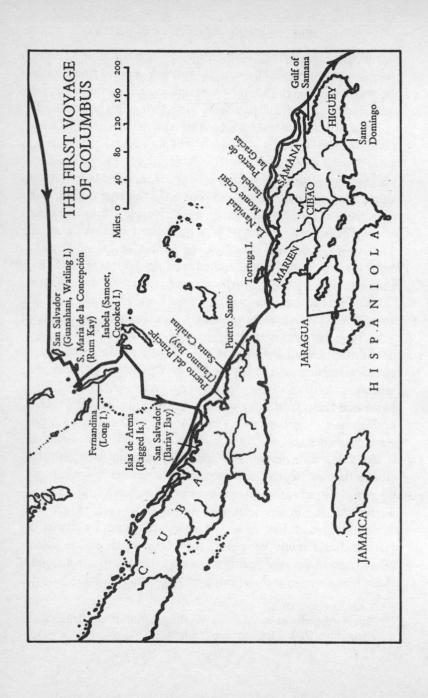

THE FIRST VOYAGE
OF COLUMBUS

Miles. 0   40   80   120   160   200

San Salvador
(Guanahani, Watling I.)

S. Maria de la Concepción
(Rum Kay)

Isabela (Samoet,
Crooked I.)

Fernandina
(Long I.)

Islas de Arena
(Ragged Is.)

San Salvador
(Bariay Bay)

C U B A

JAMAICA

Puerto del Príncipe
(Tánamo Bay)
Santa Catalina

Puerto Santo

La Navidad
Monte Cristi
Isabela
Puerto de
las Gracias

Tortuga I.

MARIEN

JARAGUA

CIBAO

SAMANA

HIGÜEY

Gulf of
Samana

Santo
Domingo

H I S P A N I O L A

'In order to win their friendship, since I knew they were a people to be converted and won to our holy faith by love and friendship rather than by force, I gave some of them red caps and glass beads which they hung round their necks, also many other trifles. These things pleased them greatly and they became marvellously friendly to us. They afterwards swam out to the ship's boats in which we were sitting, bringing us parrots and balls of cotton thread and spears and many other things, which they exchanged with us for such objects as glass beads, hawks and bells. In fact, they very willingly traded everything they had. But they seemed to me a people very short of everything. They all go naked as their mothers bore them, including the women, although I saw only one very young girl.

'All the men I saw were young. I did not see one over the age of thirty. They were very well built with fine bodies and handsome faces. Their hair is coarse, almost like that of a horse's tail and short; they wear it down over their eyebrows except for a few strands at the back, which they wear long and never cut. They are the colour of the Canary Islanders (neither black nor white). Some of them paint themselves black, others white or any colour they can find. Some paint their faces, some their whole bodies, some only the eyes, some only the nose. They do not carry arms or know them. For when I showed them swords, they took them by the edge and cut themselves out of ignorance. They have no iron. Their spears are made of cane. Some instead of an iron tip have a fish's tooth and others have points of different kinds. They are fairly tall on the whole, with fine limbs and good proportions. I saw some who had wound scars on their bodies and I asked them by signs how they got these and they indicated to me that people came from other islands near by who tried to capture them and they defended themselves. I supposed and still suppose that they come from the mainland to capture

them for slaves. They should be good servants and very intelligent, for I have observed that they soon repeat anything that is said to them, and I believe that they would easily be made Christians, for they appeared to me to have no religion. God willing, when I make my departure I will bring half a dozen of them back to their Majesties, so that they can learn to speak. I saw no animals of any kind on this island except parrots.' These are the Admiral's own words.

SATURDAY, 13 OCTOBER. At daybreak many of these men came to the shore – all young, as I have said, and all of a good height – a very fine people. Their hair is not curly but straight and as coarse as horse hair. All have very broad brows and heads, broader than those of any people I have seen before. Their eyes are very fine and not small. They are not at all black, but the colour of Canary Islanders, as could be expected, since this is in the same latitude as the island of Hierro in the Canaries. They have very straight legs and no bellies, but well-formed bodies.* They came to the ship in boats which are made from tree-trunks, like a long boat all cut out of a single log. They are marvellously carved in the native style and they are so big that forty or fifty-five men came in them. There are others smaller, so small that some carried only a single man. They row them with a paddle like a baker's shovel and they go wonderfully fast. If one capsizes they all start swimming and right it. They bale it out with gourds which they carry with them. They brought balls of cotton thread and parrots and spears and other things which it would be tedious to mention, and exchanged them for anything that was given them. I watched carefully to discover whether

---

*Las Casas appears to have quoted from two parallel accounts of the landing – the first being the Admiral's lost 'Book' which he perhaps found in the library of his son Hernando and the second from the log-book (also lost).

they had gold and saw that some of them carried a small piece hanging from a hole pierced in the nose. I was able to understand from their signs that to the south, either inland or along the coast, there was a king who had large vessels made of it and possessed a great deal. I tried hard to make them go there but saw in the end that they had no intention of doing so. I decided to remain till the afternoon of the next day and then to sail south-west, for according to the signs which many of them made there was land to the south, south-west and north-west. They indicated that men from the north-west often came to attack them. So I resolved to go south-west to seek the gold and precious stones.

This island is fairly large and very flat. It has very green trees and much water. It has a very large lake in the middle and no mountains and all is delightfully green. The people are very gentle and anxious to have the things we bring. Thinking that nothing will be given them, however, unless they give something in exchange, and having nothing to give, they take anything they can, jump into the water and swim away. But they will give all that they do possess for anything that is given to them, exchanging things even for bits of broken crockery or broken glass cups. I saw one give sixteen balls of cotton for three Portuguese *ceotis*, the equivalent of the Castilian *blanca*,* and in these balls there was more than an *aroba*† of cotton thread.

I should like to forbid this and let no one take any cotton except at my command; then if there were any quantity I would order it all to be taken for your Majesties. It grows here on this island, but owing to shortage of time I can give no exact account of it. And here too the gold is found that they wear hanging from their noses. But in order not to waste time I wish to go and see if I can strike the island of Chipangu.

* A small copper coin worth perhaps a farthing.
† About 25 lb.

Now when night fell they all went ashore in their boats.

SUNDAY, 14 OCTOBER. At dawn I ordered the ship's boat and the boats of the caravels to be made ready, and coasted the island in a north-easterly direction in order to see the other and eastward part and to look for villages. I saw two or three, whose people all came down to the beach calling to us and offering thanks to God. Some brought us water, others various sorts of food, and others, when they saw that I did not intend to land, jumped into the sea and swam out. We understood them to be asking us if we came from the sky. One old man got into the boat, and all the others, men and women alike, shouted, 'Come and see the men who have come from the skies; and bring them food and drink.' Many men and women came, each bringing something and offering thanks to God; they threw themselves on the ground and raised their hands to the sky and then called out to us, asking us to land. But I was afraid to do so, seeing a great reef of rocks which encircled the whole island. Inside there is deep water which would give sufficient anchorage for all the ships in Christendom. But the entrance is very narrow. It is true that there are some shoals within this reef, but the sea is as still as well water.

I went to view all this this morning, in order to give an account to your Majesties and to decide where a fort could be built. I saw a piece of land which is much like an island, though it is not one, on which there were six huts. It could be made into an island in two days, though I see no necessity to do so since these people are very unskilled in arms, as your Majesties will discover from seven whom I caused to be taken and brought aboard so that they may learn our language and return. However, should your Highnesses command it all the inhabitants could be taken away to Castile or held as

slaves on the island, for with fifty men we could subjugate them all and make them do whatever we wish. Moreover, near the small island I have described there are groves of the loveliest trees I have seen, all green with leaves like our trees in Castile in April and May, and much water.

I examined the whole of that anchorage and then returned to the ship and set sail. I saw so many islands that I could not make up my mind which to visit first. The men I had taken told me by signs that there were so many that it was impossible to count them. They mentioned more than a hundred by name. In the end I looked for the largest and decided to go to that one, which I am doing. It is about five leagues from this island of San Salvador, and the rest are rather more or rather less. All are very flat, without mountains and very fertile. All are populated and make war with one another, although the people are very simple and do not look savage.

[*Bartolomé de las Casas*, History of the Indies, *Bk I, Chap. 41, comments: 'I have no doubt that if the Admiral had believed that such dreadful results would follow and had known as much about the primary and secondary effects of natural and divine law as he knew about cosmography and other human learning, he would never have introduced or initiated a practice which was to lead to such terrible harm. For no one can deny that he was a good and Christian man. But God's judgements are most secret and no man can or should attempt to discover them. . . .*

'It would be well to point out two things first, the natural willingness and predisposition of these people to receive our holy faith and their readiness to adopt Christianity and moral virtues, if treated with love, charity and kindness, and how profitable this would have been to God; and secondly, how far the Admiral was from the punctual observation of divine and natural law, and how little he understood the sovereigns' obligations and his own to the natives, according to this law, since he could so lightly say that they might take all the Indians who were the natural inhabitants of

these lands to Castile, or hold them captive on their own island etc.

'*This was very far from the purpose of God and His Church, to which this voyage and the discovery of all this world and everything in and about it should have been subordinated, and by which it should have been directed.*']

MONDAY, 15 OCTOBER. I stood off that night, fearing to approach land before morning because I did not know if the coast was free from shoals. At daybreak I hoisted sail. As the island was more than five leagues away – indeed more like seven – and the tide was against me, it was midday when I reached this island. I found that the coast which faces San Salvador runs north and south for some five leagues, and the other coast which I followed runs east and west for more than ten leagues. And as from this island I saw another larger one to the west, I hoisted sail to run all that day till night, since I should otherwise not have been able to reach its western point. I named this island Santa Maria de la Concepción.* And it was almost sunset when I reached this point. I wished to learn whether there was gold there, because the men I had taken aboard at the island at San Salvador told me that here they wore very large gold bracelets round their legs and arms. I thought that this tale was probably a lie told in the hope of getting away. Generally it was my wish to pass no island without taking possession of it. Though having annexed one it might be said that we had annexed all. I anchored and stayed there until today, Tuesday, when at daybreak I approached the shore with the armed boats and landed.

There were many people all naked and like those of San Salvador. They let us go about the island and gave us all that we asked for. But as the wind was blowing from the southeast I did not wish to delay and went back to the ship. A large canoe happening to lie alongside the *Niña*, a little before

*Rum Kay.

midnight one of the men from San Salvador who was in the caravel jumped overboard and went off in it. A few minutes later another threw himself overboard also and swam after the canoe, which went so fast that no boat could overtake it, for it had a considerable start.*

So they came to land and left the canoe. Several members of my crew went ashore after them and they ran off like frightened hens. We took the canoe they had abandoned aboard the caravel *Niña*; it was approached by another small canoe with a man who had come to barter a ball of cotton. Since he would not board the caravel some sailors jumped down and seized him. Having seen all this from the forecastle where I was standing, I sent for him and gave him a red cap and some green glass beads which I put on his arm and two hawk's bells which I put in his ears. I told the sailors to give him back his canoe which they had taken on to the ship's boat, and sent him ashore. I then raised sail for the other large island which I saw to the west and ordered that the second canoe which the *Niña* was towing astern should be set adrift. Shortly afterwards I saw the man to whom I had given these gifts come ashore.

I had not taken the ball of cotton from him, although he wished to give it to me. The people gathered round him and he appeared astonished. It seemed to him that we were good people and that the man who had escaped in the canoe must have wronged us or we should not have carried him off.†

It was to create this impression that I had him set free and gave him presents. I was anxious that they should think well of us so that they may not be unfriendly when your Majesties send a second expedition here. All I gave him was worth less than four *maravedis*.

*The text is obscure at this point, but this appears to be the meaning.
†Here the text speaks of one man only but, as far as can be seen from the defective manuscript, two men escaped.

So I set sail for the other island at about ten o'clock with a south-east wind which veered southerly. It is very large and, according to the signs made by the men we had brought from San Salvador, contains much gold, which they wear as bracelets on their arms and legs and in their ears and nose s and round their necks. This other island was about nine leagues west of Santa Maria, and this part of its coast apparently runs from north-west to south-east, for upwards of twenty-eight leagues.

Like San Salvador and Santa Maria it is very flat with no mountains. All the beaches are free from rocks, although all have submerged reefs near the shore, for which reason it is necessary to look carefully before anchoring and not to anchor too near land. The water, however, is always very clear and you can see bottom. A couple of lombard shots off land the water is so deep around all these islands that it cannot be sounded. They are all very green and fertile and subject to gentle breezes. They may contain many things of which I do not know because I did not care to land and explore them, being anxious to find gold; and since these islands show signs of containing it – for the natives wear it round their arms and legs, and it is certainly gold, because I showed them some pieces which I have – I cannot fail, with God's help, to find out where it comes from.

When I was in mid-channel, between Santa Maria and this other island which I have named Fernandina,* I found a man alone in a canoe crossing from the one to the other. He was carrying a lump of their bread, about the size of a fist, and a gourd of water and a bit of red earth which had been powdered and then kneaded; also some dried leaves which they must value very highly since they gave me a present of them. He also carried a native basket containing some glass beads and two *blancas*, by which I knew that he had come from San

*Long Island.

Salvador to Santa Maria and was now on his way to Fernandina. He came alongside and I let him come aboard as he asked. I had his canoe hauled aboard also and all that he carried kept safe. I ordered that he should be given bread and honey and something to drink. I shall carry him to Fernandina and restore all his possessions to him so that he may give a good account of us. Then when, God willing, your Highnesses send others here, we shall be favourably received and the natives may give us of all they possess.

TUESDAY, 16 OCTOBER. Having left the islands of Santa Maria de la Concepción* at about mid-day for Fernandina, which appeared very large in the west, I sailed for the rest of the day in a calm and could not reach it in time to anchor, for the water was not clear enough for me to see bottom and one has to take great care not to lose the anchors. So I lay off all that night and in the morning saw a village off which I anchored. This was the native village of the man I had found on the previous day with his canoe in mid-channel. He had given such a good account of us that canoes swarmed round the ship all that night. They brought us water and something of all they had. I ordered presents to be given to all of them, that is to say, strings of ten or a dozen small glass beads and some brass clappers of a kind that are worth a *maravedi* each in Castile and some leather tags, all of which they value very highly, and when they came aboard I had them given molasses to eat. And afterwards at nine in the morning I sent a ship's boat ashore for water and they most gladly showed our men where it could be found and themselves carried the full casks back to the boat. They were delighted to give us pleasure.

This island is very large and I decided to sail round it because as I understand, in it or near it, there is a goldfield.

*There were in fact two islands close together.

The island is eight leagues west of Santa Maria and from the cape where I touched, the coast runs north-north-west and south-south-east; I saw quite twenty leagues of it and it still continued. As I write this I have set sail with a south wind intending to push on round the island until I come to Samoet, which is the island or city where the gold is, for all who have come aboard the ship have said so. Both the people of San Salvador and Santa Maria told us so.

The people here are like the people of those islands; both in language and customs, though here they seem to me rather more civilized, more tractable and more intelligent, for I see they are better able to bargain for the cotton and other trifles which they have brought to the ship than were the other peoples. And I saw on this island cotton cloths made like shawls. The people are more friendly and the women wear a small piece of cotton in front which just hides their private parts.

This island is very green, flat and fertile and I have no doubt that they sow and reap Indian corn and other crops throughout the year. I saw many trees very unlike ours. Many of them had several branches of different kinds coming from one root. One branch may be of one kind and another of another and the variation is quite marvellous. They are so extremely different, that, for example, one branch may have leaves like those of the cane and another like those of a mastic tree, and thus on a single tree there are five or six different kinds, all distinct from one another. They are not grafted, though they might be supposed to be the result of grafting; on the contrary they are wild and these people do not cultivate them.

They have no religion and I think that they would be very quickly Christianized, for they have a very ready understanding.

The fish here are surprisingly unlike ours. There are some of the shape of dories and of the finest colours in the world,

blue, yellow, red and every other hue and others variously flecked. The colours are so marvellous that everybody wondered and took pleasure in the sight. There are also whales. But I saw no kind of land animal at all except parrots and lizards. A ship's boy told me that he had seen a large snake. I saw no sheep or goats nor any other animals at all. But I was there only for a very short time; for it is now midday. If there had been any, however, I could not have failed to see some. I will describe the circuit of this island when I have made it.

WEDNESDAY, 17 OCTOBER.   At midday I set sail from the village off which I had anchored and where I had landed and taken water to make a circuit of this island of Fernandina. The wind was south-west and south. It was my intention to follow the coast of this island from where I was to the south-east, since it runs as a whole from north-north-west to south-south-east. I wanted to take my course to the south-south-east, because all the Indians whom I have aboard and others from whom I inquired tell me that southwards from here lies the island they call Samoet, where the gold is. Martin Alonso Pinzón, captain of the *Pinta*, in which I had placed three of these Indians, came to me and said that one of them had very explicitly given him to understand that the island could be rounded more quickly in a north-north-westerly direction.

I saw that the wind would not help me on the course I wished to steer and that it favoured the other course, so I steered north-north-west, and when I was about two leagues from the island's* cape I saw a marvellous harbour with an entrance, or rather two entrances, since there is an islet in the middle. Both entrances are very narrow, but it would have been large enough to provide anchorage for a hundred ships if it had been deep and free of rocks and the entrance channels

*Long Island.

had been deep also. I thought fit to examine it closely and take soundings; therefore I anchored outside and went in with all the ships' boats and we found that it was shallow. When I first saw it I thought it was the mouth of a river, so I had ordered casks to be brought to take water. On land I saw eight or ten men who quickly came up to us and pointed to a nearby village, where I sent my men for water, which they took, some going armed and others carrying the casks. As the village was some distance away I had to remain there for two hours.

During that time I walked among the trees, which were the loveliest sight I had yet seen. They were green as those of Andalusia in the month of May. But all these trees are as different from ours as day from night and so are the fruit and plants and stones, and everything else. It is true that some trees were of species that can be found in Castile, yet there was a great difference; but there are many other varieties which no one could say are like those of Castile or could compare with them. The people were all of the same kind as those already described; their condition was the same; they were naked and of the same height. They gave whatever they possessed for whatever we gave them and here I saw some ships' boys exchanging small bits of broken crockery or glass for spears.

The men who had gone for water told me that they had entered their houses and that they were very clean and well swept and that their beds and blankets are like cotton nets. These houses are like large tents. They are high and have good chimneys. But of all the villages I saw none consisted of more than a dozen or fifteen houses. Here they found that married women wear cotton drawers, but girls do not, until they reach the age of eighteen. Here there were mastiffs and small dogs and here they met one man who wore in his nose a piece of gold about half the size of a *castellano* on which they saw letters. I was angry with them because they had not bar-

gained for it and given as much as they were asked, so that we could examine it and see where the coin came from. They answered that they did not dare to bargain for it.

After taking the water I returned to the ship, raised sail and followed a north-westerly course along the shore to the point where the coast turns east-west. Later all the Indians insisted that this island was smaller than Samoet and that it would be better to turn back in order to reach that island sooner. Then the wind fell and began to blow west-north-west, which was unfavourable to the course we had been following. I therefore turned back and sailed all that night in an east-south-easterly direction, sometimes due east and sometimes south-east in order to keep clear of land, because the clouds were very thick and the weather very heavy. The wind was slight and I could not make land to anchor. In the night heavy rain fell from after midnight almost till daybreak and it is still cloudy with more rain to come.

We are now at the south-east tip of the island, where I hope to anchor until the weather clears, and I can see the other islands to which I am going. It has rained practically every day since I have been in these Indies. Your Highnesses must believe me that these islands are the most fertile, and temperate and flat and good in the whole world.

THURSDAY, 18 OCTOBER. When the weather cleared I followed the wind and got as close to the island as I could. I anchored when I could get no closer but did not land and at dawn I set sail.

FRIDAY, 19 OCTOBER. I raised anchor at dawn and sent the caravel *Pinta* to the east-south-east and the *Niña* to the south-south-east and myself went south-south-east. I ordered them to follow these courses till midday and that both should then change their courses and rejoin me, and soon, before we had

sailed three hours, we saw an island to the east, towards which we steered, and all three vessels reached its northern point before midday. Here there is an islet and a reef of rocks, on the seaward side to the north and another between this and the island itself, which the Indians whom I had with me called 'Samoet'. I named it Isabela.*

The wind was northerly and this islet lay on the course from Fernandina, from which I had sailed due west. I then followed the coast of this island westwards for twelve leagues as far as a cape which I named Cape Hermoso (Beautiful) which is on its western coast. It is indeed lovely, rounded and in deep water, with no shoals lying off it. At first the shore is low and stony, but further on there is a sandy beach which continues along most of this coast. Here I anchored on this night of Friday until morning. The whole of this coast and all of the island that I saw is more or less beach, and, beautiful though the others are, this island is the most beautiful I have seen. There are many trees, very green and tall, and the land is higher than on the other islands. On it there is a hill which cannot however be called a mountain, but which makes the whole island more beautiful. There seems to be a lot of water in the middle of the island. On this north-eastern side the coast turns sharply and is thickly covered with very large trees.

I wished to go in, anchor and land in order to see all this beauty, but the water was shallow and I could only anchor some way off shore. The wind was very favourable for sailing to this point where I am now anchored, which I named Cape Hermoso, and beautiful it is. And so I did not anchor in that bay, seeing as I did this green and lovely cape in the distance. Everything on all these coasts is so green and lovely that I do not know where to go first, and my eyes never weary of looking on this fine vegetation, which is so different from

* This is Crooked Island.

that of our own lands. I think that many trees and plants grow there which will be highly valued in Spain for dyes and medicinal spices. But I am sorry to say that I do not recognize them. When I reached this cape, the scent of flowers and trees blew offshore and this was the most delightful thing in the world.

In the morning before I sail away I will land to see what is growing on this cape. There is no village, for this lies further inland, and it is there, according to the men I have with me, that the king lives who wears so much gold. Tomorrow I intend to go so far inland as to find this village and see and speak with this king, who, according to their signs, rules all the islands in this neighbourhood and wears much gold on his clothes and person. I do not attach much belief to their statements, however, because I do not understand them very well, and know that they are so poor in gold that any small amount this king may wear will seem much to them.

I have called this cape here Cape Hermoso and I believe that it is an island separate from Samoet and that there is another small island also lying between them. I did not examine this matter minutely because I could not do all this even in fifty years, being anxious to see and discover as much as I could in order to return to your Highnesses, God willing, in April. It is true that if I find any place where there is gold or spices in quantity I shall wait until I've collected as much as I can. Therefore I continue to sail on in search of such a place.

SATURDAY, 20 OCTOBER. Today at sunrise I left the place where I was anchored off the south-west point of Samoet, which I called Cabo de la Laguna. I named the island Isabela. I intended to steer north-east and east from the southern and south-westerly end towards the place where, as I understood from the men I carried, the village with its king lay. I found the sea everywhere so shallow that I could not enter or sail to

that point and I saw that to approach it from the south-west would take me far out of my course. I decided therefore to return north-north-east by the way that I had come and round the island in that direction. The winds were so light that I could only sail along this coast at night, since it is dangerous to anchor off these islands, except in daylight, when you can see where you are dropping anchor, for the bottom is very patchy, in parts rocky, in parts clean. I made up my mind to stand off under sail for the whole of Sunday night. The caravels anchored because they had reached the coast earlier and thought that when I saw them making their accustomed signals I should anchor also. But I decided not to do so.

SUNDAY, 21 OCTOBER.   At ten o'clock I reached this Cabo del Isleo and anchored, as did the caravels. After eating a meal I went ashore, but there was no village – only one house in which I found nobody. I think they had all run away from fright, for all their things were there.

I wouldn't allow anything to be touched but went with the captains and men to examine the island. Though all the others we had seen were beautiful, green and fertile, this was even more so. It has large and very green trees, and great lagoons, around which these trees stand in marvellous groves. Here and throughout the island the trees and plants are as green as in Andalusia in April. The singing of small birds is so sweet that no one could ever wish to leave this place. Flocks of parrots darken the sun and there is a marvellous variety of large and small birds very different from our own; the trees are of many kinds, each with its own fruit, and all have a marvellous scent. It grieves me extremely that I cannot identify them, for I am quite certain that they are all valuable and I am bringing samples of them and of the plants also.

As I was walking beside one of the lagoons I saw a snake,

which we killed. I am bringing the skin to your Highnesses. As soon as we saw it, it swam into the lagoon and we followed it, for the water was not very deep, and we killed it with spears. It is almost five foot long and I believe there are many of them in this lagoon. Here I recognized aloe, and tomorrow I intend to have half a ton brought aboard, for they tell me it's very valuable. Also when we were looking for good water we found a village near by, half a league from where I am anchored.

As soon as the inhabitants saw us they ran away, leaving their houses. They hid their clothing and all that they had in the undergrowth. I allowed nothing to be taken, not even to the value of a pin. Afterwards a few of the men approached us and one of them came quite close. I gave him hawk's bells and some small glass beads, and he was very pleased and happy. In order to foster this friendship and ask for something from them, I asked them for water, and after I had returned to the ship they came down to the beach with their gourds full and gave it to us with delight. I ordered that they should be given another string of little glass beads and they said they would return the next day.

I decided to have all the vessels on board filled with water. Therefore if the weather allows I will presently set out to coast this island until I have speech with this king and see whether I can get the gold that I hear he wears. After this I shall set out for another large island which, according to the indications given me by the Indians whom I have aboard, must be Chipangu. They however call it Colba* and say that there are many large ships and sailors there. From here I shall go to another island, which they call Bohio† and say is also very large. In passing I shall see the others that lie between and according to whether I find a quantity of gold or spices I shall decide what to do next. But I am still determined to go to

*Cuba. †Hispaniola.

the city of Quinsay,* to deliver your Highnesses' letters to the Grand Khan and request his answer which I shall bring back.

MONDAY, 22 OCTOBER. I have waited here all night on the chance that the king of this place or other persons may bring me gold or other valuables. Many people came who were like the people in the other islands, all naked and painted white, red, black and in many different ways. They carried spears and some of them brought balls of cotton to barter. These they exchanged with some of the sailors for bits of glass from broken bowls and fragments of earthenware. Some of them wore pieces of gold hanging from their noses, which they happily exchanged for little bells, for bells of the kind made for the feet of a sparrow-hawk and for glass beads, but the amount was a mere trifle. Indeed, however small the things we give them, they still consider our coming a great marvel. I think they believe that we have come from the sky. We are taking water for the ships from the lagoon which lies near Cabo del Isleo, as I named it; and here Martin Alonso Pinzón, of the *Pinta*, killed another snake about five foot long and like that of yesterday. I had as much aloe collected as was to be found.

TUESDAY, 23 OCTOBER. I should like to depart today for the island of Colba, which I believe according to the indications of its size and riches given us by these people must be Chipangu. I shall not stay here any longer, to round this island or go to the village as I had intended, to have speech with the king or lord. I do not wish to delay long, since I see

*This was Hangchow – the capital of the Grand Khan – described by Marco Polo. Columbus's information about Cathay was based on the stories of old travellers, so he did not know that there had been no Grand Khan since the thirteenth century.

that there is no goldfield here and to round these islands one needs many changes of wind and the wind doesn't blow as one wishes. It is best to go where there is much to be done and so it is right not to stay here but to continue on our course, discovering many lands until we find one that is truly profitable. I think, however, that this place is very rich in spices. I am extremely sorry that I cannot recognize them, for I see a very great number of trees each bearing its own kind of fruit, and they are as green now as trees in Spain in the months of May and June. There are a thousand kinds of plants also, all in flower. But the only one I recognize is this aloe, which I ordered to be taken aboard yesterday and brought for your Highnesses.

I have not set out and I am not setting out for Colba, since there is no wind, but dead calm and much rain. It rained heavily yesterday but was not at all cold. On the contrary the days are warm and the nights mild as in May in Andalusia.

WEDNESDAY, 24 OCTOBER.   Last night at midnight I raised anchor from Cabo del Isleo on the north side of the island of Isabela, where I had lain, and set sail for the island of Colba, which these people tell me is very large and has much trade. They say that it contains gold and spices and large ships and merchandize and have told me by signs that I should steer west-south-west to find it, and I think this is right, for if I am to believe the indications of all these Indians and those I have on board – I do not know their language – this is the island of Chipangu of which such marvellous tales are told, and which in the globes that I have seen and on the painted map of the world appears to lie in this region.

So I steered west-south-west till day, and at dawn the wind dropped and it rained, as it had done almost all night, and I lay there with very little wind until after midday and then it began to blow very gently. I then raised all sail, the

mainsail and two bonnets, and the foresail and spritsail, the mizen, main topsail and the boat's sail on the poop. I continued on my course till nightfall and then Cabo Verde at the western end of the south coast of Fernandina lay to the north-west seven leagues away. It was now blowing hard and I did not know what course to follow for the island of Colba.

I did not want to go looking for it at night, for these islands lie in very deep water and no soundings can be taken at more than two lombard shots from the shore. The bottom is patchy, with rocks in some parts and sand in others, and so it is not possible to anchor safely except where you can see. I therefore decided to lower all sails, except the foresail, and to proceed under it. After a while the wind became much stronger and I made a considerable distance, which disturbed me as the clouds were thick and it was raining. I ordered the foresail to be furled and that night we went less than two leagues.

THURSDAY, 25 OCTOBER. From sunrise to nine o'clock he sailed to the west-south-west, making five leagues. After this he changed course for the west and sailed at eight miles an hour until one o'clock, and from then until three o'clock, and they made about forty-four miles. They then sighted land, seven or eight islands, in a line from north to south, and five leagues away.

FRIDAY, 26 OCTOBER. He now lay to the south of these islands. The water was shallow everywhere for five or six leagues and he anchored there. The Indians aboard told him that from these islands to Colba was a day and a half's journey in their boats which are hollowed out of tree-trunks and have no sail. These are their canoes. He now set out for Colba ... which he believed to be Cipangu.

74

SATURDAY, 27 OCTOBER.   At sunrise he raised anchor from these islands, which he named Las Islas de Arena* on account of the sandbanks that stretch southward from them for six leagues. He sailed south-south-west at eight miles an hour till one o'clock and they made about forty miles, and they continued on their course until nightfall, making another twenty-eight miles. Before nightfall they sighted land and watched all night during heavy rain. On Saturday, they made seventeen leagues to the south-south-west before sunset.

SUNDAY, 28 OCTOBER.   They sailed on south-south-west in search of the nearest point in Colba and he entered a very beautiful river very free from shoals and other dangers. And all along the coast the water was very deep up to the shore. The mouth of the river was twelve fathoms and wide enough for ships to beat about. He anchored as he says a lombard shot upstream. The Admiral says he had never seen a more beautiful country. It was covered with trees right down to the river and these were lovely and green and different from ours, and each bore its own fruit or flowers. There were many birds, large and small, which sung sweetly, and there were a great number of palms of a different kind from those of Guinea and from ours. They were of moderate height with no bark at the foot, and the Indians cover their houses with them. The land is very flat.

The Admiral got into the boat and went ashore, where he found two houses which he believed to belong to fishermen who had fled in terror. In one of these he found a dog that did not bark, and in both houses there were nets of palm fibre and lines and horn fish-hooks and bone harpoons and other fishing tackle, and there were many hearths. He believed that many people lived in each house. He gave orders that nothing should be touched in either, and his order was

*The Ragged Islands.

obeyed. The vegetation was as abundant as in April and May in Andalusia. He found much purslane and wild amaranth. He returned to the boat and went some distance up the river. He said that it was such a great joy to see the plants and trees and to hear the birds singing that he could not leave them and return. He says that this island is the most beautiful that eyes have ever seen. It has many good harbours and deep rivers, and it seems that the seas are never rough because the vegetation on the shore grows almost to the sea's edge, which is unusual where the seas are rough. So far, he had not encountered rough seas anywhere in these islands. He says that the island contains very lovely mountains, which do not form long chains but are very high. All the rest of the land is high also, like Sicily. It has plenty of water, as he gathered from the Indians from Guanahani whom he had with him, who told him by signs that it was ten large rivers and that they cannot go round it in their canoes in twenty days.

When he brought the ships close to shore, two boats or canoes came out, but on seeing the sailors entering the boat and rowing about to take soundings for an anchorage, they fled. The Indians said that there are goldfields and pearls in the island and the Admiral saw that this was a likely place for pearls, since there were mussels, which are a sign of them. The Admiral understood that the Grand Khan's ships come there and that they are large and that the mainland is ten days' journey away. The Admiral called this river and harbour San Salvador.* . . .

*This is Bariay Bay in the island of Cuba.

THE LIFE OF THE ADMIRAL
BY HIS SON, HERNANDO COLON

CHAPTER 27

The Admiral discovers the island of Cuba. What he finds there

... ON the return of the ships they followed a westerly course and discovered another, larger river, which the Admiral named the Rio de Mares. It was a much better river than the last, since a ship could both enter and turn round in its mouth, and its banks were thickly peopled. But on seeing the ships the local inhabitants fled to the mountains. These were seen to be many and high, with rounded tops and covered with trees, and they had most pleasing vegetation. Here the Indians hid everything they could carry with them, and their timidity prevented the Admiral from learning the nature of the island. Considering that if he were to land with many men the people's fear would increase, he chose two Christians, one of the Indians whom he had brought from the island of San Salvador and another, a native of Cuba, who had boldly rowed up to the ships in a small canoe. He gave them orders to go into the interior of the island and discover its character, treating any of its inhabitants they might meet on their way with friendship and courtesy. And in order that no time should be lost, the Admiral commanded that, while they were on their way, his ship should be brought ashore and caulked. They noticed that all the wood they used for the fires they needed for this job was from the *almaciga* trees, which grow in great quantity throughout the island. Both in leaf and fruit this tree is very similar to the mastic, but considerably larger.

CHAPTER 28

*The two Christians return and give an account of
what they have seen*

ON 5 November, when the ship was caulked and ready to
sail, the two Christians and the two Indians returned. They
said that they had penetrated twelve leagues inland and found
a village of fifty houses, all very large and built of wood with
thatched roofs. These houses were round and tent-shaped like
all the others they had seen. There must have been some
thousands of inhabitants, since in each house lived all the
members of a family. The chief men of the place came out to
meet and welcome the Christians and carried them on their
shoulders to their town, where they gave them a large house
for their lodging. Here they made them sit down on some
strangely shaped wooden seats in the form of animals with
short fore- and rear-paws and tails slightly raised to support
the back. For comfort this back support was as wide as the
seat, and on the front was carved a head with eyes and ears of
gold. They call these seats *dujos* or *duchos*. Having made our
men sit down, all the Indians immediately sat on the ground
around them, and then, one by one, came close to them to kiss
their feet and hands, in the belief that they had come from the
sky. The Indians gave them a meal of boiled roots, which
tasted like chestnuts,* and begged them warmly to remain
there with them, or at least to stay there and rest for five or
six days. For the two Indians whom our men had brought
with them as interpreters had spoken very highly of the
Christians.

Shortly afterwards a great number of women came in to
take a look at the Spaniards and the men went out. These

* Sweet potatoes.

women also kissed the strangers' feet and hands in awe and wonder, as if they were holy objects, and proffered the presents they had brought.

When the Christians thought it was time to return to the ships many Indians wished to accompany them. But they would allow only the king with one of his sons and a servant to come, and the Admiral received them with great honour. The Christians told him that on the way there and back they had found many villages, in which they had been welcomed and treated with the same courtesy. But these villages or hamlets were no more than groups of five houses.

On the paths they had met a great number of people carrying burning coals in order to make fire with which to burn certain perfumed herbs that they had with them.* On this fire they also boiled those roots which were their staple food. The Spaniards had seen very great numbers of trees and plants that were not found on the sea coast, and a great variety of birds, very different from our own, although among them were partridges and nightingales. They had seen no four-footed animals except some dogs which did not bark. They had also seen many fields of the staple root, and of kidney-beans, and another kind of bean, also of a grain like panic-grass that the Indians call *maize*. This grain has a very good taste when cooked, either roasted or ground and made into a gruel.

They had a great abundance of cotton spun into balls, so much that a single house contained more than 12,500 lb of yarn. They do not plant it by hand, for it grows naturally in the fields like roses, and the plants open spontaneously when ripe, though not all at the same season. For on one plant they saw a half-formed pod, an open one, and another so ripe that it was falling. The Indians afterwards brought a great quantity of these plants to the ships, and would exchange a whole basket full for a leather tag. Strangely enough, none of the

*Tobacco.

79

Indians made use of this cotton for clothing, but only for making their nets and beds – which they call hammocks – and for weaving the little skirts or cloths which the women wore to cover their private parts. When the Indians were asked if they had gold or pearls or spices, they answered by signs that there were great quantities of all three to the east in a land called Bohio* – the present-day Hispaniola, which they also called Babeque. But Columbus's men did not clearly understand at that time what land they meant.

CHAPTER 29

The Admiral ceases to follow the north coast of Cuba, and turns on an eastward course for the island of Hispaniola

WHEN he had heard this account, the Admiral did not wish to stay any longer in the Rio de Mares. He gave orders that a native of the island should be taken aboard, since he wished to bring to Castile one inhabitant of each country to give an account of its nature and products. So a dozen persons – men, women and children – were taken in a peaceful way, without noise or trouble. When the time came to sail away with them the husband of one of the women captives, and father of her two children who had been taken aboard with her, came to the ship in a canoe and begged by signs that he should be taken to Castile also, so as not to be separated from his wife and children. The Admiral was highly delighted by this man's action and ordered that the whole family should be well treated and entertained.

* This was actually the Arawak word for their huts, which Columbus misunderstood as the name of an island.

On that same day, 13 November, he sailed on an eastern course, making for the island that the Indians called Babeque or Bohio. But owing to a very strong north wind he was compelled to anchor again off Cuba among some very tall islands lying close to a large harbour, which he called Puerto del Principe. He named the waters round these islands El Mar de Nuestra Señora. These were so numerous and so close together that they were not a quarter of a league apart. The majority of them in fact were within an arquebus shot of one another. The channels were so deep, however, and the shores so thickly wooded that it was a pleasure to sail between them, among the trees, which were very different from our own. They saw many *almacigas*,* aloes, palms, with smooth green trunks, and several other kinds of tree.

Although these islands were uninhabited, there were remains of many fishermen's fires on their shores. For as was afterwards observed bands of men come from Cuba in their canoes to visit these and countless other uninhabited islands near by, to feed on the fish they catch, and on birds, crabs and other things they find ashore. The Indians are accustomed to eating unclean things, such as large, fat spiders and white worms that breed among decayed wood and other rotting matter. They eat some fish almost raw, and immediately on catching them. Before they boil them they tear out their eyes and eat them on the spot. They eat many such things that would not only make any Spaniard vomit but would poison him if he tried them. They go on these hunting and fishing expeditions at fixed seasons, moving from one ground to another, like sheep in search of new pasturage when they grow tired of the old.

To return to these small islands in the Mar de Nuestra Señora, I will observe that on one of them the Christians killed with their swords an animal resembling a badger and

*A kind of mastic, already mentioned.

discovered many mother-of-pearl shells in the sea. When they cast their nets they found among their numerous and very diverse catch a fish shaped like a pig and entirely covered with a very thick hide except at the tail, which was soft. They noticed at the same time that in this sea and on the islands the tide rose higher and fell lower than anywhere they had been, and that these tides were the reverse of our own, for when the moon stood in the south-east, at its meridian, it was low water.

CHAPTER 30

One of the caravels deserts the Admiral

... DURING that voyage [from Cuba to Hispaniola] Martin Alonso Pinzón received information from some Indians whom he was carrying as prisoners in his caravel that there was much gold in the island of Bohio (which, as we have said, was Hispaniola). Impelled by greed, on Wednesday, 21 November, he left the Admiral deliberately, not as a result of wind or currents. For the wind was behind him and he could easily have rejoined him, but did not wish to. On the contrary, pushing steadily on he made the greatest possible distance. His ship being very swift, he sailed all that Thursday and by nightfall had entirely disappeared, though up to then the ships had always sailed within sight of one another. The Admiral was now left with two ships, and since the winds prevented his crossing to Hispaniola he decided to return to Cuba to take on wood and water at a harbour not far from the Puerto del Principe [where he had anchored on first reaching Cuba], which he called Santa Catalina.

While they were drawing water, he saw by chance in the

river some stones which showed traces of gold; and in this district were hills covered with pines so tall that masts could be cut from them for ships and carracks. There was timber also for planks, sufficient indeed for building as many new ships as they might want. There were also holm oaks and strawberry trees and others like those of Castile. Following the instructions of the Indians who directed him on his course to Hispaniola, the Admiral sailed ten or twelve leagues to the south-east along a shore abounding in very fine harbours and many beautiful rivers. The Admiral speaks so highly of the charm and beauty of this region that I cannot do better than quote his own words, describing his entry of a river which flows into a harbour called by him Puerto Santo.

'When I brought the ships opposite the mouth of the harbour, which faces south, I found a river easily capable of taking a galley; and yet the entrance was so concealed that it could not be seen until we came very close. It was so beautiful that I was moved to go upstream if only for a ship's length. I found a bottom from five to eight fathoms. Continuing upstream I pushed ahead for some time. The river was very cold and pleasant and the water very clear when we looked down at the sandy bottom. There were great numbers of palms of various kinds, the tallest and most beautiful that I have seen up to now, and there were also countless trees of other kinds, very large and green. The small birds and the greenness of the fields made me want to stay there for ever. This country, Most Serene Highnesses, is so enchantingly beautiful that it surpasses all others in charm and beauty as much as the light of day surpasses night. Very often I would say to my crew that however hard I tried to give your Highnesses a complete account of these lands my tongue could not convey the whole truth about them nor my hand write it down. I was so astonished at the sight of so much beauty that I can find no words to describe it. For in writing of other regions, their trees and

fruit, their plants, their harbours and all their other features, I have wrongly used the most exalted language I knew, so that everyone has said that there could not possibly be another region even more beautiful. But now I am silent, only wishing that some other may see this land and write about it. When he sees the extreme beauties of this coast, he will then be able to prove himself more fortunate than I in the use and choice of words with which to describe it.'

As the Admiral was going upstream in his boats he saw a canoe drawn up on shore under the trees beside the harbour and concealed by the branches. It was hollowed out of a single trunk and as large as a twelve-oared *fusta*.* In some houses near by they found in two baskets hanging from a post a honeycomb and the head of a dead man and later in another house they found the same. Our men concluded that the head belonged to the builder of the house, but they did not find anyone from whom they could gain any information, for as soon as they saw the Christians the people fled from their houses and made for the other side of the harbour. The Spaniards afterwards found another canoe about seventy foot long capable of taking 150 men and also hollowed out of a single trunk.

CHAPTER 31

The Admiral sails to Hispaniola; first description of the island

HAVING sailed 107 leagues along the coast of Cuba, the Admiral came to its eastern tip, which he named Alpha. He

* A light, oared vessel which was sometimes equipped with mast and sails.

left here on Wednesday, 5 December, to cross to Hispaniola, which lay sixteen leagues eastwards. On account of some local currents he did not reach it till the following day, when he entered the harbour of San Nicolas, which he named after that saint on whose feast-day he discovered it. This is a very large and fine harbour, very deep and surrounded with many tall trees, but the land is rockier and away from the coast the trees are smaller. Among them are dwarf oaks, strawberry trees and myrtles like those of Spain. A very sluggish river flowed through the plain and out into the harbour; all about the harbour were large canoes as large as fifteen-oared *fustas*.

As the Admiral could not hold conversation with these people, he followed the coast northwards until he came to a harbour which he named Concepción, which lies almost due south of a small island which he afterwards called Tortuga,★ and which is about the same size as Grand Canary. Seeing that the island of Bohio is very large, and that its fields and trees are like those of Spain and that in a net that they had made the crew caught many fish like those of Spain – that is to say sole, skate, salmon, shad, dories, gilthead, conger, sardines and crabs – the Admiral decided to give the island a name related to that of Spain; and so on Sunday 9 December he called it Hispaniola.

Since everyone was very eager to know the nature of this island, while the sailors were fishing on the shore three Christians set out through the woods, where they met a group of Indians, naked like all those they had met before. As soon as these natives saw the Christians approaching them they ran in terror to the thickest of the woods unhindered by any cloaks or skirts. The Christians ran in pursuit hoping to have speech with them but were only able to catch one girl, who had a piece of flat gold hanging from her nose. When they brought her to the ships the Admiral gave her a number of

★Tortoise.

85

small articles – trinkets and little bells. He then had her put ashore unharmed, sending three Indians whom he had brought from other islands and three Christians to accompany her to her village.

Next day he sent nine men ashore well armed, who found nine leagues away a village of more than a thousand houses scattered about a valley. When the inhabitants saw the Christians they all rushed out of the village and fled into the woods. But the Indian interpreter from San Salvador, who was with our men, went after them and shouted words of encouragement, saying much in praise of the Christians and affirming that they had come from the sky. The natives then returned reassured, and in awe and wonder they placed their hands on the heads of our men as a mark of honour and took them off to a feast, giving them everything they asked for without demanding anything in return. They begged them to stay that night in the village. But the Christians did not like to accept this invitation without first returning to the ships with news that the land was very pleasant and rich in Indian foods and that the people were fairer and handsomer than any they had seen so far on other islands; also that they were hospitable and well mannered. They said that the land where the Indians got their gold was further east.

On receiving this news the Admiral immediately had the sails raised, although the winds were most unfavourable. On Sunday, 16 December, therefore, they beat about between Hispaniola and Tortuga, and found a solitary Indian in a small canoe and were surprised that he had not sunk for the winds and seas were very high. They picked him up in the ship and took him to Hispaniola, where they put him ashore with many presents. This man told his fellow-natives of the Spaniards' kindness, saying such fine things about them that many Indians came to the ship, but they carried nothing of value except some small pieces of gold hanging from their

noses. On being asked where this gold came from, they indicated by signs that further on there were great quantities of it.

Next day a large canoe with forty men came from the island of Tortuga, near to where the Admiral was anchored. At that moment the *cacique* or lord of this part of Hispaniola was on the beach with his men bargaining over a piece of gold that he had brought. When he and his men saw the canoe they all sat down as a sign that they were unwilling to fight. Then nearly all the Indians leapt aggressively ashore and only the *cacique* got up to resist them. He sent them back to their canoe with threatening words. He then splashed them with water and picking up some stones from the beach hurled them at the canoe.

When they had all, with apparent obedience, returned to their canoe, the *cacique* picked up a stone and handed it to a servant of the Admiral, requesting him to throw it at the canoe to show that the Admiral was on his side against the Indians, but the servant didn't succeed in hitting it, for the canoe put off very quickly. After this, speaking on the subject of the island which the Admiral had named Tortuga, the *cacique* said that there was much more gold there than in Hispaniola, and greater quantities still on Babeque which was fourteen days' journey away.

CHAPTER 32

*The overlord of this island comes to the ships with
great ceremony*

ON Tuesday, 18 December, the king who had arrived on the previous day at the same moment as the canoe from Tortuga,

and whose village was five leagues from the spot where the ships were anchored, came down to the village on the coast just before midday. Some men from the ships were also there, whom the Admiral had sent ashore to see if they could find any great signs of gold. On seeing the king's approach they went to tell the Admiral, saying that he had more than 200 men with him and that he was not walking but was carried most ceremoniously in a litter by four bearers, although he was quite a young man. On arriving near the anchorage the king rested for a little and then went over to the ships with all his men. Describing this visit in his log-book, the Admiral writes:

'Your Highnesses would certainly think well of his state and the respect paid him, although they all go naked. On coming aboard he found me at table dining beneath the forecastle and politely came to sit beside me, refusing to let me get up to receive him or even to rise from the table but insisting that I should go on eating. On coming into the cabin he signed to his men that they should go outside, which they speedily did, with all the respect in the world. They all sat down on deck, except for two men of ripe age who were I supposed his counsellors and guardians and who sat at his feet. I thought that he would like to eat some of our food and immediately ordered him to be served with some. Of each dish that was placed before him he ate only a mouthful, sending the rest out to his men who all ate. He did the same with the drink, which he only carried to his lips and then sent to the others. All this was done with marvellous ceremony and very few words. All that he said, so far as I can understand, was very clear and sensible. These two counsellors watched him with great respect and spoke for him and with him. When he had eaten, one of his attendants brought a belt like those of Castile in form but differently made, and presented it to me with two pieces of worked gold which were

so thin that I think they had very little of it, although I believe they are very near the place from which it comes and where there is a great deal. I noticed that he admired a cushion that I had on my bed and gave it to him and some very fine amber beads that I wore round my neck; also some red slippers and a glass bottle of orange-flower water, and he was marvellously delighted.

'He and his counsellors were extremely sorry that they could not understand me, nor I them. Nevertheless I understood him to say that if there was anything I wanted, the whole island was at my disposal. I sent for a wallet of mine in which I keep, as a memorial, a gold coin bearing the portraits of your Highnesses and showed it to him, saying, as I had done on the previous day, that your Highnesses were lords and rulers of the greater part of the world and that no princes were greater. I showed him the royal banners and the banners of the cross, which he greatly admired. He said to his counsellors that your Highnesses must be very great princes, since you had sent me fearlessly from so far away in the sky to this place. Other conversation took place between them of which I could understand nothing except that they were clearly most astonished by everything.

'When it was late and he wished to return I sent him most ceremoniously ashore in the boat and ordered many lombards to be fired. When he came to the beach he mounted his litter and went off with more than 200 men, and one of his sons was carried on the shoulders of a very important chief. He gave orders that food should be given to all the sailors and to other men from the ships whom he found ashore, and that they should be treated with great kindness. Afterwards, a sailor who had met him on the road told me that all the presents I had given him were carried before him by a principal chieftain and that his son did not go with him, but followed behind with a number of other men. He added that one of his

brothers went on foot with an almost equal retinue, leaning on the shoulders of two attendants. I had given this man also some small present when he had come down to the ships following his brother.'

CHAPTER 33

Columbus loses his ship in the shallows through the carelessness of some sailors. He receives help from the king of the island

To continue this narrative of the Admiral's adventures, on 24 December there was a great calm, with no wind except a slight breeze that blew from the sea from Santo Tomas to Punta Santa, off which he lay at the distance of about a league. At the end of the first watch, which would have been an hour before midnight, the Admiral went down to rest, for he had not slept for two days and a night. Because of the calm, the steersman left the helm to one of the ship's boys. 'I had forbidden this,' says the Admiral, 'from the beginning of the voyage. I had ordered that whether there was a wind or not the helm should never be entrusted to a boy. To tell the truth I considered myself safe from shoals and reefs, because on Sunday, when I had sent the boats ashore to the king, I had passed some three and a half leagues east of Punta Santa and the sailors had seen the whole coast, and the rocks which run three leagues from east to south-west from Punta Santa, and they had also seen the passage by which they could enter. I had never done this at any time in the voyage, and by God's will at midnight, when I was lying in my bed, in a dead calm with the seas as smooth as water in a bowl, everyone went below, leaving the rudder to a boy.

'Thus it happened that a gentle current carried the ship on to one of those rocks, which could have been detected even in the night because the water breaking over them could be heard a full league away. The boy then, feeling and hearing the rudder scrape, began to shout; I was the first to hear him and quickly got up for I realized before anyone else that we had run on the reef. Almost immediately the ship's master, whose watch it was, came up. I told him and the other sailors to get in the boat which was towing astern and take the anchor aboard and kedge her off by the stern. The master and a number of sailors duly got into the boat, and I thought that they were carrying out my orders. But they rowed on, making all haste to the caravel which lay half a league away. When I saw that they were saving themselves in the boat and that the tide was falling and the ship in danger, I had the main mast cut away to lighten her as much as possible and see if we could pull her off. But the tide dropped still further and the ship would not move and lay rather more athwart the seas. New seams now opened and the whole hull filled with water. Then the *Niña*'s boat came to help me. The master of the caravel had refused to take on board the sailors who had fled in the *Santa Maria*'s boat and it was therefore compelled to return to the ship.

'But I could see no way of saving the *Santa Maria*, so I departed for the *Niña* in order to save my men, for the wind was now blowing off the land and night was almost over, and we did not know how to pull off those rocks. I remained on the caravel until day and as soon as it was light went back to the ship, rowing inside the shoal. Before this I had sent the boat ashore with Diego de Arana of Cordoba, the officer responsible for discipline in the fleet, and Pedro Gutierrez, your Highnesses' steward, to inform the king of what had happened, saying that on coming to visit him at his village, as he had asked me to on the previous Saturday, I had lost my

ship on a reef a league and a half offshore. On hearing the news the king wept, showing great sorrow at our disaster. Then he sent all the inhabitants of the village out to the ship in many large canoes. Thus we began to unload her and in a very short time we had cleared the decks. Such was the help that this king gave us. After this, he himself, with his brothers and relations, did everything they could both in the ship and on shore to arrange things for our comfort. And from time to time he sent various of his relatives to implore me not to grieve, for he would give me everything he had.

'I assure your Highnesses that nowhere in Castile would one receive such great kindness or anything like it. He had all our possessions brought together near his palace and kept them there until some houses had been emptied to receive them. He appointed armed men to guard them and made them watch right through the night. And he and everyone else in the land wept for our misfortune as if greatly concerned by it. They are so affectionate and have so little greed and are in all ways so amenable that I assure your Highnesses that there is in my opinion no better people and no better land in the world. They love their neighbours as themselves and their way of speaking is the sweetest in the world, always gentle and smiling. Both men and women go naked as their mothers bore them; but your Highnesses must believe me when I say that their behaviour to one another is very good and their king keeps marvellous state, yet with a certain kind of modesty that is a pleasure to behold, as is everything else here. They have very good memories and ask to see everything, then inquire what it is and what it is for.'

CHAPTER 34

The Admiral decides to make a settlement at this king's village and calls his settlement Navidad

ON Wednesday, 26 December, the chief king of the country came to the Admiral's caravel, showing great sorrow and grief. He comforted the Admiral, generously offering him any of his possessions that it would please him to receive. He said that he had already given the Christians three houses in which they could put everything that they had rescued from the ship; and he would have given them many more if they had required them. At this moment a ship arrived with Indians from another island, bringing some sheets of gold to barter for bells which they value above everything else. Sailors also arrived from the shore saying that many Indians were coming into the village from other places bringing gold objects which they were exchanging for tags and other such things of small value and offering to bring more gold if the Christians wanted it. When the great *cacique* saw that the Admiral liked gold he promised to have a great quantity bought to him from Cibao, the place that had the most.

He then prepared to go ashore, inviting the Admiral to a feast of sweet potatoes and yucca, which are their principal foods, and giving him some masks with eyes and large ears of gold and other beautiful objects which they wore round their necks. He then complained about the Caribs, who captured his people and took them away to be eaten, but he was greatly cheered when the Admiral comforted him by showing him our weapons and promising to defend him with them. But he was much disturbed by our cannon, which so frightened all the Indians that they fell down like dead men when they heard them fired.

On receiving such kindnesses and such samples of gold from these people the Admiral almost forgot his grief for the loss of the ship, for he considered that God had allowed it to be wrecked in order that he should make a settlement and leave some Christians behind to trade and gather information about the country and its inhabitants, learning their language and entering into relations with the people. Thus, when the Admiral returned with reinforcements, he would have people to advise him in all matters respecting the occupation and conquest of the country. He was the more inclined to this by the fact that many of the crew said that they would gladly remain behind and offered to make a settlement in this place. He therefore decided to construct a fort from the timbers of the wrecked ship, which had been stripped of everything that could possibly be useful.

He was greatly assisted in this by the news that came next day, Thursday, 27 December, that the caravel *Pinta* was lying in the river, towards the eastern point of the island. In order to make certain of this, he ordered the *cacique* whose name was Guacanagari to provide a canoe with some Indians to take a Spaniard to this place. When this man had gone twenty leagues down the coast he turned back, bringing no news of the *Pinta*. Consequently another Indian who claimed to have seen the caravel some days before was not believed. Nevertheless the Admiral did not halt his arrangements for leaving some Christians in this place. Everyone knew the goodness and fertility of this land, since the Indians were offering our men many gold masks and objects and giving them information about various districts in the island where they found gold.

When the Admiral was on the point of departure, he made a treaty with the king regarding the Caribs, of whom he complained so much and was in such real terror. In order that he should be pleased to have the Christians' company and also to inspire him with fear of our weapons, the Admiral had a

94

lombard fired at the side of the *Santa Maria*, the ball passed right through the ship and fell in the water, and the king was both horrified and amazed. The Admiral also showed him our other weapons, how wounds were made with some and others used for defence, and told him that with such weapons to protect him he need no longer fear the Caribs, because the Christians would kill them all. The Admiral said that he was leaving these Christians to defend him and would himself go back to Castile to fetch jewels and other things, which he would bring him back as presents. He then begged him to be friendly to Diego de Araña, son of Rodrigo de Araña of Córdoba, who has already been mentioned. He left this man, Pedro Gutiérrez, and Rodrigo de Escobedo in command of the fort with thirty-six men and many goods and provisions, arms and artillery, and the ship's boat, with carpenters, caulkers, and all other persons necessary for a settlement, that is to say a doctor, a gunner, a tailor and such like.

The Admiral then made careful preparations for a direct return journey to Castile. He decided to make no further explorations, since he now had only one ship and if this were wrecked their Catholic sovereigns would have no knowledge of these kingdoms which he had just acquired for them.

CHAPTER 35

The Admiral sails for Castile and meets the other caravel with Pinzón

ON Friday, 4 January, at sunrise, the Admiral raised sail with his helm set north-west, in order to avoid the rocks and shoals that lie off that coast, leaving the Christian settlement which he had called Puerto de la Navidad (Christmas Harbour), in

commemoration of that day on which he had escaped the perils of the sea and reached land to make the beginnings of this settlement. These rocks and shoals stretch for six leagues from Cabo Santo to Cabo de la Sierpe, and run more than three leagues out to sea. The whole coast runs from north-west to south-east and the beach and coastal plain extend for four leagues inland. Behind lie high mountains and great numbers of large villages, more numerous and larger than on other islands.

He then sailed towards a high mountain, which he named Monte Christi, which is eighteen leagues east of Cabo Santo. Therefore anyone wishing to sail to the town of Navidad, after sighting Monte Christi, which is rounded like a bell tent and appears to be a detached rock, will have to stand two leagues out to sea and sail westward at that distance from the coast, until he comes to Cabo Santo. He will then be five leagues from the town of Navidad and will enter through certain channels which thread the shoals lying before it. The Admiral thought fit to mention these details in order that men should know the position of the first Christian town and settled country in the western world.

When the Admiral had passed Monte Christi, sailing eastwards against contrary winds, on the morning of Sunday, 6 January, a caulker sighted from the main top the caravel *Pinta* sailing westwards with the wind behind her. When she came up to the *Niña* her captain, Martin Alonso Pinzón, immediately went aboard the Admiral's ship and began to explain why he had left him, inventing various excuses and false arguments. He said that he had not wished to do so but had been unable to avoid it. Although the Admiral knew that this was untrue and that Pinzón's intentions were dishonest and remembered the liberties he had taken on many occasions during the voyage, he concealed his thoughts and accepted these excuses in order not to imperil the whole enterprise. For all might easily have been lost, since the majority

of the men in the Admiral's ship were compatriots of Martin Alonso – many of them indeed being his relatives.

The truth is that when Pinzón left the Admiral in the island of Cuba, he sailed with the intention of going to the island of Babeque, where the Indians on his caravel told him there was much gold. On arriving at that island he discovered that what they told him was untrue and returned to Hispaniola, where other Indians had assured him there was much gold. This voyage had taken him twenty days and he had got no further than a small river fifteen leagues east of Navidad, which the Admiral had named Rio de Gracia. There Martin Alonso had stayed for sixteen days and had acquired much gold, in the same way that the Admiral had got it at Navidad – by exchanging it for articles of small value. Pinzón had divided half this gold among the men of his caravel in order to win their favour and leave them happy and satisfied that he as captain should keep the rest. And he afterwards tried to persuade the Admiral that he had no knowledge of any gold.

The Admiral continued on his course to anchor near Monte Christi, since the winds prevented his going any further. He took the boat up a river south-east of the mountain and found in its sand many samples of gold grains, and for this reason he called it the Rio del Oro. It lies sixteen leagues east of Navidad, and is rather smaller than the river Guadalquivir at Cordoba.

CHAPTER 36

*In the Gulf of Samana in Hispaniola the first
brush takes place between Indians and Christians*

ON Sunday, 13 January, at Cabo Enamarado, which is in the Gulf of Samana in Hispaniola, the Admiral sent the boat

ashore. On the beach our men met some fierce-looking Indians whose bows and arrows showed that they were prepared for war. These Indians were greatly excited and also alarmed. Nevertheless our men began a parley with them and bought two bows and some arrows. With great difficulty one of the Indians was persuaded to come out to the caravel and speak with the Admiral, to whom he made a speech as fierce as his appearance. These Indians were much fiercer than any we had seen before. Their faces were blackened with charcoal in the manner of all these peoples, whose habit it is to paint themselves either black, white or red in a variety of patterns. They wore their hair very long and caught back in a little net of parrot feathers.

When this man stood before the Admiral naked as his mother bore him, as were all the natives of these islands that we had so far discovered, he spoke in the proud language common to all peoples in these regions. The Admiral, believing he was one of the Caribs and that this gulf was the boundary dividing them from the rest of Hispaniola, asked him where the Caribs lived. He pointed eastwards, signifying that they lived on the other islands, on which there were pieces of *guanin* – that is to say gold of poor quality – as large as the prow of the ship, and that the island of Matinino was entirely populated by women, on whom the Caribs descended at certain seasons of the year; and if these women bore sons they were entrusted to the fathers to bring up. These answers to our questions he gave us by signs and in a few words that were understood by the Indians we had brought from San Salvador. The Admiral ordered that he should be given food and some small presents – glass beads and green and red cloth. He then had him put ashore to obtain gold for us, if the other Indians had any.

When the boat beached it was met by fifty-five Indians who were hiding in the trees, all naked, and with long hair tied

back like that of women in Castile. Behind their heads they wore tufts of the feathers of parrots and other birds. They were all armed with bows and arrows. When our men leapt ashore the Indian made his fellow-natives put down their bows and arrows and the great clubs they carried instead of swords, for, as I have said, they have no iron of any sort. Once ashore, the Christians began, on the Admiral's instructions, to buy bows and arrows and other weapons. But when the Indians had traded them two bows, they not only refused to sell any more but with a show of contempt seemed about to take the Spaniards prisoners; they picked up the bows and arrows they had laid down and also cords with which to tie our men's hands. But our men were on guard and, though only seven in number, on seeing the Indians dash forward attacked them with great courage, wounding one with a sword thrust in the buttocks and another with an arrow in the chest. Surprised by our men's courage and by the wounds dealt by our weapons, the Indians took to flight, leaving most of their bows and arrows on the ground. Certainly many of our men would have been killed if the pilot of the caravel whom the Admiral had put in charge of the boat and those in it had not come to their rescue and saved them.

This brush did not displease the Admiral, who was certain that these Indians were some of the Caribs of whom the other natives were so afraid, or were at least their neighbours. They are a bold and courageous people, as can be seen from their looks and weapons and also from their deeds, and the Admiral thought that when the islanders learnt what seven Christians could do against fifty-five very fierce Indians of that region, our men whom he had left in Navidad would be more highly respected and esteemed and no one would dare to annoy them. Later in the day the Indians made bonfires in the fields as a show of bravery, for the boat had returned to

see what their mood was, but there was no way of gaining their confidence and so the boat put back.

The Indians' bows are of yew and almost as stout as those of the French and English, and the arrows are made of the shoots produced by the cane at the point where the seeds grow. These are thick and very straight and a yard and a half long. They tip them with a stick about a foot long, sharpened and hardened in the fire. In the point they insert a fish bone or tooth which they dip in poison. On account of this engagement the Admiral named this gulf, which the Indians call Samana, Golfo de las Flechas (Gulf of the Arrows). In the bay much fine cotton could be seen, and a long fruit rounded at one end which is their pepper. This is very hot. Near the beach in shallow water a great deal of that weed was growing which they had found floating on the ocean sea. They had been right in supposing that it grew near land, was uprooted when ripe and carried a great distance by the sea currents.

CHAPTER 37

The Admiral sets out for Castile and the caravel
Pinta *is separated from the* Niña *by a great storm*

ON Wednesday, 16 January 1493, the Admiral left the Golfo de las Flechas in good weather, on a course for Castile. Both caravels let much water and the crews had great trouble in keeping them afloat. The last point of land to disappear from sight was the Cabo de San Telmo, twenty leagues to the north-east. They saw much weed as before, and twenty leagues further on they found the sea almost covered with small tunny fish, of which they also saw great numbers on the two following days, 19 and 20 January. After this they saw

many sea-birds. The weed was continually moving from east to west with the current, and they already knew that it takes this weed a very long way. However, it does not always follow the same course but sometimes drifts one way, sometimes another. They met it every day until they had gone almost half-way across the ocean.

They sailed on their course with favourable winds and at such a speed that on 9 February the pilots thought that they had reached a point south of the Azores. But the Admiral said that they were 150 leagues short of this, and this proved correct, for they were still meeting many strands of seaweed which they had not found on their voyage to the islands until they had gone 263 leagues west of the island of Hierro.

As they sailed on in good weather, the winds began to increase from day to day and the seas to rise so high that they had great difficulty in weathering them. In the night of Thursday, 14 February, they were compelled to run with the wind. And as the caravel *Pinta* was less able to withstand the seas than the *Niña*, Pinzón had to follow a northward course, driven by a south wind, while the Admiral continued northeast on the direct route for Spain. Owing to the darkness of the night, the *Pinta* could not rejoin the Admiral, although he kept his lantern lit, and at daybreak the two ships had lost one another, and the crew of each thought that the other had sunk. Resorting to prayers and devotions, therefore, the Admiral's crew vowed that one of them should make a pilgrimage on behalf of the rest to Our Lady of Guadalupe and cast lots to decide who it should be. The lot fell on the Admiral. After this they vowed a further pilgrimage to our Lady of Loreto and the lot fell on a sailor of the *Santa Maria* from Santona, called Pedro de la Villa. They then cast lots for a third pilgrimage to make a vigil in the church of Santa Clara de Moguer, and the lot for this also fell on the Admiral. The storm, however, grew fiercer and everyone on the ship made

a vow to walk barefoot and in their shirts to offer up a prayer
on the first land they came to in any church dedicated to the
Virgin. Apart from these general vows many of the men also
made private ones.

For now the storm was very high and the Admiral's ship
had great difficulty in withstanding it through lack of ballast,
which had grown less as their provisions were consumed. To
increase their ballast they conceived the idea of filling all the
barrels that were empty with seawater, which was some help.
It enabled the ship to stand up better to the storm and reduced
its great danger of capsizing. The Admiral described this great
storm in these words:

'I should have had less difficulty in withstanding this storm
if I had only been in personal danger, since I know that I owe
my life to my Supreme Creator and He has so many times
before saved me when I have been near to death that actually
to die would hardly have cost me greater suffering. But what
caused me infinite pain and grief was the thought that after
it had pleased the Lord to inspire me with faith and assurance
to undertake this enterprise, in which he had now granted me
success, at the very moment when my opponents would have
been proved wrong and your Highnesses would have been
endowed by me with glory and increase of your high estate,
the Lord might choose to prevent all this by my death.

'Even this would have been more bearable if death were
not also to fall on all those whom I had taken with me, promising them a most prosperous outcome to the voyage.
Finding themselves in such terrible danger, they not only
cursed their weakness in coming but also my threats and
forceful persuasion which had many times prevented them
from turning back, despite their resolution to do so. In addition to all this, my grief was increased by the thought that
my two sons, whom I had placed as students at Cordoba,
would be left without resources in a foreign land, and that I

had not performed, or at least proved that I had performed, my services in such a way that I could hope your Highnesses would be mindful of them. I was comforted by my faith that Our Lord would not allow a project for the exaltation of His Church, which I had carried out in the face of such opposition and dangers, to remain incomplete and myself to be ruined. Yet I thought that on account of my demerits and so that I should not enjoy so much glory in this world, it was perhaps His pleasure to humiliate me.

'In this perplexity I thought of your Highnesses' good fortune which, even were I to die and my ship be lost, might find a means of turning the victory I had gained to your advantage, and that in some way the success of my voyage might become known to you. Therefore I wrote a parchment, as brief as the exigencies of the time required, saying how I had discovered these lands that I had promised to you and in how many days and by what course I had reached them. I described the goodness of the country, the manners of its inhabitants whom I had made subjects to your Highnesses, taking possession of all the lands I had discovered. I closed and sealed this letter and addressed it to your Highnesses, undertaking the cost of carriage, that is to say promising a thousand ducats to the man who should present it to your Highnesses unopened. My purpose was that if some foreigner should find it he would be too anxious to obtain the reward to open it and master its contents. I then sent for a large cask and, after wrapping this parchment in cloth and enclosing it in a cake of wax, placed the parcel in the cask. The hoops were then secured and the cask thrown into the sea, all the sailors supposing that this was in fulfilment of some vow. And since I thought it possible that this cask would not be picked up and the ships were still following their course towards Castile, I prepared another similar package and placed it in another cask at the highest point of the prow, so that were the ship to

sink it should float on the waves and be carried wherever the storm might take it.'

CHAPTER 38

The Admiral reaches the Azores* and the people of Santa Maria seize the boat and its crew

As they sailed on in such great danger from the storm, at dawn on Friday, 15 February, one Ruy Garcia of Santona saw from the main mast land to the east-north-east. The pilots and sailors thought that it was Cintra in Portugal. But the Admiral insisted that they were at the Azores, and this was one of the islands, and although they were not far offshore they were unable to reach land that day on account of the storm. Being compelled to beat about since the wind was in the east, they lost sight of the first island and saw another, under the lee of which they ran to shelter from a strong crosswind and bad weather. Despite their hard and continuous labours, however, they were unable to make land. The Admiral writes in his log-book:

'On the night of Saturday, 16 February, I reached one of these islands, but could not tell which on account of the storm. I rested a little that night, for I had not slept since Wednesday or even been to bed and my legs were crippled by continuous exposure to the high winds and seas, and I was suffering from hunger also. When I anchored on Monday morning I immediately learnt from the inhabitants that this island was Santa Maria in the Azores. They were all astonished at my escape from this tremendous storm which had been blowing for fifteen days continuously.'

When the inhabitants were told of the Admiral's discoveries they put up a show of rejoicing, appeared to be greatly delighted, and gave thanks to Our Lord. Three of them came

*A Portuguese possession.

to the ship with some food and the compliments of the captain of the island, who was away in the town. All that could be seen in this place was a hermit's chapel, which as they were informed was dedicated to the Virgin. When the Admiral and his crew remembered that on the previous Thursday they had vowed to walk barefoot in their shirts to some church of the Virgin in the first land they came to, they all thought that they should fulfil their vow here, where the people and the captain of the island showed our men such great love and sympathy, in the territory of the king who was such a friend to the Catholic sovereigns of Castile. The Admiral therefore asked these three men to go to the town and summon the chaplain who had the key of this hermitage to say a mass for them. These three consequently got into the ship's boat with half the ship's crew who were to begin the performance of the vow; and when they had done, the other half were to go ashore after them to complete it.

When the first boatload had come to land, barefoot and in their shirts, in fulfilment of their vow, the captain and many of the town's inhabitants, who were lying hidden in an ambush, surprised them and made them prisoner. They took away the boat, certain that without it the Admiral would not escape capture.

CHAPTER 39

The Admiral encounters another storm and recovers the boat and crew

WHEN it first struck the Admiral that his men were remaining rather long on shore (for it was now midday and they had landed at dawn) he supposed that they had met with some accident, either on sea or shore. Since from the place where he had anchored he could not see the hermitage to which they

were going, he decided to move the ship to a point from which the church was visible. When he came close to land he saw many horsemen dismount and get into the boat with the intention of attacking and taking the caravel. Fearing the probable result of their attack, the Admiral ordered his men to take up their positions and their weapons, but to show no signs that they intended to put up a defence, so that the Portuguese might then approach in all boldness. The Portuguese came on to meet the Admiral and when they were close their captain stood up and asked for a safe conduct. The Admiral agreed in the belief that they would come aboard, in which case, despite the safe conduct, he would have seized the boat and its crew and held them as surety for his own wrongly seized boat and men. But the Portuguese captain was not bold enough to come closer than hailing distance.

The Admiral told him that he was astounded at the strange state of affairs: none of his men had returned to their boat, although they had landed under safe conduct, encouraged by promises of gifts and help; and what was more the Portuguese captain had sent him his compliments. The Admiral further begged him to consider that not only was he behaving in a most unfriendly way and violating the laws of chivalry, but was also greatly offending the King of Portugal whose subjects were welcomed in the lands of his lords, the Catholic sovereigns, where they were treated with great courtesy and could land and remain ashore without safe conduct in as complete security as if they were in their own city of Lisbon. He added that their Highnesses had given him letters of recommendation to all the lords and princes and nations of the world, which he would have shown to him if he had come close; and if these letters were honoured in distant parts, he said, where he and all their Highnesses' subjects were favourably received, there was far greater reason why they should be welcomed and aided in Portugal, whose princes were the

kindred and neighbours of his own lords. For he was their chief Admiral of the Ocean and Viceroy of the Indies, which he had just discovered. In proof of this he offered to show them his appointment, signed in their royal names and sealed with their seals. Indeed, he did show him these documents from a distance and assured him he could come closer without fear, since the Catholic sovereigns and the King of Portugal were at peace and friendly, and his sovereigns had instructed him to show all possible respect and courtesy to any Portuguese ships he might meet. The Admiral added that even if the Portuguese captain persisted in his discourtesy and refused to release his crew, this would not prevent his going on to Castile, for he still had enough men on board to sail the ship to Seville, and to attack him also if it should prove necessary, for he had given him due cause and he would be to blame for any punishment he received. Moreover, his own king would probably punish him too for precipitating war between himself and the Catholic sovereigns.

The captain and his men replied that they did not acknowledge the King and Queen of Castile, or their letters, and that he was not afraid of them but would show them the might of Portugal. This reply made the Admiral think and fear that since his departure from Spain some rupture or quarrel had occurred between the two kingdoms. Nevertheless he decided to answer the captain as his rashness deserved. Finally, as he drew away, the Portuguese captain stood up and shouted to the Admiral that he must bring the caravel into port, since all his own actions had been on the written instructions of his king and lord. When he heard this the Admiral called on everyone in the caravel to witness, and in answer to the Portuguese captain he swore he would not leave the caravel until they had captured a hundred Portuguese, whom they would take home as prisoners, and had depopulated the island. Having said this, he returned to anchor in the harbour where he

had been before, since the wind made it impossible for him to do anything else.

But next day, the wind increased greatly and made his anchorage impossible; he lost his anchors and had no alternative but to raise sail for the island of San Miguel. As he could not anchor here, however, because the storm was still blowing fiercely, he decided to wait with furled sails, though still in very great danger, both from the sea, which was very rough, and because he had only three sailors and a few ship's boys on board, all the rest of his men being on shore except the Indians, who had no skill in working sails or rigging. But himself performing the work of the absent crew, he passed the night in hard work and no little danger. And when day came, he found that he had lost sight of the island of San Miguel and that the weather had somewhat improved. So he decided to return to the island of Santa Maria, to see if he could rescue his crew, his anchors and the boat. He reached San Miguel on Thursday evening, 21 February.

Shortly after his arrival, a boat came with five sailors and a notary, and trusting in the Admiral's safe conduct they all went aboard the caravel, where, since it was now late, they slept the night. Next morning they said that they had been sent by the captain to make certain where the caravel had come from and under what circumstances and if it was sailing with the King of Castile's commission. For if he was truthfully informed of these facts he was prepared to pay the Admiral all respect. This change of mind was caused by the fact that he now saw clearly that they could not take the ship or capture the Admiral, and that they might be made to suffer for what they had done.

Disguising his feelings, the Admiral answered that he thanked the captain for his courtesy and his kind offer and since what he asked of him was no more than common custom at sea, he was prepared to accede to his demands. He

therefore showed the notary his general letter of recommendation from the Catholic sovereigns, addressed to all their subjects and to other princes, and also the order and commission they had given him to make this voyage. When the Portuguese had seen these documents, they returned ashore satisfied and promptly restored the boat and the sailors, from whom the Admiral learnt that, according to reports on the island, the King of Portugal had ordered his subjects to take the Admiral prisoner by any means they could.

CHAPTER 40

The Admiral leaves the Azores and sails through bad weather to Lisbon

ON Sunday, 24 February, the Admiral sailed for Castile from the island of Santa Maria, very short of ballast and firewood, which he had been unable to obtain on account of the bad weather. The wind, however, was favourable for his voyage, yet when he was a hundred leagues from the nearest land a swallow came to the boat which had, it was believed, been driven out to sea by bad weather. This belief was very soon confirmed, for next day, 28 February, they met many more swallows and land-birds; and also saw a whale.

On 3 March they encountered such a fierce storm that shortly after midnight their sails were torn away. Then, in great danger of their lives, they made a vow to send a pilgrim barefoot and in his shirt to the Virgin of the Girdle, whose church is at Huelva. The lot once more fell on the Admiral, perhaps to show that of all the vows made to Our Lord the Admiral's were most welcome; in addition to this vow, many private vows were made also.

As they ran before the wind without an inch of sail and with bare masts, in a terrible sea and high winds, the whole

sky was rent with thunder and lightning. Any one of these horrors seemed likely to send the ship to destruction. But the Lord was pleased to show them land just before midnight. Another danger confronted them. To avoid running on a reef, where they would certainly be shattered, they had to raise a little sail, saving themselves in this way from the storm. When God was pleased to show them day and dawn broke, they saw that they were near the rock of Cintra, on the coast of the Kingdom of Portugal.

Here the Admiral found himself compelled to come to land, in great fear and dread of the local inhabitants and the sailors of that coast, who ran up from all directions to see this ship which had miraculously escaped from the cruel storm, for they had heard news of many ships which had sunk in the last few days on course for Flanders and elsewhere.

Sailing up the Tagus on 4 March, the Admiral anchored near Rastelo and very quickly sent a message to the Catholic sovereigns to announce his arrival. He also wrote to the King of Portugal requesting permission to anchor near the city, for the place where he then lay was not safe against anyone who might decide to attack him on the treacherous pretext or excuse that he had received orders to do so from the King himself, in the belief that by harming the Admiral he could impair the victory of the King of Castile.

CHAPTER 41

The people of Lisbon come out to see the Admiral and to marvel at him. The Admiral visits the King of Portugal

ON Tuesday, 5 March, the master* of the large ship which the King of Portugal kept at Rastelo to guard the harbour

* Bartholomew Díaz, discoverer of the Cape of Good Hope.

came in his armed boat to inform the Admiral that he must accompany him to give an account of his presence to the ministers of the King, as was the custom for any ship reaching Lisbon. The Admiral replied that an admiral of the Kings of Castile, which he was, was not obliged to go where anyone summoned him and must not, under pain of death, leave his ship to lodge such information; and that he was resolved to act accordingly. The Portuguese officer said that he might at least send his ship's master. But the Admiral replied that he considered it the same thing if he were only to send a boy and that it would be useless to ask him to send anyone from his ship.

On hearing the boldness of the Admiral's argument, the Portuguese officer answered that in order to confirm that he came in the names of the Kings of Castile and as their subject, the Admiral might at least show him his patents, which would be enough to satisfy his captain. The Admiral considered this a reasonable demand and showed him his letters from the Catholic sovereigns, and this satisfied the Portuguese officer, who returned to his ship to report to his captain, Don Alvaro de Acuna. Very soon, Don Alvaro came to the Admiral's caravel to the accompaniment of trumpets, fifes and drums and with a grand escort and greeted the Admiral ceremoniously, making him many offers of service.

Next day, when the Admiral's arrival from the Indies had become known in Lisbon, so many people came to the caravel to see the Indians he had brought back and so learn the news that there was not room for them all, and the sea could not be seen for the great number of Portuguese boats and launches. Some of the Portuguese gave thanks to God for this great victory but others were unhappy and greatly disappointed that this triumph had slipped out of their hands owing to their King's doubts and under-estimation of the enterprise. The day passed amidst a crowd of visitors.

Next day the King instructed his agents to give the Admiral all the refreshment and other things he needed for himself and his crew; in fact, to give him whatever he asked for. He also wrote to the Admiral congratulating him on his happy arrival and invited him, since he was in Portugal, kindly to pay him a visit. The Admiral was somewhat doubtful about accepting this invitation. But considering the friendship that obtained between the King of Portugal and the Catholic sovereigns and the nature of the courtesy demanded, and also to relieve all suspicions that he was returning from territories conquered by Portugal, he thought it right to go to Valparaiso (some nine leagues from Lisbon), where the King then was, and arrived there at night on 9 March.

The King ordered all the noblemen at his court to come out and meet him, and bring him into his presence. When the Admiral arrived before him the King paid him great honour and welcomed him warmly, ordering him to cover himself and be seated. Having heard with apparent joy the details of his victorious voyage, the King offered him all he might need for the service of the Catholic sovereigns, although in his opinion, on account of the treaty* he had agreed with them, he considered that this conquest was his. The Admiral replied that he knew nothing about this treaty and that he had scrupulously obeyed the orders that he had received not to go to Mina da Ouro† or to Guinea. The King replied that all was well and he was sure that the matter would be rightly settled. After spending some time on these conversations, the King ordered the Prior of Crato, who was the chief minister then at court, to give the Admiral lodging and entertainment and show him every favour, which he did.

The Admiral remained there for the whole of Sunday and Monday until after dinner, and then took leave of the King,

---

*The treaty ending the War of Succession.
†A Portuguese goldfield on the African coast.

who treated him with great kindness, offered him many favours and sent Don Martin de Norona to accompany him. Many other noblemen accompanied him also, both to pay him honour and to hear about the great events of his voyage.

On his return journey to Lisbon, he stopped at a convent at which the Queen of Portugal was staying, since she had sent him a most urgent message, begging him not to pass without visiting her. She was delighted to see him and treated him with all the favours and honour due to a great lord. That night one of the King's gentlemen overtook the Admiral to tell him from the King that if he wished to go overland to Castile he would accompany him and find him lodgings in all places within the frontiers of Portugal, and provide him with all necessities.

CHAPTER 42

The Admiral leaves Lisbon for Castile, travelling
by sea

ON Wednesday 13 March, at two o'clock in the afternoon the Admiral raised sail for Seville; and next day, at noon, crossed the bar of Saltes and anchored in Palos harbour, from which he had sailed on 3 August of the previous year 1492, seven months and eleven days before. Here he was received by all the people in procession, who gave thanks to Our Lord for His great mercy and this great victory, from which such expansion was to be expected both of the Christian faith and the estates of the Catholic sovereigns. All the citizens were highly delighted that it was from this port the Admiral had set sail and that the majority of the greater and nobler part of the men he had taken with him were men of this district, though some of them had by Pinzón's fault behaved with treachery and disobedience.

It happened that at the time of the Admiral's arrival in Palos, Pinzón reached Galicia and decided to go independently to Barcelona to give news of the enterprise to the Catholic sovereigns. But they sent him a message not to come except with the Admiral, with whom he had sailed on this voyage of discovery. This message so pained and annoyed Pinzón that he returned home a sick man and a few days later died of grief.

Before Pinzón reached Palos, the Admiral went by land to Seville, with the intention of going from there to Barcelona, where the Catholic sovereigns were staying. He had to make some slight delays on his journey owing to the excitement in the towns through which he passed, for everyone came from everywhere in the vicinity to gaze at him and at the Indians and other strange objects that he had brought with him.

Continuing his journey in this way, he reached Barcelona in the middle of April, having sent news ahead of him to the Catholic sovereigns of the prosperous outcome of his voyage. They showed infinite joy and satisfaction at this news and ordered that he be given the solemn reception due to one who had done them such signal service. Everyone in the city and court came out to meet him, and the Catholic sovereigns, surrounded by their court, awaited him seated in all their greatness and majesty on a magnificent throne under a canopy of gold. When he came to kiss their hands, they stood up to greet him as they would a great lord, made some demur in giving him their hands to kiss and seated him at their side. Then after some short conversation about the manner and success of his voyage, they gave him leave to retire to his lodging, to which he was accompanied by the whole court. During his stay he enjoyed such honours and favours from their Highnesses that when the King rode through Barcelona the Admiral accompanied him on one side and the Infante on the other, though the King was used to being accompanied by the Infante alone, who was his close relative.

LETTER OF COLUMBUS TO VARIOUS PERSONS DESCRIBING THE RESULTS OF HIS FIRST VOYAGE AND WRITTEN ON THE RETURN JOURNEY

SINCE I know that you will be pleased at the great success with which the Lord has crowned my voyage, I write to inform you how in thirty-three days I crossed from the Canary Islands to the Indies, with the fleet which our most illustrious sovereigns gave me. I found very many islands with large populations and took possession of them all for their Highnesses; this I did by proclamation and unfurled the royal standard. No opposition was offered.

I named the first island that I found 'San Salvador', in honour of our Lord and Saviour who has granted me this miracle. The Indians call it 'Guanahani'. The second island I named 'Santa Maria de Concepción', the third 'Fernandina', the fourth 'Isabela' and the fifth 'Juana'; thus I renamed them all.

When I reached Cuba, I followed its north coast westwards, and found it so extensive that I thought this must be the mainland, the province of Cathay.* Since there were no towns or villages on the coast, but only small groups of houses whose inhabitants fled as soon as we approached, I continued on my course, thinking that I should undoubtedly come to some great towns or cities. We continued for many leagues but found no change, except that the coast was bearing me northwards. This I wished to avoid, since winter was approaching and my plan was to journey south. As the wind was carrying

---

*In the log-book and later in this letter Columbus accepts the native story that Cuba is an island which they can circumnavigate in something more than twenty-one days, yet he insists here and later, during the second voyage, that it is in fact part of the Asiatic mainland.

me on I decided not to wait for a change of weather but to turn back to a remarkable harbour which I had observed. From here I sent two men inland to discover whether there was a king or any great cities. They travelled for three days, finding only a large number of small villages and great numbers of people, but nothing more substantial. Therefore they returned.

I understood from some Indians whom I had captured elsewhere that this was an island, and so I followed its coast for 107 leagues to its eastward point. From there I saw another island eighteen leagues eastwards which I then named 'Hispaniola'.* I crossed to this island and followed its northern coast eastwards for 188 leagues continuously, as I had followed the coast of Cuba. All these islands are extremely fertile and this one is particularly so. It has many large harbours finer than any I know in Christian lands, and many large rivers. All this is marvellous. The land is high and has many ranges of hills, and mountains incomparably finer than Tenerife. All are most beautiful and various in shape, and all are accessible. They are covered with tall trees of different kinds which seem to reach the sky. I have heard that they never lose their leaves, which I can well believe, for I saw them as green and lovely as they are in Spain in May; some were flowering, some bore fruit and others were at different stages according to their nature. It was November but everywhere I went the nightingale† and many other birds were singing. There are palms of six or eight different kinds – a marvellous sight because of their great variety – and the other trees, fruit and plants are equally marvellous. There are splendid pine woods and broad fertile plains, and there is honey. There are many kinds of birds and varieties of fruit. In the interior are mines and a very large population.

* This is referred to in the log-book as Bohio or Bofio.
† Columbus was mistaken; he probably heard the mocking-bird.

Hispaniola is a wonder. The mountains and hills, the plains and meadow lands are both fertile and beautiful. They are most suitable for planting crops and for raising cattle of all kinds, and there are good sites for building towns and villages. The harbours are incredibly fine and there are many great rivers with broad channels and the majority contain gold.* The trees, fruits and plants are very different from those of Cuba. In Hispaniola there are many spices and large mines of gold and other metals. . . .†

The inhabitants of this island, and all the rest that I discovered or heard of, go naked, as their mothers bore them, men and women alike. A few of the women, however, cover a single place with a leaf of a plant or piece of cotton which they weave for the purpose. They have no iron or steel or arms and are not capable of using them, not because they are not strong and well built but because they are amazingly timid. All the weapons they have are canes cut at seeding time, at the end of which they fix a sharpened stick, but they have not the courage to make use of these, for very often when I have sent two or three men to a village to have conversation with them a great number of them have come out. But as soon as they saw my men all fled immediately, a father not even waiting for his son. And this is not because we have harmed any of them; on the contrary, wherever I have gone and been able to have conversation with them, I have given them some of the various things I had, a cloth and other articles, and received nothing in exchange. But they have still remained incurably timid. True, when they have been reassured and lost their fear, they are so ingenuous and so liberal with all their possessions that no one who has not seen them would believe it. If one asks for anything they have they never say no. On the contrary, they offer a share to anyone with demon-

*This did not prove to be true.
†These statements are also inaccurate.

strations of heartfelt affection, and they are immediately content with any small thing, valuable or valueless, that is given them. I forbade the men to give them bits of broken crockery, fragments of glass or tags of laces, though if they could get them they fancied them the finest jewels in the world. One sailor was known to have received gold to the weight of two and a half *castellanos* for the tag of a breeches lace, and others received much more for things of even less value. For newly minted *blancas* they would give everything they possessed, even two or three *castellanos* of gold or an arroba or two of spun cotton. They even took bits of broken hoops from the wine barrels and, as simple as animals, gave what they had. This seemed to me to be wrong and I forbade it.

I gave them a thousand pretty things that I had brought, in order to gain their love and incline them to become Christians. I hoped to win them to the love and service of their Highnesses and of the whole Spanish nation and to persuade them to collect and give us of the things which they possessed in abundance and which we needed. They have no religion and are not idolaters; but all believe that power and goodness dwell in the sky and they are firmly convinced that I have come from the sky with these ships and people. In this belief they gave me a good reception everywhere, once they had overcome their fear; and this is not because they are stupid – far from it, they are men of great intelligence, for they navigate all those seas, and give a marvellously good account of everything – but because they have never before seen men clothed or ships like these.

As soon as I came to the Indies, at the first island I discovered I seized some natives, intending them to inquire and inform me about things in these parts. These men soon understood us, and we them, either by speech or signs and they were very useful to us. I still have them with me and

despite all the conversation they have had with me they are still of the opinion that I come from the sky and have been the first to proclaim this wherever I have gone. Then others have gone running from house to house and to the neighbouring villages shouting: 'Come, come and see the people from the sky,' so, once they were reassured about us, all have come, men and women alike, and not one, old or young, has remained behind. All have brought us something to eat and drink which they have given with a great show of love. In all the islands they have very many canoes like oared *fustas*.

They are of various sizes, some as large as a *fusta* of eighteen benches. But they are not as broad, since they are hollowed out of a single tree. A *fusta* would not be able to keep up with them, however, for they are rowed at an incredible speed. In these they travel and transport their goods between the islands, which are innumerable. I have seen some of these canoes with eighty men in them, all rowing.

In all these islands I saw no great difference in the looks of the people, their customs or their language. On the other hand, all understand one another, which will be of singular assistance in the work of their conversion to our holy faith, on which I hope your Highnesses will decide, since they are very well disposed towards it.

I have already told of my voyage of 107 leagues in a straight line from west to east along the coast of Cuba, according to which I reckon that the island is larger than England and Scotland put together.*

One of these provinces is called Avan† and there the people are born with tails, and these provinces cannot have a

---

*Cuba is actually considerably smaller than England without Scotland.

†From which the Spaniards took the name La Habana, which they gave first to a town that they built on the southern coast of the island and afterwards to the present city of that name.

length of less than fifty or sixty leagues, according to the information I received from those Indians whom I have with me and who know all the islands.

The other island, Hispaniola, is greater in circumference than the whole of Spain* from Collioure to Fuenterabia in the Basque province, since I travelled along one side for 188 great leagues† in a straight line from west to east.

These islands are richer than I yet know or can say and I have taken possession of them in their Majesties' name and hold them all on their behalf and as completely at their disposition as the Kingdom of Castile. In this island of Hispaniola I have taken possession of a large town which is most conveniently situated for the goldfields and for communications with the mainland both here,‡ and there in the territories of the Grand Khan, with which there will be very profitable trade. I have named this town Villa de Navidad and have built a fort there. Its fortifications will by now be finished and I have left sufficient men to complete them. They have arms, artillery and provisions for more than a year, and a *fusta*; also a skilled shipwright who can build more.

I have established warm friendship with the king of that land, so much so, indeed, that he was proud to call me and treat me as a brother. But even should he change his attitude and attack the men of La Navidad, he and his people know nothing about arms and go naked, as I have already said; they are the most timorous people in the world. In fact, the men that I have left there would be enough to destroy the whole land, and the island holds no dangers for them so long as they maintain discipline.

*This also is an exaggeration.
†Reckoned to be four (Roman) miles.
‡Columbus is apparently assuming now that Cuba is part of the mainland, but that a further part of the mainland of Asia is still to be discovered.

In all these islands the men are seemingly content with one woman, but their chief or king is allowed more than twenty. The women appear to work more than the men and I have not been able to find out if they have private property. As far as I could see whatever a man had was shared among all the rest and this particularly applies to food.

I have not found the human monsters which many people expected. On the contrary, the whole population is very well made. They are not Negroes as in Guinea, and their hair is straight, for where they live the sun's rays do not strike too harshly, but they are strong nevertheless, despite the fact that Hispaniola is 20 to 21 degrees from the Equator.

There are high mountains in these islands and it was very cold this winter but the natives are used to this and withstand the weather, thanks to their food, which they eat heavily seasoned with very hot spices. Not only have I found no monsters but I have had no reports of any except at the island called 'Quaris',* which is the second as you approach the Indies from the east, and which is inhabited by a people who are regarded in these islands as extremely fierce and who eat human flesh. They have many canoes in which they travel throughout the islands of the Indies, robbing and taking all they can. They are no more ill-shaped than any other natives of the Indies, though they are in the habit of wearing their hair long like women. They have bows and arrows with the same canes as the others, tipped with splinters of wood, for lack of iron which they do not possess. They behave most savagely to the other peoples but I take no more account of them than the rest. It is these men who have relations with the women of Matinino,† where there are no men and which is the first island you come to on the way from Spain to the

*Either Dominica or Maria Galante. Reports of monsters seem generally to refer to the Carabis.

†Martinique.

Indies. These women do not follow feminine occupations but use cane bows and arrows like those of the men and arm and protect themselves with plates of copper, of which they have much.

In another island, which I am told is larger than Hispaniola, the people have no hair. Here there is a vast quantity of gold, and from here and the other islands I bring Indians as evidence.

In conclusion, to speak only of the results of this very hasty voyage, their Highnesses can see that I will give them as much gold as they require, if they will render me some very slight assistance; also I will give them all the spices and cotton they want, and as for mastic, which has so far been found only in Greece and the island of Chios and which the Genoese authorities have sold at their own price, I will bring back as large a cargo as their Highnesses may command. I will also bring them as much aloes as they ask and as many slaves, who will be taken from the idolaters. I believe also that I have found rhubarb and cinnamon and there will be countless other things in addition, which the people I have left there will discover. For I did not stay anywhere unless delayed by lack of wind except at the town of La Navidad, which I had to leave secure and well established. In fact I should have done much more if the ships had been reasonably serviceable, but this is enough.

Thus the eternal God, Our Lord, grants to all those who walk in his way victory over apparent impossibilities, and this voyage was pre-eminently a victory of this kind. For although there was much talk and writing of these lands, all was conjectural, without ocular evidence. In fact, those who accepted the stories judged rather by hearsay than on any tangible information. So all Christendom will be delighted that our Redeemer has given victory to our most illustrious King and Queen and their renowned kingdoms, in this great matter. They should hold great celebrations and render solemn thanks

to the Holy Trinity with many solemn prayers, for the great triumph which they will have, by the conversion of so many peoples to our holy faith and for the temporal benefits which will follow, for not only Spain, but all Christendom will receive encouragement and profit.

This is a brief account of the facts.

Written in the caravel off the Canary Islands.*

15 February 1493

At your orders
THE ADMIRAL

After this was written, when I was already in Spanish waters, I was struck by such a strong south-south-west wind that I was compelled to lighten ship, but today by a great miracle I made the port of Lisbon, from which I decided to write letters to their Highnesses. Throughout the Indies, I have always found weather like that of May; I went there in thirty-three days and returned in twenty-eight. I met with no storms except these which held me up for fourteen days, beating about in these seas. The sailors here say that there has never been so bad a winter nor so many ships lost.

Written on 4 March

*Actually Columbus was off Santa Maria in the Azores.

SECOND VOYAGE
1493-6

THE LIFE OF THE ADMIRAL BY HIS SON, HERNANDO COLON

CHAPTER 43

It is decided that the Admiral should return with a large fleet to settle the island of Hispaniola. The Pope confirms the conquest

AT Barcelona, orders were given with great care and dispatch for the Admiral's second expedition and return to Hispaniola. This second expedition was designed to relieve the men who had remained there, to settle more colonists and to conquer the island together with all the others that had been discovered and those that they hoped remained to be discovered. In order to make their title clear and good, the Catholic sovereigns on the Admiral's advice very promptly applied for the Supreme Pontiff's confirmation and gift of the conquests of all these Indies.

The reigning Pope, Alexander VI, most liberally granted them not only all that they had conquered so far, but also everything that they should still discover further west as far as the Orient, in so far as no Christian prince had actual possession, and he forbade all others to encroach on these boundaries. In the following year the same Pope confirmed this gift, effectively defining it in a document of many clauses.*

*The Pope issued several bulls in the course of the year. In the most important of them, *Inter coetera* of 4 May, he established the line of demarcation between the territories assigned to Spain and Portugal on the meridian passing 100 leagues west of the Azores and the Cape Verde Islands, granting to the Castilians everything that might be discovered to the west of it. In 1494, in direct negotiations with Portugal, the line was shifted to 370 leagues to the west of the Cape Verde Islands. By this

Realizing that they owed the whole of this concession so kindly granted them by the Pope to the Admiral's labours and initiative, and that all their new rights and possessions were due to his voyage and discovery, the Catholic sovereigns were resolved to reward him for everything, and therefore at Barcelona on 28 May they granted him a new patent, or rather an explanation and amplification,* in which they reaffirmed the grants and concessions which they had originally made to him. In clear and precise language they declared that his jurisdiction as Admiral, his viceroyalty and governorship extended to the full limits of the concession granted to them by the Pope, and thus confirmed the patent granted to him at Santa Fé.

---

grant, the Portuguese were later able to colonize Brazil and, at least in theory, the English and French were debarred from the New World.

*In this document Columbus was appointed captain-general of the second fleet and given power to appoint any persons he might choose to the government of the Indies. A week before he had been given the highly prized right to wear a castle and lion in his coat of arms. [Hernando Colon's note.]

THE LETTER WRITTEN BY DR CHANCA*
TO THE CITY OF SEVILLE

MOST EXCELLENT SIR: Since the contents of the private letters which I have sent to others cannot be so generally communicated as those which I am writing here, I have decided to send the news from this place in one letter and my various requests to your lordship in another. My news is as follows:

The fleet which, by God's will, the Catholic Kings, our lords, sent to the Indies under the command of Christopher Columbus, their Admiral of the Ocean Sea, left Cadiz on 25 September 1493.† The weather and wind favoured our journey and continued to do so for two days, during which we were able to make about fifty leagues. The weather turned against us for the next two days, in which we made little or no progress. After this it pleased God to give us good weather, so that in another two days we reached Grand Canary, where we put into port; which we were compelled to do in order to repair a ship which was making much water. We remained there for the whole day, and set out on the morrow and met with some calms, so that we were four or five days in reaching Gomera. We had to remain for some time at Gomera, taking on all the stores we could of meat, wood and water for the long voyage we expected to make without sighting land.

So with our stay at these ports and a day's delay owing to calm after leaving Gomera, we were nineteen or twenty days in arriving at the island of Hierro. From here, by the kindness of God, we had good weather, the best that ever a fleet had on such a long voyage. Having left Hierro on 13 October in

---

*Chanca was one of Ferdinand and Isabela's physicians whom they sent as doctor to the expedition and whose salary they paid.

†Columbus had a fleet of seventeen ships including caravels and lighter vessels for inshore work, and twelve to fifteen thousand men.

under twenty days we sighted land, and we should have sighted it in fourteen or fifteen if the flagship had been as good a sailer as the other vessels. For on many occasions the other vessels shortened sail because they were leaving us far behind. All this time we had very good weather, for on these days, indeed throughout the voyage, we met with no storms except on St Simon's Eve, when one struck us and for four hours put us in great danger.

At about daybreak on Sunday, 3 November, the first after All Saints, a pilot of the flagship cried out claiming a reward: 'Land in sight!' All the men were so delighted that it was marvellous to hear their shouts and cries of pleasure. They had good reason, for they were so exhausted by their privations and pumping out water that they all longed most fervently for land. That day the pilots of the fleet calculated that the distance was 800 leagues from the island of Hierro to the first land which we sighted. Others reckoned 780, which was not very different, and the additional 300 from the island of Hierro to Cadiz made the total figure 1,100. So I think that everyone had seen enough water! On that Sunday morning mentioned we saw an island lying ahead of the ships* and afterwards another came in sight on the right.†

The first was high and mountainous on the side that we saw, and the other flat and covered with very thick trees. As soon as it grew lighter, other islands began to appear on both sides of the ships, so that on this day six islands were seen in various directions,‡ most of them very large. We steered to examine the first that we had seen and sailed along the coast for more than a league, looking for a harbour in which to

*Dominica, so called because it was discovered on that Sunday.

†Maria Galante, named after Columbus's ship, *Santa Maria la Galante*.

‡This might have been a mistake; probably the peaks on Dominica were counted as separate islands.

THE SECOND VOYAGE
OF COLUMBUS   (First Map)

Miles 0 40 80 120 160 200

S. Maria
de la Antigua

Maria
Galante

Dominica

Nevis

Montserrat

S. Maria la
Redonda.

Guadalupe

LEEWARD
ISLANDS

Martinique

Virgin Is.

Santa Cruz

PUERTO
RICO

Mona
(Amona)

Santo
Domingo

SAMANA

CIBAO

Isabela
Monte Cristi
Puerto de
las Gracias

La Navidad

Tortuga I.

H I S P A N I O L A

anchor, but could not find one anywhere. As much of the island as we could see was all very mountainous, very beautiful and very green down to the water's edge. It was a pleasure to look at, for at this season there is hardly any green in our own country.

Since we found no harbour there, the Admiral decided to steer for the other island, which lay on the right and was four or five leagues from this one. Meanwhile one ship remained off the first island for the whole day, continuing to look for a harbour, in case it should be necessary to return there. A good harbour was eventually found, and people and houses sighted. Later at night this ship rejoined the fleet, which had found a harbour on the other island, where the Admiral and many men had landed carrying the royal standard, and had taken formal possession of the land for their Highnesses. On this island the trees were amazingly dense, and were of a great variety of species known to none of us. Some were in fruit, some in flower, and all therefore were green. We found one tree, like a laurel but not so large, the leaves of which had the finest scent of clove that I have ever smelt. I think it must have been a species of laurel. There were wild fruit* of different kinds, which some rashly tried. But no sooner did they taste them than their faces swelled, growing so inflamed and painful that they almost went out of their minds. They cured themselves with cold compresses. We found no people on this island, nor any sign of them, and believed it to be uninhabited.

We remained only two hours, for when we got there it was late evening. Next day we departed in the morning for another island, which appeared beyond this one, very large and some seven or eight leagues away. At the point where we reached it, there was a great mountain mass which seemed to

---

*This was probably the manchineal (manzanillo). The Caribs used the fruit of this tree to make poison for their arrows.

touch the sky, and in the middle a peak higher than all the rest. From here many streams flowed in different directions, particularly in the direction in which we lay. Three leagues away could be seen a waterfall of considerable breadth, which fell from so high that it seemed to come from the sky. It could be seen from so far off that many wagers were laid on board. Some said that it was white rock and others that it was water. When we got nearer, the truth was apparent. It was the most beautiful thing in the world to see the height from which it fell, and from how small a place such a force of water sprang. When we came near, the Admiral dispatched a light caravel to sail along the coast and look for a harbour. The caravel went ahead and, on reaching the land, sighted some houses. The captain went ashore in the boat and visited the houses, whose inhabitants fled as soon as they saw him. He went into the houses and saw their possessions, for they had taken nothing with them. He took two parrots, which were very large and very different from any previously seen. He saw much cotton, spun and ready for spinning, and some of their food. He took a little of everything, and in particular he took away four or five human arm and leg bones. When we saw these, we suspected that these were the Carib islands, whose inhabitants eat human flesh. For following the indications of their position given him by the Indians of the islands discovered in his previous voyage, the Admiral had set his course to discover them, since they were nearer to Spain and lay on the direct route to the island of Hispaniola, where he had left his men on the previous voyage. By the goodness of God, and thanks to the Admiral's skill and knowledge, we had reached them as directly as if we had been following a known and familiar course.

This island* is very large, and on this side the coast appeared to be twenty-five leagues in length. We sailed along

*Guadalupe.

it for more than two leagues looking for a harbour. On the side we approached there were very high mountains, and on the side from which we left wide plains appeared. On the seashore there were some small villages, and at the sight of our sails all the people fled. When we had gone two leagues and it was quite late, we found a harbour. That night the Admiral decided that some men should land early next morning and hold conversation with the natives, to find out what people they were, though he already suspected that they were Caribs and the people whom he had seen running away were naked, like those he had seen on his previous voyage.

Certain captains set out in the morning and some returned at dinner-time bringing a boy of about fourteen, who later told us that he was one of these people's captives. The other captains went in various directions. A few men returned with a boy whom a man had been leading by the hand, but had abandoned at their approach. Only these few were detached to bring him back, the rest remaining behind. These captured some women of the island, and also brought back other women who were prisoners and came of their own accord. One captain separated himself from the party with six men, not knowing that any information had been gained. He and his companions got lost and could not find their way back until, after four days, they struck the coast, which they followed until they rejoined the fleet. We thought that they were dead and eaten by these Caribs, for there seemed no other explanation of their disappearance, since among them were pilots, sailors capable of making the voyage to and from Spain by the stars, and we didn't think they could get lost in so small a space.

On the first day of our landing, many men and women walked along the seashore, gazing on the fleet and marvelling at the strange sight. And when a boat put ashore to speak with them saying 'Tayno Tayno', which means good, they waited

so long as our men did not come ashore, remaining at the water's edge, ready to escape at any moment. Consequently none of these men could be taken, either by force or by persuasion, except two, who grew confident and were captured a little later. In addition to the two who were taken by force, more than twenty of the women prisoners and some other natives of the island came of their own accord. Some boy prisoners also fled to our men, escaping from the natives of the island who were guarding them.

We remained in this harbour for eight days because of the loss of the captain I have spoken of, and landed several times on the island, visiting the dwellings and villages on the coast, where we found great numbers of human bones and skulls hanging in the houses as vessels to hold things. Very few men appeared and the reason was, as we learned from the women, that ten canoes had gone to raid other islands. These people seemed to us more civilized than those elsewhere. All have straw houses, but these people build them much better, and have larger stocks of provisions, and show more signs of industry practised by both men and women. They have much cotton, spun and ready for spinning, and much cotton cloth so well woven that it is no way inferior to the cloth of our own country. We asked the women who were held prisoners on this island what kind of people these were; and they replied that they were Caribs. When they understood that we hated these people on account of their cannibalism, they were highly delighted; and after that, if any Carib man or woman was brought in, they quietly told us that they were Caribs. For even here, where all were in our power, they showed the fear of a conquered people, and thus we learnt from the women which were Caribs and which were not. The Caribs wore round their legs two rings of woven cotton – one below the knee and one at the ankle. In this way they make their calves large and constrict the knee and ankle. They seem to regard

this as attractive, and by this feature we distinguished the Caribs from the others.

The customs of these Carib people are beastly. There are three islands. This one they call Turuqueira; the first that we saw is Ceyre and the third Ayay.*

The people were all friendly to one another as if of one family. They do not harm each other but all make war against the neighbouring islands. They travel 150 leagues to make raids in their canoes, which are small *fustas* hewn out of a single tree. Instead of iron weapons they use arrows – for they have no iron. Some of their arrows are tipped with tortoise shell, but others on another island use fish bones which are naturally serrated like very strong saws. For an unarmed people, which they all are, they can kill and do great injury with these weapons, which are not very terrible, however, to men of our nation.

These people raid the other islands and carry off all the women they can take, especially the young and beautiful, whom they keep as servants and concubines. They had carried off so many that in fifty houses we found no males and more than twenty of the captives were girls. These women say that they are treated with a cruelty that seems incredible. The Caribs eat the male children that they have by them, and only bring up the children of their own women; and as for the men they are able to capture, they bring those who are alive home to be slaughtered and eat those who are dead on the spot. They say that human flesh is so good that there is nothing like it in the world; and this must be true, for the human bones we found in their houses were so gnawed that no flesh was left on them except what was too tough to be eaten. In one house the neck of a man was found cooking in a pot. They castrate the boys that they capture and use them as

* These are probably Guadelupe, Maria Galante and Santa Cruz, but the identification is not certain.

servants until they are men. Then, when they want to make a feast, they kill and eat them, for they say that the flesh of boys and women is not good to eat. Three of these boys fled to us, and all three had been castrated.

After four days the captain who had been lost returned. We had abandoned all hope of his coming. For search parties had twice gone out to look for him, and only that day one party had returned with no certain news of him. We were as glad at his coming as if we had found him for the first time. In addition to the men who had gone with him, he brought in ten natives, boys and women. But neither this party nor those who had gone in search of them found any men, for they had all fled. But perhaps there were very few men left in the district, because as we learned from the women ten canoes had gone to raid the other islands. This captain and his companions returned so weary from the forest that they were a pitiful sight. When we asked how they had got lost, they answered that the trees were so thick they could not see the sky and that some of them who were sailors had climbed trees to look at the stars, but had not been able to see them, and if they had not found the sea it would have been impossible for them to rejoin the ships.

We left this island eight days after we arrived. Then at noon next day we saw another island which was not very large and was twelve leagues from this one.* We were becalmed for the greater part of the day after we left and remained near the coast of this island. The women whom we brought with us said that it was uninhabited, because the Caribs had removed the whole population. So we did not stay there. Then in the evening we sighted another island† and at nightfall found some shoals close to it, for fear of which we dropped anchor, nor daring to go further until daylight.

*Montserrat.
†Santa Maria la Redonda, the round island.

Next morning another island of considerable size appeared.*
We visited none of these, being anxious to relieve those who
had been left on Hispaniola. But it did not please God that we
should do so, as will appear later.

Next day at dinner-time we reached another island† which
seemed to us to be a very good one, for, to judge by the
many tracts of cultivation upon it, it was thickly inhabited.
We went there and put into a coastal harbour. Then the
Admiral sent a boat ashore with a landing party, whom he
instructed to speak with the inhabitants and find out if possible what people they were. We also wished for information
about our course, though, despite the fact that the Admiral
had never sailed that way before, he had, as it appeared later,
followed a very direct line. But because matters of doubt
should always be looked into with the greatest possible care,
he wished to make inquiries there also. Some of those in the
boat landed and made their way to a village, whose inhabitants had all gone into hiding. The landing party took some
women and boys, most of whom were the people's captives,
for like the inhabitants of the other islands these people were
Caribs, as we learnt from the women whom we took with us.

When this boat was about to return to the ships with the
captures it had made down the coast below this place, there
appeared along the coast a canoe with four men, two women
and a boy, and when they saw the fleet they were so amazed
that they remained motionless for a full hour about two
lombard shots from the ships. The crew of the boat and indeed the whole fleet saw their stupefaction. Soon those in the
boats went after them, keeping so close to the shore that
these Indians, lost in amazement and wondering what the
strange sight might be, failed to see them, until they were
almost upon them and consequently could not escape though

*Santa Maria de la Antigua.
†San Martin.

they tried hard to do so. Our men rowed after them so fast that they did not get far. When the Caribs saw that flight was useless they very boldly snatched up their bows, men and women alike; I say 'very boldly' because they were only four men and two women and there were twenty-five or more in our boat, but they succeeded in wounding two of them, one with two arrows in the chest and the other with an arrow in his side. If our men had not carried shields of wood and leather and had not come close to the canoe and upset it, most of the others would have been wounded too. When the boat was upset, the Indians remained in the water, sometimes swimming and sometimes standing, since there were shallows there, and our men had some difficulty in catching them, for they continued to shoot when they could. There was indeed one that they could not take until he was mortally wounded with a spear-thrust and they brought him thus wounded to the ships.

[*An incident of this time recorded by one of the Admiral's Italian lieutenants, Michele de Cuneo, throws additional light on the Christians' behaviour to the Indians:*

'*While I was in the boat, I captured a very beautiful Carib woman, whom the said Lord Admiral gave to me. When I had taken her to my cabin she was naked – as was their custom. I was filled with a desire to take my pleasure with her and attempted to satisfy my desire. She was unwilling, and so treated me with her nails that I wished I had never begun. But – to cut a long story short – I then took a piece of rope and whipped her soundly, and she let forth such incredible screams that you would not have believed your ears. Eventually we came to such terms, I assure you, that you would have thought she had been brought up in a school for whores.*']

The difference in appearance between these Indians and the others is that the Caribs wear their hair very long and the others have it cut irregularly and decorate their heads in a great number of different patterns, each according to his

fancy. They make these patterns – crosses and such-like devices – with sharpened reeds. Both the Caribs and the others are beardless; only very rarely will you find anyone with a beard. The Caribs who were captured there had their eyes and brows stained, which I think they do for show. It makes them look more terrifying. One of these Indians told us that in one of these islands, called Ceyre, which is the first we saw but did not visit, there is much gold.* They go there with studs and nails to build their canoes and bring away as much gold as they want.

Later that day we left this island after a stay of only six or seven hours and made for another land,† which came in sight on the course we were following. We came near to it at nightfall, and next morning followed its coast. There was much land though it was not very continuous, for there were more than forty islets. It was very high and unlike any of the islands we have seen before or since, and mostly barren. It seemed the sort of land in which there might be metals, but we did not go ashore, though a lateen-rigged caravel went to one of the islets where they found some fishermen's huts. The Indian women who were with us said they were uninhabited.

We followed this coast for the greater part of the day and in the evening of the next came in sight of another island called Burenquen‡ whose coast we followed for the whole of the next day. The island was reckoned to be thirty leagues long on this side. It is most beautiful and appears to be very fertile. The Caribs have come here on raids and taken many of the people. The natives have no canoes and no knowledge of navigation, but according to the Caribs whom we captured they use bows like their own, and if they manage to capture

---

*If this refers to Dominica it is not true. There is no gold but plenty of wood. There is perhaps a mistake in the text.

†The island of Santa Cruz.   ‡Puerto Rico.

any of the raiders they eat them in the same way as the Caribs themselves. We stayed in a harbour on this island for two days, and many of our men landed, but we were never able to have speech with the people, for they were terrified of the Caribs and all fled.

All these islands were discovered on this voyage, for scarcely one of them had been seen by the Admiral when he came here before. They are all very beautiful and have good soil, and this one seemed the best of all. It was almost the last of the islands facing Spain which the Admiral had not already seen, but we consider it certain that there is land forty leagues nearer to Spain than these first islands, because two days before we sighted land we saw some of those birds called frigate-birds, sea-birds of prey, which never alight or sleep on the water, and towards evening they were circling high in the air and flying off in search of land on which to sleep. As it was now almost night they could not have been going to roost more than twelve or fifteen leagues away. We sighted them on our right as we sailed on our course from Spain and everyone reckoned therefore that there must be land there. But we did not go to look for it because this would have deflected us from our course. I hope that during the next few voyages it will be discovered.*

We left the island of Burenquen at dawn and at nightfall came within sight of land which was also unknown to those who had accompanied the Admiral on his previous voyage, but which, on the information of the Indian women whom we had aboard, we guessed must be Hispaniola, where we lie at present. Between this island and Burenquen there appeared another small one in the distance. When we reached His-paniola the land on that side was at first low and very flat, and on seeing this everyone was uncertain what land it was, for neither the Admiral nor any of those who had sailed with him

*The remaining Leeward Islands.

had seen this part of the island. It is so large that it is divided
into provinces. This part which we reached first is called Haiti,
the one next to it they call Jamana, and the one after that in
which we now are is Bohio.* These provinces are themselves
divided into districts, for Hispaniola is very large. Those who
have seen the whole length of the coast suppose it to extend
for 200 leagues. In my opinion it is not less than 150 leagues
long, and its breadth is still unknown. Forty days ago a
caravel left to circumnavigate it and has not yet returned.

The land is very remarkable; it contains many large rivers,
great mountain ranges, wide open valleys and high mountains. I suspect that the vegetation remains green right through
the year. I do not believe that there is winter either in this
island or any of the others, for many birds' nests were found
at Christmas, some containing fledglings and some eggs. No
four-footed animal has been seen in any of them, except for
some dogs of various colours like those in Spain, which are
of the build of large mastiffs. There are no wild beasts, only a
creature the size of a young rabbit, with a coat of the same
kind and colour and a long tail and hind and forefeet like those
of a rat. It climbs trees and many who have tried it say the
flesh is very good to eat.†

There are many small snakes but only a few lizards, because the Indians consider them as great a delicacy as we do
pheasants at home. They are of the same size as our native
lizard but differently formed, though on one small island
beside a harbour called Monte Christi, where we stayed for a
day or two, a very large lizard was seen many times and was
said to be as big as a calf and the length of a lance from tip to
tail.‡ They often went out to hunt it, but owing to the thick-

*Haiti and Bohio were both native names for the whole island and
Jamana was a district lying on the north coast.

†Aguti, a kind of edible rat.

‡According to Oviedo an alligator.

ness of the undergrowth it escaped into the sea and they never came face to face with it.

In Hispaniola and the other islands there are a great number of birds like those of our country and many others of kinds never seen there. No domestic fowls have been found here at all except in Zuruquia, where there were some ducks in the houses, most of them white as snow but a few black. They had flat crests and were larger than those at home, though smaller than geese.

We sailed along the coast of this island for about a hundred leagues, to the place where the Admiral had left his people, which must have been about half-way along the island. As we coasted the province of Jamana, we put ashore one of the Indian captives of the previous voyage, clothed, and with a few small objects which the Admiral had given him. That day a Basque sailor died who had been wounded by the Caribs on the occasion when we surprised them by keeping close to the shore. Since we were near the coast the opportunity was taken of sending a boat ashore to bury him, and two caravels were sent in to escort it. Many Indians came out to meet the boat as it beached, some of whom had gold round their necks or in their ears. They wanted to come out to the ships with the Christians, but the sailors refused to bring them since they had no permission from the Admiral. When they realized that we were not going to row them out, two of them got into a small canoe and went to one of the caravels which had put in towards the shore.

They were kindly received and were then conveyed to the Admiral's ship, where they said through an interpreter that they had been sent by a certain king to learn who we were and to beg us to land because they had much gold and would give us some, as well as some food. The Admiral ordered that they should be given a shirt each and a cap and other trifles. He told them, however, that as he was going to the

place where Guacamari* lived, he could not wait now, but would be able to visit their king at some other time, and with that they went away. We sailed continuously along our course until we reached a harbour called Monte Christi, where we stayed two days to inspect the ground because the Admiral did not think that the place where he had left his people was suitable for a settlement. There was a large river of very good water, but the land around is all swampy and unsuitable for habitation. During their inspection of the river and the land some of our men found two corpses at a place near the bank, one with a noose round his neck and the other with his feet tied. This was on the first day. On the next they found two other corpses further upstream, one of which was so well preserved that it was possible to see that he had been heavily bearded. Some of our men suspected the worst and with justification, for the Indians have no beards, as has already been observed.

This harbour was two leagues away from the place where the Admiral had left his people and two days later we set sail for it. The Admiral had left them in the company of a king called Guacamari, who was I think one of the principal kings of this island. That day we arrived off the place, but it was already evening and because of the shoals on which the Admiral's ship had been lost on the previous voyage we did not dare to go inshore and enter the harbour until next day, when soundings could be taken and we could do so in safety. We remained that night rather less than a league from shore.

During the evening a canoe appeared in the distance with five or six Indians who were rowing rapidly after us, but, believing it was safer for us to keep our sails set, the Admiral would not allow us to wait for them. They pressed on, however, and came within a lombard shot of us, where they stopped to look at us and when they saw that we were not

* Guacanagari.

144

stopping they turned round and rowed back. After we had anchored offshore that evening, the Admiral ordered that two lombards should be fired in hope that the Christians who had remained with Guacamari would reply, for they also had lombards. But there was no reply and no sign of fires or houses in that place. This greatly disturbed our people, who drew the natural conclusion and were very sad.

Four or five hours after nightfall the same canoe returned. The Indians shouted to the captain of the first caravel they approached, asking for the Admiral. They were taken to his ship but would not go aboard until the Admiral himself had spoken to them. They asked for a light in order to recognize him, and when they had done so came on board. One of them was a cousin of Guacamari who had sent them on the previous occasion. When they had returned to him on that first evening, he had given them two gold masks, one to be taken as a present to the Admiral and the other to one of the captains who had accompanied him on his previous voyage. They remained aboard for three hours, talking with the Admiral in the presence of the whole crew, and seemed highly delighted. When the Admiral asked them about the Christians and how they were, Guacamari's cousin answered that they were all well, although some of them had died of disease and others of quarrels which had arisen between them. He said that Guacamari was lying at another village with a wound in his leg and for this reason had not come, but that he would come the next day. He said that two other kings, Caonabo and Mayreni, had attacked him and burned the village. And they went ashore later saying that they would return the next day with Guacamari, and so they left us comforted for that night.

Next morning we were waiting for Guacamari to come, and in the meantime several men landed, on the Admiral's orders, and went to the place where they had often been in the past. They found the palisaded blockhouse in which the

Christians had been left, burnt, and the village demolished by fire, and also some clothes and rags that the Indians had brought to throw into the house.* The Indians whom they met there went about very warily and did not dare to come near us, but ran away. This seemed a bad sign, for the Admiral had told us that on our arrival so many canoes would put out to come alongside and see us that we should not be able to fend them off, as had been the case on the previous voyage. When we saw that they were now very shy with us, we came to the worst conclusions.

Nevertheless that day we made advances to them and threw them some small things, such as hawks' bells and beads, in order to reassure them. Two or three of them, including Guaca-mari's cousin, became sufficiently confident to enter the boat and came aboard the ship. When asked about the Christians, they answered that they were all dead. Although one of the Indians who had come with us from Castile had reported that he had learned this from the two natives who had come to the ship and remained alongside in their canoe, we had not believed the story. Guacamari's cousin was asked who had killed them. He replied King Caonabo and King Mayreni and that they had burnt down the village. He said that many Indians had been wounded and that Guacamari himself had a wound in the thigh and was at present at another village where he proposed to go immediately and call him. He was given some presents and departed for the place where Guaca-mari was.

We waited all that day, and when we saw that they were not coming many of us suspected that the Indians who had done so on the day before had been drowned, because we had given them two or three glasses of wine and they had come in a small canoe which might easily have overturned. Next

* These would have been thrown alight to set fire to the straw roofs; possibly they are the same as the clothing mentioned later.

morning the Admiral and some of us landed and went to the site of the village. We found it completely burnt and the Spaniards' clothing lying on the grass. At that time, we did not see any corpses.

There are many opinions among us. Some of us suspected that Guacamari had taken part himself in the betrayal or murder of the Christians. Others thought not, since it was his village that had been burnt down. The whole matter was therefore extremely doubtful. The Admiral ordered that all the ground within the Christians' fortifications should be searched, since he had instructed them to bury any quantities of gold they might obtain. During this search he decided to inspect a place about a league away which seemed to us a suitable site for a town, since the time had now come to build. Some of us went with him along the coast, examining the country until we came to a small village of seven or eight houses which the Indians had abandoned when they saw us coming. They had taken what they could and hidden the rest of their possessions in the grass near them. These people are so like animals that they have not the intelligence to find a proper place to live. Those who live on the seashore build in a surprisingly primitive way. The houses there are so covered with green or damp that I am astonished they survive.

In these houses we found many possessions of the Christians, which it was incredible they should have bartered, among them a very fine Moorish cloak, which had not been unfolded since it had been brought from Spain, and also stockings and pieces of cloth and an anchor from the ship which the Admiral had lost there on the previous voyage and other things which greatly strengthened our suspicions. On examining the contents of a wicker basket which they had carefully sewn up and well concealed, we found the head of a man, carefully wrapped. We concluded that this must be the head of a father or mother or of someone whom they greatly loved. I have since

heard that many heads like this have been found, from which I conclude that our opinion at that time was correct. After this we returned.

That day we again visited the place where the village had been and found many Indians there who had gained confidence and were bartering gold. They had bartered almost a mark's worth. We learnt that they had pointed out where eleven Christians lay covered with grass that had grown over them. They all told us through an interpreter that Caonabo and Mayreni had killed them, but complained at the same time that the Christians had taken three or four women apiece, from which we concluded that they had been murdered out of jealousy.

Next morning, since there was no suitable place for a settlement anywhere in that locality, the Admiral dispatched a caravel elsewhere to look for a site, and took some of us with him in another direction, where we found a very safe harbour and a very pleasant tract of land for a town. But as it was very far from the place where we wanted to be, which was near the goldfield, the Admiral decided not to make a settlement there but in another nearer place, assuming a suitable site might be found.

On our return we found the other caravel which had sailed in the opposite direction, with Melchior* and four or five important men. As they went along the coast in search of a suitable place a canoe had come out to them with two Indians, one of them Guacamari's brother, who was recognized by a pilot on that caravel. The Indians asked who were in the ship and had been told 'men of importance'. They then said that Guacamari invited them to land and come to a village of some fifty houses where he was staying. The Spaniards landed in the boat and went to the place where

* Melchior Maldonado, who had been sent on the expedition by the sovereigns Ferdinand and Isabela.

Guacamari was, and found him on his bed apparently suffering from a serious wound. They spoke with him and asked about the Christians, and he answered, telling the same story as the others, that it was Caonabo and Mayreni who had killed them, and that they had wounded him in the thigh, which he showed them bandaged. Seeing him in this state they believed that his story was true, and when they left he gave to each a golden jewel, small or great according to what he supposed to be their importance. These Indians beat their gold into very thin sheets from which they make masks, setting it in bitumen which they prepare for the purpose. They could not make their masks without it. They also shape gold to be worn as head ornaments or in the ears or nose. It always has to be beaten thin, since they do not prize it as riches but only for its ornamental uses. Guacamari intimated by signs as best he could that because of his wounded state we must ask the Admiral kindly to come and see him, and the Indians told this same story to the Admiral when he arrived.

Next morning the Admiral decided to go to that village, which was about three leagues from where we were, but as the journey would take just under three hours it would have been dinner-time when we arrived. So we ate before landing, and when we had finished the Admiral ordered that all the captains should come in their boats to go ashore, since earlier in the morning before we set out Guacamari's brother had visited the Admiral urging him to hasten his visit to Guacamari. The Admiral and all the chief officers landed so richly dressed that they could have graced a capital city. He took some presents, since he had already received a considerable amount of gold from Guacamari and it was right that he should respond to this demonstration of goodwill. Guacamari had himself prepared a further present for the Admiral and on our arrival we found him stretched on his bed, which was of their native kind, made of woven cotton mesh and hung

above the ground. He did not get down but from his bed made the best gestures of courtesy that he could. He showed great feeling for the death of the Christians; the tears sprang to his eyes as he began to talk, demonstrating as best he could how some had died of disease and others had gone to Caonabo in search of the goldfield and had been killed there and how the rest had been killed in his own village. To judge from the condition of the bodies this had happened less than two months ago.

At this point Guacamari presented the Admiral with eight and a half marks worth of gold, and five or six hundred carved stones of various colours, and a head-dress of these same stones, of which I think they have great quantities. In this head-dress was a jewel to which they attached great value. It seems to me that they value copper more than gold.

I was present and so was a surgeon of the fleet. The Admiral said that we had knowledge of men's ailments and asked him to show us his wound. He agreed and I said that it would be best for him to go out of the house if he could, since the crowd of people inside made it dark and it was impossible to see clearly. He agreed to this, I think rather out of fear than goodwill, and left the house supported by an attendant. When he had sat down the surgeon went up and began to remove his bandages. Then Guacamari told the Admiral that he had been wounded by a *ciba*, which means a stone. When the bandages were off we began to examine him, and it was quite obvious that he was no more wounded in this thigh than in the other, although he made a cunning pretence of being in great pain.

What had occurred remained uncertain, for the facts were still not known, though there were many undoubted signs that some hostile people had attacked Guacamari. Consequently the Admiral could not decide what to do. He and many others thought that for the present and until the facts were

better known it would be best to dissemble. When they learned the truth they could demand whatever reparation they chose from him.

That evening Guacamari accompanied the Admiral to the ships, where he was shown the horses and everything aboard, which greatly astonished him as things never seen before. He took supper on the ship and later in the evening returned to his house. The Admiral said that he wished to settle there with him and build houses, and Guacamari replied that this would please him but that the place was unhealthy because it was very damp, which it certainly was. All this conversation was conducted through two Indian interpreters, the only survivors of the seven who had been taken to Castile on the previous voyage. Five of them died on the way back and these two almost did so.

Next day we remained at anchor in that harbour and Guacamari inquired when the Admiral intended to depart. A reply was sent that we would leave on the following day, and on that day Guacamari's brother and some others came to the ship bringing gold for barter. This next day a fair amount of gold was exchanged.

There were ten women on board, who had been rescued from the Caribs, most of them from the island of Boriquen, and Guacamari's brother talked with them, and I think instructed them to do what they did that night, which was quietly to jump overboard during the first watch and swim ashore. By the time they were missed they had swum so far that only four were taken by the boats and not until they were just coming out of the water. They had swum a good half league. Next morning the Admiral went to Guacamari demanding that he should return the women who had escaped during the night, and sent to look for them immediately. When his messengers arrived they found the village deserted – not a person remained in it. Many people then reaffirmed their

suspicions; others said that Guacamari had merely moved on to another village, as was their custom.

We remained anchored there that day because the weather was against us. On the morning of the next day the Admiral decided that since the weather was still unfavourable it would be a good idea to go and examine a harbour some two leagues up the coast and see if it offered a suitable site for settlement. We rowed there with all the boats, keeping close to the shore and leaving the ships in harbour. There too the natives were apprehensive. On arriving we discovered that the inhabitants of the village had all fled, but we found an Indian hidden in the undergrowth with a gaping dart wound in his back which had prevented him from escaping any further. The Indians of this island fight with darts which they shoot from slings like those with which small boys shoot in Castile. They can shoot both far and accurately, and for a people without iron weapons they can certainly do great damage. This man said that he had been wounded by Caonabo and his people and that they had burned Guacamari's houses. Since we understood them so little and their equivocal statements were so obscure, we have not yet been able to determine the truth about the death of our men, nor did we find a suitable site for a settlement near that harbour.

The Admiral decided that we should return up the coast in the direction from which we had come because he had news that there was gold there. But the weather was so much against us that to sail back thirty leagues was harder than to come from Castile. Indeed, it was so bad and the voyage so long that it was a full three months before we landed. By God's will, which prevented us going further, we had to land at the best and most favourable site we could find. Here there is a very good harbour and large fisheries, of which we were in great need, owing to lack of meat.

In this country the fish are very strange to us and more

wholesome than those of Spain. Nevertheless the climate does not allow of their being kept from one day to the next, for it is hot and damp and perishable foods quickly go bad. The soil is most favourable for all crops. At this site there is one main river and another of moderate size with extremely good water.

A town* is being built beside the river and it stands immediately above the water at the top of a steep ravine, so that no defensive works are needed on this side. On the other side it is bounded by a forest so thick that a rabbit could hardly get through. The forest is so green that it would be impossible to burn it at any time of year. They have begun to divert an arm of the river which the workmen say they will bring through the centre of the town, and they intend to place mills and waterwheels on this channel and anything else that can be driven by water. They have sown many vegetables, which grow more in eight days than in twenty in Spain. Many Indians come here continually, among them *caciques*,† who are, so to speak, their chieftains, and many women as well.

They all bring yams, which are like turnips and very good food, and we prepare them for eating in a variety of ways. They are so nourishing that we are all greatly restored by them, for we have been living on the smallest possible rations during our months at sea. This was necessary, since we did not know what weather we should meet or how long it would please God that the voyage should take. So it was only prudent that we should limit our consumption in order to have enough to keep alive however long the voyage might last. The Indians barter gold and provisions and all that they

*The town was called Isabela, after the Queen. It was abandoned after two years in favour of Santo Domingo, and fell into ruins.

† This word, Arawak in origin, was applied to chieftains throughout Spanish America, though the word was proper to the West Indies alone.

bring for tags of laces, beads, pins and bits of dishes and plates. This yam is called by the Caribs *nabi* and by the Indians *hage*.

All the people go about as I have said, naked as their mothers bore them, except the women of this island, who cover their private parts with woven cotton which they tie round their hips or with grasses or the leaves of trees. Their way of decoration is to paint their faces black, or red and white, making themselves such sorry sights that we cannot help laughing at them. Their heads are partly shaved and partly covered with tangled locks in such a variety of patterns that it is impossible to describe them. In fact, the best of them delight to crop themselves in a way that in Spain we would only crop a madman. In their neighbourhood there are many goldfields, none of which, according to their reports, is more than twenty or twenty-five leagues away. Some are said to be in Niti, in the territory of Caonabo, who killed the Christians. Others are in another district called Cibao, and if it is God's pleasure we shall know and see all these with our own eyes before many days have passed. We would make the journey now were it not for the fact that there are so many things to be seen to that we cannot manage everything. For a third of the people have fallen sick in the last four or five days, most of them I think from hard work and the rigours of the voyage, and because of differences of climate. But I trust God that all will recover.

These Indians seem so well disposed that they could be converted if we had an interpreter, for they imitate everything that we do. They bend their knees at the altars, and at the *Ave Maria* and other moments, and cross themselves. They all say that they wish to be Christians, although actually they are idolaters. There are idols of all kinds in their houses. When I ask them what these are they answer that they belong to *Turey*, that is to say to the sky. I once made a show

of wanting to throw these in the fire, which so upset them that they were on the point of tears. They also think that whatever we bring comes from the sky, for they call it all *Turey*, that is to say sky.

The first day on which I landed and slept ashore was Sunday. The short time that we have spent ashore has been devoted rather to preparing our settlement and searching for what we need than to exploring the land, but the little that we have seen is marvellous. We have seen trees that bear very fine wool, so fine that those who understand weaving say that good cloth could be woven from it.* These trees are so numerous that the caravels could be fully laden with the wool, though it is hard to gather, since they are very thorny, but some means of doing so could easily be devised. There is also an infinite amount of cotton growing on trees the size of peach trees, and there are trees that bear wax the colour and taste of bees' wax and as good for burning. Indeed, it is not very different. There are a great number of trees producing turpentine which are very remarkable and very fine; also much tragacanth, which is very good too, and some trees which I think bear nutmegs but at present no fruit. I say I think because the smell and taste of the bark is like that of nutmegs. I saw a root of ginger, which an Indian had tied round his neck. There is also aloe, and though not of a kind which has hitherto been seen in our country it is no doubt one of the species used by doctors. A kind of cinnamon has been found as well, though it is true that it is not so fine as the cinnamon we know at home. This may be because we do not know the right season to gather it, or possibly there are better trees in the land. Yellow mirabolans† have also been found, but at the time they were lying beneath the tree and as the soil is very damp they had gone rotten. They taste very bitter, I

*This is the Ceiba or silk cotton tree.
†'Hog plum.'

155

think because they are rotten. But in every respect except their taste, which is foul, they are the true mirabolan. There is also very good mastic.

None of the people we have met so far have iron. They have quantities of tools such as hatchets and axes, made of stone, which are so beautifully worked that it is a wonder they have been able to make them without iron. They live on bread made of the roots of a vegetable* which is half-way between a plant and a tree and on *age*, the turnip-like fruit, already mentioned, which is an extremely good food. They use as seasoning, a spice called *agi*,† with which they also season their fish and birds when they can get them. There are great numbers of birds of many different kinds. They have also some nuts like hazels, very good to eat. They eat any snakes, lizards or spiders and worms that they find on the ground, and their habits seem to be more bestial than those of any beast in the world.

Although, on account of the many cases of sickness among his people, the Admiral had previously decided to postpone the search for the goldfields until he had dispatched the ships that were to go to Castile, he now resolved to send two parties under different captains, one to Cibao and the other to Niti, the residence of Caonabo. They went and returned, one on 20 January and the other on 21 January. The captain who went to Cibao found gold in so many places that no one dared to guess the number. Indeed, they found it in more than fifty streams and rivers, and on dry land also. He says that where-ever you look, anywhere in this province, you will find gold. He bought samples from many parts from the sand of rivers and from springs on land. It is believed that, if we dig as we know how, it will be found in larger pieces, for the Indians cannot mine, since they have nothing with which to dig more than eight inches deep. The other captain who went to Niti

* Yucca. † Red pepper.

also bought news of much gold in three or four places, and he too brought a sample.

Our sovereigns therefore can certainly consider themselves henceforth the richest and most prosperous on earth, for nothing comparable has ever been seen or read of till now in the whole world. On the next voyage which the ships make they will be able to carry away such quantities of gold that anyone who hears of it will be amazed. Here I think it will be well to end my story. I believe that those who do not know me and hear all this will consider me longwinded and exaggerative. But as God is my witness I have not departed one iota from the truth.

CHAPTER 51

Events after the settlement of Isabela

NOT only was the Admiral too pressed for time to chronicle events in his usual way, but he also fell ill and therefore left a gap in his diary from 11 December to 12 March 1494.

In the interval, after arranging things in the town of Isabela as well as he could, he sent Alonso de Hojeda in the course of January with fourteen men to look for the gold-fields of Cibao. Later, on 2 February, twelve ships* of the Spanish fleet returned home, under the command of Captain Antonio de Torres, brother of the governess of the Prince Don Juan, a man of honour and sound judgement, much trusted by the Catholic sovereigns and the Admiral. This gentleman carried an extended account of all that had occurred, a description of the country and of what was required to be done there.†

After a few days Hojeda returned, and in giving an account of his journey observed that on the second day after leaving Isabela he had spent the night beside a harbour somewhat difficult to enter and from there had met at intervals of a league a number of *caciques*, who had treated him with great

---

*On one of these, Dr Chanca, writer of the preceding letter, departed.

†The letter carried by de Torres in fact made a great number of demands by the Admiral both for himself and for the benefit of others. Most of these were fulfilled, but the general effect must have been somewhat disconcerting to the sovereigns, for in fact there was less news of the expedition and its achievements than demands for payments and concessions.

courtesy. Continuing on his way he had reached the gold-fields of Cibao on the sixth day of his journey, where very shortly after his arrival some Indians had panned gold from a stream, which they had also done at many other places of this same province. He affirmed it was very rich in gold. On receiving this news, the Admiral, who had now recovered from his sickness, was greatly delighted and decided to land in order to examine the nature of the country and decide on a course of action.

On Wednesday, 12 March 1494, he left Isabela for Cibao in order to see these goldfields with all his men that were fit, both foot and horsemen, leaving a good guard on the two ships and three caravels, all that remained of his fleet. He had had all the shot and weapons of the other ships put aboard his flagship, so that no one could raise a revolt in the others, as many had plotted to do while he was ill. For many had come on this voyage with the idea that the moment they landed they would load themselves with gold and would im-mediately be rich men (though in fact where gold is found it takes pains, time and industry to seek and collect it) and as things had not succeeded for them according to their hopes they were discontented. This exasperated them, as did also the labour of building the town; they were exhausted too by sickness due to the nature of this new country, the climate and the food. They had been plotting in secret to renounce the Admiral's authority and after taking the remaining ships to return in them to Castile. The chief instigator of the plot was a court official named Bernal de Pisa, who had joined the expedition as accountant for their Catholic Majesties, and when the Admiral learnt of the plot, out of respect for them he punished him only by imprisoning him in the ship, intending to return him to Castile with a list of his crimes: both his attempted revolt and certain libels written against the Admiral which were found in a secret place.

After making these provisions and leaving persons both at sea and on shore, to attend jointly with his brother Don Diego* the discipline and safety of the fleet, he continued his journey to Cibao. He took with him all the tools and other things necessary for building a fort, with which to keep that country at peace, and the Christians who went to look for gold safe from any harm or offence that the Indians might attempt against them.

In order to intimidate the Indians further and deprive them of all hope that they might be able to repeat in the Admiral's presence what they had done at Navidad in his absence to Arana and the thirty-eight settlers, he took with him all the Spaniards he could. Thus the Indians in their villages would see and recognize the Christians' power and realize that if they were to harm a single one of them travelling alone in that country there would be a great force of men ready to punish them. As a greater display of his might, on leaving Isabela and all the other places he came to, he drew up his men in military formation as if marching to war, fully armed with trumpets sounding and banners displayed.

On marching out of Isabela, he crossed the river which was a gun-shot away and another smaller stream a league further on; and from there went to spend the night at a village three leagues away on a plain with fine level fields stretching up to a rough pass two crossbow shots† high which he called the Puerto de los Hidalgos, in honour of the gentlemen who went ahead to see that the way was clear. This was the first pass ever cleared in the Indies, because the Indians only make their paths wide enough for one man travelling on foot. After crossing this pass he came to a great plain, across which he marched five leagues on the following day. He slept the night

*Columbus had summoned this younger brother (born 1468) from Italy on his return from the first voyage.

†A crossbow could shoot about 300 yards.

beside a great river, which his men crossed in large and small canoes. This river, which he called the Rio de las Canas, flowed into the sea near Monte Christi.

On his journey he passed many Indian villages with round houses thatched with straw. The doors are so low that you have to bend to get in. On entering these houses, the Indians whom the Admiral brought from Isabela promptly seized anything that pleased them and the owners showed no sign of resentment. They seemed to hold all possessions in common. Similarly, whenever any of the natives went up to a Christian, they took from him whatever they liked, in the belief that similar customs obtained among us. But they were quickly undeceived when they saw that this was not the case. In the course of their journey the Christians passed through woods full of most beautiful trees, among which they saw wild vines, aloe trees, wild cinammon and some others which bear a fruit like a fig; these have very stout trunks and leaves like an apple tree and are said to produce scammony.*

CHAPTER 52

The Admiral marches to Cibao, where he finds the goldfields and builds the fort of Santo Tomas

ON Friday, 14 March, the Admiral left the Rio de las Canas and a league and a half further on found another large river, which he called the Rio del Oro, because as they crossed it they picked up some grains of gold. On reaching the other side with some difficulty, he came to a large village, a great number of whose inhabitants rushed out into the woods; the rest fortified themselves in their houses, barring the doors with

*A purgative oil produced by a quite different plant in Asia Minor.

crossed canes as if these formed a great defence and would prevent anyone from entering. According to their customs, no one will enter a door that is barred in this way, for they have no doors of wood or other material with which to shut themselves in and these canes seem to suffice. From here the Admiral went on to another most beautiful river, which he named the Rio Verde, the banks of which were covered with round shining pebbles. Here he spent the night.

Continuing his journey next day he passed through some large villages, whose inhabitants also had barred their doors with crossed sticks. Since the Admiral and his men were tired, they spent the next night at the foot of a rough wooded pass, which he called the Puerto de Cibao, about eleven leagues beyond the first mountain pass he had come to. The land is on the whole flat and the general direction of the road is to the south. On setting out next day, they followed a track along which the leading horses had difficulty in passing. From this place the Admiral sent some mules back to Isabela to fetch wine and bread, for they were already running short of food and the journey was proving long. Their hardships were increased by the fact that they were not yet accustomed to eating the food of the Indians, as people do now who live and travel in these parts. Indeed, they find the native food easier to digest and more suitable to the climate of the country than that which is brought from Spain, although it is not as nourishing.

On Sunday, 16 March, the men returned with the food, and the Admiral, having crossed the mountain, entered the district of Cibao, which is rough and craggy, full of stony places and patches of grass, and watered by many rivers in which gold is found. The further they went, the rougher and more mountainous the country became, and in the streams they found grains of gold. For, as the Admiral says, the rain washed it down from the mountain tops in small grains. This province

is as large as Portugal and throughout there are many gold-fields* and much gold in the rivers. But generally there are few trees, and these are found on the river-banks. The majority of them are pines and palms of various sorts.

As has been said, Ojeda had already travelled through this country, and from him the Indians had received news of the Christians. Hence it was that wherever the Admiral went the Indians came out on the paths to receive him with presents of food and some quantity of gold grains which they had gathered on learning that this was what he had come for. Reflecting that he had come eighteen leagues from Isabela and all the land through which he had travelled was very rough, the Admiral ordered the building of a fort on a strong and pleasant site. This he called the fort of Santo Tomas.† It was intended to dominate the region of the goldfields and to be a place of safety for Christians going to them.

In this new fort he stationed Pedro Margarit, a man of great authority, with fifty-six men, among whom were experts in all crafts necessary for the construction of the fort, which was built of earth and timber – strong enough materials to resist any number of Indians who might attack. Here they dug the ground to sow seeds and on gathering certain rocks to line the ditches found at a depth of about six feet nests made of

---

* There were no goldfields in Cibao and very little gold. Ojeda had reported goldfields, and Dr Chanca, although generally a careful witness, took this report on trust. Columbus also believed it and on this legendary gold of Cibao the whole belief in the riches of Hispaniola was founded. Nevertheless, Hernando repeats his father's original optimistic tales about the wealth of Cibao. In fact, Hispaniola was rich in nothing but potential slaves and it was on the slave trade that Columbus, despite the disapproval of the Catholic sovereigns, founded his hopes. He had already made a proposal in the letter that he entrusted to Antonio de Torres for the importation of slaves captured in war.

† He is said to have chosen this name in order to confute the doubting Thomases who (more or less rightly) said there was no gold in Cibao.

clay and straw, containing in place of eggs three or four round stones each the size of a large orange which seemed to have been made purposely as cannon balls. They were much astonished by these. In the river which flows at the foot of the hill where they had built their fort, they found some most beautiful marble stones of various colours (some of them large); also some pieces of jasper.

CHAPTER 53

The Admiral returns to Isabela and finds the whole land very fertile

WHEN the Admiral had done everything possible to ensure the strength of his fort, he returned on Thursday, 21 March, to Isabela, and when he reached the Rio Verde met mules coming with more food. He was unable to cross the river on account of the heavy rains, and remained there, sending the food on to the fort. At the same time he looked for fords by which he could cross that river and the Rio del Oro, which is greater than the Ebro, and stopped for some days in the Indian villages, eating their cassava bread and peppers, which were both good and cheap. On Saturday, 29 March, he came back to Isabela, where they had grown melons ripe enough to eat, although the seed had only been sown two months before. Cucumbers also were grown in twenty days, and a wild vine of the country though not fully grown had produced good, large bunches of grapes.

The next day, 30 March, a farmer gathered ears from wheat which had only been sown at the end of January. They also gathered chick-peas bigger than the stock from which they were grown. The seeds of all the plants they sowed came up in

three days and on the twenty-fifth day were ready to eat. Fruit stones produced seedlings and vine shoots produced tendrils, both in seven days, and unripe grapes could be gathered in twenty-five. Sugar cane germinated in seven days also. All this was attributable to the mildness of the climate, which was much like that of our own country, being cool rather than hot, but also to the rains in these parts, which are very cold, light and good for growth.

The Admiral was delighted with the nature of the climate, and with the fertility and people of the country. On Tuesday, 1 April, however, there came a messenger sent by Pedro Margarit from the fort of Santo Tomas, where he had been left as captain, with news that the Indians of the district were fleeing from their villages and that a *cacique* called Caonabo was preparing to come and burn the fort. But the Admiral, knowing that these Indians were cowards, did not make much of this rumour, especially as he trusted in the horses, of which the Indians were much afraid, fearing that they would eat them. In fact, they were in such dread of horses that they dare not enter any building in which one of them was. But as an added precaution the Admiral decided to send more men and food, for he intended to go in the three caravels remaining, to discover the mainland, and thought it wise to ensure the complete peace and security of the island. On Wednesday, 2 April, he sent seventy men to the fort with food and munitions, twenty-five of them for defence and the rest to help in the construction of a new road, for on the original road it was difficult to cross the river fords.

These men set out, and while the ships were being prepared to start on a new voyage of discovery, the Admiral attended to all the necessary planning of the town he was founding. He divided it into streets with a convenient central square and endeavoured to bring the river to it in a broad canal, for which he would construct a dam that would also serve to drive mills.

For since the town was almost a cannon shot away from the river it would have been very difficult for the population to draw water from such a great distance, the more so since the majority of the people were very weak and enervated by the thinness of the air, which did not suit them. In fact, they suffered from various sicknesses; what is more they had no provisions from Spain except biscuits and wine, since the captains of the ships had failed to look after their stores, and they do not keep as well in that country as in ours. And although they received plenty of victuals from the Indians, these disagreed with them badly, since they were not used to them. For this reason the Admiral had decided not to leave more than 300 men on the island, and to send the rest back to Castile, since he considered this number sufficient to keep it at peace and obedient to the rule of the Catholic sovereigns. And because by this time the biscuit was used up and they had wheat but no flour, he decided to construct mills; but there was no spate of water to drive them within a league and a half of the town.

In order to hurry the workmen on this job and all the others, the Admiral had himself to supervise them, for they all tried to avoid work. He decided to send everyone who was fit except the master craftsmen and workers to march through the Vega Real in order to pacify it and strike fear into the Indians and also gradually to accustom his men to the local food, because the stores they had brought from Castile were diminishing every day. He put Hojeda in command of this force to remain so until they reached Santo Tomas, when he was to hand over his men to Pedro Margarit, who was to lead them on a further march through the country. Hojeda was then to remain behind as commander of the fort, because he had exhausted himself in the previous winter exploring the province of Cibao (which in the Indian language means 'stony').

Hojeda left Isabela on Wednesday, 9 April, on his way to Santo Tomas with all the men given to him (amounting to more than 400) and immediately after crossing the Rio del Oro seized the *cacique* of the district and a brother and nephew and sent them in chains to the Admiral. He took one of their chieftains too and had one of his ears cut off in the centre of his village because of his treatment of three Christians on their way from Isabela to Santo Tomas; this chieftain had lent them five Indians to carry their clothing across the river ford, and when the Christians were half-way across these Indians had run off to his village with their clothes and the *cacique* instead of punishing their crime had taken the clothing for himself and refused to return it. The *cacique* who ruled on the other side of the river, however, relying on the services he had rendered to the Christians, decided to accompany the prisoners to Isabela and intercede for them with the Admiral. The Admiral received him politely and ordered that the Indians with their hands tied should be sentenced to death by public proclamation. The good *cacique* wept at the sight and their lives were granted him, the guilty Indians promising by signs that they would never commit another crime.

No sooner had the Admiral set these Indians at liberty than a horseman from Santo Tomas arrived with bad news. On passing through the town of the *cacique* who had been made prisoner he had found that this man's subjects had seized five Christians on their way back from Santo Tomas to Isabela. Arriving suddenly on his horse he had terrified the Indians and freed his fellow-Christians, putting more than 500 of the natives to flight, and wounding two of them in the chase. He said that on reaching the further side of the river he had seen the Indians coming back to attack the Christians, but when they saw his horse they had again run away, terrified that the creature might fly back across the river.

THE SECOND VOYAGE OF COLUMBUS
(Second Map)

Miles 0 20 40 60 80 100

Archipelago de
los Canarreos

Isla de
Evangelista

Santa
Marta

Jardin de la Reina

Cabo de la Cruz

C U B A

Montego Bay

Rio Bueno

JAMAICA

Cabo del
Farol

Portland Bight

Santiago Bay

Puerto Grande

C. San
Nicolas

C. San Miguel

La Navidad

Isabela

Beata I.

HISPANIOLA

Mona
(Amona)

CHAPTER 54

Having settled matters on Hispaniola the Admiral
sets out to explore the island of Cuba, which he
supposes to be the mainland

HAVING decided to go and explore the mainland, the
Admiral formed a council to take his place and govern the
island for him. This council consisted of his brother Don
Diego Colon, with the title of President; Father Buil and
Pedro Hernandez Coronel, as regents; Alfonso Sanchez de
Carvajal, a magistrate from Baeza, and Juan de Lujan, a
gentleman of Madrid and servant of the Catholic sovereigns.

In order that the people should not be left short of flour, he
took great pains to have the mills finished, although the rains
and the great swelling of the rivers made this very difficult.
These rains, says the Admiral, were the cause of the humidity,
and consequently of the fertility of this island, whose trees
were so marvellously rich that the Spaniards were still eating
their fruit in November. In fact, they produced a crop in that
month from which the Admiral concluded that they bore
two crops a year. Wheats and grasses bear flowers and fruit
continuously, and all through the year birds' nests are to be
found in the trees with eggs and fledglings. The general
fertility of the island was so great that news came in every
day of fresh riches. For every day men returned from different
parts with news of mines that had been discovered, and in
addition accounts were brought by Indians of great quantities
of gold to be found in various parts of the island.

But not content with this the Admiral decided to resume
his discoveries along the coast of Cuba. He was uncertain
whether it was an island or not.* Setting out with three ships

* On his first voyage, Columbus had accepted the natives' statement

on Thursday, 24 April, he raised sail immediately after dinner and anchored that night at Monte Christi, to the west of Isabela. On Friday he reached Guacanagari's harbour, believing he would meet the *cacique* there. But as soon as he saw the ships Guacanagari fled in fear; his subjects, however, stated untruthfully that he would very soon be back. The Admiral did not wish to stop unless for important reasons, and left on Saturday, 26 April, for the island of Tortuga, which lies six leagues further west. He passed the night near the island in a great calm with his sails spread. The sea was choppy on account of the currents. Next day, with a north-wester blowing and the currents flowing from the west, he was forced to return eastwards and anchored in the river Guadalquivir, in this same island, to wait for a wind to counteract the currents. Both then and on his first voyage in the previous year, he had met with very strong eastward currents in these parts.

On Tuesday, 29 April, in good weather, he reached the port of San Nicolas and from there made for Cuba, the southern coast of which he began to follow. When he had sailed a league past Cabo Fuerte, he entered a large bay which he called Puerto Grande. The entrance was very deep and 150 yards wide. Here he cast anchor and they made a meal of baked fish and hutias,* of which the Indians have great quantities. On the following day, which was 1 May, he left this place and sailed along the coast, on which he found very convenient harbours, most beautiful rivers and very high wooded hills, and in the sea, ever since leaving the island of

---

that Cuba was a very large island. However, he was most anxious to identify Hispaniola with Chipangu or Japan, as described by Marco Polo. So if Hispaniola were indeed Japan, then in defiance of all probability – for he had sailed some distance along its north and south coasts– Cuba *must* be the mainland of Asia. As will be seen, Columbus clung to this belief as long as he could.

*A kind of edible rat.

Tortuga, he found great quantities of that weed which he had met in the ocean on his way from and to Spain. As he sailed along the coast many natives of the island came out to the ships in canoes, believing that our people had come down from the sky. They brought us their bread, water and fish, which they gave us gladly, asking for nothing in return. But in order to leave them happy, the Admiral ordered that everything should be paid for and gave them glass beads, hawks' bells, little brass bells and suchlike.

CHAPTER 55

The Admiral discovers the island of Jamaica

On Saturday, 3 May, the Admiral decided to go from Cuba to Jamaica, not wanting to pass this island without discovering whether the reports of much gold there, which he had heard in all the other islands, were true. And in good weather he sighted it on the next day, Sunday, while still half-way there. On Monday he anchored close to it and it seemed to him the most beautiful island of any he had seen in the Indies. An amazing number of natives came out in canoes great and small.

Next day, wishing to examine the harbours, the Admiral went down the coast and, when the boats went out to sound the harbour entrances, so many canoes came with armed warriors to defend the land that they were obliged to put back to the ships, not so much out of fear of the Indians as from reluctance to break friendly relations. But on reflecting that if they seemed afraid they would increase the pride and confidence of the natives they turned to another harbour on the island, which the Admiral called Puerto Bueno. And when

the Indians came out from there also, and hurled their spears, the crews of the boats fired such a volley from their cross-bows that the natives were compelled to retire with six or seven wounded. Once the fight was over great numbers of canoes came out very peaceably, from neighbouring villages, bringing to the ships various foods and other articles for sale and barter. These they exchanged for the smallest trinket.

In this harbour, which is shaped like a horseshoe, repairs were made to the Admiral's ship, whose timbers had sprung and were letting water. When the leak was repaired, on Friday, 8 May, sail was raised and they continued down the coast westwards so close to the land that the Indians followed in their canoes, anxious to barter and to possess some of our trinkets.

As the winds were somewhat contrary, the Admiral could not make as much headway as he wished and on Tuesday, 13 May, decided to return to Cuba in order to follow its southern coast. He was resolved not to turn back until he had sailed five or six hundred leagues and made certain whether it was island or mainland.

Just as the ships were putting to sea a very young Indian came out and said he wanted to go to Castile. He was followed by many of his relatives and other people in canoes, who begged him most insistently to return to the island, but they could not deflect him from his purpose. Indeed, to avoid the tears and groans of his brothers he hid in a place where no one could see him. The Admiral was amazed at this Indian's persistence and ordered that he should be well treated.

CHAPTER 56

The Admiral returns from Jamaica and follows
the coast of Cuba in the belief that it is
the mainland

ON leaving the island of Jamaica, on Wednesday, 14 May, the Admiral reached a cape on the coast of Cuba which he named Santa Cruz. As he followed the coast he was overtaken by a heavy thunderstorm with terrible lightning which put him in great danger. His difficulties were increased by the many shallows and narrow channels which he found, and he was compelled to seek safety from these two dangers which demanded opposite remedies. To protect himself from the storm he should have lowered the sails; to get out of the shallows he had to keep them spread. Indeed, if his difficulties had continued for eight or ten leagues he would never have escaped.

But the worst thing of all was that the further he sailed along this coast to the north and north-east the more low islets they found. Though they saw large trees on some, the rest were sandbanks which scarcely rose above water level. These islets were about a league round, some larger and some smaller. But in actual fact, the nearer they came to Cuba the higher and more beautiful these islets were. Since it would have been useless and difficult to give a name to each one, the Admiral called them collectively El Jardin de la Reina. But if they saw many islands that day, they saw even more on the next and they were on the whole bigger than those they had sighted before. They lay not only to the north-east, but also to the north-west and to the south-west. That day they sighted as many as 160 of these islets, which were divided by deep channels through which the ships sailed.

On some of these islands they saw cranes of the size and

kind of those of Spain but scarlet in colour. On others they saw a great number of turtles and turtle eggs which are like hen's eggs, though their shells are very hard. The turtles lay these eggs in holes which they make in the sand. These they cover and leave until the heat of the sun hatches the young turtles, which grow with time to the size of a buckler and some to the size of a large shield. They also saw on these islands crows and cranes like those of Spain; also goosanders and great numbers of small birds, which sang most sweetly, and the air that blew from the land was so soft that they seemed to be in a rose garden full of the most delightful scents in the world. Nevertheless as we have said navigation was extremely dangerous, for the channels were so many that it took them a long time to find their way out.

In one of these channels they saw a canoe, with Indian fishermen who remained calm and unperturbed, motionlessly awaiting the boat's approach, and when it came close they signed to it to wait a little until they had finished their fishing. Their way of fishing appeared so odd and strange to our men that they complied with this request. Their method is this: they tie thin cord to the tails of certain fishes which we call 'remora' and send these after the other fish. These remora have a rough patch on their heads which extends down the spine and attaches itself to any other fish that comes near. When the Indian feels that the other fish has stuck he pulls on the cord and brings the two fish out together; and our men saw these fishermen bring out a turtle to whose neck this fish had attached itself. They generally attach themselves to the neck of their victims, since in this way they are certain not to be bitten. I have seen them cling in this way to big sharks. After the Indians in the canoe had pulled the turtle aboard and two fish that they had caught previously, they came very peacefully to the boat to see what our men wanted.

At the Christians' request they came with them to the ships

where the Admiral treated them very courteously. He learnt
from them that there were a great number of islands in that
sea. They willingly offered the Christians everything they
had, but the Admiral would not have anything taken from
them except this fish, for they had nothing else but nets, hooks
and the gourds in which they carried their drinking water.
Having given them a few small objects he sent them off very
happy and continued on his course. But he did not intend to
follow it much further, since he was now running short of
victuals. If he had still had plenty he would not have returned
to Spain, except by way of the East.

The Admiral was utterly exhausted both by poor food
and because he had not taken off his clothes or slept in his
bunk from the day he left Spain to 19 May, and at the time
when he wrote this he had been sleepless for eight nights on
account of a severe illness. On previous voyages he had sustained great difficulties, but on this voyage they were twice as
severe, because of the large number of islands through which
they were sailing. They were so many indeed that on Wednesday, 20 May, he saw seventy-one for the first time and in
addition many more which appeared in the sunset to the
west-south-west. These islands and shallows are very dangerous on account of their numbers, for they appear on all sides,
but even more so because of the thick mist which rises every
evening and muffles the eastern sky. This mist appears to
threaten a heavy hailstorm and is accompanied by severe
thunder and lightning, but when the moon rises it all vanishes,
partially breaking up in rain and wind. This is so common a
happening in these parts that not only did it occur every
evening during the Admiral's voyage there, but I also saw it
myself in those islands in the year 1503 on the way back from
the discovery of Veragua.* The prevailing wind at night is
from the north, since it blows off the island of Cuba, and

* On the fourth voyage.

175

when the sun has risen it changes to the east and follows the sun until at sunset it blows from the west.

CHAPTER 57

The Admiral suffers great hardships and perils
sailing among the many islands

FOLLOWING his course westwards through great numbers of islands, on Thursday, 22 May, the Admiral reached one a little larger than the rest, which he named the island of Santa Marta. On it was a village, but when they landed they found that all the Indians had left it and no one remained to talk to the Christians. They found nothing in the houses except fish, the sole food of these Indians, and a number of mastiff-like dogs which also live on fish. So without speaking to anyone or seeing anything of note the Admiral continued his voyage north-eastwards through many other islands, in which were many scarlet cranes, parrots and other birds and dogs like those in the village and vast quantities of that weed that they had found on the sea during the first voyage of discovery. The Admiral was much exhausted by having to steer among all these islands and shallows, for no sooner did he make course for the west than he had to veer either north or south according to the disposition of the channels. Despite all his care and precautions in sounding the bottom and keeping a look-out in the rigging to observe the depth, the ship very often ran aground, which was unavoidable since there were so many shoals everywhere.

Nevertheless, sailing in this fashion he once more landed on the island of Cuba, to take aboard water, of which he was very short. But although the place where they landed was

too thickly wooded for them to make out any village, a sailor who landed with a crossbow to kill some beasts or birds in the woods met thirty Indians armed with their usual weapons; that is to say spears, and those sticks which they carry in place of swords and call *macanas*. The sailor reported that he had seen one of them wearing a white robe which reached to his knees, and two others who had robes down to the ground. All three were as white as ourselves. However, he had been unable to hold any conversation with them, for being afraid of their great numbers he had started shouting to his companions and the Indians had taken flight, and had not returned.

Although the Admiral sent men ashore next day to discover the truth of the sailor's story they were not able to go more than half a league owing to the great thickness of the trees and vegetation and because the whole of that coast was swampy and full of mud patches from the beach to the hills and mountains, which rose some two leagues inland. So all they saw were the traces of fishermen and some cranes of the Spanish kind but larger.

Sailing on a further ten leagues westwards they saw houses on the beach from which some canoes put out with water and the food these Indians eat and brought it to the Christians, who paid well for everything. The Admiral had one of these Indians seized, saying to him and his comrades, through an interpreter, that as soon as he had shown the Spaniards their course and given them some information about the country, they would free him and let him go home. The Indian was quite content with this and told the Admiral as a positive fact that Cuba was an island and that the king or *cacique* of the western part only spoke to his subjects by signs, which they obeyed promptly doing everything he commanded.* The Indian said that the water was shallow and full

* This was probably true. The original inhabitants of the island were Siboney, who were related to the Indians of Florida and they had been

of islands all along this coast, which proved to be the case. For next day, which was 11 June, in order to bring the ship from one channel into another deeper one, the Admiral had to have it towed with ropes over a sandbank where there was not a fathom of water and which was two ship-lengths wide. Drawing closer to Cuba in this way they saw turtles three to four feet long in such vast numbers that they covered the sea. Afterwards, at dawn, they saw a cloud of birds so numerous that they darkened the sun; these flew towards the island from the open sea and settled a little way inland. Various doves and other kinds of birds were seen also. And next day such a swarm of butterflies flew out to the ship that they filled the air. They stayed right through the day but were dispersed at evening by a heavy shower of rain.

CHAPTER 58

The Admiral turns back towards Hispaniola

SEEING that the coast of Cuba stretched much further to the west and that navigation remained extremely difficult owing to the great number of islands and shoals which he found everywhere, and since food was beginning to run out, the Admiral saw that he could not continue the voyage according to his intention. On Friday, 13 June, therefore, he decided to turn back to Hispaniola and the town which he had left, still hardly begun. To stock himself with water and firewood he put in to the Isla de Evangelista, which is thirty leagues in circumference and 700 leagues from the first landfall at Dominico.

conquered and enslaved by the Arawaks, who were akin to various tribes of South America and would have had an entirely different language from that of their slaves.

When he had taken aboard all that he needed he directed his course southwards in the hope of finding a better way out in that direction. Choosing the channel which seemed to him clearest of shoals, he followed it for some leagues but found it blocked. This greatly frightened and depressed the crew, who saw themselves almost entirely surrounded by shoals and without either food or comfort. But the Admiral, being a man of prudence and courage and seeing that his men were in a weak state, said with an appearance of optimism that he gave thanks to God for compelling him to return by the way he had come, since if they had continued along their initial course they might well have got into waters from which it would have been very difficult to sail out. They might then be so short of food and the ships be so damaged that they would be unable to sail back, which they could now easily do. Thus, all were comforted and satisfied and he returned to the island of Evangelista, where he had recently taken aboard water.

On Wednesday, 25 June, he sailed from here to the northwest in the direction of certain islets which they had seen about five leagues away. A little further on they came into a sea so full of green and white patches that it seemed one great shallows, though it actually had a depth of three fathoms. He sailed through this for seven leagues till he came to another sea as white as milk, which greatly perturbed him, for the water was very cloudy. This sea baffled everyone; it seemed to all who saw it to be nothing but shallows, without sufficient depth for the ships, although in fact there were three fathoms of water. After sailing through this sea for about four leagues, he came to another, as black as ink, which had a depth of five fathoms, and he sailed through this till he reached Cuba.

From here he sailed eastwards with only very slight winds, through channels between sandbanks. On 30 June, while he was writing the log of his voyage, his ship ran aground so violently that they could not pull her off by the anchors or

cables. By God's grace, however, they were able to tow her off by the bow, though she had sustained great damage from striking the sand. Having got off finally with God's help, he sailed, in so far as the winds and shallows allowed him, through seas that remained white and had a depth of two fathoms, which neither increased nor grew less except when they came close to one or another of the banks, when it had hardly any depth at all. On top of these difficulties, they met every day at sunset with violent squalls of rain, which blew down from the hills on the further side of the lagoons which border the sea. They were greatly afflicted and troubled by these until they reached the eastern coast of Cuba, along which they had sailed on their outward voyage. From here, as when they had passed before, there blew a scent as of the sweetest flowers.

On 7 July he landed and heard mass. Here an old *cacique*, who was ruler of that province, came up and listened attentively. When the mass was finished, he indicated by signs, as best he could, that it was a very good thing to give thanks to God, since if the soul was good it went straight to heaven and the body remained on earth and that the souls of wicked men must surely go to hell. Among other things, he said that he had been in the island of Hispaniola, where he knew the Indian chieftains, and also in Jamaica; and had travelled a great deal in the west of Cuba, where the local *cacique* dressed like a priest.

CHAPTER 59

*The great hardships and sufferings of the Admiral
and his crew. They return to Jamaica*

AFTER leaving this place on Wednesday, 16 July, to the accompaniment of great winds and squalls of rain, he made for

the Cabo de la Cruz in Cuba. On his way he was suddenly assailed by so violent a rain storm and such heavy squalls that the ship was almost submerged. But, thanks be to God, they were able quickly to strike sail and anchor with all their heaviest anchors. Nevertheless, so much water entered the ship through the bottom planks that the sailors could not get it out with the pumps, for they were all weak and exhausted from shortage of food. Their daily ration was a pound of rotten biscuit and a pint of wine, no more; and if they were lucky enough to catch a fish, they could not keep it from one day to the next, for victuals in those parts are more perishable and the heat is always greater than in our country. This short supply of food being shared by all, the Admiral wrote in his log: 'I receive the same ration myself. Pray God that it be in His service and in that of your Highnesses. Otherwise I would never subject myself to these hardships and dangers. Every day we seem about to be engulfed by death.'

Through these hardships and dangers he came to Cabo de la Cruz on 18 July, where he was welcomed by the Indians, who brought him plenty of their cassava bread, which they make from grated roots, much fish and a great quantity of fruit and other things that they eat. Finding no favourable winds for a return to Hispaniola, on Tuesday, 22 July, the Admiral crossed to Jamaica and sailed westwards along its coast, close to the land, which was most beautiful and fertile. It has fine harbours at a league's distance from one another, and the whole coast is thick with villages, whose inhabitants followed the ships in their canoes, bringing their habitual foods, which the Christians greatly preferred to those they had eaten on other islands.

The skies, temperatures and climate here were like those of all the other islands. In this western part of Jamaica at dusk every day a great cloud forms from which rain falls for more or less an hour. The Admiral says that he attributes this to the

great forests and trees of that country and that he knew this by his experience of the Canaries, Madeira and the Azores, where they have felled many of the trees which were once so thick, and the clouds and rain are not now so heavy as they were.

The Admiral sailed on, though with constant headwinds, which compelled him to shelter every night in the lee of the coast. The land continued to be so green and pleasant, so fertile and rich in food, and so thickly populated that he considered it unrivalled by any other, especially the part that bordered a channel which he called de las Vacas, since it had seven islets close to land. He writes that the land here is as high as any he has seen and that he believes he has emerged from the climatic zone that produces the storms. Nevertheless it is all very thickly populated and most beautiful and fertile.

He considered that this island would be about 800 miles in circumference, though when he had discovered it all it proved to be no more than twenty leagues in breadth and fifty in length. Entranced by its beauties, he was seized by the desire to stay there and discover its qualities in detail. But the food shortage of which we have spoken and the great amount of water still not pumped out of the ships prevented him from doing so. So, as soon as he had a little good weather, he sailed away eastwards and, losing sight of this island, on Tuesday, 19 August, set course for Hispaniola. He called the easternmost cape on the southern coast of Jamaica, Cabo del Farol.

CHAPTER 60

The Admiral explores the southern part of
Hispaniola, and returns eastwards to Isabela

ON Wednesday, 20 August, the Admiral sighted the western point of Hispaniola, which he named the Cabo de San Miguel

and which was thirty leagues from the eastern point of Jamaica. Owing to the ignorance of sailors, however, this cape is now known as the Cabo del Tiburon. At this cape, on Saturday, 23 August, a *cacique* came to the boats and hailed the Admiral by name. But he knew more about him than his name, which proved that the place was part of Hispaniola.

At the end of August the Admiral anchored at an island which he called Alto Velo and, since he had lost sight of the other two ships which he had in convoy, he had some men landed on this island. For it was so high they could see very far from it in all directions. But they did not see either of his ships. As they returned to the ship, however, they killed eight seals that were sleeping on the beach. They also took many pigeons and other birds. For, since the island was uninhabited and these creatures were not used to the sight of men, it was possible to kill them with sticks.

They killed more on the two following days, while waiting for the two ships which had been missing since the previous Friday. After six days, however, these returned and the three ships together sailed to the island of Beata, which lies twelve leagues east of Alto Velo. Here they coasted beside a pleasant plain, which ran back a mile from the sea and which was so thickly populated that it seemed like one large town a league in length. The whole plain was seen to stretch for three leagues from east to west. When the people of the island observed the Christians' approach, they came out in their canoes to the caravels with news that some other Christians from Isabela had visited them, and that they were all well. The Admiral was greatly delighted by this news; and in order that the settlers at Isabela should learn that he and his men were safe and had returned, when he had gone a little further to the east, he sent nine men to cross the island to Isabela by way of the forts of Santo Tomas and Magdalena. As he with his three ships followed the coast eastwards, he sent the boats ashore

to take water at a beach where he saw a large village. The Indians came out to meet the Spaniards, armed with bows and poisoned arrows and carrying cords, with which, as they showed by signs, they intended to bind any Christians they might capture. But as soon as the boats came ashore, these Indians threw down their arms and offered to bring bread, water and anything else they had, and asked in their language for the Admiral.

As they continued on their voyage, the Admiral and his men saw a fish in the sea as big as a whale. It had a large shell on its back, like that of a turtle, and kept its head, which was the size of a barrel, out of the water. It had a tail like that of a tunny fish, very long with a large fin on either side. By the presence of this fish and by other signs, the Admiral judged that the weather was about to change, and began to look for a harbour in which to take refuge.

On 15 September, by God's will, he sighted an island lying off the eastern coast of Hispaniola and close to it, which the Indians call Adamaney. The storm had now blown up, and he cast anchor in the channel between this island and Hispaniola, near an island that lies between them. Here, when night fell, they saw an eclipse of the moon, by which he calculated that the distance between Cadiz and his anchorage at the time was five hours, twenty-three minutes. I believe that this eclipse was the reason for the long spell of bad weather which compelled him to remain in that channel until the 20th of the month, in some fear for the other two ships, which had not been able to enter. But God was pleased to save them. When the fleet was reunited on 24 September he sailed on to the most eastern point of Hispaniola, and from there to a small island lying between Hispaniola and San Juan, which the Indians called Amona.

From this point the Admiral ceased to record the voyage in his log-book. He does not say how he returned to Isabela, but

only notes that he sailed from the island of Amona to San Juan. The reason for this was his exhaustion from the great hardships he had suffered and his weakness from lack of food. He was afflicted by a serious illness, something between an infectious fever and a lethargy, which suddenly blinded him, dulled his other senses and took away his memory.*

Owing to the Admiral's illness, the men of all three ships decided to abandon the enterprise of exploring the Carib islands and to return to Isabela, which they reached in five days, on 29 September. Here God was pleased to restore the Admiral's health, although the illness did not entirely abate for five months. It was generally attributed to the hardships he had undergone on his voyage and to his very weak state. For he had sometimes spent a whole week without so much as three hours' sleep, a thing which would have appeared impossible if he had not himself noted it in his log-book.

CHAPTER 61

The Admiral reduces Hispaniola to submission.
His methods of making it profitable

ON returning from his expedition to Cuba and Jamaica the Admiral found that his brother, Bartolomé Colon, who had been his agent in his negotiations with the King of England, had arrived in Hispaniola. On returning to Castile with the completed agreement,† he learnt in Paris, from King Charles of France, that his brother had already discovered the Indies and had left him 100 escudos to pay for his journey. Although

* Morrison, in *Admiral of the Ocean Sea*, suggests that this is some form of nervous breakdown.

† In fact no agreement was concluded.

on receiving the news he hastened to meet the Admiral in Spain, by the time of his arrival he had already left Seville with his seventeen ships.

In order to arrange certain matters which his brother had left in his charge, Bartolomé immediately went, at the beginning of the year 1494, to see the Catholic sovereigns, taking with him my brother Don Diego Colon and myself to serve as pages to that most serene prince Don Juan – may he dwell in glory! – at the command of the Catholic Queen Isabela, who was then at Valladolid. As soon as we arrived the King sent for my uncle Don Bartolomé and dispatched him to Hispaniola with three ships. Here he served for some years, as appears from an account written by him, which I found among his papers, and in which he says: 'I served as captain from 14 April 1494 to 12 March 1496, on which day the Admiral left for Castile. I then began my service as Governor, which lasted till 28 August 1498, on which day the Admiral sailed to discover Paria. On this day I resumed my service as captain, which lasted till 11 December 1500, when I returned to Castile.'

But let us return to the story of the Admiral's voyage back from Cuba. Finding his brother in Hispaniola he made him *adelantado*,* or governor, of the Indies. There was subsequently some difference of opinion about this, however, since the Catholic sovereigns said that they had not given the Admiral the right of appointment to such an office. In order to settle this difference amicably, the sovereigns granted Bartolomé the governorship anew; and so from that time onwards he was called *adelantado* of the Indies.

By his brother's advice, and with his help, the Admiral now took some rest and lived quietly, although he was still much

---

*Strictly the military governor of a frontier province. In fact the difference between *adelantado* and governor is one of title rather than office.

distressed both by his illness and by the fact that he had found all the Indians of the island in revolt, owing to the misconduct of Pedro Margarit, whom we have already mentioned. The Admiral had to consider and deal with the following situation: on departing for Cuba he had left this man in command of 360 foot and fourteen horsemen with instructions to patrol the island and reduce it to the service of the Catholic sovereigns and obedience to the Christians, especially the province of Cibao, from which the Admiral expected the greatest profit and found just the opposite. No sooner had he departed than Pedro Margarit left with all his people for the Vega Real, ten leagues from Isabela, making no efforts to control and pacify the island. On the contrary, by his fault quarrels and factions arose in Isabela. He tried to persuade the council, which the Admiral had formed there, to obey him, and most shamelessly sent them his orders.

On finding that he could not make himself supreme commander, he decided not to wait for the Admiral, to whom he would have to give a complete account of his office, and with his men boarded one of the first ships to come from Castile, in which he returned home without giving any account of himself or reducing the population to order according to his instructions. As a result every Spaniard went out among the Indians robbing and seizing their women wherever he pleased, and doing them such injuries that the Indians decided to take vengeance on any Spaniards they found isolated or unarmed. The *cacique* of Magdalena, whose name was Guatigana, killed ten Christians and secretly ordered the firing of a house in which forty men lay sick. On the Admiral's return, this *cacique* was severely punished. Although it was impossible to lay hands on *him*, some of his chieftains were seized and sent to Castile in the four ships which Antonio de Torres took home on 24 February 1495.

Six or seven other *caciques* were also punished for injuries

done to the Christians in various parts of the island. Indeed they had killed a great number, but would have killed many more if the Admiral had not arrived in time to prevent them. He found the island in a bad state: the Christians were committing innumerable outrages for which they were mortally hated by the Indians, and the Indians were refusing to return to obedience. All the *caciques* and kings had agreed not to resume obedience, and this agreement had not been difficult to obtain. For, as we have said, there were only four principal rulers under whose sovereignty all the rest lived.

The names of these kings were Caonabo, Higuanama, Behechio and Guarionex, each of whom ruled over seventy or eighty *caciques*, from whom they did not exact tribute or provisions, but who were obliged, when called upon, to aid them in their wars or sow their fields. Guacanagari, who was one of these, and ruler of the district in which the Spaniards had founded the town of Navidad, had remained friendly to them. As soon as he heard of the Admiral's coming, he visited him and said that he had not agreed to the plans of the other *caciques* or aided them, as the courtesy with which Christians had been treated by his people would testify, for there had always been about a hundred of them in his territory and they had always been welcomed and provided with all they needed, to the best of his ability. For this reason, the rest of the *caciques* were hostile to him, especially Behechio, who had killed one of his women, and Caonabo, who had stolen another. He requested the Admiral to have this woman returned to him and to help him revenge his other injuries. The Admiral accepted what he said as true and decided to do so. For he still wept every time he thought of the men who had been killed at Navidad, and mourned them as if they had been his own sons. He was encouraged in this resolution by the thought that the disagreements among the *caciques* themselves would facilitate the conquest of the country and the punishment of the

Indians for their rebellion and for the murder of the Christians.

On 24 March 1495, therefore, the Admiral left Isabela, prepared for war. He took with him as ally Guacanagari, who was most eager to conquer his enemies, although this might have seemed a very difficult undertaking, since they had assembled more than 100,000 Indians and the Admiral had with him 200 Christians, twenty horses and about the same number of hunting dogs.*

Knowing the nature and habits of these Indians, the Admiral divided his army with his brother, the *adelantado*, two days after they left Isabela. His intention was to make an attack from two different directions on the Indians, who were scattered about the fields, for he thought that fear on hearing the sound of firing from various sides would be more likely than anything else to put them to flight, as was effectually demonstrated by events. When the infantry squadrons of both armies had attacked the mass of Indians, and they had begun to break under the fire of muskets and crossbows, the cavalry and hunting dogs charged wildly upon them to prevent them re-forming. The Indians fled like cowards in all directions, and our men pursued them, killing so many and wreaking such havoc among them that, to be brief, by God's will victory was achieved, many Indians being killed and many others captured and executed. Caonabo, the principal king of all, was taken alive with his sons and women.

Caonabo confessed to the murder of twenty of the Christians who had remained with Arana in the town of Navidad on the Admiral's first voyage, when he discovered the Indies, and that afterwards, under pretence of friendship, he had come to spy out the town of Isabela, though the Christians had suspected his purpose in doing so: which was to see how best he

* These were used by the Spaniards not only for hunting, but for bringing down Indians.

could attack it and repeat what he had previously done at Navidad. About all this the Admiral had received complete knowledge from various informants; and it was to punish the king for this crime and for his subsequent rebellion and raising of the Indians that the Admiral had marched against him. Having captured Caonabo and one of his brothers, he sent them to Spain, since he did not want to execute justice on so important a person without the knowledge of the Catholic sovereigns. He contented himself with sentencing many of the most guilty.

After this victory and the capture of those *caciques*, the Christians' fortunes became extremely prosperous. Although they were no more than 630 in number, most of whom were sick and many of them women and children, in the space of a year, during which the Admiral travelled about the island without once having to unsheath his sword again, Hispaniola was reduced to such peace and obedience that all promised to pay tribute to the Catholic sovereigns every three months. That is to say: in the province of Cibao, where the goldfields lay, every person over the age of fourteen would pay a large bell-full of gold dust, and everywhere else twenty-five pounds of cotton. And in order that the Spaniards should know what person owed tribute, orders were given for the manufacture of discs of brass or copper, to be given to each every time he made payment, and to be worn around the neck. Consequently if any man was found without a disc, it would be known that he had not paid and he would be punished.

There is no doubt that these measures would have been successful had not quarrels broken out among the Christians, about which we shall speak later. After Caonabo's capture the region became so peaceful that a Christian could go anywhere he pleased alone and in complete safety. Indeed, the Indians would carry him on their shoulders in the way they carry letters, wherever it pleased him to go. The Admiral attributed

this peace to God's providence and the good fortune of the Catholic sovereigns and to no other cause, since he thought it impossible that 200 men, ill-armed and half of them sick, would have been sufficient to conquer such a multitude, if the Lord had not wished to bring them beneath His hand. In order to make it more patent that these marvellous victories and the conquest of these people were the work of His will and His mighty hand, and not the result of our strength and intelligence and the cowardice of the Indians, He had inflicted on the Christians shortage of food and severe illness, which reduced them to a third of their former strength. Even if our force had been stronger, the great number of Indians would certainly have been enough to outweigh any advantage they might have had.

CHAPTER 62

Certain things seen in the island of Hispaniola.
Description of the customs, ceremonies and religion
of the Indians

WHEN the people of the island had been pacified and were on better terms with our men, many unknown facts about the country were discovered: in particular that there were copper mines, sapphires, amber, brazil-wood, ebony, incense, cedars, many fine gums and various kinds of spices, which were in a wild state but could be greatly improved by cultivation. Among them was cinnamon of a fine colour, though bitter in flavour, ginger, red pepper, various kinds of evergreen mulberry for the silkworm, and many other useful trees and plants of which we have no knowledge in our lands.

Our men also learnt many other things about the customs

of the Indians that seemed to me worth mentioning in this history. I will begin on the subject of religion and copy the Admiral's own words, which are as follows:

'I have not been able to discover any idolatry or other religious belief among them. However, each of the many kings in Hispaniola and the other islands and on the mainland has his special house apart from the village. This house contains only wooden images carved in relief, and called by them *cemies*. Here there is no other activity except the service of the *cemies* and the Indians perform certain prayers and ceremonies here as we do in church. In these houses are highly carved tables, round in shape like a chopping table, on which lies a special powder which they place on the heads of their *cemies* with certain rites. They then sniff up this powder through a double-branched cane, which they place in their nostrils. This powder intoxicates them and they babble like drunkards, but none of our men understand the words they use.

'Each of these images has a name, and I think that some represent the father, others the grandfather and others both. Some houses contain more than one and some more than ten, commemorating, as I have said, various ancestors. I have noticed that they do not value all of them alike but pay more devotion and respect to some than to others, as we do on the occasion of religious processions. Each *cacique* and his people take pride in having better *cemies* than their neighbours. They conceal their visits to the *cemi* from the Christians and do not let them enter the image house. If they think that a Christian is coming they pick up the *cemies* and conceal them in the woods, fearing that the Christians will take them from them, since they have the ridiculous custom of stealing one another's *cemies*.

'It once happened when they were most suspicious of us that some Christians entered an image house with them. A *cemi* emitted a shout in words of their language, and this

revealed the fact that it was hollow. A hole had been cut in the lower part, into which a trumpet or speaking tube had been fitted, which communicated with a dark corner of the house obscured by branches. Behind these branches stood a servant who spoke whatever words the *cacique* wished, as we do through a speaking tube. Our men suspected this, kicked the *cemi* over and discovered the contrivance we have described. When the *cacique* saw that we had discovered the trick, he most insistently begged our men not to reveal it to his subjects or anyone else, since by this device he kept everyone obedient to him. We can therefore say there is some tinge of idolatry, at least in those who do not suspect the tricks and devices of their *caciques*, since they believe that it is the *cemi* that speaks and the deception is fairly general. The *cacique* alone knows and preserves their superstitious belief, by which he exacts all the tribute he desires from his people.

'Most of the *caciques* have also three stones, to which they and their people pay great devotion. They say that one of them is beneficial to the plants and grains they sow, another brings painless childbirth, and the third rain and sun when they are needed. I have sent your Highnesses three of these stones by Antonio de Torres, and I will bring another three myself.

'Their funeral rites are of various kinds. They prepare their *caciques* for the tomb by cutting open the body and drying it over a fire so as to preserve it entire. Of some common people they preserve only the head; others they bury in a grave, placing above the head bread and a gourd of water; and yet others they burn in the houses where they die. When they see a man on the point of death, they strangle him, and this is their practice with *caciques*. Others they carry out of the house, and yet others they place on hammocks or string beds, laying bread and water beside their heads. They then leave them and do not come back to see them again. When some men are gravely

sick, they take them to the *cacique*, who decides whether they should be strangled or not, and they do as he says.

'I have made strenuous efforts to discover what they know and believe about the place to which they go at death. I inquired particularly of Caonabo, the chief king of Hispaniola, a man of mature years, great knowledge and very lively intelligence. He and others answered that they go to a certain valley which each principal *cacique* imagines to lie in his own country. They state that here the dead meet their fathers and ancestors, eat, have wives and take their pleasure and consolation with them. This and other information I received from Fray Ramón Pane* who made inquiries on my behalf.'

CHAPTER 63

*The Admiral returns to Castile to give an account
of the island of Hispaniola to the Catholic
sovereigns*

To return to the principal thread of our narrative, I will say that, after pacifying the island and building the city of Isabela, small though it was, and three forts in the country, the Admiral decided to return to Spain to give an account to the Catholic sovereigns of many matters that he thought it to their advantage to know. This seemed to him particularly important because various wicked and libellous persons, prompted by envy, were continuously conveying to their Majesties false and spiteful stories concerning the state of the Indies, greatly to the prejudice and dishonour of the Admiral and his brothers.

*Fray Ramón Pane or Pan, a Spanish priest otherwise unknown, who drew up a considerable report on the manners and customs of the Indians.

Therefore on Thursday, 10 March 1496, he embarked with 225 Christians and thirty Indians. He raised sail shortly after dawn from the port of Isabela and beat about in an east wind, sailing up the coast with two caravels, the *Santa Cruz* and the *Niña*, in which he had made his voyage of discovery to Cuba. On Tuesday, 22 March, the eastern point of Hispaniola disappeared from his view, and he sailed eastwards as fast as the winds would let him. But since they blew principally from the east, he found himself on 6 April very short of provisions and his crew depressed and exhausted. So he decided to turn south and make for the Carib islands, which he reached three days later, anchoring at Maria Galante on Saturday, 9 April.

Next day, although it was his custom, if in harbour, not to raise anchor on Sunday, he hoisted the sails, because the crew were complaining that since they had come to look for victuals they should not be so strict in religious observance. He therefore went to the island of Guadalupe, anchored there and sent the boats ashore well armed. But, before they arrived, a number of women came out of the woods carrying bows and arrows, and with feathers on their heads, apparently resolved to defend the island. For this reason, and because the sea was somewhat choppy, the crew of the boat did not land but made two of the Indians they brought from Hispaniola swim ashore and tell the women who the Christians were. On learning that all they wanted was to barter food for the small objects they carried, the women told them to take their ships to the northern islands where their menfolk were who would provide them with all they wanted. When the ships came very close to shore, they saw many Indian men coming out on to the beach with bows and arrows, which they shot at our men with great daring and loud shouts. But they shot in vain, for their arrows fell short. On seeing that the armed boats were about to beach, the Indians retired into an ambush and, just as our men were approaching the shore, attacked them to pre-

vent their landing. Frightened by the lombards which were fired from the ships, they were forced to retire to the woods and to abandon their houses and possessions. The Christians then entered these houses, pillaging and destroying everything. Knowing the Indian way of making bread, they seized their dough and began to knead it, thus providing themselves with the food that they needed. Among the objects that they found in the houses were large parrots, honey, wax, small iron hatchets used for cutting, and weaving frames on which they make their cloth. The houses were square, not round as on other islands, and in one of them a human arm was found cooking in a stewpot.

While the bread was being made, the Admiral sent forty men into the island to investigate its character and geography; and on the following day these men captured ten women and three boys. The rest of the inhabitants had fled. Among the women whom they captured was a *cacique*'s wife, who almost succeeded in escaping from one of the Admiral's men, a native of the Canaries, who was a very swift runner. Indeed, she would have got away if she had not thought that she could capture him, since he seemed to be alone. She closed with him and brought him to the ground, and would certainly have strangled him if his fellow-Christians had not come to his rescue, for he could not have overcome her unaided.

These women have their legs swathed in cotton cloth from their calf to the knees in order to make them seem stout; they call this practice *coiro* and consider it extremely beautiful. They bind these cloths on so tightly that if one of them happens to get loose this part of the leg is seen to be very thin. This custom is also general among both men and women in Jamaica, where they bind their arms under the shoulder by means of bracelets, which we too wore in ancient days. These women are extremely fat, some of them being two yards or more round, though well proportioned in other ways. As soon

as their children are able to stand and walk they put a bow in their hands and teach them to shoot. They all wear their hair long and loose on their shoulders, and cover no part of their bodies. The lady or female *cacique* whom they captured said that the whole island was inhabited by women and that the people who had prevented their boats from landing were women also, though there were four men with them who had landed by chance from another island. For at a certain period in the year men come from other places to lie with them. The same practice is followed by the women of another island called Martinino, from which arose the story of the Amazons, which the Admiral believed when he saw these women and their strength and courage. They are said to be more intelligent than the women of the other islands, since in other places time is only reckoned by the sun in the day and the moon at night, whereas these women reckon time by the stars also, saying, 'When the Great Bear rises or some other star sets, then it is time to do this or that.'

CHAPTER 64

The Admiral leaves the island of Guadalupe for Castile

WHEN they had supplemented the bread they had aboard with enough to give them twenty days' supply, the Admiral decided to resume his voyage to Castile. But seeing that this island could be a provisioning place and was the first to be reached on a voyage to the Indies, he resolved to pacify these women with some gifts to make good the injuries done to them. So he sent the prisoners ashore, with the exception of the woman *cacique*, who agreed to go to Castile with her

daughter in the company of the other Indians who had been brought from Hispaniola. One of these was Caonabo, who, owing to the fact that he was a Carib and not a native, was the greatest and most famous king in the island. The woman *cacique* went willingly to Castile with the Admiral.

Having taken aboard water, bread and firewood on Wednesday, 20 April, the Admiral hoisted sail and left the island of Guadalupe. With little wind and many calms, he followed a course along the 23rd parallel, leaving it much or little according to the winds. For they had not then the experience we have today by which we steer north to find the strong westerlies. Since they had made little way and had great numbers on board, by 20 May they began to be in great trouble owing to shortage of food. Each man's ration was reduced to six ounces of bread and a pint and a half of water, and that was all. Although there were six or eight pilots in the two caravels, none of them knew where they were, though the Admiral was quite certain that they were a little west of the Azores, as he notes in his log-book, saying, 'This morning the Flemish compass needles pointed a quarter north-west, as usual, and the Genoese, which generally agree with them, deviated very little. The further east we go the more they deviate to the north-west: I reckon therefore that we are about a hundred leagues west of the Azores. Because when we were exactly a hundred leagues west and there were a few scattered strands of weed on the sea, the Flemish compasses deviated a quarter and the Genoese pointed due north, and as we went further east-north-east there was a slight variation.'

These observations were quickly confirmed the following Sunday, 22 May. By these signs, his own assurance and the point he had marked on the chart, he knew that he was in fact a hundred leagues west of the Azores. This amazing difference between the compasses must be attributable to differences in the loadstone with which they were magnetized, since up to

that line they all pointed a quarter north-west, and there some continued to do so while others – those from Genoa in fact – pointed directly to the Pole Star. The same observation was made on 24 May.

Later on their course, on Wednesday, 8 June, when all the pilots were confused and lost, they sighted Odmira, which is between Lisbon and Cape St Vincent. Although for some days they had been nearing land, all the pilots were still at a loss except the Admiral, who ordered the sails to be struck for fear of running aground, and gave as his reason that they were now near Cape St Vincent. The pilots laughed, some of them saying that they were in the English Channel and others off the English coast. Yet others who were rather less in error, said that they were off the coast of Galicia and protested that sails should not be struck, since it would be better to perish on land than to die miserably of hunger at sea. For they were so near starvation that some of them wished to imitate the Caribs and eat the Indians they had aboard. Others, in order to economize the little food they had, were in favour of throwing the Indians overboard, which they would have done if the Admiral had not taken strict measures to prevent them. For he considered them as their kindred and fellow-Christians and held that they should be no worse treated than anyone else. And God was pleased to reward him next day with the sight of land, and the Admiral's assurance that they were near the coast of Portugal was confirmed. From that day onwards he was held by the seamen to have great and heaven-sent knowledge of the art of navigation.

THIRD VOYAGE
1498-1500

THE LIFE OF THE ADMIRAL BY HIS SON, HERNANDO COLON

CHAPTER 65

The Admiral comes to court. The Catholic
Sovereigns entrust him with a commission to
return to the Indies

ON arriving on Castilian soil, the Admiral made ready to go to Burgos, where he was well received by their Catholic Majesties, who had come there for the wedding of their son Don Juan with Princess Margarita of Austria, daughter of the Emperor Maximilian of Austria. The princess had been brought to that city and solemnly received there by the greater part of the nobility and the largest and most distinguished company that had ever been assembled in Spain. But although I was present as page to his serene Highness, I will not enumerate the titles and distinctions of those present, since it has nothing to do with my story, and their Majesties' chroniclers have, in any case, attended to this matter.

To return to the Admiral's affairs, I will mention that on reaching Burgos he made a handsome present to their Majesties of many objects, including samples of the products of the Indies. Among them were birds, beasts, trees and plants, tools and other things used by the Indians for work and pleasure; also masks, belts and various images in which the Indians had put small gold plates in place of ears and eyes, and many grains of unworked gold, some very small and some as large as a bean or a chickpea, and a few the size of a pigeon's egg. These were valued more highly then than at a later date when nuggets were found weighing as much as thirty pounds. But in hopes of greater things to come, the Catholic sovereigns

accepted this gift most joyfully, and thanked the Admiral for the great services he had performed.

Having given an account of all that he had done for the improvement and settlement of the Indies, the Admiral desired to return as quickly as possible for fear that some disaster or misadventure might occur in his absence, since he had left the settlers very short of much that was indispensable to them all. But greatly though he insisted on this matter, affairs at court are subject to long delays, and this business was not disposed of promptly. Ten or twelve months elapsed before two ships were equipped for him and laden with provisions for the settlers, and put under the command of Captain Pedro Fernandez Coronel.

These ships sailed in February 1497, and the Admiral remained behind, still begging for the rest of the fleet that was necessary for his return to the Indies. But he did not obtain them quickly and was compelled to wait for more than a year in Burgos and Medina del Campo. While the court was in the latter city in the year 1498, the Catholic sovereigns granted the Admiral many favours and privileges not only in the matter of his own rank and affairs, but also the government and provisioning of the Indies. I will give an account of these favours and privileges, so that their Majesties' will at that time to reward the Admiral for his merits and services shall be known to all;* also that all may know how greatly their minds were afterwards changed by the misinformation of malicious and envious persons. For soon they allowed him to be injured and insulted in a way that will be described.

Let me resume the Admiral's story after he left the court for Seville. Here he met with further delays owing to the faults and mismanagement of the royal officials, especially of Don

*In fact, Hernando does not do so. The sovereigns confirmed the Admiral's former privileges and in some respects increased them.

Juan de Fonseca,* archdeacon of Seville, and the dispatch of the fleet was unreasonably postponed, and there arose in the said Don Juan, afterwards bishop of Burgos, a mortal and unceasing hatred of the Admiral and everything to do with him. He was chief of the plotters who procured the Admiral's disgrace with the sovereigns. So that my brother Diego and I, who had been pages to the Prince Don Juan until his recent death, should not be prejudiced by this delay and remain absent from court until he sailed, our father sent us on 2 November 1497 from Seville to resume our service, as pages to her serene highness Doña Isabela of glorious memory.

*Fonseca, who was chief of the royal office for the Indies, was disliked and censured by all the Conquistadores. Bernal Díaz del Castillo was even more hostile in his judgement of Fonseca than Columbus or his son.

NARRATIVE OF THE THIRD VOYAGE OF CHRISTOPHER COLUMBUS TO THE INDIES, IN WHICH HE DISCOVERED THE MAINLAND, DISPATCHED TO THE SOVEREIGNS FROM THE ISLAND OF HISPANIOLA

[... ON my second voyage] by the Grace of God I discovered in a very short time 333 leagues of mainland,* the end of the East, and 700 islands of importance in addition to those discovered on my first voyage, and I sailed round the island of Hispaniola, which is greater in circumference than all Spain, and has a vast population, all of whom should pay tribute.

Then abuse broke out and disparagement of the undertaking began, because I had not immediately sent back ships laden with gold. No one considered the shortness of the time or the many difficulties that I described in my letters. And so for my sins, or, as I think it will prove, for my salvation, I became an object of loathing and objections were made to all my wishes and demands. I therefore decided to come to your Highnesses and prove to you how right I had been in every respect. ... Your Highnesses replied by smiling and telling me that I need not worry because they did not believe any of those who maligned this enterprise.

I left the town of San Lucar on Wednesday, 30 May, very weary from my journey. I had hoped for some rest on this new voyage to the Indies, but my distresses were doubled. I sailed to Madeira on an unaccustomed route to avoid possible trouble from a French fleet, which was waiting for me near Cape St Vincent.† From there I went to the Canaries, from

* In spite of all evidence Columbus still insisted that Cuba was the extreme eastern extension of the Asiatic mainland.

† France and Spain were now at war.

which I sailed with one ship and two caravels. I sent the other ships straight to the Indies, to the island of Hispaniola, and sailed south with the intention of going to the Equator and following it westwards to a point immediately south of Hispaniola.

Having reached the Cape Verde Islands – a false name since they are so barren that I saw nothing green there, and all the inhabitants were so sick that I did not dare to stay there – I sailed 480 miles (which is 120 leagues) south-westwards, where I found the North Star in the fifth degree at nightfall. There the wind failed me and the heat grew so great that I was afraid my ships and crew would be burnt. Suddenly everyone was so prostrated that no one dared go below and attend to the casks and provisions. This heat lasted for eight days. The first day ,was clear, but on the seven that followed it rained and was cloudy, and yet we found no relief. If these days had been as sunny as the first I do not think any of us would have survived.

I remembered that on each of my voyages to the Indies, as soon as I passed a hundred leagues beyond the Azores, I found a change of temperature, which is the same at all points from north to south. So I resolved that if the Lord should grant me a wind and fair weather to carry me from the place where I was, I would sail no further south and would not turn northwards either but go directly westwards, in hope of finding the same temperatures as I had found when sailing in the parallel of the Canaries, and if this proved so I would then be able to resume my southward course.

It pleased the Lord, when these eight days were passed, to give me a good east wind, but I did not dare to sail further south, because I found a great change in the sky and the stars, but none in the temperature. So I decided to carry on due west on the parallel of Sierra Leone, and not to change course until I reached the point where I expected to find land. There I

THE THIRD VOYAGE OF COLUMBUS

Miles 0 10 20 30 40

TRINIDAD

La Galea
(Cape Galeota)

Orinoco

Cabresse Pt

Boca del Drago

Chacachacara I.

Promontorio
de Paria

GULF OF PARIA

Punta del Aguja

Golfo de
las Perlas

Paria Peninsula

Rio Guarapiche

Punta del
Arenal

Boca de la Sierpe

Mouths of the

G R A C I A

Los Testigos

Las Guardias

MARGARITA I.

would repair the ship and, if possible, take fresh supplies and water, which had run short.

After seventeen days, during which Our Lord gave me favourable winds, at midday on Tuesday, 31 July, land appeared. I had expected it on the previous day, and had maintained my course till then. But as the sun came up on Monday, because of our shortage of water, I decided to go to the Carib islands, and so changed course.

As proof that the Lord has always shown mercy towards me, on that Tuesday a sailor climbed up to the main top and sighted a cluster of three peaks, at which we said the *Salve Regina* and other prayers and gave many thanks to Our Lord.

I then abandoned my northerly course and made for the land, which I reached about nine o'clock at a cape which I called La Galea.* I had already called the island Trinidad.† The harbour would have been very good if we could have found bottom. There were houses and people and fine cultivated land, as green and lovely as the orchards of Valencia in March. I was sorry that I could not enter the harbour and ran along the coast of this island westwards. After five leagues I found a good bottom and anchored. Next day I continued on my course looking for a harbour where I could repair the ships, take water, and supplement the corn and the scanty provisions that I was carrying. Here I took aboard a hundred gallons of water and then continued until we reached the cape, where I found shelter from the east winds and a good bottom. So I gave orders to anchor, repair the ship and take in wood and water; and I put the men ashore to stretch their limbs after the fatigue of the long voyage. I called this point 'del Arenal'. Here all the ground was printed with the footmarks of some animals which had hooves like goats, but

* Cape Galeota, the south-eastern point of Trinidad.

† From the three peaks and Columbus's special devotion to the Trinity.

although they are apparently numerous we caught sight of none except one carcase.

That day there appeared from an eastward direction a large canoe with twenty-four men, all young and very well equipped with arms, bows and arrows, and wooden shields and, as I have said, they were all young, well built and not black but fairer than the other natives I have seen in the Indies. They were handsome, with fine limbs and bodies, and long straight hair cut in the Spanish manner, and round their heads they wore a cotton cloth elaborately patterned in colours, which I believed to be *almaizares*.* They wore another of these scarves round the body in place of breeches. As this canoe approached, they shouted to us from a distance, but neither I nor anyone else understood them. I gave orders, however, that they should be signalled to approach, and more than two hours passed in this way. Each time they came a little nearer, they immediately sheered off again. I ordered pans and other shining objects to be displayed in order to attract them and bring them closer, and after a while they came nearer than they had come before. I greatly desired conversation with them, but it seemed that I had nothing left to show them which would induce them to come nearer still. So I had a tambourine brought up to the poop and played, and made some of the young men dance, imagining that the Indians would draw closer to see the festivities. On observing the music and dancing, however, they dropped their oars, and picked up their bows, and strung them. Each one seized his shield, and they began to shoot arrows at us. I immediately stopped the music and dancing and ordered some crossbows to be fired. The Indians then put off, making for another caravel, and hastily sheltered under its stern. The pilot hailed them and gave a coat and hat to the man who seemed to be their chief, and arranged with him that he would meet and talk

* Moorish head-dresses.

with them on the beach, to which they immediately rowed their canoe to await him. But he did not wish to go without my permission. When they saw him come to my ship in his boat, they got back into their canoe and rowed away, and I never saw them again or any other inhabitants of this island.

When I reached the end of this Cape Arenal, there was a gulf two leagues wide from east to west between the island of Trinidad and the land of Gracia,* and it was necessary to enter it in order to sail north. I saw some lines of waves crossing this estuary with a great roaring sound, which made me think that there was a reef here with rocks and shallows which would prevent us from entering. Beyond this line of waves was another and yet another, which made a great noise like seas breaking on a rocky beach. I anchored here at Cape Arenal, outside this gulf, and observed that the water was flowing from east to west as furiously as the Guadalquivir in flood. It flowed continuously both day and night, which made me think I could neither turn back on account of the waves, nor go forward on account of the shallows. Late at night standing on the deck I heard a terrible roar approaching the ship from the south. I remained watching and saw the seas rising from west to east, with a swell as high as the ship, which gradually came nearer. On top was a crest of advancing water which rushed onwards with a tremendous noise like that of the other waves I had observed before. Even today I can recall my physical fear that the ship might be swamped when it broke over her. This swell passed and flowed into the gulf, where it was held up for a considerable time.†

The next day I sent the boats out to take soundings, and

---

*This was the mainland of South America at the mouth of the Orinoco.

†This would appear to describe a tidal bore, but in fact there is none at this place. Morrison, in *Admiral of the Ocean Sea*, attributes it to a volcanic disturbance.

found that the shallowest part of the gulf was six or seven fathoms, and all the time these currents continued to flow, some into and some out of the strait. The Lord was pleased to give me a favourable wind, which enabled me to sail into this strait where I soon found calm. By chance we drew some water from the sea and I noticed it was sweet.

I sailed northwards towards some very high mountains about twenty-six leagues from Cape Arenal. Here there were two other capes,* both very high, the one on the east belonging to this island of Trinidad, and the one on the west belonging to the land which I have called 'Gracia'. Here the strait was very narrow, narrower than at Cape Arenal, and here there were the same waves and the same great roaring of the waters as at that place, and here too the sea water was fresh. So far I had had no conversation with the natives of this country, though I greatly desired it. So I sailed westwards along the coast of this land, and the further I went the sweeter and fresher I found the sea water. When I had gone some distance I noticed a place where the soil seemed to have been cultivated. I anchored and sent the boats to land, where they observed that some people had recently been. The sailors found all the mountains full of wild monkeys, and returned. The whole of this territory was mountainous, but further west the land appeared to be flatter, and might have been inhabited.

I ordered the anchors to be raised and sailed along the coast to the seaward point of this range, where I anchored in a river. Many people then came to us and told us that the name of this land was 'Paria', and that further west it was more thickly inhabited. I took four of them aboard and sailed westwards. When I had gone eight leagues to the west, beyond a cape which I called Punta del Aguja (Needlepoint), I found some

* These are probably Promontorio de Paria and Cabresse Point, which is not on Trinidad but on Chacachacara.

of the most beautiful country in the world, which was thickly populated. I reached it in the morning at nine o'clock, and, on seeing this green and beautiful country, anchored in order to meet its people.

Some Indians immediately came to the ship in canoes to ask me, on behalf of their king, to land; and when they saw that I was not disturbed, great numbers more came to the ship in their canoes, many of them wearing pieces of gold round their necks, and some with pearls tied round their arms. I was delighted by this last sight, and tried hard to discover where they found these pearls. They told me that they found them there and in the northern part of the country.

I should have liked to have stayed, but the provisions – corn, wine and meat – which I had brought so far and at such great labour for the people here* were beginning to perish. All I wanted, therefore, was to bring them to safety and I did not stop for anything. I tried to get some of these pearls and sent the boats to land. These people were very numerous and of good appearance. They were all of the same colour as the natives I had seen before and very obliging. Our men who landed found them very pleasant and were very well received. They said that as soon as the boats reached shore two chieftains (a father and son) came, with their whole people, and led them to a very large house, with a double-pitched roof. It was not round like a field tent, as the others are. In it there were many seats on which they invited their guests to sit and others on which they sat themselves. They brought in bread and various kinds of fruit and different wines, white and red, made not from grapes but probably in various ways from various fruits.† Some of it must be made from maize,‡ which

* In Hispaniola, where the Admiral was writing.
† Perhaps made from the agave and related to pulque, the common drink of modern Mexico.
‡ This is the chicha of present-day Venezuela.

is a cereal with an ear like that of wheat. I have brought some back and there is now much in Castile. The best is apparently considered excellent and most highly prized.

The men all sat together at one end of the house and the women at the other. Both the Indians and the Spaniards were much grieved that they did not understand one another, since they wanted to ask us about our country and we wanted to learn about theirs. When the Christians had been given a meal at the house of the elder chieftain, the younger took the Spaniards to his own house and gave them another. They then got into the boats and returned to the ship. I immediately raised anchor, since I was in great haste to save my provisions, which were beginning to perish and which I had brought at such great labour, and also to cure myself, since my eyes were inflamed with sleeplessness. For although, on my previous voyage to discover the mainland,* I was without sleep for thirty-three days, and blind for all that time, my eyes were not so inflamed as now, nor did they run with blood and give me so much pain.

These Indians, as I have said, are all very well built, tall and with finely proportioned limbs. Their hair is very long and straight, and they wear woven cloths round their heads, which look from the distance like silk and resemble, as I have said, Moorish scarves. They wear another, somewhat longer cloth which they wrap round themselves, men and women alike, instead of breeches. These people are fairer than any others I have seen in the Indies. They all wear some jewel round their necks or on their arms, in the local fashion. Many of them have pieces of gold hanging round their necks. Their canoes are very large and better made and lighter than those of the other Indians, and in the middle of each they have a small shelter, like a cabin, in which, as I saw, the chieftains sat

* This was the second voyage and the mainland was – according to Columbus's theory – Cuba.

with their women. I called this place Los Jardines (The Gardens), for the name suited it.

I inquired very carefully where this gold came from, and they all pointed to a land bordering on theirs, to the west, which was very high and not far away. But they all told me not to go there because the inhabitants ate men. I presumed from this that these inhabitants were Caribs like the other cannibals I had met. But I have thought since that they may have meant not cannibals but wild animals. I also asked them where they got their pearls, and they again pointed to the west, and to the north as well, to show that it was beyond their own country. I did not confirm this on account of my supplies and the bad state of my eyes, and because my ship was too large for such an expedition. As the time was short, it all went in questions, and we returned to the ship at evening, as I have said. I immediately raised anchor and sailed westwards.

I sailed on for the whole of the next day in the belief that this was an island, and that I should be able to come out to the northward. I discovered, however, that there were hardly three fathoms of water, and sent a caravel ahead to discover whether the channel was landlocked or if there was some way out. I sailed for some distance, as far as a very large gulf into which four other moderate-sized gulfs seem to open, one of which was the mouth of a very large river.*

We found a constant depth of five fathoms and plenty of very fresh water, of which I have never drunk the like. I was very disturbed, however, that I could not sail out either to the west or north, since I was surrounded on all sides by land. So I raised anchor and turned back to sail north up the passage I have already described. I was not able to go back to the village where we had been, since the currents bore me away from it. Always at every cape I have found the water fresh and clear; the current carried me very swiftly towards the two

* This is probably the Rio Guarapiche.

straits of which I have already spoken. I surmised from the ribbons of current and the swelling seas which flowed into and out of these straits with a great roaring of water that there was a battle between the fresh water and the salt. The fresh water struggled to prevent the entrance of the salt, and the salt strove to prevent the fresh from flowing out. I also surmised that where these straits are there may once have been land connecting the island of Trinidad with the country of Gracia, as your Highnesses can see from the map which I am sending with this letter. I sailed out northwards through this strait and found that the fresh water all the time predominated. When, on the crest of one of these waves, I was blown out by a strong wind, I noticed that behind the swell the water was fresh and in front of it salt.

Each time I sailed from Spain to the Indies I found that when I reached a point a hundred leagues west of the Azores, the heavens, the stars, the temperature of the air and the waters of the sea abruptly changed. I very carefully verified these observations, and found that, on passing this line from north to south, the compass needle, which had previously pointed north-east, turned a whole quarter of the wind to the north-west. It was as if the seas sloped upwards on this line. I also observed that here they were full of a vegetation like pine branches loaded with fruit similar to that of the mastic. This weed is so dense that on my first voyage I thought we had reached shallows, and that the ships might run aground. We had not seen a single strand of weed before we came to that line. I noticed that when we had passed it the sea was calm and smooth, never becoming rough even in a strong wind. I found also that westwards of this line the temperature of the air was very mild and did not change from winter to summer. Here the Pole Star describes a circle of five degrees in diameter, and when it is at its lowest the Guards* point

* These are the Pointers.

towards the right. It then rises continuously until they point to the left. It then stands at five degrees, and from there it sinks until they are again on the right.

On this present voyage I sailed from Spain to Madeira, from Madeira to the Canaries, and then to the Cape Verde Islands. From here, as I have already said, I followed a southward course in order to cross the Equator. On reaching a point exactly on the parallel which passes through Sierra Leone in Guinea, I found such heat and such strength in the sun's rays that I was afraid I might be burnt. Although it rained and the sky was overcast, I remained in a state of exhaustion until the Lord gave me a fair wind and the desire to sail westwards, encouraged by the thought that, on reaching the line of which I have spoken, I should find a change in temperature. On coming to this line I immediately found very mild temperatures which became even milder as I sailed on. But I found no corresponding change in the stars. At nightfall the Pole Star stood at five degrees, with the Guards pointing straight overhead, and later, at midnight, it had risen to ten degrees, and at daybreak stood at fifteen degrees, with the Guards pointing downwards. I found the sea as smooth as before, but not the same vegetation. I was greatly surprised by this behaviour of the Pole Star and spent many nights making careful observations with the quadrant, but found that the plumb line always fell to the same point. I regard this as a new discovery, and it may be established that here the heavens undergo a great change in a brief space.

I have always read that the world of land and sea is spherical. All authorities and the recorded experiments of Ptolemy and the rest, based on the eclipses of the moon and other observations made from east to west, and on the height of the Pole Star made from north to south, have constantly drawn and confirmed this picture, which they held to be true. Now, as I said, I have found such great irregularities that I have

come to the following conclusions concerning the world: that it is not round as they describe it, but the shape of a pear, which is round everywhere except at the stalk, where it juts out a long way; or that it is like a round ball, on part of which is something like a woman's nipple. This point on which the protuberance stands is the highest and nearest to the sky. It lies below the Equator, and in this ocean, at the farthest point of the east, I mean by the farthest point of the east the place where all land and islands end.

In support of this belief, I urge all the arguments which I have stated concerning the line from north to south a hundred leagues west of the Azores. As we passed it in a westerly direction, the ships mounted gently nearer to the sky, and we enjoyed the mildest weather. On account of this mildness the needle shifted by a quarter north-westwards, and continued to shift farther to the north-west as we sailed on. It is this increase of height that causes the changes in the circle described by the Pole Star and the Guards. The closer I came to the Equator the higher they rose, and the greater the alteration in these stars and their orbits.

Ptolemy and the other geographers believed that the world was spherical and that the other hemisphere was as round as the one in which they lived, its centre lying on the island of Arin, which is below the Equator between the Arabian and Persian gulfs; and that the boundary passes over Cape St Vincent in Portugal to the west, and eastward to China and the *Seres*.* I do not in the least question the roundness of that hemisphere, but I affirm that the other hemisphere resembles the half of a round pear with a raised stalk, as I have said, like a woman's nipple on a round ball. Neither Ptolemy nor any of the other geographers had knowledge of this other hemisphere,

---

*This was the Romans' name for the Chinese, of whom they knew nothing except that they produced the silk which arrived along the caravan trails.

which was completely unknown, but based their reasoning on the hemisphere in which they lived, which is a round sphere, as I have said.

Now that your Highnesses have commanded navigation, exploration and discovery, the nature of this other hemisphere is clearly revealed. For on this voyage I was twenty degrees north of the Equator in the latitude of Hargin★ and the African mainland, where the people are black and the land very parched. I then went to the Cape Verde Islands, whose inhabitants are blacker still, and the farther south I went the greater the extremes. In the latitude in which I was, which is that of Sierra Leone, where the Pole Star stood at five degrees at nightfall, the people are completely black, and when I sailed westwards from there the heats remained excessive. On passing the line of which I have spoken, I found the temperatures growing milder, so that when I came to the island of Trinidad, where the Pole Star also stands at five degrees at nightfall, both there and on the mainland opposite the temperatures were extremely mild. The land and the trees were very green and as lovely as the orchards of Valencia in April, and the inhabitants were lightly built and fairer than most of the other people we had seen in the Indies. Their hair was long and straight and they were quicker, more intelligent and less cowardly. The sun was in Virgo above their heads and ours. All this is attributable to the very mild climate in those regions, and this in its turn to the fact that this land stands highest on the world's surface, being nearest to the sky, as I have said. This confirms my belief that the world has this variation of shape which I have described, and which lies in this hemisphere that contains the Indies and the Ocean Sea, and stretches below the Equator. This argument is greatly supported by the fact that the sun, when Our Lord made it, was at the first point of the east; in other words the first light

★ Arguin, an island off the west coast of Africa.

was here in the east, where the world stands at its highest. Although Aristotle believed that the Antarctic Pole, or the land beneath it, is the highest part of the world and nearest to the sky, other philosophers contest it, saying that the land beneath the Arctic Pole is the highest. This argument shows that they knew one part of the world to be higher and nearer to the sky than the rest. It did not strike them however that, for the reasons of shape that I have set down, this part might lie below the Equator. And no wonder, since they had no certain information about this other hemisphere, only vague knowledge based on deduction. No one had ever entered it or gone in search of it until now when your Highnesses commanded me to explore and discover these seas and lands.

It was discovered that the distance between these two straits which lie, as I have said, opposite one another on a line from north to south, is twenty-six leagues. There can be no mistake in this because I took the readings on a quadrant. From these two straits westward to the gulf which I have mentioned and I called the Golfo de las Perlas* is another sixty-eight leagues of four miles (as is generally reckoned at sea). The water runs continuously and very fiercely out of these two straits towards the east, which accounts for its battle with the salt water outside. In that southern strait which I named the Boca de la Sierpe, I found that at nightfall the Pole Star stood at about five degrees above the horizon, and in the northern strait, which I called the Boca del Drago, it was at about seven. I found that the Golfo de las Perlas itself is almost 3,900 miles westwards of the first meridian of Ptolemy, which is nearly seventy degrees along the Equator, reckoning each degree as fifty-six and two-thirds miles.

Holy Scripture testifies that Our Lord made the earthly Paradise in which he placed the Tree of Life. From it there

*The extreme western end of the Gulf of Paria. No pearls were actually found here.

flowed four main rivers: the Ganges in India, the Tigris and the Euphrates in Asia, which cut through a mountain range and form Mesopotamia and flow into Persia, and the Nile, which rises in Ethiopia and flows into the sea at Alexandria.

I do not find and have never found any Greek or Latin writings which definitely state the worldly situation of the earthly Paradise, nor have I seen any world map which establishes its position except by deduction. Some place it at the source of the Nile in Ethiopia. But many people have travelled in these lands and found nothing in the climate or altitude to confirm this theory, or to prove that the waters of the Flood which covered, etc., etc.* . . . reached there. Some heathens tried to show by argument that it was in the Fortunate Islands (which are the Canaries); and St Isidore, Bede, Strabo, the Master of Scholastic History,† St Ambrose and Scotus and all learned theologians agree that the earthly Paradise is in the East, etc.*

I have already told what I have learnt about this hemisphere and its shape, and I believe that, if I pass below the Equator, on reaching these higher regions I shall find a much cooler climate and a greater difference in the stars and waters. Not that I believe it possible to sail to the extreme summit or that it is covered by water, or that it is even possible to go there. For I believe that the earthly Paradise lies here, which no one can enter except by God's leave. I believe that this land which your Highnesses have commanded me to discover is very great, and that there are many other lands in the south of which there have never been reports. I do not hold that the earthly Paradise has the form of a rugged mountain, as it is shown in pictures, but that it lies at the summit of what I have described as the stalk of a pear, and that by gradually approaching it one begins, while still at a great distance, to climb

*These abbreviations are Columbus's own.
†Petrus Comestor, author of *Historia scolastica*.

towards it. As I have said, I do not believe that anyone can
ascend to the top. I do believe, however, that, distant though
it is, these waters may flow from there to this place which I
have reached, and form this lake. All this provides great evidence of the earthly Paradise, because the situation agrees
with the beliefs of those holy and wise theologians and all the
signs strongly accord with this idea.* For I have never read
or heard of such a quantity of fresh water flowing so close to
the salt and flowing into it, and the very temperate climate
provides a further confirmation. If this river does not flow
out of the earthly Paradise, the marvel is still greater. For I do
not believe that there is so great and deep a river anywhere
in the world.

We left the Boca del Drago, which is the more northerly
of the two straits I named, on the following day, which was
the August Feast of the Virgin, and I found the sea running so
strongly towards the west that from ten in the morning to
nine at night we made sixty-five leagues of four miles. The
wind was not too violent but very gentle, and this confirms
the fact that from there to the south there is a continuous
ascent, and to the north, where we were then going, a continuous descent.

I strongly believe that the waters of the sea flow from east
to west, following the course of the heavens, and that here,
in passing this region, they flow more rapidly and have consequently eaten away a large part of the land, which will
account for the great number of islands hereabouts. The
islands themselves supply evidence of this, for all those that
lie west and east or a little more obliquely north-west and

---

*Las Casas, in Bk I, Chap. 141, refutes this theory on the grounds of
Columbus's lack of grounding in Holy Scripture, ancient history and
the teaching of the Holy Fathers and secular writers. He excuses the
Admiral's poor choice of language and lack of simile by his humble
origins and foreign birth.

south-east are broad, and those lying north and south and north-east and south-west are narrow, for they stand in the way of these prevailing winds. All these islands produce precious things, because of the mild climate which comes to them from heaven and because of their proximity to the highest point of the earth. It is true that at certain places the waters do not appear to flow in this direction, but this is only so in particular places where it is interrupted by land, which apparently causes the current to change course.

Pliny writes that the sea and the land together form a sphere, and states that this ocean sea forms the greatest body of water and lies towards the heavens, that the land is beneath it and supports it, and that the two are related like the kernel of the nut and the containing shell. The Master of Scholastic History commenting on Genesis says that the waters are very small, although on the day of creation they covered the whole land. They were then gaseous like a mist. But when they became solid and compact they occupied a very small space. This is confirmed by Nicholas of Lyra, and Aristotle says that the world is small with very little water, and that it is easy to go from Spain to the Indies. This view is supported by Averroes and by Cardinal Pedro de Aliaco, who confirm his statement and that of Seneca (who is of the same opinion). The Cardinal says that Aristotle was able to learn many of the world's secrets through Alexander the Great, Seneca through the Emperor Nero, and Pliny by way of the Romans, who devoted men and wealth and great effort to the discovery of the world's secrets, and their explanation to the peoples. The Cardinal accords greater authority to them than to Ptolemy and the other Greeks and the Arabs. In confirmation of the belief that the seas are small and cover only a small part of the world, the Cardinal opposes to the belief of Ptolemy and his followers a passage from II Esdras,* in which he says that, of

* II Esdras vi, 42 (Authorized version): 'Upon the third day thou didst

the seven parts of the world, six are revealed, and the seventh covered with water. Such Saints as Augustine and Ambrose (in his *Exameron*) quote II Esdras 28, 29, 'Here my son Jesus shall come and my son Christ shall die',* as proof that Esdras was a prophet, which is the belief also of Zacharias, father of St John, and of the Blessed Simeon.† Francisco de Maironis also cites these authorities. As to the area of dry land, many voyages have shown that it is much greater than is commonly believed, which is not surprising, for the further one travels the more one learns.

I will return to my subject of the land of Gracia, the river and the lake that I discovered. This lake is so large that it could rather be called a sea than a lake, because a lake is a small sheet of water, and when it is large, as in the case of the Sea of Galilee and the Dead Sea, it is called a sea. I would say that if this river does not spring from the earthly Paradise it comes from a vast land lying to the south, of which we have hitherto had no reports. But I am firmly convinced that the earthly Paradise truly lies here, and I rely on the authorities and arguments that I have cited.

May the Lord grant your Highnesses long life and health, and leisure to pursue this most noble enterprise in which I believe a great service is being performed for Our Lord, and by which the territories of Spain are being greatly extended and from which all Christians are receiving great joy and comfort, since in this way the name of Our Lord will be spread abroad.

In every land to which your Highnesses' ships sail, I have a tall cross erected on each cape, and I proclaim your Highnesses' greatness to all the people informing them that you

---

command that the waters should be gathered in the seventh part of the earth: six parts hast thou dried up. . . .'

* This is the Vulgate version of II Esdras vii, 28 and 29.

† Luke ii, 25–35.

are lords of Spain. I tell them as much as I can about our Blessed Faith and the creed of Holy Mother Church, which has members throughout the world. I tell them of the civilization and nobility of all Christians and their faith in the Holy Trinity.

May it please Our Lord to forgive the persons who have libelled and do libel this noble enterprise and who oppose and have opposed its progress without considering what honour and glory it brings to your royal estate throughout the world. They do not know what arguments to urge against it except that much money is expended on it, and so far no ships have been sent back loaded with gold. They do not consider how brief the time has been or the many difficulties that have been encountered, nor that in your Highnesses' household in Castile many earn by their merits more in a single year than is needed to finance this whole undertaking. They do not consider either that no princes of Castile have ever before won lands abroad, that your Highnesses have now another world in which our Holy Faith can be greatly extended and from which such great profits can be derived. Although no great cargoes have arrived, enough samples of gold and other valuables have been sent back to prove that great profit will very shortly accrue from these lands. They do not consider either the great courage of the princes of Portugal, who have prosecuted for so long the enterprise of Guinea and are now prosecuting that of Africa, to which they have devoted half the inhabitants of their kingdom, and that the King of Portugal is as much resolved on this enterprise as ever. May Our Lord provide in this matter, as I have said, and lead them to consider what I have written; which is not a thousandth part of what I might write about the deeds of princes who have devoted themselves to gaining knowledge, and making and maintaining conquests.

I have not said all this because I disbelieve in your

Highnesses' will to pursue this enterprise as long as you live. I trust most firmly in your reply to me on a certain occasion by word of mouth, and have seen no change of mind in your Highnesses. But I am frightened by what I have heard about certain persons, since constant dripping wears a stone. Your Highnesses answered me with that magnanimity for which you are famous throughout the world, telling me to take no account of these fears because it was your will to prosecute and maintain this enterprise, even should it produce nothing but rocks and stones.

You said that you thought nothing of the expense, since you spent a great deal more on matters of less importance and regarded the wealth you had devoted and would devote to it as well invested, for you believed that by it the Christian faith and your royal dominions would be greatly extended. You said furthermore that those who maligned this enterprise were no friends of your royal Majesties, and now just as you are receiving information about these lands which I have newly discovered and in which I fervently believe the earthly Paradise to lie, the *adelantado* Bartolomé Colon* is going with three ships well equipped for the purpose, to carry on the exploration. They will discover as much as they can in those regions. In the meantime I will send your royal Highnesses this letter and a map of the land, and you will decide what is to be done in the matter and send me your commands which, with the help of the Holy Trinity, I will carry out with all diligence in such a way as to give service and pleasure to your Highnesses. Thanks be to God.

*Columbus's brother had just arrived in Santo Domingo. After making him *adelantado* or governor, Columbus planned to send him to continue exploration.

THE LIFE OF THE ADMIRAL BY HIS SON, HERNANDO COLON

CHAPTER 73

The Admiral crosses from the mainland to Hispaniola

THE Admiral sailed along the coast of Paria, gradually departing from it in a north-westerly direction, in which he was driven by the calm and the prevailing currents. Consequently at midday on Wednesday, 15 August, he left the Cabo de las Conchas and Margarita Island to the west. I do not know whether God inspired him to give the island this name on account of its nearness to that of Cubagua, from which a vast quantity of pearls (or margaritas) have since been brought. For, in a similar way, after he left Jamaica he named certain mountains on Hispaniola the Golden Range, and soon afterwards the greatest quantity of gold ever brought to Spain was discove red in them.

But, to return to his voyage, he sailed past six islands which he named Las Guardias and another three which lay further north which he named Los Testigos. And although he discovered much land to the west of the coast of Paria, the Admiral says that he could not give as detailed an account of them as he wished since his eyes had begun to bleed because of many sleepless nights, and he was therefore compelled to leave the greater part of these matters to be recorded by the pilots and sailors who accompanied him. He adds that on this same night of Thursday, 16 August, the compasses, which had so far not deviated to the north-west, suddenly did so by a point and a half, and some of them by a whole quarter, and that there could be no error about this, since they had all the

time been most careful in noting their readings. Astonished by this and disappointed that it was impossible for him to follow the coast of the mainland any further, he sailed on an almost unvarying course to the north-west till, on Monday, 20 August, he anchored between La Beata and Hispaniola. From here he sent some Indians with letters to his brother, the *adelantado*, announcing his arrival and the success of his voyage. He was surprised to find himself so far west, for although he knew that the currents had been strong he did not think they could have driven him so far from his course.*
Therefore, in order that his provisions should not run out, he steered east on a course for Santo Domingo, whose river and harbour he entered on 30 August. For the *adelantado* had chosen the site for his city on the eastern bank of this river, where it now stands, and had called it Santo Domingo† in memory of their father, whose name was Domenico.

CHAPTER 74

*The rising and disturbances which the Admiral
finds in Hispaniola, instigated by the malice of
Roldan, whom he had left as* alcalde mayor‡

HAVING entered the city of Santo Domingo almost blind, from continual watches, the Admiral hoped to rest after the hardships of his voyage and find great peace among his own

---

* Morrison considers Columbus's navigation from Paria to Hispaniola one of the greatest proofs of his seamanship. Sailing from one uncharted point to another equally unknown he was only deflected from his course by currents which he could not be familiar with.

† Columbus had been away from Hispaniola for two and a half years, and in the interval the settlement of Isabela had been abandoned in favour of the present Santo Domingo.

‡ Chief magistrate.

people. But he found quite the opposite. For all the house-
holds on the island were in a state of great unrest and rebellion;
a number of the settlers he had left were dead and more than
a hundred and sixty were suffering from syphilis. In addition
many others had revolted with Roldan, and he did not find
the ships there which he had sent with supplies from the
Canaries.

However, I must now describe events in their due sequence
in order to resume and unravel the thread of this story, and I
will begin from the day on which the Admiral departed for
Castile. This, as we have said, was in March 1496, and thirty
months before he returned. At the beginning of this time in
expectation of his swift return with fresh supplies the settlers
remained fairly peaceful. But at the end of the first year, when
provisions from Castile were running short, and their sickness
and hardships were increasing, they grew weary of their present state and could see no hope of any improvement in the
future. The complaints of the many malcontents remained un-
voiced until a ringleader appeared. For in such cases there is
always someone at hand to foment the trouble and assume
leadership. The leadership fell to Francisco Roldan, a native of
Torre de Domjimeno, whose reputation and authority the
Admiral had himself established among both Indians and
Christians by making him *alcalde mayor*, to whom obedience
was due as to the Admiral himself. As a result there was not
the full agreement between Roldan and the *adelantado* who had
been left as governor that was necessary for the public good,
as the Admiral was to discover with time and experience. For
when his absence became prolonged and no fresh supplies
arrived, Roldan began to think of making himself master of
the island and then killing the Admiral's brothers, for they
would provide the chief resistance. And he waited for an opportunity to put this plan into effect.

It happened that one of the Admiral's brothers, the

adelantado, had gone to a western province called Jaragua, eighty leagues from Isabela, while Roldan remained behind under the authority of the Admiral's other brother, which so annoyed him that, although the *adelantado* had ordered that all the tribute that the Admiral had imposed on the natives of the island should be paid to the Catholic sovereigns, he, Roldan, began secretly to levy tribute on his own behalf.

But since revolt dare not raise its head all of a sudden and without pretext, Roldan found a convenient excuse for his rebellion. A caravel had been brought to land at Isabela and was being prepared to make the voyage to Castile, should necessity demand it. In fact, through lack of rigging and other tackle it could not put to sea, but Roldan suggested that there was another reason, and publicly proclaimed his suspicions, protesting at the same time that it would be for the general good if some men were to go in it to Castile with news of their difficulties.

Therefore, under the pretext of the public interest, Roldan pressed very hard for the ship to be launched, and when Don Diego demurred because of the lack of rigging, Roldan with increased boldness and effrontery began to plan with certain others that the ship should be launched in defiance of Don Diego. He said to those whom he thought to be in agreement with him that if the *adelantado* and Don Diego opposed the launching it was because they wanted to retain their command of the country and keep them in perpetual subjection without a ship that could carry news to the Catholic sovereigns of the brothers' tyranny and disobedience. For, he continued, they were all well acquainted with the terrible cruelties of the *adelantado* and Don Diego, who compelled them to work on the land and build forts and led them a miserable life, and since they had no hope that the Admiral would return with supplies, they must now seize the caravel and win their liberty. They must no longer serve for pay that they never re-

ceived, or obey a foreigner, when they might enjoy a comfortable life and all make a good profit. Everything that could be found or bartered in the island ought to be divided equally among them, and they should put all the Indians to service without interference from anyone. For at present they could not even take an Indian woman that pleased them. What was worse the *adelantado* made them observe the three Christian vows* and there was no lack of fasts and penances, penal punishments and imprisonment, imposed on them for the mildest faults. Roldan assured them that since he wielded the royal wand of justice no harm could come to them for anything that might happen and urged them to follow his counsel, since they could not be wrong in doing so.

Inspired by hatred of the *adelantado* and hopes of self-advantage, Roldan won so many adherents with such speeches that one day some of his faction decided to attack and stab the *adelantado*, who had by then returned to Isabela from Jaragua. They thought that the attack would be so easy that they brought ropes with them to hang him when he was dead. What particularly incited them to this crime was the imprisonment of Barahona, a friend of the conspirators, and if God had not inspired the *adelantado* to refrain from carrying out his sentence, they would undoubtedly have assassinated him at that time.

CHAPTER 75

*Roldan attempts to raise a rebellion at Concepción
and sacks Isabela*

O N seeing that the *adelantado*'s death could not be contrived as he wished, and that his plot was now discovered, Roldan
*Poverty, chastity and obedience.

decided to take possession of the town and fort of Concepción, since he thought that from here he could easily conquer the whole island. The execution of this plan was facilitated by his nearness to the place, for during the *adelantado*'s absence Don Diego had sent him to this province with forty men to put down the Indians who had revolted also and were planning to seize the town and kill the Christians. So under the pretext that he had come to put down the rising and punish the Indians, Roldan assembled his people at the village of a certain *cacique* called Marque, with the intention of putting his plan into effect at the first favourable opportunity. But as the *alcalde* Balesta had some suspicion of his intentions he put a good guard on the fort and informed the *adelantado* of the danger in which he stood. Collecting such men as he could, the *adelantado* came immediately, and speedily established himself in the fort. Seeing that his plot was now discovered, Roldan went to Concepción under a safe conduct, but rather to see what harm he could do to the *adelantado* than with the intention of coming to an agreement with him. With excessive boldness and effrontery, he demanded that the *adelantado* should either put the caravel to sea or give him permission to do so, for he and his friends would not find it difficult.

This proposal greatly annoyed the *adelantado*, who replied that neither Roldan nor his friends were sailors or knew the proper and necessary procedure for launching a ship, and that even if they could launch it they could not sail it owing to the shortage of rigging and other tackle. Any attempt to do so would endanger both the caravel and its crew. Because the *adelantado* was a seaman and understood these matters, and they, not being sailors, did not, an argument ensued, and after various differences had been expressed Roldan departed in a fury, refusing either to resign his wand of office or to obey the *adelantado*'s orders, saying that he would do both when the King, on whose behalf he was in the island, should com-

mand him, since he knew that he would never receive justice from the *adelantado*, who by hook or by crook would find an opportunity of killing him or doing him some injury. In the meantime, however, he agreed to do what was reasonable and take up his residence where the *adelantado* might choose. But when the *adelantado* directed him to the village of the *cacique* Don Diego, Roldan refused to go, saying that he would not have enough food there for his men and that he would look for a more suitable place.

Roldan then departed for Isabela, having collected sixty-five men and, seeing that he could not put the caravel to sea, opened the store-houses, he and his followers taking whatever arms, clothing or food they liked, and Don Diego Colon, who was in the town, could not prevent them. Indeed, if he and some of his servants had not taken refuge in the fort they would have been in some danger, notwithstanding the fact that, at the court inquiry that was instituted afterwards to look into this matter, some witnesses affirmed that Roldan had promised to obey Don Diego in return for Don Diego's agreement publicly to take sides against his brother. But in fact Don Diego refused this offer and Roldan was powerless to do him any more harm. In fear of the reinforcements which the *adelantado* had sent and which were just arriving, Roldan left Isabela with all the mutineers, and fell on the flocks that were grazing in the vicinity, killing enough beasts for their food and taking many more as pack animals for their journey to the province of Jaragua which the *adelantado* had just left. Here they intended to stay, since it was the most pleasant and fertile part of the island, and had a more tractable and civilized population than other places, and more especially because its women were more beautiful and accommodating than those elsewhere – which was the chief attraction that drew them there.

But in order not to depart without trying his strength

before the *adelantado* arrived with his reinforcements and dealt him due punishment, Roldan decided to march to Concepción, take it by surprise and kill the *adelantado*, who was still there, and, if this plan failed, to besiege the town. Having received warning of this, the *adelantado* encouraged his men with a speech in which he offered them various favours and two slaves each for their private service. For he thought that most of the men with him were attracted by the life that Roldan offered to his men, since they listened to his emissaries. Indeed this had encouraged Roldan to hope that they would all very soon come over to his side, and this hope had emboldened him to undertake and pursue his enterprise. But things did not go as he wished. The *adelantado* had not only been warned, as we have said, but was a man of great courage, and his men remained loyal to him. He resolved therefore to achieve by arms what he had not been able to achieve by reason and good counsel. So having assembled his men, he left Concepción to attack Roldan on the road.

CHAPTER 76

Roldan stirs up the Indians against the adelantado *and departs for Jaragua*

FINDING that he had been cheated in his hopes and that none of the *adelantado*'s men were going to join him, as he had expected, Roldan decided to make a timely departure and continue his original march to Jaragua. He had not the courage to wait for the *adelantado*, but did not lack a tongue to attack him with vituperations and to incite the Indians of the lands through which he passed to hatred of the *adelantado* and rebellion against him. He said that the reasons why he and his

men had parted company with the *adelantado* had been Don
Bartolomé's violent nature and his vengefulness against
Christians and Indians alike, and the unbearable greed which
he displayed in piling burdens and tributes on them. If they
were to pay them regularly each year, he would constantly
increase them, though this was against the will of the Catholic sovereigns, who wanted nothing but obedience from
their subjects and the maintenance of freedom, peace and
justice among them. In case they were afraid to defend themselves, continued Roldan, he with his friends and followers
would come to their aid, and he would declare himself their
protector and defender. At the conclusion of this speech, an
agreement was reached to withhold the payment of tribute
and as a result nothing could be obtained from those who lived
far from the place where the *adelantado* happened to be because of the great distances, nor from those who lived near
by either, for fear of annoying them and causing them to take
the rebels' side.

But despite this considerate treatment of the Indians, when
the *adelantado* left Concepción, Guarionix, the chief *cacique*
of the province, with Roldan's help, boldly planned to besiege
the town and fort and to kill the Christians who were guarding it. The better to achieve his purpose, he collected all the
caciques, and came to an agreement with his allies that each
one should kill the Christians in his province. For the lands of
Hispaniola were not so big that any of them could support
many men, and the Christians had been compelled to split up
into bands or companies of eight or ten, one for each zone.
This encouraged the Indians to think they had only to surprise
each band separately and simultaneously, and not one of them
would be left alive. But the Indians have no numbers by
which to determine dates or anything else that requires calculation; they can only count on their fingers. So it was
agreed that on the day of the next full moon each one of them

would be ready to kill his Christians, and Guarionix had instructed his *caciques* to do so. But one of them, who was the most anxious to gain honour and considered the whole thing very easy, although he was not a good enough astronomer to be certain when the moon was full, attacked before the agreed day. The attack miscarried and he was forced to flee to Guarionix, from whom he expected help. But this was his undoing; he met with the punishment he deserved for betraying the plot by giving the Christians warning.

The rebels were greatly discomfited by this disaster. For, as we have said, the plot had been hatched with their help and connivance, and they had been waiting to see if Guarionix would bring it off, hoping with his support to overthrow the *adelantado*. But when they learnt that he had failed they did not think themselves safe in the province where they were, and left for Jaragua, still proclaiming that they were the protectors of the Indians, though in mind and deed they were more like thieves, since their greed knew no restraint of God or man. They had no master but their own ungovernable appetites, and each one stole as much as he wished, and their leader Roldan was the greatest thief of them all. Yet he still continued to persuade and command the principal Indians and all the *caciques* to give him everything he asked in return for his promise to defend them and their people from the *adelantado*'s demands for tribute. But in fact he took a great deal more from them than the *adelantado* asked as tribute. From one *cacique* alone, called Manicaotex, he exacted a gourd full of fine gold weighing three marks* every three months, and to make certain of his payment he kept a son and a nephew of this *cacique* with him, under guise of friendship. (And let no one be surprised that we measure marks of gold by the gourd! We merely wish to show that the Indians used this measure, having no knowledge of scales.)

*A mark was 230 grams.

CHAPTER 77

*Ships arrive from Castile with food and
reinforcements*

THUS the Christians were divided, and the ships that were
to bring food and reinforcements from Castile were delayed,
and neither the *adelantado* nor Don Diego could pacify those
who remained with them, most of whom were men of low
character and were attracted by the better life and treatment
that Roldan promised them. For fear of being entirely deserted, therefore, the brothers hesitated to punish the guilty.
This made them so disobedient that it was almost impossible
to find any way of keeping them quiet, and the brothers were
compelled to put up with the insults of the rebels. But the
Lord desired to give them some comfort, and the two ships
arrived which we have already mentioned and which were
dispatched a year after the Admiral sailed home from the
Indies and had cost him great efforts and perseverance at
court. When he considered the nature of the land and the
character of the men he had left there, and the great danger
that might be occasioned by his delay, he begged and obtained from the Catholic sovereigns the dispatch of two of
the eighteen ships which they had ordered to be equipped for
him, ahead of the rest.

Their arrival, the food and reinforcements that they carried,
and the news that they brought of the Admiral's safe return
to Spain, gave fresh spirit to the *adelantado*'s men and encouraged them to serve him more loyally, and at the same
time inspired Roldan's men with fear of punishment.
Wishing to learn some news and obtain some of the
things they lacked, Roldan's men went to Santo Domingo
where the ships had arrived. And an additional reason for

going there was the hope of gaining recruits for their party.

But as the *adelantado* had received warning of their coming and was nearer the port, he marched out to meet them and block their road. Having placed guards at certain passes on the way, he entered Santo Domingo to see the ships and impose order on the town. Anxious that the Admiral should find the island at peace and disturbances put down, he made a new proposal of peace to Roldan, who was with his followers six leagues away, and entrusted it to the captain who had come with the two ships, whose name was Pedro Fernandez Coronel. He chose him as an honest man of authority, but also in the hope that his words would be the more effective, since he could speak as a witness of the Admiral's arrival in Spain, of his warm welcome there and of the great solicitude shown to him by the Catholic sovereigns, who loved him and valued him highly. But the chief rebels feared the impression that this emissary might make on the majority of their followers and refused to let him speak in public. They came out to meet him on the road, carrying crossbows and arrows, and he was only able to address a few words to those chosen to hear him. So he went back without achieving any agreement, and they returned to their quarters in Jaragua.

They were in some fear, however, that Roldan and some of his chief men might write to their friends among the *adelantado*'s followers, warmly entreating them to intercede with the Admiral on his arrival and urging that their just complaints were not against him but only against the *adelantado* and that they were anxious to resume their obedience and be restored to his favour.

CHAPTER 78

*The three ships sent by the Admiral from the
Canaries put in at the scene of the rebellion*

Now that we have described the arrival of the two ships
which the Admiral sent to Hispaniola from Spain, we must
speak of the three that separated from him at the Canaries to
continue their voyage in good weather as far as the Carib
islands, which are the first to be met by sailors on their way
to the port of Santo Domingo. Since the pilots were not very
familiar with the course through these islands that is generally
followed today, they were unfortunately unable to find that
port, and were dragged westwards by the currents to the
province of Jaragua, where the rebels then were. As soon as
they saw that the ships were off course and knew nothing of
the rebellion, the rebels quietly went aboard, pretending that
they were in these parts on the *adelantado*'s orders to ensure
the provision of food and preserve peace and obedience there.
But as it is easy to discover a secret known to many, before
very long the most astute of the ship's captains, Alonso Sanchez de Carvajal, suspected the discord and rebellion and began to discuss terms of peace with Roldan, believing that he
could persuade him to obey the *adelantado*. But the friendship
and familiarity which now obtained between all the rebels and
those aboard the ships prevented Carvajal's persuasion from
having the desired effect.

Roldan had privately received promises from many of the
new arrivals that they would join his company, and with this
advantage he strengthened his position. When Carvajal saw
that his negotiations would not quickly reach a successful
conclusion, he decided, with the agreement of the other two
captains, that it would be well if the many whom he had

brought to work for wages in the mines and for other jobs and services were sent by land to Santo Domingo. For since the seas, winds and currents made the voyage there very difficult, it might possibly take as much as two or three months, and in this case not only would all the food be exhausted and the men fall sick but much time would be lost in which they should have been working at the tasks they had come to do.

When this resolution was taken Juan Antonio Colombo was put in trust of the workmen, of whom there were forty, to supervise their journey, Pedros de Arana was given the task of bringing back the ships, and Carvajal was to remain behind and see if there was any way of coming to an agreement with Roldan. While Juan Antonio was making preparations for his departure, on the second day after their landing, those workmen – they could be more properly described as idlers – who had been brought over to do the jobs we have specified went over to the rebels, leaving their captain with only six or seven men who remained loyal. In answer to this barefaced treachery the captain without the least fear of danger went to see Roldan and told him that since he claimed to esteem and serve their Catholic Majesties he should not allow these men, who had been brought to settle and cultivate the land and perform various tasks in return for the wages they had received, to remain there, wasting their time and doing none of the duties for which they had been brought. Should Roldan send them away, said the captain, he would show that his deeds were in accordance with his words, and that the reason for his presence in Jaragua was defiance and hatred of the *adelantado* rather than any wish to prejudice the public weal or the royal service. But recent events had greatly compromised Roldan and his followers, and they were determined to persist in their rebellion. Moreover, a crime shared by many is easier to disguise than that of one individual.

Roldan therefore refused this request, on the plea that he could not compel his followers, and that theirs was a free brotherhood of which no one could be denied membership. Seeing that it would be foolish to expose himself to further danger by insisting without hope of success on what he would never obtain, Juan Antonio decided to return to the ships with his few remaining followers. Thereupon, to prevent a similar defection among those who remained with them, the other two captains hastened to sail to Santo Domingo in weather as unfavourable as they had met with before. The voyage took them many days, they lost their provisions, and Carvajal's ship was severely damaged. Running on some shoals, it lost its rudder and received a hole in the keel, through which so much water entered that it was all they could do to keep up with the rest.

CHAPTER 79

The captains find the Admiral at Santo Domingo

ON returning to Santo Domingo with their ships the captains found that the Admiral had arrived there from the mainland, and had full information about the rebels and the prosecution which the *adelantado* had launched against them. Although he recognized their crime and that they deserved punishment, he thought it advisable to make another inquiry and set up a fresh prosecution, in order to inform the Catholic sovereigns about the course of events. He was resolved to use all possible moderation in this and by skill to bring the rebels to obedience. For this reason, and in order that neither party should have any complaints against him, or say that he kept them there by force, on 22 September he gave orders for them to

be called together in the name of the Catholic sovereigns, and promised them food and a passage home. Also, having been informed that Roldan was marching on Santo Domingo with part of his company, he ordered Miguel Ballester, commander of Concepción, to guard the district and its fort carefully, and, should Roldan pass that way, to tell him in the Admiral's name that he greatly regretted the hardships Roldan had undergone and various recent events, to which he would make no further reference. The Admiral offered a general pardon and at the same time invited Roldan to come and visit him without fear, since he wished to consult him about matters concerning the service of their Catholic sovereigns. If Roldan should think that a safe conduct was necessary, he had only to ask and the Admiral would send him one.

Ballester answered this message on 24 September, saying that he had reliable information that Riquelme had arrived on the previous day at the town of Bonao, and that Adrian de Mujica and Roldan, the leaders of the faction, were to join one another six or eight days later, at a time and place which would enable him to take them prisoner. For he had talked with them according to the Admiral's instructions, and found them unabashed and stubborn. Roldan had said that they had not come to make an agreement, and that they neither wanted nor required peace, since he had the Admiral and his authority in his grasp, and could support or destroy it, as he wished. Roldan added that they should not speak of pacts or agreements until they had sent back all the Indians captured at the siege of Concepción, since they had gathered only in the King's interest and to do him service, and had all trusted in the *adelantado*'s word. Roldan had said more to the effect that he wanted no agreement except on terms greatly to his advantage. To negotiate such a pact or agreement, he asked the Admiral to send Carvajal, who was the only man with whom he would care to talk, since he had shown himself to be both

242

reasonable and prudent at the time when the three ships arrived at Jaragua.

This answer made the Admiral suspicious of Carvajal, and not without serious cause. Firstly because before Carvajal came to Jaragua, where the rebels then were, they had often written and sent messengers to his friends who were with the *adelantado*, saying that when the Admiral came they would put themselves at his disposal, and begging these friends of Carvajal graciously to act as mediators and placate him.

Secondly, if they had done this on the arrival of the two ships, bringing aid from the Admiral, they would have had greater reason to do so on learning that the Admiral had himself come, if they had not been dissuaded by the long discussion that Carvajal had held with them.

Thirdly, if Carvajal had done his duty he could have detained Roldan and the chiefs of his band as prisoners in his caravel, since they had spent two days with him under no safe conduct.

Fourthly, that knowing as he did that they were in revolt he should not have let them buy from the ships the fifty-four swords and forty crossbows they had acquired.

Fifthly, because having already seen signs that the men who had disembarked with Juan Antonio to go to Santo Domingo intended to join the rebels he should never have let them go ashore; or when they had joined the rebels he should have made greater efforts to secure their recapture.

Sixthly, because Carvajal was spreading it abroad that he had accompanied the Admiral to the Indies in order that the Admiral should do nothing without him, since they were afraid in Castile that he might commit some error.

Seventhly, because Roldan had sent a letter to the Admiral by Carvajal to the effect that he had come to Santo Domingo on Carvajal's advice in order to be at hand and ready to negotiate an agreement with the Admiral on his arrival in Hispaniola;

and that when the Admiral arrived and the facts were seen not to conform with this letter, it seemed more probable that Carvajal had brought Roldan to Santo Domingo so that in the event of the Admiral's delay or non-arrival, he, Carvajal, as the Admiral's companion, and Roldan, as *alcalde*, could have governed the island in despite of the *adelantado*.

Eighthly, because when the other two captains came by sea with the three caravels and he came to Santo Domingo by land the mutineers left one of their chiefs, Gomez by name, under his protection, and this man had spent two days and nights with him in his ship and accompanied him to within six leagues of Santo Domingo.

Ninthly, because he had not only written to the rebels when were at Bonao but sent them presents and provisions.

Tenthly and lastly, because the rebels would not treat with anyone but him, but all said unanimously that in case of necessity they would have chosen him as their captain.

On the other hand, the Admiral considered that Carvajal was a prudent and wise gentleman, and that each of the suspicions set out might have a legitimate explanation or what he had been told might be untrue, for he thought of Carvajal as a man who would do no wrong. Being anxious to quench the flames, the Admiral decided to consult all the principal men around him concerning the best way of replying to Roldan and what should now be done in this matter. All were in agreement, and he ordered Carvajal together with the *alcalde* Ballester to negotiate terms.

The only reply that they could get from Roldan, however, was that since they had not brought the Indians he had asked for there could be no talk of any kind about an agreement. Carvajal met this refusal with his characteristic tact and argued so well and reasonably with them all that Roldan and three or four of his chiefs were moved to visit the Admiral in

order to reach an agreement with him. This so displeased the rest of the rebels that, as Roldan and the others were mounting their horses to go with Carvajal to see the Admiral, the rest objected, saying that on no account must they go, and that if any agreement were made it must be by exchange of letters so that everyone could approve its terms. Consequently some days later, on 15 October, Roldan wrote a letter to the Admiral with the general consent, in which he laid the whole blame for his disaffection on the *adelantado*, who had caused the trouble. He told the Admiral also that since he had sent them no written safe conduct enabling them to come and give him an account of what had happened they had decided to set out in writing the objects and terms they demanded. These included payment for the works they had carried out so far, of which more later.

Though their demands were exorbitant and quite shameless, Ballester wrote next day to the Admiral, highly praising the reasonableness of Carvajal's earlier speech, and saying that, since it had been powerless to dissuade the rebels from their evil purposes, there was no other course but to grant them their demands. For he had found their spirit so high that the majority of those at present with his Illustrious Lordship would go over to them. The Admiral might rely on his servants and the men of rank who were with him, continued Ballester, but they could not be enough to oppose all the many who were daily going over to the rebels.

The Admiral already observed these defections. For since Roldan was close to Santo Domingo, he had held a muster of those who would have to go out and fight, if necessary, and had noted that some pretended to be lame and others sick, and that less than seventy men had turned out, of whom not forty were reliable. Under these circumstances, on the following day, which was 17 October 1498, Roldan and the other chiefs who had been willing to accompany him on his

visit to the Admiral sent him a letter signed by them all, saying that they had left the *adelantado* to save their lives, since he had been seeking a means of killing them. As servants of his most Illustrious Lordship, they had awaited his coming in the expectation that he would accept what they had done as in his interest, and had prevented their followers from in any way harming or prejudicing his office, as they could easily have done. But since his arrival the Admiral had not only shown them no gratitude, but had endeavoured to hurt and take vengeance on them. Therefore, in order honourably to carry out their resolutions and preserve their liberty to do so, they were removing themselves from his authority and service.

Before this letter was handed to the Admiral, he had already sent Roldan an answer by Carvajal in which he expressed the confidence that he had always had in him and the good account of him that he had given to the Catholic sovereigns, and added that he had not put this account in writing since he was afraid that it might cause Roldan some difficulties with the common people who, if they had seen it, might have done him some injury. Instead of a signed letter, he went on, he had sent them the *alcalde* Ballester, a person whom he knew to be much trusted by them – and whom he could consider as reliable as the Admiral's own seal; and he would be right to do so since he would find him in every way well disposed.

Then on 18 October the Admiral commanded that five ships should sail for Castile, by which he sent the Catholic sovereigns very detailed information about all that was going on. He said that he had detained these five ships for so many days after his arrival, since he believed that Roldan and his followers wished to return on them, as they proclaimed. As for the other three ships that he had with him, these needed refitting, so that the *adelantado* could sail in them to continue the exploration of the mainland of Paria and supervise the fishing and purchase of pearls, a sample of which he sent them.

CHAPTER 80

*Roldan goes to see the Admiral, but reaches no
agreement with him*

On the third day after receiving the Admiral's letter Roldan
replied, showing every sign that he was willing to do as he
was asked. But since his men would not allow him to visit the
Admiral without a safe conduct, he begged that one should be
sent him, as had been requested in the document which he had
sent to the Admiral, signed by himself and ratified by his chief
lieutenants. The Admiral sent him the safe conduct immediately, on 26 October. As soon as he received it Roldan set out,
though rather with the intention of attracting people to his
cause than of reaching a settlement, as was evident from the
shameless nature of his demands. He returned therefore without coming to any agreement and saying that he would give
an account of things to his men and that he would write to
the Admiral to tell him what they had decided; and in order
that someone should be there on the Admiral's behalf to
negotiate and conclude any agreement that might be reached
a steward of the Admiral's, Diego de Salamanca by name,
accompanied Roldan back to his men.

After much argument Roldan sent a deed of agreement for
the Admiral to sign, and wrote to him on 6 November that
this was all he had been able to obtain from his people, and
that if his Illustrious Lordship approved it, he should send his
acceptance to Concepción, since they had now run out of
food at Bonao, and that they would wait for his reply until
the following Monday.

When he saw the terms of their reply, the Admiral considered their demands to be shameless and refused on any account to agree for fear of prejudicing justice or staining the

honour of himself and his brothers. But in order that they should have no cause for fresh complaint or say that he was acting with severity in this matter, on 11 November he ordered a proclamation of safe conduct to be published and displayed for thirty days – which it was – on the doors of the fort. In it he stated that during his absence in Castile, although some differences had arisen between the *adelantado* and the *alcalde mayor* Roldan and other persons who had joined him, all in general and each man separately could come in complete safety to serve the Catholic sovereigns as if nothing had happened, and that if anyone wished to depart for Castile he would receive his passage and an order for the payment of his salary, as had been the usual practice in all other cases; and that this promise would be put into effect if they would appear before the Admiral within thirty days to take advantage of this safe conduct. But should they not appear within that time, proclaimed the Admiral, he would take judicial action against them. He then sent Roldan this safe conduct, duly signed, and carried by Carvajal, giving him in writing the reasons why he neither would nor should accept the terms sent to him and reminding Roldan of what he and his followers should rightly do if they wished to fulfil their duties to the Catholic sovereigns.

Carvajal took these documents to Concepción and saw the rebels, whom he found very bold and arrogant. They laughed at the Admiral's safe conduct, saying that very soon *he* would be asking for one from them. This business lasted three weeks, during which time, under the pretext that they wanted to arrest a man whom Roldan wished to execute, they kept the *alcalde* Ballester besieged in the fort, cutting off the water in the hope that thirst would compel him to surrender. But on Carvajal's arrival they raised the siege, and after a great deal of argument the two parties reached the following agreement.

[*The terms of the agreement set out in the next chapter (81)*

248

guarantee the return of Roldan and his followers to Castile in two ships to be provided by the Admiral. Their seaworthiness would be approved by competent sailors, and they were to depart from the port of Jaragua suitably stocked with provisions. The exact amounts of bread and flour were specified. The returning settlers were to be confirmed in all their possessions, including the slaves that had been granted them, and were to take back all women pregnant by them and all their children. The Admiral was to give them a letter addressed to the Catholic sovereigns, which would speak well of them and entitle them to payment for all their services up to the date of their departure; Roldan, in particular, who seems to have been the richest, was guaranteed the fair price ruling in the island for his large herd of pigs, also the right to sell the rest of his estates, as he should think fit. Various other grievances, mainly concerning slaves and possessions, were settled in favour of Roldan's party, and the Admiral gained very little beyond the concession that Roldan would recruit no more of those still loyal during the ten days between the handing over of the terms and their signature by the Admiral, and that his officials who came to see the ships off at Jaragua would be respected as servants of the Catholic sovereigns.

The document was agreed on 16 November 1498 at Concepción.]

CHAPTER 82

After the agreement is concluded the rebels go to Jaragua, saying that they are going to embark on the two ships that the Admiral is sending them

ON the conclusion of the agreement described, Carvajal and Salamanca returned to Santo Domingo and at their instance the Admiral signed the terms they brought him. He issued a

fresh safe conduct and licence for all those who did not wish to go to Castile with Roldan, promising them wages or settler's rights in the island – whichever they preferred – and that the rest could come and negotiate their affairs as they wished, and in complete liberty. This document was handed to Roldan and his followers by Ballester, and they then set out on their journey to Jaragua to pursue the policy of their faction in a way that was not known till later.

The Admiral was to some extent aware of their wickedness and was much grieved when he saw that the *adelantado*'s mission, which was to continue the exploration of the mainland of Paria and organize the fishing and barter of pearls, would be greatly hindered if these ships were given them. Nevertheless he did not wish to give the rebels cause to reproach him for refusing to provide the promised passage. He therefore began to prepare the ships in the manner agreed, but their departure was somewhat delayed by shortage of necessary materials. In order to collect these materials and cut short the delay he ordered Caravajal to go to Jaragua by land so that, while the ships were on the way, the final preparation could be made for the equipment and departure of Roldan's people in conformity with the detailed conditions that had been agreed. The Admiral decided that he would himself go to Isabela without delay to inspect the country and make it safe, leaving Don Diego at Santo Domingo to gather all necessary supplies.

So after the Admiral's departure, the two caravels sailed at the end of January 1499, with all that was necessary for the voyage to pick up the rebels. But owing to a storm which overtook them on the way they were compelled to put into another port and stay there till the end of March. Since one of the caravels, the *Niña*, was in a bad condition and required considerable repairs, the Admiral ordered Pedro de Arana and Francisco de Garay to go to Jaragua in the other and less dam-

aged ship, the *Santa Cruz*, and Carvajal followed afterwards in the *Niña*, thus breaking off his journey by land. The voyage took him eleven days and on reaching Jaragua he found the *Santa Cruz* already there.

CHAPTER 83

The rebels change their minds about going to Castile and make a new treaty with the Admiral

SINCE the caravels were delayed and most of Roldan's men had no wish to sail, they used this as an excuse for remaining where they were and blamed the Admiral for not having sent them off with the greatest possible dispatch. On hearing of this, the Admiral wrote to Roldan and Adrian de Mujica, with fair arguments exhorting them to carry out the agreement and not break their promises. In addition Carvajal, who was with them at Jaragua, protested to the rebels on 20 April before the notary Francisco de Garay (afterwards governor of Panuco and Jamaica) to the effect that since the Admiral was sending the two caravels duly equipped they should accept them and fulfil their side of the bargain. But as the rebels refused to comply, on 26 April Carvajal ordered the ships back to Santo Domingo, because they were being destroyed by shipworm and the crews were suffering from a severe shortage of provisions.

The rebels were not much concerned by Carvajal's action. On the contrary they were delighted and proud that he should treat them so seriously. They did not acknowledge the Admiral's courtesy but blamed him in writing for their continued stay at Jaragua, saying that in his desire to take revenge on them he had delayed the caravels and then sent them in

such a bad state that no one sailing in them could possibly hope to reach Castile safely. But even if they had been in good condition, the rebels had, so they said, exhausted all their provisions while waiting, and it would be some time before they could collect more. Under these circumstances, therefore, they had decided to wait there for redress from the Catholic sovereigns.

Carvajal returned to Santo Domingo by land, carrying this reply, and at the time of his departure Roldan told him that if the Admiral would send him another safe conduct he would be glad to visit him and see if they could come to new terms agreeable to both. Carvajal sent this information to the Admiral in a letter dispatched from Santo Domingo on 15 May. The Admiral replied on the 21st, thanking Carvajal for his great efforts in this matter, and enclosing a letter for Roldan, brief in words but weighty and forceful in content, exhorting him to keep the peace and remain the obedient servant of their Catholic Majesties. On the messenger's return to Santo Domingo the Admiral wrote at greater length on 24 June.

On 3 August six or seven of the Admiral's chief lieutenants sent Roldan another safe conduct enabling him to come and treat with his Lordship. But as the distance was great and it suited the Admiral to make a journey into the country, he agreed to come to the port of Asua in the same island of Hispaniola and to the west of Santo Domingo, with two caravels, in order to be nearer to the province where the rebels were. A good number of them came to this port and, on arriving with his ships almost at the end of August, the Admiral began to enter into negotiations with the chief of them. Exhorting them to abandon their evil purposes, he promised them liberal grants and favours, and the rebels offered to do as he wished if he would concede them four points: first, to send fifteen of their number to Castile in the first ships that should arrive;

secondly, that those who remained on the island should be given land and a living in lieu of the wages due to them; thirdly, that an edict should be published to the effect that all the recent happenings were due to false witness and some mischievous persons; and fourthly, that Roldan should immediately be appointed *alcalde mayor* in perpetuity.

When these terms were agreed between them, Roldan went ashore from the Admiral's caravel and sent his men the articles, but so maliciously perverted the meaning of the clauses to his own advantage as to state in conclusion that, should the Admiral default in any way, they would be entitled to obtain his compliance by force or as they thought fit. But the Admiral was anxious to see the end of all these difficulties. When he considered that his enemies had been growing continuously stronger for the last two years and remained defiant, and that many of those still with him were gathering into factions intending to march to other places in the island, as Roldan had done, he decided to sign whatever he was asked. He published two edicts, one appointing Roldan *alcalde mayor* in perpetuity and the other agreeing to the four demands already specified. He also confirmed the other orders that he had given, in writing, a copy of which I have given above.

Afterwards, on Tuesday, 5 November, Roldan began to exercise his office and, in virtue of the authority permitted to him alone, appointed Pedro de Riquelme judge at Bonao with the right of trying all malefactors, except those liable to the death penalty, who were to be sent to the fort at Concepción to be judged by him. And since the pupil had as malignant intentions as the master, Riquelme immediately began to plan the building of a fort at Bonao, and would have built it if he had not been prevented by Pedro de Arana, who clearly recognized that Riquelme was acting against his duties to the Admiral.

CHAPTER 84*

*On returning from his voyage of exploration Ojeda
raises fresh disturbances in Hispaniola*

'ON the day after Christmas 1499,' writes the Admiral, 'when everyone had left me, I was attacked by Indians and evil Christians and reduced to such straits that to avoid death I had to abandon everything and put to sea in one small caravel. Then the Lord rescued me, saying: "O man of little faith, be not afraid. I am here." And so He scattered my enemies, and showed me how to fulfil my obligations, unhappy sinner that I am, who depended utterly on the hopes of this world.'

On 3 February 1500 the Admiral intended to go to Santo Domingo in order to make preparations for his return to Castile and give an account of everything to the Catholic sovereigns.

To continue the thread of our story, let me say that, having settled the affair of Roldan, the Admiral appointed a captain and some men to patrol the island in order to pacify it and exact tribute from the Indians. Their further duty was to give early warning of any incipient unrest or disturbance among the Christians or any Indian rebellion, so that it might be suppressed and things be put right immediately. He took this measure because he intended to leave for Castile, taking the *adelantado* with him, since they would find it difficult to forget recent events if he were to remain governor.

As he was preparing for his departure, Alonso de Ojeda†

---

* The first two paragraphs of this chapter appear out of sequence in the original.

† Ojeda had obtained a patent of exploration from Fonseca, and had sailed to the then unknown coast of Brazil, from which he had gone along the mainland as far as Venezuela, named by him 'Little Venice'

arrived in the island, having made a voyage of exploration with four ships. And since such men sail with no fixed purpose, on 5 September 1499 he had entered a harbour which Christians call the port of Brasil* (the Indians call it Yaquimo), with the intention of getting whatever he could from the natives and taking a cargo of slaves and brasil-wood. While this was going on he devoted himself wholeheartedly to doing mischief. To prove himself a loyal henchman of Bishop Fonseca, already mentioned, he set about stirring up fresh trouble by proclaiming as a fact that Queen Isabela was at the point of death and that once she was dead there would be no one left who favoured the Admiral, and that he as a true and trustworthy servant of the bishop could do anything he liked to the Admiral's prejudice on account of the enmity between the two men. He then began to write to some not very reliable men who had been involved in the late disturbances, exciting them with these tales, and entering into negotiations with them.

On learning of Ojeda's actions and proposals, Roldan went against him with twenty-six men, on the Admiral's orders, to prevent him from doing the mischief he was plotting. On 29 September, being within a league and a half of Ojeda, Roldan learnt that he, with fifteen men, was at the village of a *cacique* called Haniguayaba, baking bread and biscuit. So Roldan went that night to catch him by surprise. Knowing that Roldan was pursuing him, however, Ojeda made a virtue of necessity. Not having the strength to resist Roldan, he went out to meet him and told him that he had come there to get

---

on account of the number of offshore islands. He had visited the pearl fisheries of Margarita, which Columbus had missed and to which he had intended to send his brother. With Ojeda sailed the Italian clerk Amerigo Vespucci, who by the whim of a cartographer gave his name to the continent.

*Named from the dye wood which grew in the vicinity.

provisions, of which he was very short, and that he was on his sovereigns' land and had no harmful intentions. He gave Roldan an account of his voyage, saying that he had sailed along the coast of Paria westwards for 600 leagues, and had met a people who had fought against the Christians on equal terms, wounding twenty of them, but he had not been able to take advantage of the wealth of the country, in which he said he had found deer, rabbits, the skins and paws of tigers, and base gold. These he showed Roldan in the caravels, telling him that he wished to go quickly to Santo Domingo in order to give an account of all this to the Admiral.

The Admiral was at that time greatly troubled by a letter he had received from Pedro de Arana, telling him that Riquelme, whom Roldan had nominated *alcalde* of Bonao, had on the excuse of wishing to build a cattle shed chosen a commanding hill from which with a few men he could do all the harm he chose. Arana said that he had prevented this. But Riquelme had drawn up a protest with witnesses against the violence done him by Arana and sent it to the Admiral, begging for redress, in default of which some disorder might break out between them. As for Ojeda, the Admiral was well aware that he had some ulterior design. But he decided to put aside his suspicions, while remaining on his guard, thinking that it might be enough to correct Ojeda's obvious mistake without inflaming a situation which could be met by pretending to ignore it.

Ojeda, however, persisted in his evil purposes. In February 1500, having taken leave of Roldan, he went with his ships to Jaragua, where many of the former rebels were living. Since greed and profit are the best means of fomenting evil, Ojeda began to proclaim among these people that the Catholic sovereigns had appointed him counsellor to the Admiral, jointly with Carvajal, to prevent him from doing anything that they considered against their Majesties' interest, and that

the first of many things that they had been ordered to do was to pay immediately, in cash, the wages of everyone in the island who was engaged in the royal service. But since the Admiral did not seem disposed to make these payments, he offered to go with them himself to Santo Domingo and compel the Admiral to pay promptly. After that, if they agreed, he could be thrown out of the island alive or dead. For they must not rely on the agreement the Admiral had made with them nor on his promise to them, for he was not a man who kept his word except under compulsion.

Tempted by this offer, many decided to follow him, and with their support he fell one night on the group that opposed him. There were dead and wounded on both sides. Since they thought it certain, as it indeed was, that Roldan had returned to the Admiral's service, and would not join the new conspiracy, these followers of Ojeda decided to attack him by surprise and take him prisoner. But Roldan received warning of this plan and marched against Ojeda with enough men to remedy the trouble or punish him, as he thought fit. Ojeda then retired in fear to his ships, and from the sea negotiated with Roldan, who remained on land, concerning a suitable place for an interview, for each of them was afraid of putting himself in the power of the other.

When Roldan saw that Ojeda would not trust himself ashore, he offered to go and talk with him aboard ship, and for that purpose sent to ask him for a ship's boat. Ojeda sent it with a strong guard and when Roldan with six or seven of his lieutenants were in the boat and Ojeda's guard felt completely secure Roldan's party attacked them with naked swords, killing some and wounding others and seizing the boat which they brought to land. Ojeda was now left with only one boat to serve all his ships, and in this he calmly went to his interview with Roldan. There, excusing himself for his violence, Ojeda freed some prisoners he had captured, asking in ex-

change for the boat and its crew that had been taken by Roldan, saying that if it was not restored he and his ship would be wrecked, for they had no other boat to serve them. Roldan restored it gladly in order that Ojeda should have no cause for complaint, and not be able to say that because of Roldan he was going to his doom. But before this he exacted a binding promise from Ojeda that he and his men would leave Hispaniola within a certain time, and Ojeda was compelled to put to sea because Roldan placed a strong guard on the shore.

But as it is difficult to destroy weeds so thoroughly that none spring up again, so a disorderly people cannot fail to return to their old errors, as some of the rebels did a few days after Ojeda's departure. A certain Don Hernando de Guevara, a malcontent who was in disgrace with the Admiral, had joined Ojeda out of hatred for Roldan for which he was himself to blame. Roldan had refused to let him marry a daughter of Anacaona, the principal queen of Jaragua, and Guevara then began to gather many of the old conspirators with the intention of capturing Roldan and taking over the work of destruction. He incited Adrian de Mujica in particular, one of the principal malcontents, who, with two other criminals, in the middle of June 1500, had planned the capture or murder of Roldan.

But Roldan was very much on his guard, since he knew what they were discussing, and arrested Guevara, Mujica and the rest of the band. He then informed the Admiral of the course of events and asked his opinion as to what he should do. The Admiral replied that, since they had wantonly attempted to raise the country, total destruction would ensue if they were not punished. He must therefore do justice on them according to their crimes and the provisions of the law. The *alcalde* immediately carried out this advice. He tried the rebels and condemned Adrian de Mujica to be hanged as the author and

leader of the conspiracy. He sentenced others to various terms of exile according to their guilt and held Guevara in prison until 13 June, when he handed him and other prisoners over to Gonzalo Blanco, to be taken by him to the Admiral.

These sentences quietened the country, the Indians returned to their obedience and again served the Christians, and goldfields were discovered in such plenty that everyone resigned the royal service and set up on his own account, industriously extracting gold, a third part of which was given to the Crown. This work went on so successfully that one man extracted, in a single day, five marks of fair-sized gold grains, and among them was one worth more than 196 ducats. The Indians were very docile and much afraid of the Admiral. So anxious were they to please him that, to oblige him, they voluntarily became Christians, and if an Indian chief had to appear before him he endeavoured to come clothed.

CHAPTER 85

Owing to false information and lying stories and
the complaints of certain persons the Catholic
sovereigns send a judge to the Indies to discover
what is going on

DURING the course of the disturbances many of the rebels sent false information in letters from Hispaniola, and others who had returned to Castile also gave lying reports against the Admiral and his brothers to the sovereigns and their Council, alleging that they were not only very cruel but incompetent to govern. For not only were they foreigners from another country, but they had never before been in a position of authority, and had no experience of controlling people of

quality. These people affirmed that unless their royal Highnesses were to intervene the Indies would come to total ruin,
and if they were not destroyed by his perverse administration,
the Admiral would himself rebel and make a pact with some
foreign prince who would support him on the assumption
that all these lands were his, since he had discovered them by
his own skill and labour. They said that, in furtherance of this
project, the Admiral was concealing the riches of the land
and preventing the Indians from working for the Christians
and becoming converted to our faith. For he hoped by flatter-
ing them to win them to his side and to make them do everything possible to their Highnesses' disservice.

By repeating these and similar calumnies, they greatly disturbed the Catholic sovereigns, libelling the Admiral, and
complaining that the Spaniards had not been paid their wages
for many years, and this aroused much talk and scandal among
those then at court. In fact, when I was in Granada, at the time
of His Most Serene Highness Don Miguel's death,* fifty or
more shameless fellows around the court bought large quantities of grapes and sat down in the great court of the Alhambra, crying that their Majesties and the Admiral had reduced
them to this sort of diet by low wages. They said much else
that was offensive, and were so brazen that if his Catholic
Majesty came out they would surround him and bar his way,
shouting: 'Pay! Give us our pay!' And if my brother and I,
who were pages to the Queen, happened to pass, they would
shout to heaven and pursue us crying: 'There go the sons of
the Lord Admiral of the Flies, the men who discovered lands
of vanity and deceit for Spanish gentlemen to starve and die
in!' And they uttered many more obscenities, so that we tried
to avoid any place which they frequented.

As a result of their complaints and their importunate
approaches to the King's favourites, his Majesty decided to

* Grandson of the sovereigns. He died on 20 July 1500.

send a judge to Hispaniola to inquire into all these complaints, and ordered him, should he find the Admiral guilty of the matters complained of, to send him back to Castile and himself remain as governor. This examining judge sent by their Catholic Majesties was Francisco de Bobadilla, a poor knight of the order of Calatrava. He was appointed in Madrid on 21 May 1499, with plenary powers and blank patents bearing the royal seal and signatures, which were to be presented to anyone he thought fit in Hispaniola and which commanded them to give him all help and service.

Bobadilla arrived at Santo Domingo with these documents at the end of August 1500,* while the Admiral was away at Concepción setting to rights the affairs of that province, where the *adelantado* had been attacked by the rebels, and where there were a greater number of Indians than in the rest of the island, who were also of better quality and intelligence

---

*Hernando presents the case for his father far too favourably. Las Casas, who is seldom unfair to Columbus, gives a more objective account in his *History* (I, 178). On arriving Bobadilla met the spectacle of two Spaniards swinging on the gallows. Don Diego was punishing the former rebels, of whom many more, among them Guevara and Riquelme, were in prison awaiting execution. The town was full of gossip, and for a day or two the settlers waited 'to see which of the two worlds would come out on top'. Bobadilla demanded the release of the prisoners; Diego refused to let them out. Then Bobadilla proclaimed that arrears of wages would be paid either out of the royal funds in the island or from Columbus's possessions. The *adelantado* was putting down the rebellion in Jaragua, Columbus himself was pacifying Concepción. Bobadilla dealt rather tactlessly with the Admiral, treating him with less respect than Roldan, to whom he sent a personal letter. Columbus may have attempted armed resistance. Perhaps he thought Bobadilla a second Ojeda. But the Admiral was generally loathed, the settlers were unpaid and his only remedy for the disorders was one of violent suppression. Bobadilla, like other royal officials sent out to clear up after the Conquistadores, was peremptory and unsentimental. It is hard to accept Hernando's judgement, however, that the 'poor knight' was greedy for his father's fortune and governorship.

than those of other regions. So, when Bobadilla arrived, he was met by no one who commanded his respect. The first thing he did, therefore, was to lodge himself in the Admiral's palace, taking possession and making use of everything there, as if it were his by lawful right of succession. He favoured and encouraged all the former rebels whom he met, and many others who hated the Admiral and his brothers, and proclaimed himself governor. And, in order to gain the goodwill of the people, he issued an edict exempting them from the payment of tribute for twenty years. He then summoned the Admiral to come to him without delay, saying that this was his duty as a servant of the Catholic sovereigns. To confirm this order he sent him by Brother Juan de Trasiera, on 7 September, a royal patent to the following effect:

'To Don Cristobal de Colon, our Admiral of the Ocean Sea. We have sent the *comendador* Francisco de Bobadilla, the bearer of this patent, to speak with you on our behalf about certain matters of which he will tell you. We ask you to give him faith and credence. From Madrid, 26 May 1499. I the King, I the Queen. Written at their command by Miguel de Almazan.'

CHAPTER 86

The Admiral is arrested and sent to Castile in chains, together with his brothers

IMMEDIATELY he saw this letter from the Catholic sovereigns the Admiral hastened to Santo Domingo, where the judge was, and Bobadilla, in his anxiety to maintain himself as governor, with no further delay or inquiry, at the beginning of October arrested the Admiral and his brother Don Diego,

sending them aboard ship where he put them in chains and under a strong guard, ordering that no one, under the severest penalties, should even speak of them. Afterwards, with the proverbial justice of King Crane, he began to draw up a case against them, citing as witnesses the Admiral's enemies who had rebelled against him, publicly favouring and encouraging anyone who came forward to abuse the prisoners. These witnesses were so malevolent and abusive in their declarations that a man would have had to be more than blind not to recognize that what they said was prompted by passion, not by truth. For this reason the Catholic sovereigns afterwards refused to accept these charges and absolved the Admiral, repenting of having sent this man with such powers. And they had good cause to be sorry, for Bobadilla destroyed the island and dissipated the royal rents and tributes in order to win support for himself. To this end he proclaimed that the Catholic kings wanted nothing more than the titular sovereignty, and that the profit from it was for their subjects.

But however wrong, Bobadilla did not fail to raise adherents. On the contrary, allying himself with the richest and most powerful, he gave them Indians to work for them on the understanding that they would divide with him all the profit that they made by the labour of these Indians; and he sold by public auction all the possessions and lands that the Admiral had won for the Catholic sovereigns, saying that the sovereigns were neither farmers nor merchants, and did not need these lands for their profit but for the aid and comfort of their good subjects. On this pretext he sold them everything, taking care, on the other hand, that some of his companions should buy what he offered at a third of its proper price. In addition to this, he perverted the course of justice to the same end, and had no other aim but to enrich himself and gain the affection of the people. For he was still in some fear that the *adelantado*, who had not yet come back from Jaragua, might

obstruct him and attempt to free the Admiral by armed force.

But in fact Don Bartolomé exercised great restraint in this matter, having received a message from the Admiral requesting him, in the royal interests and in order not to disturb the country, to come peacefully, since on reaching Castile they would find it easier to secure the punishment of a certain person and remedy for the injuries they were suffering.

Nevertheless Bobadilla imprisoned Don Bartolomé with his brothers and allowed the ill-disposed mob to speak all kinds of libels against them in public places, blowing horns on the landing-stage as they were taken aboard, and posting abusive notices at the street corners. What is more, on hearing that Diego Ortiz, governor of the hospital, had read out a libellous statement in the main square, Bobadilla not only failed to punish him but showed great delight at the reading. Consequently each man did his utmost to rival his neighbour in such displays of effrontery.

At the time of the Admiral's departure, fearing that he might swim ashore, Bobadilla took care to order the ship's captain, whose name was Andres Martin, to hand him over still in chains to the bishop Don Juan de Fonseca, on whose favour and counsel he unwaveringly relied in doing what he did. Afterwards, however, when they were at sea, recognizing Bobadilla's malice, the captain wished to release the Admiral from his chains. But the Admiral would not consent. Since the Catholic sovereigns, he said, had commanded him in their letter to do whatever Bobadilla might order to be carried out in their name, and the chains had been put on him by their commission and authority, he was unwilling for anyone else but their Highnesses to exercise judgement in this matter. In fact he was determined to keep these chains as relics to remind him of the way in which his many services had been rewarded; which is more or less what he did. For he kept them always in his room and wished them to be buried with his bones.

LETTER SENT BY THE ADMIRAL OF THE INDIES TO THE GOVERNESS* OF DON JUAN OF CASTILE IN THE YEAR 1500, IN WHICH HE WAS BROUGHT FROM THE INDIES A PRISONER

MOST VIRTUOUS LADY: If it is new for me to complain against the world, its habit of ill-treating me is an old one. It has made many attacks on me, all of which I have resisted till now, when neither arms nor precautions have availed me. It has cruelly thrown me to the depths, but hope in my Creator sustains me, since His aid has always been very swift. On another occasion not long ago when I was cast even lower, He raised me with His right arm, saying, 'Oh man of little faith, arise, it is I, be not afraid!'

I came with such earnest love to serve these princes and have given them unparalleled service.

Of the new heaven and the new earth, which Our Lord made – as St John writes in Revelations – following the words given to Isaiah, 'He made me the messenger and he showed me where to go' – all men were incredulous. But the Lord gave to my Lady the Queen the spirit of understanding and great courage, and He made her His dear and much beloved daughter, heiress to it all. I took possession of all these lands in her royal name. All tried to justify the ignorance in which they were sunk by speaking of difficulties and expense. The Queen, on the other hand, approved my scheme and supported it with all her power. Seven years passed in discussions and nine in the enterprise itself. Remarkable and memorable

*Juana de la Torre, a close friend of Queen Isabela who had been 'nurse' or governess to Prince Juan, the heir to the throne.

events took place in those years, which no one could have conceived beforehand.

Now I have reached a state in which even the vilest creature feels capable of insulting me, and in this state I now am. It will be accounted a virtue in anyone to hold back from reviling me. If I had stolen the Indies or the holy city of which St Peter was bishop and delivered them to the Moors, they could not treat me in Spain with greater hostility. Who would believe this of a country that has always been so noble?

I would most gladly abandon the whole business if I could do so without dishonour to my Queen. But Our Lord's support and the Queen's compel me to go on with it. To provide some alleviation for the sorrows which death* had caused her, I undertook a new voyage to new skies and lands which had been concealed till now, and if this is not regarded with the same amazement as my other voyages, it is not surprising, since by my efforts these lands are now known.

The Holy Spirit inspired St Peter and the twelve apostles with him and they all fought valiantly in the world. Their trials and labours were many: and in them all they were finally victorious.

I thought that this voyage to Paria would somewhat comfort her on account of the pearls and the finding of gold in Hispaniola, and I ordered the people to fish for pearls and keep them until I returned to fetch them. I made this agreement with them and as I understood it they promised me about a bushel and a half. If I did not write to inform their Highnesses of this it was because I wanted to assess the amount of the gold first. I should have lost neither the pearls nor my honour if I had pursued my own advantage and allowed Hispaniola to be ruined, or if my grants and privileges had been respected. I say the same of the gold which I had by that

* This refers to the death of Prince Juan, of whom Juana de la Torres had been governess.

time collected, and which with such toil and loss of life I have brought back complete.

On my return from Paria I found almost half the settlers in Hispaniola in revolt, and they have fought me to this day as if I were an infidel. At the same time there has been grave trouble with the Indians. Then came Ojeda, who endeavoured to complete my ruin. He said that their Highnesses had sent him with promises of gifts, privileges and payments. He gathered a great following, for nearly all the settlers in Hispaniola are adventurers. There is no one there with wife and children. This man Ojeda caused me great trouble and I had to send him away. He went, saying that he would soon return with more ships and men, and said also that he had left her royal Majesty at the point of death.

At this moment Vicente Yanez arrived with four caravels. He aroused suspicion and disturbance but did no damage. The Indians reported that many other ships had arrived at Paria and in the Carib islands and afterwards came news of six other caravels brought by a brother of the chief magistrate, but these reports were malicious. This was at a moment when there was very little hope that their Highnesses would ever send ships to the Indies. We did not expect them and it was commonly said that her Highness was dead.

One, Adrian, led another uprising at this time but the Lord did not allow him to effect his evil purpose. I had made up my mind not to harm a hair of anyone's head, but unhappily on account of his ingratitude I could not spare him as I intended. I would not have dealt more mercifully with my own brother if he had plotted to kill me and rob me of the command which my King and Queen had entrusted to me. This Adrian as it has proved sent Don Fernando to Jaragua to collect some of his followers and there was argument there with the *alcalde mayor*, which led to a deadly quarrel, but he did not attain his purpose. The *alcalde mayor*

arrested him and some of his band, and in fact punished him without my orders. They were kept prisoner, awaiting a caravel to take them home, but Ojeda's news made us lose hope that any ship would come.

For six months I had been ready to leave and bring their Highnesses the good news of the gold and escape from this governorship of dissolute people, who fear neither God nor their King and Queen, and are full of perversity and malice.

I should have been able to pay the people six hundred thousand *maravedis* and for this purpose I had four million and more from the tithes as well as a third of the gold. Before departing I many times begged their Highnesses to send someone out at my expense to take over the administration of justice; and when I found the *alcalde mayor* in revolt I begged them once more for some men or at least for a servant bearing their letters, for such is my reputation that were I to build churches and hospitals they would always be called dens of thieves. Their Highnesses at last acceded to my request, but not at all as the situation demanded. But so let it be, since that is their pleasure.

I stayed there two years, without being able to secure any provision in favour of myself or the other settlers, and he★ brings a chestful. Whether all these will be used in the royal service, God knows. Grants have been made for twenty years which is a lifetime, and gold is being collected so freely that a man may have five marks in four hours. I will say more about this later.

May it please their Highnesses to rebuke this mob who know that I am exhausted. I have suffered so greatly from their abuse that my services to their Highnesses and my endeavours to preserve their estates and authority have availed me nothing. It would be only charitable if they would shame these people and restore my honour, and their action

★Francisco de Bobadilla.

would be spoken of throughout the world, for this matter is of such importance that it it is more widely discussed and more highly valued every day.

At this juncture the knight Bobadilla arrived in Santo Domingo. I was in the Plains and the *adelantado* was where this man Adrian had raised a revolt, but things were now settled, and the country rich and at peace. On the day after his arrival, he made himself governor, appointed officials, performed executive acts, granted licences for the collection of gold, and tithes, and all sorts of other things for a period of twenty years, which, as I have just said, is a lifetime. He said that he had come to pay everyone, including those who have not yet completed their service, and to send me and my brothers back in irons, as he has done, and that I must never return to Hispaniola and nor may any member of my family. He also said many unjust and abusive things about me.

He did all this, as I have said, on the day after his arrival, when I was far away and did not even know that he had come. He filled a number of blank letters signed by their Majesties, which he had brought with him, with favours and flatteries and sent them to the *alcalde mayor* and his followers, but he sent no letter or message to me and has not done so to this day.

Imagine, Madam, what a man with my responsibilities must think of this! Honours and favours for one who was palpably robbing their Highnesses of their authority and doing so much evil and damage, and disgrace for one who supported that authority at such peril! When the news of this reached me, I thought that this would be like the affair of Ojeda or one of the others. I restrained myself when I learnt for certain from the friars★ that their Highnesses had sent him. I wrote to welcome his arrival, saying that I was ready to go to court and had put all my possessions up for sale. I begged him not to be in a hurry over the grants, and said

★Las Casas speaks of one friar only.

that I would soon give him a very thorough account both of this matter and my governorship. I wrote the same thing to the friars, but neither they nor Bobadilla sent me any reply. He adopted a hostile attitude and compelled all who came to Santo Domingo to swear allegiance to him as governor for twenty years, as they told me.

When I heard of the grants that he was making, I resolved to repair his great mistake, thinking he would be glad that I should do so, for without cause or reason he was conferring vastly more on idle adventurers than would have been needed by a man who had brought out a wife and children. I proclaimed by word and letters that he had no right to exert his powers since mine had greater authority and showed him the privileges conveyed to me by Juan de Aguado.

I did all this to gain time, so that their Highnesses might be informed of the state of the country, and be able to send fresh orders proclaiming their will in these matters.

It is not to their advantage that such grants should be made in the Indies, but much to the advantage of the settlers, who receive the best lands, which at a low estimate will be worth 200,000 *maravedis* by the time they have established their rights as residents, even if they do not turn a single sod in the whole four years. I would not speak like this if the settlers were married men, but there are not half a dozen of of them who do not aim to amass all they can and return home speedily. It would be a good thing if men were to come from Castile, but only men of good reputation, and if the country could be settled by honest people.

I had arranged with those settlers that they should pay a third of the gold and the tithes and this at their request. They accepted this as a great favour from their Highnesses and I took them to task when I heard that they were breaking the agreement. I expected the *comendador* to do the same, but he did quite the contrary. He inflamed them against me saying

that I wanted to take away what their Highnesses had given them. He did all he could to stir them up, and he succeeded. He made them write to their Highnesses that they should entrust me with no more commissions (and this is my entreaty also, I want nothing for myself and nothing done for me, so long as the people remain unchanged). He ordered an inquiry to be made into my crimes, which were more heinous than any known in hell.

Our Lord is in heaven, who saved Daniel and the three children, with all His wisdom and power. May it please Him to save me also by a similar manifestation of His will. I should have been able to repair all this and everything else that has been said and done since I came to the Indies if I had allowed myself to act for my own advantage and if it had been honourable for me to do so. But the continuous maintenance of justice and the increase of their Highnesses' estates has brought me to ruin.

Just at the moment when so much gold is being found, men argue whether it is better to go about plundering or go to the mines. The cost of a woman is 100 *castellanos*, the same as that of a farm. The trade is very common and there are now many merchants who go about looking for girls; some of nine or ten are now on sale, but whatever their age they command a good price.

I declare that the slanders of disaffected persons have done me more harm than my services have done me good. This is a bad example both for now and the future. I swear on oath that there are plenty who have come to the Indies who were not deserving of baptism in the eyes of God and the world, and now they are returning home with the *comendador* Bobadilla's agreement.

I declare that in saying that the *comendador* had no right to make grants I was doing what he himself wished. I told him, however, that it was in order to gain time until their High-

nesses were advised of the state of the country and on reconsideration could send fresh orders.

The *comendador* put all the settlers against me, and it appears from his actions and behaviour that he came in a hostile frame of mind. It is said that he spent a great deal to come on this business: but about this I know no more than I have heard. I have never heard of a Judge of Inquiry collecting rebels and taking them or other godless and untruthful men as witnesses against their own governor. If their Highnesses would order a general inquiry, to be held there, they would be greatly astonished I assure you that the island has not sunk beneath the sea.

I think that you will remember, Madam, that when I was driven without sails into Lisbon I was falsely accused of having gone there to see the King of Portugal and give the Indies to him. Their Highnesses afterwards learnt that this was an untrue story invented out of malice.

So far as I know, no one considers me so stupid as to imagine that even if the Indies were mine I could hold them without the aid of some prince. This being the case, where could I find better support and certainty of not being completely expelled from them than in our Lords the King and Queen, who have raised me from nothing to such honours and who are the greatest princes in the world, both on sea and land? They believe that I have served them and they preserve my rights and privileges, and if anyone infringes them they will extend them to my advantage, as was seen in the case of Juan Aguado. Their Highnesses command much honour to be paid me, and as I have already said they have received services from me and taken my sons to be their servants, which could never have happened with any other prince, since where there is no love everything else is lacking.

Only most unwillingly have I spoken with such severity against these abuses, which I would not wish to remember

even in my dreams. By his actions and behaviour the *comendador* Bobadilla has openly displayed his malice in this matter. But I will show with the utmost ease that his ignorance, laziness and inordinate greed have proved his undoing.

I have already said that I wrote to him and to the friars and then set out as I informed him, absolutely alone because all the men were with the *adelantado* and because I wished to relieve his suspicions. On hearing this, he imprisoned Don Diego in a caravel and put him in irons, and on my arrival did the same to me and to the *adelantado* also when he came. I had no more conversation with him and he has allowed no one to speak to me to this day. I swear on oath that I cannot imagine why I have been made prisoner.

The first thing he did was to take the gold, which he did without measuring or weighing it and in my absence. He said that he was going to pay the people from it, and as I hear he took the first part for himself and sent out new officials to superintend the barter. I had set aside for their Highnesses' pleasure certain samples of this gold, various nuggets of different sizes, some as large as goose, hen's and pullet's eggs, which a few men were able to gather in a short while to show them that this trade might be very profitable; I added several pieces of ore bearing rich veins of gold. Bobadilla's first malicious stroke, however, was to hold these samples back, so that their Highnesses should attach little importance to the business until he had feathered his own nest, and he is doing this very fast. The gold, stored for melting, has diminished in the fire. A necklace weighing anything up to twenty marks has disappeared. I have been even more upset over this business of the gold than over that of the pearls, for I was most anxious to bring it to their Highnesses.

The *comendador* was very active in doing everything that he thought might injure me. As I have already said, with 600,000

maravedis I could have paid everybody without defrauding anyone, and I had more than four million in tithes and protection dues without touching that gold. He made some absurdly generous gifts, the first of which I think he took for himself. Their Highnesses will discover the truth of this when they ask him for an account, especially if I may be present at the time. He is continually saying that a great sum is owing, though it is only so much as I have reported, or even less.

I am very much aggrieved that a man should have been sent out to examine my affairs who knows that if he makes a very damaging report he will be left in charge of the government. Would to God that their Highnesses had sent him or another two years ago, for I know that in that case I should now be free of scandal and disgrace and my honour would neither be lost nor called into question. God is just and He will in due course make known all that has happened and why.

In Spain they judge me as if I had been sent to govern Sicily or some province or city under settled government, and where the laws can be strictly applied without fear of a complete upheaval. This does me great harm. I should be judged as a captain sent from Spain to the Indies to conquer a large and warlike people, with customs and beliefs very different from ours. These people live in mountains and forests without settled townships, and we have none there either. Here by God's will I have brought under the dominion of our sovereigns a new world, whereby Spain, which was called poor, has now become rich. I should be judged as a captain who has borne arms for a long time and bears them still, not laying them aside for a single hour, and I should be judged by knights of conquest and experience, not by men of letters,* unless they be Greeks or Romans or their peers of the present day, of whom there are so many noble examples in Spain.

*Lawyers.

In default of this I shall be greatly wronged, since in the Indies there are neither towns nor seats of justice.

The gateway is already opened to gold and pearls, and we can safely expect quantities of other precious stones, spices and countless other things. I pray that no fresh disaster may fall on me, so that I may soon undertake the first voyage to open up trade with Arabia Felix as far as Mecca, as I wrote to their Highnesses by Antonio de Torres when commenting on the division of sea and land with the Portuguese. And after that I will go to Colucuti,* as I have said and set down in writings that are at the monastery of La Mejorada.

Concerning the gold that I promised to give, the news is that on Christmas Day, when I was hard pressed by the attacks of wicked Christians and the Indians and on the point of leaving everything and escaping if possible with my life, the Lord miraculously comforted me, saying: 'Take courage. Be not dismayed nor afraid: I will provide for everything: the seven years of the gold concessions have not elapsed. And in this matter, as in all others I will remedy your fortunes.' On that day I learned that there were eighty leagues of land containing mines from end to end; it now appears that it is all one single mine; some have collected 120 *castellanos* in a day and others ninety and the amount has risen to 250. To gather from fifty to seventy or in many cases from fifteen to fifty is considered a good day's work and many are still gathering an average of between six and twelve. Anyone who falls below it is dissatisfied. This mine appears to be like all others, which do not give the same yield every day; it is new and so are the miners. The general opinion is that even if all Castile were to go there the idlest man would not collect less than one or two *castellanos* a day, which has been the case up to now. It is true that they employ Indian servants, but the yield depends entirely on the Christians.

*Calicut (?).

Note the intelligence of Bobadilla! He gave everything and received nothing, handing over four millions of tithes unasked and for no reason and without first notifying their Majesties – and this is not the only damage he has done. I am conscious that my errors have not been committed for the sake of doing ill and I believe that their Highnesses will accept my word for this. I know and see that they are merciful with those who do them ill-service out of malice, and I most certainly believe that they will treat me much better and with greater mercy, for I fell into error unwittingly and under compulsion, as they will soon entirely understand. I am their humble creature, and if they will examine my services they will see that they gain greater advantage from them day by day. They will weigh everything in the balance even as, according to Holy Scripture, good and evil will be weighed on the Day of Judgement. If they still demand that I be tried before another judge (which I do not expect) and that an inquiry be held about the Indies, I beg them most humbly to send two honest and conscientious persons there at my expense. I think they will speedily discover that gold is brought in at the rate of five marks in four hours. Be this as it may it is most necessary that their Highnesses should inquire into the whole matter.

When the *comendador* arrived in Santo Domingo, he lodged at my house and took everything he found there for himself. He was welcome. Perhaps he had need of it. No pirate ever treated a merchant like this. My greatest complaint is about my papers which he took from me in this way. I have not been able to get a single one from him, and those that most firmly prove my innocence he has kept most carefully hidden. What a just and honest inquisitor! They tell me that in all his actions he has ceased to regard justice and has behaved purely as a despot. The Lord God still wields his power and wisdom as of old and punishes all wrongs, especially ingratitude.

CHAPTER 86 (*continued*)

ON 20 November 1500 the Admiral wrote to the sovereigns that he had arrived at Cadiz, and when they heard of his coming they immediately gave orders for his release. They wrote him letters which were full of benevolence and expressed great displeasure at his ordeal and the gross discourtesy with which he had been treated by Bobadilla. They told him to come to court, where his affairs would be attended to and orders would be given that everything should be dealt with most honourably and with great dispatch.

Despite these amends I cannot fail to blame the Catholic sovereigns for entrusting this matter to a person of such malice and so little experience. For if he had been a man who knew how to perform his duties properly, the Admiral himself would have welcomed his coming. He had himself begged in his letters for someone to be sent to draw up a true account of the people's crimes and the outrages they were committing, so that they might be punished by some other person. For since they had been the instigators of the revolt against his brother, he did not wish to proceed against them with the full vigour that would have been exercised by another person who was beyond suspicion. And although it may be said that even if the Catholic sovereigns had received most damaging information against the Admiral they should not have sent Bobadilla with such marks of their favour and such letters, yet it may be urged in excuse that it was not surprising they did so, since the complaints which they had received against the Admiral were, as we have already said, very numerous.

CHAPTER 87

The Admiral goes to court to give an account of himself to the Catholic sovereigns

As soon as the sovereigns heard of the Admiral's arrival and his imprisonment, they sent orders, on 17 December, that he should be set at liberty, and summoned him to Granada, where he was received by their Highnesses with smiling faces and affectionate speeches. They told him that his imprisonment had not been by their will or command. On the contrary, it had much displeased them, and they would see that those guilty of it were punished and that this wrong should be redressed.

With favourable words like these, the sovereigns commanded that the Admiral's affairs should be dealt with. Their decision was, in brief, that no governor should be sent to Hispaniola who had displeased the Admiral and his brothers, that Bobadilla should restore to him everything he had taken, that the Admiral should be given everything to which he was entitled by the terms of agreement, that the courts should inquire into the case of the rebels, and that their crimes should be punished according to the degree of their guilt. Don Nicolas de Ovando *comendador* de Lares, a prudent man of sound judgement, was then sent out, and although he later proved himself violent to impartial eyes he controlled his passions with cautious astuteness. He confirmed the suspicions of his detractors, however, by behaving, according to them, in a cruel and vengeful spirit on such occasions as the execution in Jaragua of eighty *caciques*.

But to return to the Admiral in Granada, at the same time as the Catholic sovereigns decided to send Ovando to Hispaniola, they thought fit to send the Admiral on another

voyage which they expected would bring profit to themselves, and which would keep him occupied until their new emissaries had quietened the unrest in Hispaniola. They thought that it would be harmful to him to be kept for too long from his rightful possessions, without due cause. For it was clear to them that the information against him sent to them by Bobadilla was full of lies and malice, and provided no grounds for depriving him of his estates.

As the execution of this business took some time and they were now running into late October 1501, and the Admiral's enemies were demanding further delays to await fresh information, he decided to speak to their Highnesses and ask for their promise to defend and protect him in his danger. He afterwards confirmed this request in a letter.

[*Hernando now gives a letter from the Catholic sovereigns, expressing their regret for the Admiral's ill-treatment, and confirming, 'if such confirmation be necessary', the privileges previously granted him, for himself and his son. They promised also to favour his brothers and to send him on his next voyage without undue delay.*]

FOURTH VOYAGE
1502–4

LETTER WRITTEN BY CHRISTOPHER COLUMBUS, VICEROY AND ADMIRAL OF THE INDIES, TO THE MOST CHRISTIAN AND MIGHTY KING AND QUEEN OF SPAIN, OUR SOVEREIGNS, NOTIFYING THEM OF THE EVENTS OF HIS VOYAGE AND THE CITIES, PROVINCES, RIVERS AND OTHER MARVELS, ALSO THE SITUATION OF THE MANY GOLDFIELDS AND OTHER OBJECTS OF GREAT RICHES AND VALUE

MOST serene, exalted and mighty King and Queen our sovereigns: I crossed from Cadiz to the Canary Islands in four days, and thence to the Indies in sixteen, where I wrote that my intention was to hasten my voyage while I had good ships, crews and provisions, and that my course was for the island of Jamaica, and at the island of Dominica I wrote this. Till I reached there I had as good weather as I could have wished for, but the night of my arrival there was a great storm, and I have been dogged by bad weather ever since.

On reaching Hispaniola I sent the bundle of letters and asked as a favour to be provided with a ship at my own cost, since one of those that I had with me was unseaworthy and could not carry sail. The letters were taken and your Highnesses will know if they were delivered to you. I was commanded from Spain not to touch or land there.

[*In sending Columbus on his fourth voyage, their Majesties, in a letter written from Valencia on 14 March 1502, reiterated their assurances that they regretted his imprisonment, asked him to leave*

THE FOURTH VOYAGE OF COLUMBUS

Miles 0   50   100   150   200

the matter of his estates to be settled with his son Don Diego, and requested him on the outward journey not to put in at Hispaniola but to press on with his exploration. They gave him permission to put in briefly on his return, but not to delay there long. They also warned him on no account to get embroiled with the Portuguese. In his dealings with his crew he must think of them as royal servants and he must on no account bring back slaves. See Las Casas, Bk II, Chap. 4.]

My crew was disheartened by the fear that I was taking them further. They said that if any danger occurred there would be no help in these distant places and they would rather meet with disaster now than sail on. Moreover, anyone who pleased could say that the *comendador** would receive control of any lands that I might gain.

The storm was terrible, and on that night my fleet was broken up. Everyone lost hope and was quite certain that all the rest were drowned. What mortal man, even Job himself, would not have died of despair? Even for the safety of myself, my son, brother and friends, I was forbidden in such weather to put into land or enter harbours that I had gained for Spain by my own blood and sweat.

But, to return to the ships, which the storm had taken from me, leaving me alone, the Lord sent them back when it pleased Him. The unseaworthy vessel had put out to sea for safety. Near the island the *Gallega* lost her boat and all lost great part of their provisions. The ship in which I was travelling, though amazingly storm-tossed, was saved by Our Lord and was completely unharmed. My brother was in the unseaworthy vessel and he (after God) was her salvation.

In this storm I struggled on painfully till I reached Jamaica. There the high seas fell to a calm and there was a strong current which carried me as far as the Jardin de la Reina with-

*Nicolas de Ovando, the governor of Hispaniola, who had succeeded Bobadilla.

out sighting land. From there I sailed as soon as I could to the mainland and on the way the wind and a terrible current were against me. I struggled with them for sixty days and in the end had not made more than seventy leagues. For all that time I did not put into harbour nor could I have done, since the storm did not let up at all. Rain, thunder and lightning was so continuous that it seemed the end of the world. Finally I reached Cape Gracias a Dios* and from there the Lord gave me good winds and currents. This was on 12 September. This terrible storm had lasted for eighty-eight days and all this time I had never seen the sun or the stars on account of the high seas. My ships were stripped, the sails torn, anchors, rigging and cables were lost, and also the boats and many stores. The crew were very sick and all repented their sins, in turning to God. Everyone made vows and promised pilgrimages, and very often men went so far as to confess to one another. Other storms have been seen but none has ever lasted so long or been so terrifying. Many whom we thought very brave were reduced to terror on more than one occasion. The distress of my son,† who was with me, racked my soul, for he was only thirteen and he was not only exhausted but remained so for a long time. But the Lord gave him such courage that he cheered the others and he worked as hard in the ship as if he had been a sailor for eighty years. He comforted me, for I had fallen ill and was many times at the point of death. I directed the course from a little shelter which I had erected on the deck. My brother was in the worst ship, which was in the greatest danger, and this distressed me greatly, especially as I had brought him against his will. As for myself I had won little profit in twenty years of toilful and dangerous service, for today in Castile I have no roof to shelter me. When I want a meal or a bed I must go to an inn or tavern,

*On the Central American coast.
†Hernando, afterwards the Admiral's biographer.

and more often than not I have not the money to pay the bill. Another sorrow tore at my very heart and that was grief for my son Don Diego, whom I had left an orphan in Spain, stripped of the honours and estates that should have been mine. But I certainly trusted that, as just and grateful princes, your Majesties would restore everything to him with increase.

I reached the land of Cariay,* where I stayed to repair the ships, replenish the stores and rest the crews, who had become very weak. I had myself, as I have said, several times come near to death. Here I received news of the goldfields in the province of Ciamba which I was seeking. Two Indians brought me to Carambaru, where the people go naked, wearing shining gold discs round their necks, but they would not sell or barter them.

They gave me the names of many places on the sea-coast where they said there was gold and goldfields too. The last of these was Veragua, about twenty leagues away. I set out with the intention of inspecting them all, but when I was half-way there I learnt that there were other goldfields only two days' journey away, and decided to send and inspect these. The expedition was to have left on the Eve of St Simon and St Jude, but such seas and winds arose that night that we had to run before it and the Indian who was to have guided us to the goldfields remained on board.

In all these places I had visited, I had found the information given me true, and this assured me that the same would be so of the province of Ciguare,† which, as they told me, lies inland nine days' journey westward. They say that there is a vast quantity of gold there and that the people wear coral ornaments on their heads and stout bracelets of the same material on their wrists and ankles. They also embellish and

---

* Somewhere on the Mosquito Coast of Nicaragua.

† These accounts must refer to the Maya cities of Guatamala, the first places of high civilization of which the Spaniards heard.

inlay stools, chests and tables with it. I was told too that the women wore circlets on their heads that hung down to their shoulders. All the people of these parts agree about this and from all that they say I should be glad of a tenth of those riches. According to reports they are all acquainted with red pepper.

In Ciguare the custom is to trade in fairs and markets, and I was shown this people's method of trading. It was also said that their ships carry cannon, bows and arrows, swords and shields, and that they wear clothes and that there are horses in that country. It was said that these people wage war, wear rich clothing and have good houses.* They say also that Ciguare is surrounded by water, and that ten days' journey away is the river Ganges. These lands seem to lie in the same relation to Veragua as Tortosa to Fuentarabia† or Pisa to Venice.‡

When I left Carambaru and reached these places I have mentioned, I found the customs of the people to be the same, except that anyone who had a gold disc would barter it for three hawks' bells, even if it weighed as much as ten or fifteen ducats. In their general manners they are like the people of Hispaniola but have different ways of collecting gold, all incomparably poorer than the Christians' methods. These

---

*This clearly shows the extent of the Spaniards' misunderstanding of the Indian signs or language. The Mayas had clothing and houses and waged war, but they had no horses and certainly no cannon or swords as the Spaniards understood them, since they did not know steel. So anxious was Columbus still to prove that he was in the neighbourhood of China or India that he accepted anything that contributed to this persistent and mistaken belief.

†From the Mediterranean coast of Spain to the Bay of Biscay.

‡It has been argued from this passage that Columbus had heard reports of the Pacific and realized that there was another sea on the further side of the Maya country. But if this was so he would scarcely have referred to the river Ganges in his previous sentence.

reports are from hearsay, however. All that I know for certain is that in the year '94 I sailed to longitude 135, which is 24 degrees westward or nine hours of the sun's course. There can be no mistake about this, because there was an eclipse; the sun was in Libra and the moon in Aries. All this that I learnt by report I knew in greater detail from books.

Ptolemy believed that he had thoroughly corrected Marinus, who is now seen to be very near the truth. Ptolemy places Catigara twelve 'lines' from his meridian, which he fixed $2\frac{1}{3}$ degrees from Cape St Vincent, in Portugal. Marinus includes the full extent of the earth in fifteen lines. In Ethiopia this same Marinus draws more than 24 degrees on the further side of the equinoctial line, and now that the Portuguese have made their voyages they find this to be correct. Ptolemy says that the most southerly land is the first place and that it does not lie more than $15\frac{1}{3}$ degrees south. The world is small and six parts of it are land, the seventh part being entirely covered by water. Experience has already shown this and I have already written in other letters with illustrations drawn from Holy Scripture concerning the site of the earthly Paradise accepted by Holy Church. I say that the world is not as great as is commonly believed and that one degree on the Equator is $56\frac{2}{3}$ miles, which may be exactly proved.*

But I will leave this subject, since it is not my intention to speak of these matters but to give an account of my long and arduous voyage, which was however both noble and profitable.

As I said, on the Eve of St Simon and St Jude, I ran where the wind carried me, and could not resist it. I sheltered in a harbour from the great violence of sea and storm and decided there not to turn back to the goldfields, but left them, con-

* Columbus is anxious to defend Marinus of Tyre against Ptolemy, since according to Marinus's theories the world was sufficiently small for Asia to lie in the region of the newly discovered America.

sidering them gained already. I set out to continue my voyage in rain and reach the harbour of Bastimentos,* into which I was driven against my will. Storm and the strong current held me there for fourteen days and when I finally left it was in bad weather. Having with difficulty made fifteen leagues, I was driven back by the furious wind and current to the port which I had just left. I found 'El Retrete',† where I entered in great danger and distress, the ships being in bad condition and both the crews and myself greatly fatigued. I stayed there fifteen days, compelled to do so by the cruel weather, and when I thought that it was ending I found it was only beginning. So I decided not to go to the goldfields or do anything else until the weather should be favourable for me to set out and put to sea.

When I had gone four leagues the storm returned and so exhausted me that I did not know what to do. There my wound reopened.‡

For nine days I was lost with no hope of life. Eyes never saw the sea so rough, so ugly or so seething with foam. The wind did not allow us to go ahead or give us a chance of running, nor did it allow us to shelter under any headland. There I was held in those seas turned to blood, boiling like a cauldron on a mighty fire. The skies had never looked more threatening. For a day and a night they blazed like a furnace and the lightning burnt in such flashes that every moment I looked to see whether my masts and sails had not been struck. They came with such terrifying fury that we believed the ships would be utterly destroyed. All this time water fell unceasingly from the sky. One cannot say that it rained, for it

*Nombre de Dios.
† The Narrows, Escribanos or Port Scrivan.
‡ What wound is not clear. Las Casas speaks only of his gout. This reference has been used to substantiate the dubious story that Columbus served and was wounded in the Moorish wars.

was like a repetition of the deluge. The crews were now so broken that they longed for death to release them from their martyrdom. The ships had already twice lost their boats, anchors and rigging and were stripped bare of their sails.

When it pleased our Lord I returned to Puerto Gordo, where I made the best repairs I could. I then set course for Veragua, but although I was bent on continuing my voyage the winds and currents were still against me. I arrived at about the same place as before, and here again I was prevented by winds and currents. So I returned once more to port so battered by the tempestuous seas that I did not dare to await the opposition of Saturn with Mars, which generally brings storms or bad weather. At ten o'clock on Christmas morning I was back at the spot from which I had departed so laboriously. At the beginning of the New Year I resumed my efforts. But even though I had struck good weather for my voyage, the ships had become unseaworthy, and the crews sick or dying.

On the day of Epiphany (6 January) I reached Veragua, completely broken in spirit. Here Our Lord gave me a river and a safe harbour, although it was less than eight feet deep. I got in with difficulty and next day the storm returned. If it had found me outside I should not have been able to get in because of the bar. It rained without stopping until 14 February, so I never had an opportunity of exploring the country or of repairing my condition in any way. On 24 January, when I was lying there in safety, the river suddenly became very high and violent. The cables and bollards were broken and the ships were almost swept away. I had never seen them in greater danger, but Our Lord saved us as ever. I know of no one who has suffered greater trials.

On 6 February, when it was still raining, I sent seventy men inland and at five leagues away they found many gold-fields. The Indians whom they had with them led them to a

very high hill and from there showed them all the surrounding country as far as the eye could reach, saying that there was gold everywhere and that there were goldfields twenty days' journey to the west. They named the towns and villages and showed where they lay thickest or thinnest. I afterwards learned that the Quibian* who had given us these Indians had told them to point to distant goldfields which belonged to a rival chieftain, though within his own territory a man could collect a full load of gold in ten days whenever he wished.

I have with me these Indians who were his servants, and they will bear witness to this. The boats went to the place where his township lay, and my brother returned with his men all carrying the gold they had gathered in the four hours they had been ashore. The quantity must be great, since none of them had ever seen goldfields and most of them had never seen unrefined gold before.†

The majority of them were sailors and almost all of them only lads. Having plenty of building materials and stores I established a settlement. I gave many gifts to the Quibian, as the chief of the country is called, but I knew that friendly relations would not continue for long, since they were very uncivilized and our men very peremptory and I had taken possession of land in his territory. When he saw the houses built and trade increasing, he decided to burn them down and put us all to death, but his plan went wrong and he was himself taken prisoner, with his wives, children and servants, though his imprisonment did not last long. He had been entrusted to a reliable man and a small guard but succeeded in making his escape. His sons escaped also from a shipmaster to whose care they had been entrusted.

*A chief.
†I take this to be Columbus's meaning: that if they had had more experience in recognizing gold they would have brought a great deal more back and therefore the quantities must be very great.

In January the mouth of the river had silted up. In April, the ships were all worm-eaten and could not be kept afloat. At this time the river formed a channel by which I brought three of them out empty, and with great difficulty. The boats then went back into the river for salt and water and the Indians who had gathered together in great numbers attacked their crews, killing them all. My brother and the rest of the company were all aboard one ship which was left in the river and I was completely alone outside on this dangerous coast in a high fever and a state of great exhaustion. All hope of escape was dead.

I clambered up to the highest point of the ship, crying in a trembling voice, with tears in my eyes, to all your Highnesses' war captains at every point of the compass to save me, but there was no reply. Tired out and sobbing I fell asleep and heard a very compassionate voice saying: 'O fool, slow to believe and serve thy God, the God of all! What more did he do for Moses or David his servant than he has done for thee? . . . He gave thee the Indies, which are so rich a part of the world, for thine own and thou hast divided them at thy pleasure, and He has enabled thee to do this. He gave thee the keys of the barriers of the ocean seas which were closed with such such mighty chains. Thou hast been obeyed in many lands and gained an honourable fame throughout Christendom. . . . His mercy is infinite. Thine old age will not prevent thee from attaining all thy great objects. He has many mighty heritages to bestow. . . . Now He has shown thee the reward for the anguish and danger thou has endured in the service of others.'

I heard all this as if in a swoon, but I could find no answer to words of such assurance: I could only weep for my transgressions. Whoever it was ended with the words: 'Fear not, have trust, all these tribulations are inscribed on marble and are not purposeless.'

I got up as soon as I could, and nine days later the weather improved, but not sufficiently to get the ships out of the river. I collected the men who were on land and as many more as I could, for there were not enough both for a settlement and to man the ships. I would have remained with all of them to hold the settlement if your Highnesses had known of it: but the fear that ships would never reach there, and the thought that if help were to be sent it should find us all together, decided me to abandon it.

I sailed in the name of the Holy Trinity on the night of Easter Monday in ships that were rotten, leaky and worm-eaten, leaving one of them (the *Gallega*) at Belen with a number of objects and another (the *Viscaina*) at Belpuerto. I had only two left, which were in as bad a state as the others and without boats and stores. In these I must sail seven thousand miles of sea or die on the way with my son and brother and all these men. Let the habitual critics and fault-finders sitting safely at home ask me now: 'Why did you not do this in those circumstances?' I should like to have had them there on that voyage. But I truly believe that another journey of a different character is in store for them if there is any reliance to be placed upon our Faith.

I arrived on 13 May at the province of Mago,* which borders on Cathay, and from there set out to Hispaniola. I sailed for two days with good weather, but after that it turned against us. I was steering a course which would avoid the great number of islands in order to keep clear of the adjoining shoals. The stormy sea compelled me to turn back without sail: I anchored at an island where at one blow I lost three anchors and at midnight it seemed as if the world were coming to an end. The other ship broke its cables and bore down

* The district of Macaca in Cuba. It is difficult to understand by what logic Columbus still supposed that Cuba was part of the Asiatic mainland.

on me, so it was a wonder we were not dashed to pieces. It was my one remaining anchor that (after Our Lord) saved me.

Six days later when good weather returned I had lost all my tackle but resumed course. The ship was as riddled with holes as a honeycomb and the crew exhausted and dispirited, but I sailed a little beyond the point I had reached before, when the storm had driven me back and put into a safer port in the same island.

Eight days later I resumed my voyage and reached Jamaica at the end of June with the wind always against me and the ships in a worse state than ever. With three pumps, pots and cauldrons and all hands at work, I still could not keep down the water that entered the ship, and there was nothing we could do to meet the damage done by the shipworm. I steered the course that would bring me nearest to Hispaniola, which was twenty-eight leagues away, but afterwards I wished I had not done so. The other ship, which was half awash, was obliged to run for port, but I struggled to keep at sea in spite of the weather. My ship was almost sinking when by a miracle Our Lord brought us to land. Who would believe what I have just written? Yet I swear that I have not told a hundredth part of the story in this letter. Those who sailed with the Admiral can testify to this.

If it please your Highnesses to aid me with a ship of about sixty-four tons with 200 bushels of biscuit and some other provisions, this will be enough to bring me and my crew back to Spain. As I have said it is no more than twenty-eight leagues from Jamaica to Hispaniola, but I should not have gone there even if the ships had been fit to do so, since I had received orders from your Highnesses not to do so. God knows whether these orders have served a good purpose. I am sending this letter by way of Indian messengers* and it will be a great miracle if it reaches its destination.

* It was actually entrusted to Diego Mendez, whose narrative follows.

To resume, I had with me on this voyage 150 men, among whom there were some very capable pilots and fine sailors. But none of them can give a certain account of where I went or from where I came, and the reason is very obvious. I set out from above Puerto del Brasil in Hispaniola and a storm prevented me from following the course I wished. I was forced to go where the wind drove me, and at the same time I fell very sick. No one had ever sailed in that direction before. After a few days the winds and high sea abated and the storm yielded to calm with strong currents. I put in at an island named 'de las Pozas'* and from there went to the mainland. No one can give an accurate account of this, for there are no sufficient records, since we had to follow the current out of sight of land for so many days. I followed the mainland coast, relying on my own skill and the compass. No one could make observations by the heavens and when I left there for Hispaniola the pilots believed we should strike the island of St Juan,† but we actually struck the land of Mango, 400 leagues further west than they said. Let them state if they can the position of Veragua. I declare that the best account they can give is that they went to a land where there is much gold and this they will swear to. But they do not know by what route they could return to it. In order to return they would have to make a new voyage of discovery. There is a method of calculation based on astronomy which is reliable and a sufficient guide for anyone who understands it. This resembles a prophetic vision.

In the Indies, ships only sail with a following wind. This is not because they are badly built or clumsy. The strong cur-

---

This letter contains many inaccuracies, attributable perhaps to Columbus's exalted and exhausted state of mind.

*Probably one of the Jardin de la Reina.

†Apparently Puerto Rico. Columbus is said to have taken away all the charts.

rents that flow there and the winds together make pilots distrustful of the bow-line,* for in a day they may lose as much way as they have gained in seven and on this account I do not bring out caravels, or even Portuguese lateens.

Because of those winds and currents, ships only sail with a regular breeze and sometimes lie in port waiting for it for six or eight months, and this is not remarkable, because the same very often happens in Spain.

The people of whom Pope Pius II writes in describing the region and its characteristics have been found, but not the horses with saddles, breast-plates and bridles of gold,† which is not surprising, for the lands along the seaboard are only suitable for fishermen. I did not stay there because I was in haste. In Cariay and in the adjoining districts there are great and very terrifying magicians who would have done anything to prevent my remaining there an hour. On my arrival they sent me two magnificently attired girls, the elder of whom could not have been more than eleven and the other seven. Both were so shameless that they might have been whores, and had magic powders concealed about them. On their arrival I ordered that they should be given some of our trinkets and sent them back to land immediately.

Here I saw on a mountain a sculptured tomb as big as a house, on top of which a corpse lay embalmed.‡ I was also

* Bow-lines are ropes employed to keep the windward edges of the principal sails steady, and are only used when the wind is so unfavourable that the sails must be all sideways-braced, or close-hauled to the wind.

† The reference is to the *Cosmographia* of Pope Pius, descriptive of the Far East.

‡ Neither Las Casas nor Ferdinand Columbus suggests that the Admiral landed here. How he could have seen this tomb is consequently not clear. In writing of the magicians and the girls they are less dramatic than Columbus. They describe the girls as older and say nothing of the magic powders.

told of other excellent works of art. There are many kinds of animals both small and large and very different from ours. I took aboard two hogs* and the Irish wolfhound was always afraid of them. A crossbowman wounded a creature that was like an ape, only much larger and with a human face. He had pierced him with an arrow from the breast to the tail but had to cut off a fore and hind paw because he was so fierce. When one of the hogs saw this ape-like creature it bristled and fled, and when I saw this I ordered the *begare*, as the natives call this animal, to be thrown to the hog. Though he was dying with the arrow still through his body he coiled his tail round the hog's snout as soon as he got within reach of him, gripped him very tight and with his remaining forepaw struck him hard on the head as if he were his enemy. The hunting of this animal was so strange and splendid that I have had to describe it.

They have many kinds of animals, all of which die of *barra*.† I saw a great number of large fowl, with feathers like wool, pumas, deer, also fallow-deer and birds. During our arduous voyage through these seas some got the pagan notion that we had been bewitched and still persist in the belief. I found other tribes who ate human flesh, as their brutal appearance showed.

It is said that there are large mines of copper, of which they make axes and other objects, worked or cast and soldered; also forges, goldsmith's tools and crucibles. The people here are clothed, and in that district I saw large cotton sheets worked with very fine embroidery, and also cloths finely painted with designs of various colours. It is said that inland in the country lying towards Cathay they have gold-embroidered materials. However, we were not able to get very exact information about these lands and what they contained, owing to the lack of an interpreter.

*Peccaries.
†A disease unknown to the dictionaries, perhaps a skin disease.

Although the villages are very close together, each has a different language and consequently the people of one do not understand those of another, any more than we understand the Arabs. I think this is true of the uncivilized people on the sea-coast but not of those in the interior.

When I discovered the Indies I said that they were the richest domain in the whole world in respect of gold, pearls, precious stones, spices, and trade and markets, and because all these things were not produced at once I was subjected to abuse. Because of this ill-treatment I now report nothing except that which I learnt from the natives of the land. One thing I dare say, since there are so many witnesses to it, and this is that in the land of Veragua I saw more evidences of gold in the first two days than in four years in Hispaniola, that the lands hereabouts could not be more beautiful or better cultivated, that the people could not be more timid, and that there is a fine harbour, a lovely river, which could be defended against the world. All this makes for the safety of the Christians, and their security of possession, and also offers great hopes of honour and expansion to the Christian faith. The voyage there will be as short as that to Hispaniola, since it can be made with a following wind. Your Highnesses are as much lords of this country as you are of Jerez or Toledo. Your ships can come here as safely as if they still lay at home. They will bring back gold from here, whereas if they wish to take the products of other lands they would have to take it by force or come back empty-handed, and inland they must entrust themselves to savages.

Concerning the other things of which I have refrained from speaking I have given the reasons for my reticence. I have not stated the sixth part of what I have learnt in all that I have said and written, nor do I swear to it, nor do I claim to have reached the fountainhead. The Genoese, Venetians and all other people who have pearls, precious stones and other

valuables take them to the ends of the world to sell and turn into gold. Gold is most excellent. Gold constitutes treasure, and anyone who has it can do whatever he likes in the world. With it he can succeed in bringing souls to Paradise. When the people of these lands in the district of Veragua die, their gold is buried with their bodies, or so it is said.

Solomon was brought 666 talents of gold from a single expedition, in addition to what he received from merchants and sailors and his payments from Arabia. With this gold he made 200 lances and 300 shields, and the overlay of his throne, which was of solid gold adorned with precious stones; also many other objects and great vessels inlaid with jewels.*

Josephus writes of this in his chronicle of *Antiquities*, and it is also mentioned in the Book of Chronicles and in the Book of Kings. Josephus believes that this gold came from Aurea. If this is so, the goldfields of Aurea are in my opinion the same as these of Veragua, which, as I have said, extend twenty days' journey westwards, and are everywhere the same distance from the Pole and the Equator. Solomon bought all this gold, precious stones and silver, but your Majesties may send orders for them to be collected at your pleasure. David, in his will, left 3,000 talents of gold from the Indies to Solomon to help in the building of the Temple, and according to Josephus it came from these same lands.

Jerusalem and Mount Sion shall be rebuilt by Christian hands; whose they are to be is said by David in Psalm 14. Abbot Joachin said that this builder would come from Spain.†
St Jerome showed the holy woman how it was to be done. Some time ago the Emperor of Cathay sent for some scholars to instruct him in the Christian faith.‡

*II Chronicles ix, 13-17.
†A reference to the *Oraculum Turcicum* of Joachin, Abbot of Flores, in Calabria. There is actually no reference to Spain in his prophecy.
‡This refers to the Embassy sent by the Grand Khan to Pope

Who will offer himself for this task? If Our Lord will bring me back to Spain, I pledge myself in God's name to convey that man here in safety. These men who have accompanied me have undergone incredible toils and danger. I entreat your Highnesses, since they are poor, to have them paid immediately, and to grant favours to each one of them according to his merits, for in my belief they are bringing the best news that ever came to Spain.

Although I have information that the gold belonging to the Quibian of Veragua and the chiefs of the surrounding districts is very abundant, I do not think it would be well, or to your Highnesses' advantage, for it to be seized by way of plunder. Fair dealing will prevent scandal and disrepute, and bring this gold into the treasury down to the last grain.

Given a month of good weather, I could complete my whole voyage. Being short of ships I have not delayed any longer but resumed my journey. I trust in my Creator that I shall be of service to your Highnesses in every respect, so long as my health lasts. I hope that your Highnesses will remember that I wished to have ships constructed in a new way.* Lack of time did not allow this, and I certainly foresaw what the result would be. I rate this trade and the possession of these extensive goldfields more highly than anything else we have achieved in the Indies. This is no child to be entrusted to a stepmother, and I never think of Hispaniola or Paria or these other countries without tears in my eyes. I thought that our settlements there would be an example to others. But on the contrary they are in a state of exhaustion. Although they are not dead their sickness is incurable or at least very extensive. Let him who brought them to this state produce the remedy if he knows it. Everyone is a master of

Eugenius IV, mentioned by Toscanelli in the letter accompanying his chart. See Introduction, p. 12.

*This is the only mention of Columbus's wish.

disorder. It was always the custom to give thanks and rewards to those who exposed themselves to danger. It would not be right that one who has so opposed this business should enjoy the profits from it and bequeath them to his children. Those who left the Indies to avoid hardships, and spoke evil both of them and of me, have returned with official employment,* and the same thing will surely take place in respect of Veragua. This is a bad example, detrimental both to trade and justice in the world. Fear for all this, and other serious reasons which I saw clearly, caused me to beg your Highnesses, before I discovered these islands and the mainland, to let me govern them in your royal name. It pleased you, and the privilege and agreement was granted under the royal seal and oath. You gave me the title of Viceroy Admiral and Governor-General of all these lands, fixing the boundaries of my governorship a hundred leagues west of the Azores and the Cape Verde Islands on a line passing from one pole to the other. It was to comprise everything which should be discovered and you granted me wide powers, as is stated in the document at greater length.

But there is another very important matter, inexplicable to this day, which cries loudly for redress. I spent seven years at your royal court, where everyone to whom I spoke of this undertaking said that it was ridiculous. Now even tailors are asking for licences of exploration. Probably they intend only to come out and plunder, but the licences granted are greatly to the detriment of my honour and to the prejudice of the undertaking itself. It is right to render unto God the things that are His, and unto Caesar what belongs to Caesar. This is a just sentiment and based on justice. The lands that here obey your Highnesses are greater and richer than all the rest of

*It is not clear whether Columbus is making a general attack or thinking of one man in particular, perhaps Ojeda, whose discovery of the pearl fisheries of Margarita Island he resented.

Christendom. I had, by God's will, placed them under your royal and exalted rule, and was on the point of securing very great revenues. I was happy and I was secure. Then, when I was waiting for ships to carry me into your royal presence, a victor bearing great news of gold, I and my two brothers were suddenly arrested and put aboard a ship, naked, ill-treated and loaded with chains; and this without trial or sentence. Who will believe that a poor foreigner could without cause rebel in such a place and without the support of another prince, alone among your vassals and subjects and with all his children at your royal court?

I came to serve at the age of twenty-eight and today I have not a hair on my head that is not grey. My body is sick and wasted. All that I and my brothers had has been taken from us, down to our very coats, without my being heard or seen, and I have suffered great dishonour. It is incredible that this could have been done by your royal command. The restoration of my honour and of what has been taken from me and the punishment of the man who inflicted this damage on me will redound to your Highnesses' good name. The man who robbed me of the pearls* and infringed my privileges as Admiral should be punished also. It would be a most virtuous deed and a famous example if you were to do this, and would leave to Spain a glorious memory of your Highnesses as grateful and just princes.

The honest devotion which I have always paid to your Highnesses' service and the unparalleled wrong that I have suffered will not let me keep silence, although I would gladly do so. I beg your Highnesses' pardon. I am ruined, as I have said; till now I have wept for others. May Heaven now have pity on me and earth weep for me. Of worldly possessions I have not even a farthing to offer for my spirit's good.† Here

*Alonso de Ojeda.
†That is, for the purpose of masses.

in the Indies I am cut off from the prescribed forms of religion, alone in my troubles, sick, in daily expectation of death and surrounded by a million hostile savages full of cruelty, and so far from the Holy Sacraments of the Blessed Church that my soul will be forgotten if it leaves my body. Weep for me whoever has charity, truth and justice!

I did not sail on this voyage to gain honour or wealth. This is certain for by that time all hope of this was dead. I came to your Highnesses with sincere devotion and true zeal, and this is no lie. I beg your Highnesses' leave if it please God to bring me back from this place, to go to Rome and other places of pilgrimage. May the Holy Trinity preserve your lives and high estate and grant you increased prosperity.

Written in the Indies on the island of Jamaica, 7 July 1503.

ACCOUNT BY DIEGO MENDEZ
OF CERTAIN INCIDENTS ON
CHRISTOPHER COLUMBUS'S LAST
VOYAGE

[*Diego Mendez,* citizen of Santo Domingo on the island of Hispaniola, being in the town of Valladolid, where their Majesties' court was at that time, made his will on 6 June 1536 before Fernan Perez, clerk to their Majesties and public notary at the court and throughout their dominions.*

It was witnessed by Diego de Arana, Juan Diez Miranda de la Cuadra, Martin de Orduna, Lucas Fernandez, Alonso de Angulo, Francisco de Hinojosa and Diego de Aguilar, all servants of the lady Vicereine of the Indies,† and among the clauses of the said will is one that runs as follows:]

I served the great Admiral Christopher Columbus, accompanying him in his discovery of islands and of the mainland, and many times exposed myself to great danger of death in order to save his life and that of his companions, especially when we were confined to the harbour at the mouth of the Belen or Yebra river. We were forced to remain here by the violent seas and winds which swept in and piled up sand in such quantities as to block the entrance to the harbour. His Lordship was greatly distressed, since large numbers of the local Indians had gathered with the intention of coming to

---

*A young gentleman who sailed on this voyage in the caravel *Santiago de Palos*. He was a friend of the Columbus family and defended their claims in the lawsuit that followed Columbus's death.

†Maria de Toledo, widow of Columbus's son Diego, whom she married in 1508 and with whom she sailed to Hispaniola. She was granddaughter of the Duke of Alba and a relative of the royal family. She held a brilliant court at Santo Domingo and actively defended the Columbus family's claims.

burn our ships and kill us all, though the reason for this gathering was, they said, to attack other Indians of the province of Cobrava and Aurira, with whom they were at war. Many of these Indians visited the harbour in which our ships were moored, but no one in the fleet noticed this except myself. I went to the Admiral and said: 'My Lord, these men who have been going about here in battle array say that they are going to join the men of Veragua to attack the people of Cobrava and Aurira, but I do not believe them. On the contrary, they are gathering to burn the ships and kill us all.' And this was the truth.

The Admiral then asked me what precautions we should take. I proposed to his Lordship that I should set out in a boat and go up the coast towards Veragua and see where they had pitched their camp. And I had not gone half a league before I saw a thousand warriors with great provisions and stores. I leaped ashore alone, into the midst of them, leaving my boat afloat, and spoke to them as well as I knew how, offering to accompany them on their war in their armed boat. They stoutly refused my aid, saying that they had no need of it. So I returned to my boat and kept watch on them all through the night. As they saw that they could not come near the ships to burn and destroy them as they intended without being seen by me, they changed their plan, and returned that night to Veragua, and I returned to the ships to relate what I had seen to his Lordship. He did not take this lightly, but discussed with me how we could make certain of these people's intentions. I offered to go to them with a single companion, which I did, in greater expectation of death than survival. I then followed the shore to the Veragua river, where I found two canoes manned by strange Indians who informed me very clearly that these people were going to burn our ships and kill us all, but had delayed because a boat had surprised them. Nevertheless they intended to return and do so in two

days' time. I asked them to take me up-river in one of their canoes and offered to pay them for the service. They refused and advised me on no account to go, for if I did so both I and my companion would certainly be killed.

Despite their warnings I made them take me to the villages upstream, where I found the Indians drawn up in battle array. They would not let me go to the principal hut of the *cacique*. But I pretended that I had come to him as a surgeon to treat a wound that he had in his leg, and in return for the presents I gave them they let me go to his house, which stood on a levelled hill-top with a large space around it and was surrounded by the heads of 300 warriors whom they had killed in battle. When I had crossed the whole open space and reached the *cacique*'s house, there was a great commotion among the women and children gathered round the door and they went screaming into the palace, from which emerged one of the *cacique*'s sons in a great rage, talking furiously in his language. He laid hands on me and thrust me away with a single push. To calm him I said that I had come to cure his father's leg and showed him some ointment which I had brought for this purpose. He replied that on no account was I to go in to his father. When I saw that I could not appease him in this way I took out a comb, scissors and a mirror and asked Escobar my companion to comb and cut my hair. The chief's son and others who were standing around were astonished. I then made Escobar comb the young man's hair and cut it with the scissors, and after that I gave him the comb and the mirror and at this he was pacified. I asked him to send for some food, which they brought immediately, and we ate and drank in love and comradeship and remained friends.

I then took my leave of him and returned to the ships, where I gave an account of all this to my Lord the Admiral, who was quite delighted to hear this story of my adventures. He ordered careful watch to be kept from the ships and in

some straw huts which he had built on the shore, since I and certain others intended to remain there and learn the secrets of the land.

Next morning the Admiral sent for me to discuss what should now be done about the Indians. My opinion was that we must seize the *cacique* and all his captains, because once we had them in our power the common people would be subdued. His Lordship was of the same opinion, and I suggested the ruse by which this plan might be achieved. The Admiral ordered his brother the *adelantado* and myself with eighty men to execute this plan. We set out and, by God's good fortune, captured the *cacique* and most of his captains; also his wives, children and grandchildren and all the chief members of his family. As we were taking them as prisoners to the ships the *cacique* escaped through the carelessness of his captor and subsequently did us great harm.

At this juncture it pleased God that there should be heavy rains. The river flooded and the harbour was opened for us. The Admiral then took the ships out to sea in order to sail for Castile, leaving me on shore to stay as their Highnesses' agent with seventy men. He left me the greater part of the stores of biscuit and wine, oil and vinegar.

When the Admiral had put to sea, I was left at the settlement with only twenty men, for the rest had gone down to the harbour to take their leave of him. Suddenly I was attacked by a host of about 400 natives armed with spears, darts and slings. Lying concealed in the wood they suddenly gave a great shout, then another and another, and thus thanks be to God gave me time to prepare for the battle and organize my defence. We remained on the shore among the huts we had built and they on the wooded mountain an arrow's flight away. They began to shoot their arrows and hurl their darts as if attacking a bull. The arrows and darts fell as thick as hail, and some warriors left the woods to come and attack us with

clubs, but none of them returned, for all lost an arm or a leg or were killed outright by our swords. At this the rest took such fright that they ran away, having killed seven of the twenty men with whom we had started the battle, and lost nine or ten of those who had attacked us so boldly. The battle had lasted for more than three hours and by a miracle the Lord gave us the victory, for we were very few and they were very many.

When the battle was over, Captain Diego Tristan came from the ships with the intention of taking boats up-river to fetch water for the voyage. Despite my earnest warnings not to go, he overruled me and went up-river with two boats and twelve men. There the natives fell on him by surprise and killed him and all his men except one, who escaped to bring the news. They took the boats and broke them to pieces, which left us in great difficulties. The Admiral lay offshore in his ships with no boats, and we had no boats either in which to go out to him, and all the time the Indians continued to attack us, ceaselessly sounding their trumpets and drums and shouting wildly in the belief that they had conquered us. To defend ourselves against these warriors we had two very good brass falconets and plenty of powder and ball with which we so terrified them that they did not dare to approach. This situation continued for four days, during which I had many bags made from the sails of the one ship still lying in harbour,* and in these we put all our remaining biscuit. I then took two canoes, and, fastening them together with poles across the tops, loaded all the biscuit and casks of wine, oil and vinegar aboard, and secured them with hawsers and ropes. They were then towed out to sea when it was calm, and in seven journeys everything was carried aboard. The men who had been left with me were also taken out a few at a time and I remained with five men to the last and entered the last boat

* This was the *Gallega*, which was being left behind as unseaworthy.

at nightfall. The Admiral was highly delighted with this action and repeatedly embraced me, kissing me on both cheeks, in gratitude for the service I had done him. He gave me command of the *Capitana* and of its whole crew, to take responsibility for the voyage, and I accepted this in order to oblige him as it was a service of great responsibility.

On the last day of April 1503 we left Veragua with three ships, intending to return to Castile, but as the ships were all riddled and worm-eaten we could not keep them afloat, and after making thirty leagues we abandoned one of them, remaining with two, which were in an even worse condition. With all hands at the pumps, pots and cauldrons, we were still unable to draw off all the water that entered through the worm-holes. Nevertheless with great toil and in danger we sailed for thirty-five days on our course to Castile, at the end of which time we reached the lowest point of the island of Cuba in the province of Homo, where the town of Trinidad now stands. Here we were 300 leagues further from Spain than when we left Veragua and as I have said the ships were rotten and unseaworthy and our provisions were almost exhausted. It pleased Our Lord, however, that we should come to the island of Jamaica, where we beached our two ships and built two straw-roofed huts from their timbers. Here we established ourselves, though in considerable danger from the natives of the island, who had not been subdued or conquered and who might set fire to our dwellings by night, which they could easily do though we kept careful watch.

Here I gave out the last ration of wine and biscuit, and taking a sword in my hand went with three men into the interior of the island, since no one had yet dared to search for food for the Admiral and his men. By God's mercy I found the natives so gentle that they did me no harm. On the contrary they welcomed me and willingly gave me food, and in the village

of Aguacadiba I arranged with the chief and his men to make cassava bread, hunt and fish and give a certain amount of food to the Admiral each day, which they were to bring to the ships in exchange for blue beads, combs and knives, fish-hooks, bells and other articles which we carried for the purposes of barter. After making this agreement, I sent one of the Christians who were with me to the Admiral, asking him to appoint someone who could pay for these provisions and make sure of their dispatch.

From there I went to another village three leagues away and made a similar agreement with its *cacique* Indians and sent another Christian to the Admiral asking him to appoint someone to act for him in the same way here. From there I went on to visit a great *cacique*, whose name was Huareo, at a place now called Melilla, which was thirteen leagues from the ships. This chief received me kindly, gave me a good deal of food and ordered his subjects to bring him a quantity of provisions in three days' time. These were brought and I paid for them in such a way as to leave them content. I arranged that more supplies should be regularly brought and that someone should stay there to pay for them and, having made this arrangement, sent another Christian to the Admiral with the food I had obtained. I also asked the *cacique* to give me two Indians who could accompany me to the extreme end of the island, one to carry the hammock in which I slept, the other to carry the food.

Thus I travelled to the easternmost cape of the island, where I visited a chief, whose name was Ameyro, with whom I swore fraternal friendship, giving him my name and taking his, which is considered a great sign of brotherhood among them. I bought from him a very good canoe, giving him in exchange a very fine brass helmet which I was carrying in a bag, also a coat and one of my two shirts. I embarked in the canoe with six Indians whom the *cacique* had given me to

help me row it, and put out to sea in search of the other places I had visited. On arriving at these places where I had gathered food I found the Christians there whom the Admiral had sent, and entrusted them with the provisions I had brought with me. I then went to the Admiral, who gave me a fine welcome. He was so delighted to see me that he embraced me again and again, asking me about all that had happened on my journey and thanking God for having brought me back safely and delivered me from all these savage people. On the day that I got back to the ships they had no bread left to eat. They were delighted to see me, since they were so short of everything that they were dying of hunger.

From that time onwards the Indians came every day, carrying provisions to the ships from the villages where I had arranged for supplies, which were enough for the 230 persons who were with the Admiral.

Ten days later the Admiral called me aside and told me of the great danger he was in. 'Diego Mendez, my lad,' he said to me, 'none of my people realize the danger of our situation except you and myself. We are very few, these savage Indians are very many, and we cannot be certain that their mood will not change. One day, when the fancy seizes them, they may come and burn us here in these two ships which we have turned into houses. For since the roofs are of straw, they will easily be able to set them alight from the landward side and roast us all alive. It is true that you have made this arrangement with them to bring us food every day, and at present they are doing so willingly. But tomorrow the fancy may seize them to act otherwise, and supplies will cease. If they do not choose to bring us food, we are not in the position to take it by force. I have thought of a remedy, about which I should like your opinion. Suppose that in this canoe you have brought someone were to risk making the crossing to the island of Hispaniola, he could there buy a ship in which we

could escape from our very great danger. Let me hear your opinion about this.'

I answered him: 'Sir, I can clearly see our danger, which may be even greater than it appears. To cross from this island to Hispaniola in a vessel as small as this canoe would in my opinion be not merely dangerous, but impossible. I know no one who would dare to make the passage across those forty leagues of sea. For since among these islands the waters are subject to violent currents, and seldom calm, the dangers are only too obvious.'

His Lordship did not contradict me but firmly persuaded me that I was the man to undertake the voyage.

I replied: 'My Lord, I have often put my life in danger to save yours and those of your companions, and Our Lord has marvellously preserved me. Yet many people have complained that your Lordship entrusts all the most honourable responsibilities to me, although there are others in the company who would perform them as well as I. I should like you therefore, Sir, to call everyone together and offer this mission to them all. We shall then see if there is anyone among them who will undertake it, which I doubt, and if they all hold back, as they will, I shall risk my life once more in your service as I have done many times already.'

Then on the following day the Admiral called all his men together and proposed the mission to them just as he had proposed it to me. They listened but were all silent. Some of them said that it was absurd even to talk of such a thing, because it was impossible in a small canoe to cross a strait forty leagues wide, which had such strong currents and was so seldom calm. For great ships had been lost on voyages of discovery between these two islands, powerless to stem or resist the violence of the currents. I then got up and said: 'My Lord, I have only one life but I will risk it in your Lordship's service and for the good of all those here present. For I trust the Lord

God, that being witness to the motives from which I act, He will preserve me as He has done many times before.'

On hearing my resolution the Admiral got up, embraced me and kissed me on both cheeks, saying: 'I knew very well that nobody here except yourself would dare to undertake this mission. I trust in the Lord God that you will emerge from it as successfully as you have from the other missions you have undertaken.'

Next day I drew my canoe ashore, fixed a false keel to it, pitched and greased it, and nailed some boards to the prow and stern to prevent the water from coming in, which it might, owing to the low freeboard. I also added a mast and sail and put sufficient stores aboard for myself, one other Christian and six Indians, eight men in all, for the canoe would hold no more. I said good-bye to the Admiral and all his men and went up the coast of Jamaica for thirty-five leagues from the place where the ships were to the extreme end of the island. I met with great hardships and dangers on the voyage, for I was taken prisoner by Indian sea-raiders, from whom God miraculously delivered me. As I was waiting beside the cape at the tip of the island for the sea to grow calm before beginning my voyage, many Indians gathered with the intention of killing me and taking the canoe and its contents. Once gathered, they drew lots for my life to see who should be fated to carry out their plan. When I saw this I slipped off to my canoe, which I had beached three leagues away, raised my sail and returned to the place where I had left the Admiral fifteen days before.

I told him all that had happened, and how God had miraculously rescued me from the hands of those savages. His Lordship was very glad that I had come, and asked me if I was prepared to set out again. I replied that I would if I could take some men with me to remain at the tip of the island until I had put to sea on the second lap of my voyage. His Lordship gave me seventy men, among them his brother the *adelantado*,

to go with me and remain at the cape until three days after I had embarked. Thus accompanied I returned to the cape, where I stayed for four days. When I saw the seas growing calm I very sadly took leave of my escort and they of me. I commended myself to God and Our Lady of Antigua, and rowed for five days and four nights, never taking my hand off the oar and steering the canoe while all my companions rowed. Thanks be to our Lord God, after five days I reached the island of Hispaniola at Cape San Miguel.* During the last two days we neither ate nor drank, since our stores were exhausted. I steered my canoe up a most beautiful river where many natives came to us, bringing plenty of things to eat, and we remained there resting for two days. I then took six local Indians, leaving my own behind, and began to row along the coast of Hispaniola. It was 130 leagues from there to the city of Santo Domingo, to which I had to go since the governor, the *comendador* de Lares, was there.

After travelling eighty leagues along the coast, not without great peril and toil, for the island was not yet subdued and pacified, I reached the province of Azoa, which is twenty-four leagues from Santo Domingo. Here I was informed by the *comendador* Gallego that the governor had gone to pacify the province of Jaragua, which was fifty leagues away. On learning this, I left my canoe and set out on foot for Jaragua, where I found the governor, who kept me with him for seven months, during which time he burnt or hanged eighty-four ruling *caciques*, among them the lady Nacaona, the greatest chieftain in the island, who was obeyed and served by all the others. When the province was pacified I left on foot for Santo Domingo (which was seventy leagues away) and waited there for ships to come from Castile. None had come for more than a year, but thanks be to God three arrived during my stay, one of which I bought and loaded with pro-

* Cape Tiburon (Shark Point), the south-west point of the island.

visions: bread, wine, meat, hogs, sheep and fruit. I then sent
it to the place where the Admiral was, so that he and all his
men might come in it to Santo Domingo and from there return to Castile. I myself went ahead with the other two ships
to give the King and Queen an account of all that had happened on that voyage.

I think that I should say something about what happened
to the Admiral and his company during the year in which
they were left on the island. A few days after my departure
the Indians rebelled and refused to bring them the accustomed
food. The Admiral had the *caciques* summoned and told them
that he was astonished at this discontinuance of supplies, since
they knew very well that he had come there at God's command. He said that God was very annoyed with them and
would show His anger that night by signs that would appear
in the heavens. That night there was an eclipse of the moon,
which was almost completely obscured, and the Admiral told
them that the cause of this was God's anger with them for no
longer supplying him with food. They believed him and in
great fear promised always to bring him food, which in fact they
did, until the ship which I had sent with provisions arrived.

[*Diego Mendez does not mention the rebellion of Francisco de
Porras, one of the ships' captains, which took place before the incident of the eclipse. Porras reproached the Admiral in January for
making no attempt to return to Spain and tried to get away with a
number of his men in canoes rowed by Indians. They made two
attempts but both failed, with loss of life. After the eclipse, they
remained recalcitrant, and the* adelantado *kept them at a distance
from the Admiral's camp. They accused the Admiral of keeping
them on Jamaica by necromancy, and finally Porras was arrested
and put in chains. When Columbus finally brought him back to
Hispaniola, however, Ovando released him and removed him from
the Admiral's jurisdiction, a great humiliation for the Viceroy of the
Indies. (See Las Casas, II, Chaps. 32–36 passim.)*]

The Admiral and all his companions were highly delighted with the ship's arrival. Afterwards in Castile his Lordship told me that in all his life he had never known so joyful a day, since he had never expected to leave Jamaica alive. He went aboard this ship and set out for Santo Domingo and from there for Spain.

[*Diego Mendez concludes with the story that afterwards in Castile he asked the Admiral to reward him for this service and for strongly defending him in the lawsuits which followed concerning the governorship of the Indies. He says that the Admiral conferred on him the post of* alguacil mayor (chief magistrate) *of Santo Domingo, which would have made him one of the richest men in the New World. The gift however was not honoured and in this testament of 1536 he requests lesser offices from Maria de Toledo, the Admiral's daughter-in-law, if not for himself, for his sons.*]

THE LIFE OF THE ADMIRAL BY HIS SON, HERNANDO COLON

CHAPTER 108

*The Admiral arrives in Hispaniola and from there
returns to Castile, where the Lord raises him to
His Holy Glory at Valladolid*

ONCE the Christians were brought to obedience the Indians
were more punctual in bringing provisions for barter. We
had now been in Jamaica for a year, less only a few days, when
the vessel arrived which Diego Mendez had bought and
stocked at Santo Domingo with the Admiral's money; and
all, friends and foes alike, went aboard. On 28 June we set sail
and had a very laborious passage, since the winds and currents
were continuously against us, as we have said they always are
on the crossing from Jamaica to Santo Domingo, which we
entered on 13 August 1504 with a great longing to rest. The
governor gave the Admiral a great reception and offered him
his house for a lodging. But though the governor flattered he
also stung: for at the same time he released Porras, who had
been the leader of the rebellion, and tried to punish those who
had been responsible for his imprisonment. He also presumed
to pronounce judgement on other matters and misdemeanours
which were the concern of the Catholic sovereigns alone,
since they had assigned responsibility for them to the Admiral
as captain general of their fleet. The governor conferred many
favours on the Admiral but always with a false smile and a
pretence of friendship to his face. This continued until our
ship was refitted and another equipped, in which the Admiral embarked his relations and servants, most of the others
remaining in Hispaniola.

We raised sail on 12 September, and had gone two leagues beyond the river mouth when the mast of the other ship broke at deck level and it had to put back to port. We in our ship, however, continued on our voyage enjoying good weather until we were a third of the way across the ocean. Then one day we were struck by a most violent storm, which put the ship in great danger. On the following day, Saturday, 19 October, when the weather had turned fair and we were taking a rest, our mast broke in four pieces. But thanks to the *adelantado*'s bravery and the ingenuity of the Admiral, who was confined to his bed by gout and did not get up, a jury mast was constructed from one of the lateen yards and partially braced with ropes and timbers from the forecastle and the sterncastle, which we demolished. Our mizzen mast was brought down by another storm, and it was God's will that we should sail on in this sorry plight for 700 leagues, at the end of which we entered the harbour of San Lucar de Barameda, on 17 November 1504. From here we went to Seville, where the Admiral took some rest from the hardships he had suffered.

Then in May 1505 he left Seville for the court of the Catholic King whose glorious Queen had been summoned to a higher life at the end of the previous year. The Admiral felt great grief at the death of Queen Isabela, for it had been she who had supported and favoured him, and he had always found the King somewhat abrupt and unfavourable to his projects, and this attitude was clearly shown by the King's reception on this occasion. Although Ferdinand received him with apparent favour and pretended that he was about to restore him to his old authority, he planned to strip him of it altogether, and would have done so if he had not been prevented by shame, which, as we have said, has great power over noble minds. His Highness himself and her most serene Majesty had conferred this authority on him when he set out on the voyage we have just described. But when the affairs of

the Indies showed signs of turning out as they did, and the Catholic King saw the large share that the Admiral would receive by virtue of the agreement which they had made with him, he tried to retain sole jurisdiction over the Indies for himself and to fill at his own will and pleasure those offices that were rightfully in the Admiral's appointment. He therefore proposed fresh terms of agreement and a new way of rewarding the Admiral. But God did not permit these changes to take place, for his most serene Majesty Philip I arrived to assume the crown of Spain,* and at the very moment when the Catholic king came out of Vallalolid to receive him, the Admiral, suffering more severely still from his gout and other ills and from grief at seeing himself so fallen from his high estate, yielded his soul to God on Ascension Day, 20 May 1509, in that city, after receiving with great devotion all the sacraments of the Church and pronouncing these last words: 'Into Thy hands, O God, I commend my soul.'† And we can believe that of His great goodness He indeed received the Admiral into His glory, into which may He lead us with him. Amen.

*Philip of Hapsburg, husband of Joanna the Mad, the daughter of the Catholic sovereigns.

†The words are given in Latin.